Camp Club Girls
Bailey

4-in-1 Mystery Collection

Camp Club Girls
Bailey

Linda Carlblom

BARBOUR BOOKS
An Imprint of Barbour Publishing, Inc.

Bailey's Estes Park Excitement © 2010 by Barbour Publishing, Inc.
Bailey's Peoria Problem © 2010 by Barbour Publishing, Inc.
Bailey and the Santa Fe Secret © 2011 by Barbour Publishing, Inc.
Bailey and the Florida Mermaid Park Mystery © 2019 by Barbour Publishing, Inc.

Print ISBN 978-1-68322-828-8

eBook Editions:
Adobe Digital Edition (.epub) 978-1-64352-127-5
Kindle and MobiPocket Edition (.prc) 978-1-64352-128-2

Published by Barbour Books, an imprint of Barbour Publishing, Inc., 1810 Barbour Drive, Uhrichsville, Ohio 44683, www.barbourbooks.com

Our mission is to inspire the world with the life-changing message of the Bible.

 Member of the
Evangelical Christian
Publishers Association

Printed in the United States of America.
06367 0119 BP

Camp Club Girls:
Bailey's Estes
Park Excitement

CHAPTER
1

Two Mysteries, Five Days!

Crsiiish!

The ground shook.

Bailey Chang grabbed her father's arm.

"Does Colorado have earthquakes?" she shouted over the sudden noise.

"Stampede!" someone yelled.

Bailey's dad grabbed her. With his other hand he snatched her friend Kate Oliver. He dragged them to the safety of the Stanley Hotel's front porch. Bailey's mom and older sister, Trina, ran up the steps.

A herd of beautiful elk thundered across the lawn of the old hotel. Within seconds, only a cloud of dust and an unnatural silence remained.

Moments earlier Bailey's greatest fear was of the historic Stanley Hotel itself. Nestled in the majestic Rocky Mountains in Estes Park, Colorado, it had stared menacingly at Bailey, each window a glaring eye, as her family drove up and parked. Its deathly white walls and bloodred tile roof eerily reminded her of the ghosts rumored to live in it. The bright sun hid behind clouds on this early October afternoon.

Bailey swallowed hard, her dark brown almond eyes wide. In her nine years, she had never stayed in a haunted hotel. Nor had she almost been trampled by a stampeding herd of elk.

"Is everyone okay?" Mr. Chang asked as the dust settled.

"I think so," Mrs. Chang answered. "Are you girls all right?"

"Except for being almost killed in a stampede, we're great!" fourteen-year-old Trina mouthed off.

"A—are we really going to stay here?" Bailey asked her father, George Chang, who had brought the family along on a business trip.

"Yes," he answered matter-of-factly. "It's a well-known hotel, highly recommended. I'm sure that stampede was merely a fluke."

Bailey looked at her eleven-year-old friend, Kate Oliver. Kate's eyes were as big as twin full moons behind her black, rectangular glasses. She nervously tucked her sandy, shoulder-length hair behind her ears. Biscuit the Wonder Dog whined and hid behind Kate's leg. Bailey, Kate, and the other four Camp Club Girls had rescued Biscuit when they first met at Camp Discovery. Though Biscuit lived with Kate, he still took part in some of the girls' mysteries.

"But what if it's true, Dad?" Bailey asked.

"What if what's true?"

"What if there really are ghosts in there?" Bailey pointed at the hotel.

"Bailey." Mrs. Chang's hands rested firmly on her hips, her blond head tilted. "Do you really think your father would let you stay in a dangerous place?"

"Think about it, Bales," Trina said, relaxing now that the threat had passed. "Mom and Dad barely let us go to sleepovers without interrogating our friends' parents first. They're pretty picky about where we sleep."

Bailey's shoulders slumped slightly. "I guess you're right."

Kate looked over a pamphlet for the hotel that she'd picked up at the Denver, Colorado, airport. "Maybe we can study this brochure about the hotel and investigate the ghost sightings and mysterious sounds people have reported."

She grinned at Bailey and grabbed Biscuit. "And Biscuit the Wonder Dog will sniff out clues for us." Biscuit's whole body wriggled and wagged as he licked Kate's face.

With the stampede over, Bailey's family returned to unloading their Honda CR-V in front of the hotel. "Come on. Let's go get checked in," Mr. Chang said, starting toward the main entrance.

The huge front porch seemed friendly enough, Bailey thought, now that she didn't need to escape from rampaging elk. Cushioned white wicker rocking chairs, love seats, and tables sat waiting for people to relax in their comfort. *Maybe it won't be so bad.* Bailey took a deep breath and stepped through the doorway.

The smell of old wood and lemon oil greeted Bailey as she entered the magnificent lobby, pulling her pink camouflage suitcase. Gleaming hardwood floors reflected her awestruck face. She was so busy looking around that she nearly ran into an enormous flower bouquet on a round, glass-topped table.

A wide, grand staircase with a white banister and glossy wood handrail invited—or dared—guests to go upstairs and explore ghostly nooks and crannies. On each end of the lobby overstuffed couches and chairs rested on large area rugs in front of fireplaces. An old green car with yellow wooden wheels in mint condition stood on display near one of the fireplaces, protected by thick red velvet ropes.

"That car's called the Stanley Steamer," Kate explained to Bailey. "Here's a picture of it in this brochure. The guy who started this hotel, F. O. Stanley, invented it. See, there's his picture."

The girls surveyed antique black-and-white portraits of F. O. Stanley on gray-green wallpapered walls.

"Wow," Bailey said. "This looks like where a movie star would stay."

"I've never stayed in a place this fancy before." Kate shoved her glasses up her small, roundish nose. "Sure beats the Super Six where we usually stay."

"Sure does." Mrs. Chang turned a slow circle to take it all in. "I'm glad George's company is paying for this."

Bailey parked her suitcase and joined her dad, who was standing at the registration desk. Her mom, Trina, and Kate followed close behind.

"Usually the elk are quite friendly as they roam about the town," the clerk with a name badge that said "Barbara" was saying. "But for some reason they've become aggressive in the last few weeks, so be cautious around them."

"What made them become so aggressive?" Bailey asked, standing on tiptoe to see over the counter.

The registrar shrugged her shoulders. "One minute they're calm and the next thing you know, they're charging. No one knows why."

"That's unusual." Kate scratched her head. "There must be a reason for their sudden change."

"Don't worry," Mrs. Chang said, putting one protective arm around Bailey's shoulder while patting Kate's back with the other. "We'll be careful. Right, girls?"

The two nodded but smiled at each another. Biscuit yawned and whined at the same time.

Barbara leaned over the counter. "Is that your dog?"

"He's mine." Kate smiled proudly then picked up the wiggly fur ball. "This is Biscuit." The dog's whole body wagged in a friendly Biscuit greeting.

Barbara frowned. "Is he house-trained?"

"Of course!" Kate answered.

"Does he bark?"

Bailey almost blurted out, *Not as much as you!* but Kate answered coolly, "Only when threatened."

Mr. Chang quickly stepped in. "I'm sure Biscuit will be no trouble. We'll make sure he stays quiet and doesn't make a mess. And if he does, we'll take full responsibility for any extra cleaning charges."

"Just make sure you keep him on a leash." Barbara gave the Changs their keys and a map of the hotel, and then she called a bellhop to take the suitcases to room 412. "The elevator is right over there or you can take these stairs," she instructed the Changs, pointing to her left.

"Let's ride the elevator," Kate suggested after hooking a leash to Biscuit's collar.

"After walking through the airports, I'll be glad to take the easy way to our room." Mrs. Chang smiled. "I can't wait to get out of these shoes!"

The five climbed into the elevator and Bailey pushed the button for the fourth floor. A ding signaled their arrival. The doors opened to a long hallway with plush burgundy carpet.

"Look at that wallpaper," Bailey said in awe. The lower portion of the wall was painted white, and the upper was papered with a white-on-white embossed design. Bailey touched it. "It's not wall*paper*—it's wall *fabric!*"

"Whoa!" Kate reached out to feel it before following the arrow directing them to room 412.

As the girls walked down the hall, two boys who looked about their ages came out of one of the rooms. Lunging, Biscuit growled and barked at them.

Kate yanked him back with the leash. "Biscuit!" She picked up the little dog and looked at the boys. "Sorry."

One of the boys shrugged while the other gave her a fiery glare.

"I hope that isn't any indication of how this week will be." Mr. Chang stopped outside of room 412. He slid his magnetic card through the slot and pushed the door open.

Bailey walked in and eyed the sparsely furnished room. "Cool! It looks so old-fashioned!" Two full-size beds with tall posts at each corner stood against one wall. A wooden table and chair sat in another corner. Bailey looked around. "Look how high these beds are! They even have little steps to help you get into them!"

A rollaway bed was pushed along one wall, ready to open.

"Let me guess," Trina said. "That's my bed."

"You girls can trade off if you want." Mrs. Chang looked softly at her older daughter.

"That's okay. At least I won't have to sleep with anyone."

"I'll let you use our stairs if you want help getting into your rollaway," Bailey offered.

Trina laughed. "I think I can get into this bed without steps. But thanks."

"No way!" Kate shouted. "Come see this bathroom!"

Bailey hustled to the door and peered in. A claw-foot bathtub sat next to the toilet. A freestanding toilet paper holder and a pedestal sink completed the décor.

"I can't wait to take a bath in that tub," Bailey said. "It's just like in the old movies. I'll need lots of bubbles."

Back in the bedroom, Mrs. Chang put her suitcase on the bed and began to unpack. "Dad and I will take this bed and you can have the one by the window," she said to Bailey and Kate.

"I have a meeting this afternoon, but you can get settled while I'm gone," Mr. Chang said. "I should be back before supper."

"Okay. See ya later, Dad." Bailey hugged her dad's neck. "Don't get run over by any wild elk!" she joked.

Kate climbed onto the bed by the window. "Let's look at this brochure to see what we can find out about this place."

"Yeah, maybe we'll learn where the ghosts hang out." Bailey shuddered, then grinned. She sprawled out on the bed beside Kate.

"Let's see." Kate laid out the brochure before her like a map. "This tells the history of the hotel, and about F. O. Stanley, inventor of the Stanley Steamer automobile, who came to Estes Park for health reasons. He and his wife spent a summer here in 1903 and fell in love with the area. Because of his health improvement and the beauty of the valley they decided to stay and opened the Stanley Hotel in 1909."

"Interesting," Bailey remarked.

"Sorta, but listen. . ." Kate's eyes sparkled. "The hotel was the inspiration for a novel by Stephen King. It's also been used as a location for a bunch of films."

"Cool! We're actually staying where they made movies!" Bailey exclaimed. "Maybe we'll see some stars. Or *maybe* some of their stardom will rub off on *me*!"

"You don't need anything to rub off on you to become a star," Mrs. Chang said. "You're special in your own right. But remember, you need to finish your education before you run off to Hollywood."

Bailey laughed and sat up. "But wouldn't it be awesome? To be a famous actress making big movies?"

Trina rolled her eyes as she hung one of her sweaters in the closet. "You've dreamed that dream for sooo long."

Bailey glared at her sister. "So what?"

"So you have to do something besides sit around and dream about it, that's what." Trina poked her younger sister in the ribs. Bailey rolled to her side, giggling.

Biscuit jumped onto the bed to check out the commotion then nested comfortably against Bailey's back.

"All right. Now, where were we?" Kate asked, looking at the brochure. "Oh yeah! I was just getting to the part about the ghosts!"

"Oooooo!" Bailey gave her best ghost shriek, making Biscuit howl.

Kate laughed as she scooped the little dog into her arms. "Don't worry, boy. Ghosts aren't real."

"What's it say?"

Kate pushed up her glasses. "It says F. O. Stanley's ghost is the most notable one seen. It usually appears in the lobby or the Billiard Room, which was his favorite room when he was alive. His wife, Flora, has been seen playing the piano in the Music Room. Cleaning crews also have heard strange noises coming from room 418, as well as finding the bed rumpled when the room has been empty. And guests say they hear children playing in the halls at night. One guest saw a man wearing a cowboy hat and a mustache staring out of the window of room 408 when no one was in the room."

"Since even numbers are on one side of the hall and odd on the other, that makes room 408 only two doors down from ours!" Bailey exclaimed. "Do you think we'll see any of the ghosts?"

Kate answered in her scariest voice, "You never know," then laughed evilly.

"Stop it! You'll scare Biscuit." Bailey petted the dog.

"Biscuit?" Trina glanced sideways at her sister. "You sure he's the only one you're worried about Kate scaring?"

"Well, I'm not scared of any fake ghosts, if that's what you mean." Bailey crossed her arms defiantly and lifted her chin.

Trina smirked. "Right."

Kate pushed her glasses up. "Since ghosts aren't real, these sightings and sounds must be done by some special effects." Bailey could see the wheels turning in Kate's head. "Maybe we can uncover how they do them."

"Yeah!" Bailey agreed. "Another Camp Club Girls mystery! Does the brochure say anything else that might help us figure it out?"

"Not much. Just that room 401 is usually the ghost hunters' favorite room." Kate put the pamphlet on the nightstand.

"Hey, check this out," Trina called, pulling back the curtains.

Bailey and Kate jumped up from the bed.

"Awesome!" Bailey pressed her nose to the window. Below their fourth floor window was a grassy courtyard where elk wandered among the guests as if they'd checked in and paid for a room themselves.

"They don't seem aggressive," Kate said.

"Maybe not now, but you can't be too careful around wild animals," Mrs. Chang warned.

"I wonder what they eat," Bailey said. "Maybe we could get some elk food and feed them."

"No way." Mrs. Chang shook her head in no uncertain terms. "You heard what the lady at the desk said. They can become aggressive without warning. Wildlife can be very unpredictable."

Trina moved away from the window and went back to unpacking her suitcase. "I wonder what makes them get angry and charge people."

"Maybe they're afraid the people will hurt them," suggested Bailey.

"Or maybe someone did hurt them and it has made them skittish," Kate offered.

"Maybe they've got some hideous sickness like mad elk disease and it will gradually infect the whole elk population!" Bailey grimaced.

Trina laughed. "You two have a lot of crazy ideas. Maybe they're just sick of tourists like us invading their town."

"Looks like we'll have two mysteries to work on while we're here." Bailey held up one finger. "One, what makes the ghosts and spooky sounds, and two, what made the elk turn mean."

Bailey looked at Kate, two fingers still raised like a peace sign. A grin spread slowly across her face. Kate beamed back then raised her hand and Bailey high-fived it. The Camp Club Girls had two mysteries and only five days to solve them.

Ghost Hunt

"Mom, can Kate and I go explore the hotel?"

Placing clothes into the dresser drawers, Bailey's mother answered, "I suppose. But take the hotel map with you and your cell phone, just in case you get turned around."

"Okay, thanks!" Bailey turned toward the door.

"And don't forget Biscuit," Trina added with a smile.

"We would never forget you!" Kate cooed in a baby voice to her dog.

"And stay together," Mrs. Chang warned.

"We will," Kate promised.

"You still have the brochure about the hotel?" Bailey asked her friend.

"Right here." Kate patted her back pocket before hooking Biscuit's leash to his collar. "Let's go, boy."

"Don't let any ghosts sneak up on you!" Trina called as they left.

Bailey laughed. "That shouldn't be a problem since ghosts don't exist!"

"Let's find room 401 while we're on this floor," Kate suggested as the door closed behind them. "Since it's the ghost hunters' favorite room, maybe we'll see something that will explain how they do some of the special effects."

"Good idea." Bailey looked both ways down the hall. "Our room number is 412, and I think the numbers were smaller nearer the elevator, so let's go that way."

"Even-numbered rooms are on our side, and odd on the other."

Bailey studied the oval plates outside each door that showed the room numbers. "Here it is," she whispered when she spotted room 401.

"Why are we whispering?" Kate asked.

Bailey laughed. "I don't know. I feel like I'm spying or something."

Kate examined the walls and then inspected the carpet. "I don't see anything suspicious. Do you?"

Bailey shook her head as she inspected the hallway. "There's a speaker, but that's where the music is coming from. Nothing weird about that."

"We'll have to keep our eyes and ears open," Kate said, still searching. "I'm sure this isn't that complicated if we just keep thinking."

Trying to peer underneath the door, Bailey ventured, "The tricks could be hidden inside the room." She stood back up. "I can't see anything. Maybe we'll have better luck at room 217, the room where they say the author of that scary book stayed."

"It's worth a try," Kate said.

The girls found an elevator and stepped inside.

"Did you read that book or see the movie that was made from it?" Bailey asked as the doors closed.

"No, it's a horror movie. My parents won't let me watch scary movies like that. Did you see it?"

"Nope." Bailey grinned mischievously. "I think our parents are just alike. Mine would never let me see scary movies either."

"Hey, I wonder if Elizabeth saw it." The elevator bell dinged as the doors opened onto the second floor. Kate stepped out first with Biscuit in tow. "She's fourteen. Maybe her parents let her watch those kind of movies."

Bailey flipped open her cell phone and pushed *E* in her contacts. Elizabeth's number showed up and Bailey pushed TALK. Kate spotted a sign that pointed to room 217 and they followed its arrow.

"Elizabeth? It's Bailey."

"And Kate!" Kate shouted into the phone.

"Well, this is a surprise!" Elizabeth said. "What are you two up to? Are you really together or are we conferenced in?"

"We're together," Bailey said, and went on to explain where they were and why. "And guess what? We've already got two mysteries to solve!"

"Two?" Elizabeth asked.

"Yeah, the elk here have gone bonkers," Bailey explained. "I think they might need a counselor or something!"

Elizabeth laughed. "Maybe we should have them talk to McKenzie. She's good at figuring people out. Maybe she could help the elk too!"

"Maybe! So that's our first mystery." Bailey's voice rose with excitement. "Our second one is hunting ghosts. People say ghosts live in this hotel. But since we know ghosts aren't real, we're trying to figure out who is making them seem real, and what special effects they use."

"Wow! Sounds exciting!" Elizabeth paused a moment. "So how can I help? You know I love a good mystery."

Bailey told her that a book by Stephen King was inspired by the hotel, and that a movie had been made from the book. "Have you ever seen it?" Bailey looked expectantly at Kate.

"If it's a Stephen King movie, I haven't seen it," Elizabeth answered. "My folks won't let me. Too scary." She added, "And I'm glad."

Bailey laughed and then shook her head at Kate to relay Elizabeth's answer. "Yeah, I know what you mean. I don't really want to see those scary movies either. We just thought since you're older you might have seen it."

"Let me talk!" Kate grabbed the phone. "Hi, Elizabeth! Biscuit says hi too."

The girls chatted for a minute and then Elizabeth said, "Well, you know I'm praying for you two! Keep me posted on what you find out."

"We appreciate your prayers," Kate said. "We'll let you know what we find out and if you can help out on anything else. If you talk to any of the others, let them know we'll be calling or emailing them soon with all the mystery details."

Kate flipped the phone closed just as they came to the end of the hall.

A metal room plate by the door read 217.

"Here we are! Just think. Movie stars stood at this very place we're standing." Bailey nearly felt faint from the rush.

"And just think," Kate repeated just as dreamily. "A future movie star is standing here right now!"

"Oh, stop." Bailey waved her hand. "You're just saying that."

"You never know. It could happen." Kate dug in her pocket and brought out a pen. "Here. Let me take your picture, just in case. Then we can say I predicted your fame on this very day at this very moment outside this very door!"

"Hold it! That's not a camera. It's a pen." Bailey shook her head.

"Ah, you *think* it's a pen, but it's really a tiny camera!" Kate smiled brightly. "I've been dying for the right moment to show you my latest gadget!"

"Let me see that." Bailey took the pen from Kate. She clicked the top of it, and the ballpoint came down just like a real pen. She scribbled on the corner of the brochure. Blue ink looped round and round. "So it's a real pen *and* a camera. How does it work?"

"You look into the silver clip to see what the camera sees. Then click the top and it takes the picture."

"Did I take a picture when I clicked it before?" Bailey asked.

Kate shook her head. "It only functions as a camera when it's held on its side. Up and down, it's just your ordinary, average blue pen. Turn it over and it switches to camera mode."

"That's awesome!" Bailey squealed. "Let's try it. Take my picture." She struck her most glamorous pose.

Kate held the pen on its side and clicked the top.

"How do we see the picture?"

"We have to unscrew the pen and remove the memory chip inside. I have a special stick to put it into that will fit the computer, then we download the pictures."

"I can't wait to see how it turns out." Bailey bounced up and down on her toes.

"Me too." Kate looked around. "Let's see if we can find any clues here."

A door burst open down the hall and a man bolted out. "Oh no! We've got to go help them!" he shouted to the woman behind him.

"I hope no one was hurt!" she cried as she and the man ran past the girls.

Bailey looked at Kate and they took off after the man and woman, who had stopped in front of the elevator. The elevator doors opened just as the girls caught up and they all climbed inside.

"What's going on?" Bailey asked.

"We were looking out our window when we saw an elk run through the courtyard knocking a boy to the ground," the man answered. "We're going to see if he needs help."

"My husband is a doctor," the woman explained.

Bailey nodded somberly, and Kate petted Biscuit.

The elevator door opened into the main lobby. The doctor and his wife rushed to the courtyard where the elk had charged.

Bailey and Kate stood a short distance away but stayed close enough to see and hear what was going on. In the courtyard, a boy who looked about six years old was stretched on the ground. He didn't appear to be injured, but his father was kneeling over him. The doctor hurried to them.

"Sir, I'm Doctor Gibbins," the man said, kneeling by the father. "I saw what happened from my room and came immediately in case the boy was injured. Is he your son?"

"Yes," the father answered. "Thank you."

The boy moaned and turned his head.

"Did the elk step on him or just knock him down?" asked Doctor Gibbins.

"He was knocked down and bumped his head."

The little boy tried to sit up.

"Hold on there, son." The doctor gently checked his arms and legs to make sure no bones were broken.

"Daddy!"

"I'm right here, Robby," his father answered tenderly.

"I think he's going to be fine," the doctor told him. "Seems to have gotten the wind knocked out of him and a good bump on his head when he went down, but nothing too serious." He helped the child sit up.

"Thank you," the father said again, clasping the doctor's hand.

Robby's dad stood up and picked up his son. "Let's go see Mommy."

From the sidelines, Bailey looked at Kate. "Wow! That was scary."

"Guess what they said about the elk was true." Kate stuffed her pen back in her pocket.

"Did you have that out the whole time?" Bailey asked.

Kate nodded. "I took a few shots just in case it turned into a major news story or something." She laughed. "They might need some pictures for the evening news."

Bailey rolled her eyes. "You're always thinking."

"It'll be a good test to see how well the pictures turn out since we were farther away."

"I wonder what made the elk run like that?" Bailey eyed the courtyard.

"Something must have set him off."

The two girls strolled through the courtyard looking for any clue of what might have spooked the elk but found nothing.

"This really is a mystery." Bailey sighed. "A mystery with no clues."

"There's bound to be something we're missing," Kate encouraged. "We'll figure it out."

"Come on. Let's head back to the room."

●━━●━━●

That night, while Mr. Chang and Trina went to get ice, and Mrs. Chang read a book, the girls reviewed their day.

"After looking around here a bit I think we're starting to learn our way around, don't you?" asked Bailey.

"Yeah, the map in the brochure was helpful," Kate replied. Then wrinkles lined her forehead. "I felt bad about that little boy getting hurt by the elk."

"I know. Me too," Bailey said.

"I'm glad he seemed to be all right."

"That camera-pen of yours is awesome!" Bailey grinned like she'd just won a prize at the fair. "I can't wait to see the pictures you took today."

The hotel room door opened and Mr. Chang and Trina walked in with a full ice bucket. "Anyone want some ice for a bedtime drink of water?"

"Yeah!" Bailey ran into the bathroom to grab the plastic-wrapped glasses. They scooped ice into each one and added water from the tap. "Thanks!"

"Are we ready for lights-out?" Mr. Chang asked.

"Just a minute," Kate replied. "Let me spread Biscuit's blanket at the foot of the bed." She and Bailey laid out the paw-printed fleece blanket, and Biscuit turned a tight, complete circle before plopping down on it. "All set!"

Mr. Chang flipped off the light. "Good night."

" 'Night, Dad." Bailey lay in the dark with her eyes open. Moments later, she heard soft giggling.

"Girls, get to sleep." Mrs. Chang used her no-nonsense voice.

"We're *trying* to," Bailey answered, confused.

The giggling came again, this time followed by childlike voices.

"Bailey, you heard your mother," Mr. Chang warned sternly.

"Dad, it isn't us!" Bailey complained.

"Then who is it?" Trina smarted off.

"How should I know?"

The voices came again, the words unclear, but sure.

"It's the ghost children in the hallway!" Bailey yelled, sitting straight up.

Ghost Children of the Night

Biscuit gave a low, throaty growl.

"Ghost children?" Mrs. Chang said, getting up. "Really, Bailey, I think you've been reading too many mysteries."

Bailey switched on the bedside lamp. "Hand me that hotel brochure, Kate." She pointed to Kate's suitcase, where she could see the brochure sticking out.

Again they heard faint laughing and children's voices.

"Did it ever occur to you that those could be real children out there, rather than 'ghost children,' as you call them?" Trina leaned on one elbow in her bed.

"Listen to this," Bailey said, folding the pamphlet back. "Guests often say they hear children playing in the hallway at night. One couple even checked out of the hotel very early in the morning complaining that the children in the hallway kept them up all night. However, there were no children booked in the hotel at the time. The children have since been called 'ghost children of the night.'" Bailey lowered the hotel brochure and nodded emphatically. "See? Ghost children."

"I seem to recall seeing some boys in this hallway when we brought our luggage to our room," Mr. Chang said. "Two boys. We could be hearing them, or any other children who are checked in."

"If we hear the voices again, can I peek out the door to see if anyone's out there?" Bailey asked.

"If you promise to get right to sleep afterward," Mr. Chang answered with a yawn.

"Me too?" Kate asked.

"You too."

"Yeah, that way there'll be a witness when the body snatchers grab Bailey," Trina teased.

"Trina!" Mrs. Chang scolded. "That will be enough from you. Can we all just relax and get to sleep?" She flipped the light off.

"Hee-hee-heeeeee!"

"That's them!" Bailey said, jumping into her slippers and bathrobe. "I'm out of here!"

Trina groaned. Biscuit barked fiercely then bounded off the bed and ran to the door.

"Me too!" Kate felt her way through the dark after Bailey.

Cautiously, Bailey slid the security chain off the door and slowly opened it. Light from the hallway spread into the room in a giant wedge. She poked her head out into the hall and looked from side to side. "I don't see anyone."

"No surprise there," Kate said, joining her in the doorway.

"Mom, can we go down the hall?" Bailey whisper-yelled.

"Just grab the key off the table first. And stay in our hall," Mrs. Chang instructed in a tired mumble. "I don't want you wandering the entire hotel in your pajamas."

Bailey felt her cell phone on the table and opened it, shining its light to find the key. "Got it," she told her mom. "We'll be back in just a minute."

"Stay, Biscuit," Kate commanded. "We'll be right back."

With the phone lighting their path, the girls crept back to the door and stepped into the lighted hallway. Bailey shoved her phone into her bathrobe pocket. A high-pitched giggle greeted them, followed by muffled children's voices that sounded like they were telling secrets.

"There it is again!" Kate's eyes scanned the walls then moved up and down from floor to ceiling as if looking for some clue as to where the voices came from.

"Sounds like they're coming from down here," Bailey whispered loudly, walking to the far end of the hall. The voices spoke again, though still not clearly.

"There must be wires to a speaker somewhere," Kate said. She ran her hand along the wall, stopping at the corner. "Here!"

Bailey hustled over to her friend.

"Feel right here," Kate instructed.

Bailey touched the wallpaper on one wall then continued around the corner. "Aha! A bump!" She ran her hand vertically along the bump and found that it went higher than she could reach. "Our wire!"

"Now we just have to figure out where it runs to and we may have our first solution to the ghost sounds." Kate's eyes sparkled like diamonds, and she gave Bailey a victorious high five.

"Come on," Bailey said. "We'd better go back so my mom doesn't worry."

The two tiptoed back to the room. Bailey lit her cell phone up again once they arrived in the dark room and led the way to their bed. Biscuit jumped at their legs, excited to see them as if they'd been gone for months. Kate and Bailey pulled back the sheets and climbed in, followed by Biscuit, who snuggled into his little nest of blankets on the bed.

"We'll have to investigate some more tomorrow," Kate whispered.

"Should be a great way to start the day!" Bailey smiled and then drifted off to sleep.

●━━●━━●

The next morning, Bailey woke to the sound of the phone and her father's voice. She rolled over and pulled her pillow over her head.

"Yes, I'll be available in an hour. Thank you. See you then."

Mr. Chang flipped his cell phone closed and said to Mrs. Chang, "William Perkins will meet me in the hotel lobby in an hour for our conference. His wife and children are here with him, and he's bringing them to meet us. They're also staying at this hotel."

"Guess I'd better clean up." Mrs. Chang sprang from the bed and headed to the shower.

"Will has two boys, so I don't imagine the girls will be too interested in hanging out with them much."

"Or will they?" Mrs. Chang said with a sly smile. She laughed and shook her head. "Probably not, but it will be nice to meet them anyway. It's always nice to have a friendly face, just in case you need something." Mrs. Chang turned on the water. "Will you get the girls up while I shower?"

Mr. Chang moved to the girls' bed and whispered, "Biscuit!" The dog stretched and yawned, but soon he was prancing all over Bailey and Kate, nudging Bailey's pillow off her head, licking hands, faces, and feet.

"Biscuit! Stop!" Kate howled, hiding her face in the covers.

"We're too tired. Go away." Bailey rolled over.

"Come on, girls," Mr. Chang said. "Time to get up. Some people are meeting us downstairs in an hour."

"Ugghh," Bailey moaned.

"You too, Trina." Mr. Chang shook his older daughter's shoulder.

"Mr. Perkins is bringing his family to meet us."

"How could you do this to me?" Trina wailed, with all the dismay she could muster at seven a.m.

"Easy!" Mr. Chang chuckled. "Watching you writhe around and moan is good early morning entertainment."

Trina threw a pillow at her father, which he deftly dodged. When she saw him pick up the pillow and pull his arm back to throw it, she jumped up. The pillow landed with a *whoosh* in her empty bed.

"Ha!" Trina laughed. "Missed me!"

"Ha, yourself." Mr. Chang laughed. "I got you up."

Bailey and Kate had pillows in hand ready to throw but put them back down when the action wound down so quickly. "Shucks," Bailey said. "We missed our chance."

An hour later, they stepped out of the elevator into the hotel lobby.

The Perkins family was looking at the old Stanley Steamer car in the lobby when the Changs arrived.

"Will! Great to see you." Mr. Chang and Will Perkins shook hands.

"George, I'd like you to meet my wife, Janice, and my sons, Joseph and Justin."

Bailey inhaled sharply and elbowed Kate. Joseph and Justin were the two boys Biscuit had nearly attacked in the hall the day before. Good thing they'd taken Biscuit for an early morning walk and left him in the room before coming to meet the Perkinses.

"It's a pleasure to meet you," Mr. Chang replied, shaking each of their hands. "This is my wife, Dory, and my two daughters, Trina and Bailey. And this is Bailey's friend, Kate."

Bailey smiled politely.

"Hey, aren't you the ones who had that dog in the hallway yesterday?" Justin asked.

Mr. Chang cleared his throat. "I guess we are. I'm sorry, I didn't recognize you. We're terribly sorry about Biscuit barking at you. He's a little skittish being in a new place and off his usual routine."

"No harm done," Mr. Perkins assured him.

Bailey noticed that Justin, the older of the two, was scowling. *What's his problem?*

Her thoughts were interrupted by a friendly looking older man and his wife approaching them. "There they are!" the man said.

"Grandpa!" Joe ran to the couple, who greeted the boy with warm hugs.

"Hungry for some breakfast?" Grandpa asked him.

"Starving!"

Mr. Perkins introduced his parents, Glen and Clara Perkins, to the Changs.

"They live here in Estes Park. That's why I brought the family along," Mr. Perkins explained.

"We're off to have breakfast at the Waffle House," Grandma Perkins said. "You're welcome to join us."

"George and I need to get to our conference," Mr. Perkins said. "But maybe Dory and the girls would like to."

"That would be lovely," Mrs. Chang said before Bailey could signal that she did not want to eat with these grouchy boys. She turned her back to the group and rolled her eyes at Kate.

After getting directions to the Waffle House, Mrs. Chang, Trina, Bailey, and Kate piled into the car. "That was nice of them to invite us to join them for breakfast," Mrs. Chang said.

"Nice if you like eating with Oscar the Grouch," Bailey retorted.

"Bailey!" her mother warned.

Bailey looked down at her lap. "But Mom, those boys are so rude!"

"Maybe they're not morning people," Mrs. Chang said.

"Apparently they're not afternoon people either, since they were so grouchy yesterday when Biscuit barked at them."

"Maybe they're afraid of dogs," Trina said.

"Who could be afraid of sweet little Biscuit?" Kate asked.

"As I recall, Biscuit wasn't exactly his usual, sweet little self when he barked at the boys." Mrs. Chang turned into the Waffle House driveway. "Let's just give them a chance. We don't know what's going on in their lives. Maybe they're having some kind of problems at home or something."

Bailey nodded. She never thought of that.

"Right this way." The hostess grabbed menus and motioned for them to follow her to two tables pushed together.

Bailey sat next to Kate, with Justin and Joe directly across from them. While the adults chatted pleasantly, the children were silent. Bailey cleared her throat. "So how old are you?"

The dark-haired boys shifted in their seats. They seemed uncomfortable making conversation with the girls.

"I'm twelve," Justin said, eyes narrowed.

"And I'm ten," Joe added less than enthusiastically.

"You're about our ages then," Kate volunteered. "I'm eleven and Bailey's nine."

"What about her?" Justin nodded in Trina's direction.

"That's Trina. She's fourteen."

"Umph," Joe said.

Whatever that means, thought Bailey. She eyed the boys more closely. They weren't bad looking. They could even be considered cute if they smiled more. Freckles sprinkled Joe's nose and round cheeks. Justin's face was more chiseled and his build was more muscular than his younger brother's. His eyes burned with anger or hurt or something Bailey couldn't quite identify. His eyebrows pointed downward in what looked like a permanent frown.

"Did you hear about the elk problem they're having?" Kate asked, trying to be polite.

"Of course we did," Joe snapped. "Our grandparents live here."

"Oh, right," Bailey said. She added, "Did we say something wrong?"

"What do you mean?" Justin placed his hands on the table, palms down as if he were about to jump up.

Bailey shrugged. "Well, you just seem mad at us."

"Why should we like you?" Joe scowled.

"Why shouldn't you?" Kate smiled in spite of herself.

"We don't have anything against you. We just don't like your dog." Justin leaned back and folded his arms.

"Have you had a bad experience with dogs before?" Bailey asked.

Joe watched his older brother, waiting for his answer. "Maybe, maybe not."

"Well, I'm sorry if you did," Kate said. "Biscuit is a really nice dog, and he'd never hurt a flea."

"Whatever." Justin picked up his menu and hid behind it.

"Have you eaten here before?" Bailey asked, changing the subject.

"Our grandparents bring us here all the time," Joe said, suddenly sounding almost friendly.

"What do you recommend?" Kate asked.

"I usually get the Belgian waffles with strawberries and whipped cream." Joe licked his lips.

"What about you, Justin?" Bailey asked.

"I don't have a favorite," he said from behind his menu.

"I'm thinking of the ham and cheese omelet," Kate said. "Ever had it?"

Justin lowered his menu slowly. Bailey saw his jaw clench. "I've had it and it's fine," he said through gritted teeth.

Were those tears in his eyes? Bailey blinked to see more clearly. Too late. The menu was back up again.

The waitress took their orders and they ate their breakfast without much conversation.

Afterward, Mrs. Chang and Trina went to do some shopping while Bailey and Kate took Biscuit for a walk and talked about their strange encounter with the Perkins boys.

"Something was definitely bothering Justin," Kate said.

"No kidding!" Bailey's eyes nearly popped out of her head. "Did you see when you asked him if he'd had the omelet before? I thought he was going to cry!"

"We need to get on our Camp Club Girls website to let the other girls know what's going on around here. So far we have elk gone mad, unexplained ghost noises, and two crabby boys who hate us for no reason." Kate stopped to let Biscuit sniff some bushes.

"Maybe Justin and Joe don't hate us, but they sure do act weird," Bailey said.

Back at their room, Bailey opened her laptop and signed onto the CCG website then clicked on the chat room. Kate pulled out her cell phone and also went to the site.

Bailey: *Hi CCGs. Who's out there?*

Elizabeth: *I'm here.*

McKenzie: *Me too.*

Sydney: *Me three!*

Alex: *Me four!*

Bailey: *Perfect! Kate and I are in Estes Park and have some weird stuff we may need your help with. We're staying at the Stanley Hotel, which is supposedly haunted. We've heard some strange noises and voices and are trying to find out what causes them.*

McKenzie: *Oooo! Sounds spooky!*

Elizabeth: *How can we help?*

Bailey: *We heard the ghost children of the night in our hall last night.*

Kate: *I found a wire running along the wall under the wallpaper. It probably goes to a speaker somewhere. It was higher than I could reach, so I lost track of it.*

Alex: *Sounds just like a* Scooby Doo *episode! They always have fake ghosts. Maybe you'll run into Shaggy and Scooby while you're there!*

Bailey: *Any hints you can give us?*

Alex: *I think you're on the right track with the speaker wire. You just have to find the speaker.*

Kate: *I figure it's probably a recording. Something probably trips a circuit to start it. But what would be tripping the recording to play?*

Alex: *Look for a switch of some kind. It will most likely be hidden. Something people would touch unknowingly. Or at least that's how they did it in* Scooby.

Kate: *Great. We'll look around some more.*

Bailey: *We also are trying to find out why the elk (which roam around town just like people!) are suddenly going crazy and are charging for no reason.*

Kate told Bailey, "Tell them about Justin and Joe."

Bailey: *Kate wants me to tell you about these two boys we met.*

Alex: *Oooo! Sounds interesting!*

Kate rolled her eyes at Bailey. Leave it to Alex to get the wrong idea about boys.

Bailey: *It's not like that. These boys are crabby. Even Biscuit doesn't like them. We're not sure what's up with them, but we hope to find out.*

Kate: *Bailey has already nicknamed the older one Oscar the Grouch.*

Alex: *And the younger one?*

Bailey: *I'm thinking of Slimey, you know, like Oscar's worm friend on* Sesame Street.

McKenzie: *LOL. Maybe they're insecure and trying to make up for it by being tough.*

Bailey: *Maybe. We don't know too much about them yet except their dad works with my dad and their grandparents live here in Estes Park.*

Elizabeth: *Do you know much about elk? What would spook them?*

Bailey: *We haven't researched elk yet. Any volunteers?*

Sydney: *I can check them out. My Uncle Jerome lives in a cabin on South Twin Lake near the Nicolet National Forest in Wisconsin and has elk around his property.*

Bailey: *Great. Thanks. If anyone reads anything about special effects that could be used to make ghost sounds, let us know. We'll keep you posted on any new developments. Bye!*

Bailey closed the laptop and sighed. "I wish we could all be together to work on our mysteries."

"It's great that we can at least stay in touch so easy, though." Kate suddenly sat up straight. "Hey! We never finished exploring the wire we found under the wallpaper last night."

"Let's go!" Bailey was off the bed faster than you could say "ghost children of the night."

"You stay here, Biscuit," Kate said. "We won't be long."

Kate brought along her camera-pen, and Bailey her camera-watch. There were no ghost noises in the bright sunlight of afternoon. A neighboring door opened and Justin and Joe came out, binoculars hanging around Justin's neck. They stopped short when they saw Bailey and Kate.

"Hi, Justin. Hi, Joe," Bailey said. "Where you going?"

"Hiking." Justin kept his eyes to the floor.

"That sounds like fun," Kate said. "Maybe we can go with you sometime."

"Yeah, maybe," Joe answered, his eyes meeting Bailey's.

"We don't know our way around the trails like you probably do since your grandparents are from here," Bailey said, trying to build the boys up just in case McKenzie's idea about them being insecure had any truth to it.

"Hmmph," Justin grunted. He pushed past them.

"What's that long thing under your jacket?" Bailey asked.

"Huh? Oh this?" Justin looked flustered and pulled his jacket closed even more. "It's just my walking stick."

Bailey and Kate nodded as the brothers dashed to the elevator. The girls turned to each other.

"That was no walking stick," Kate said. "It was way too short."

"And it looked like it was made of metal." Bailey frowned.

"Bailey!" Kate's eyes were wide with alarm. "I think you're right! That metal walking stick was really the end of a long gun!"

The Angry Elk

When the elevator doors closed behind Justin and Joe, Bailey and Kate went to a hallway window to see if they could spot the brothers leaving the hotel. They were about to give up when the boys came into view and walked across a grassy field into a wooded area.

"Where do you think they're going?" Bailey asked.

"And why do they need that gun?" Kate added.

Bailey turned from the window and started back down the hall. "Those two are up to no good."

Kate followed then stopped. "Bailey, look!" She pointed to a high corner where the hall had a sudden small turn.

Bailey's eyes followed Kate's finger to a flat circle with tiny holes in it. "A speaker!"

"Exactly!" Kate ran her hand along the wall. "Aha!"

"Aha what?" Bailey asked.

"What do you wanna bet our wire ends there? I can see a bump under the wallpaper up higher than I can reach, but then it snakes over from the corner to the speaker."

"They probably put it there figuring no one would look up since the hall jogs to the left here. People would have to watch where they're going so they don't run into the wall."

"Perfect reasoning!" Kate high-fived Bailey. "I mean, look how they wallpapered the edges of the speaker so you barely even see it. A definite attempt to hide it."

"If we hear those ghost children again tonight, let's see if the voices are coming from this speaker."

The elevator dinged, and Mrs. Chang and Trina stepped out, arms loaded with shopping bags. "Oh Bailey! I thought you and Kate were taking Biscuit for a walk."

"We already did," Kate said. "Now we're investigating the ghost children's voices we heard last night. We think we may have figured it out!"

Bailey wound her hand through the crook of her mom's arm and pulled her toward the corner speaker. "See that flat, round thing up there?"

"Yeah," Mrs. Chang said, craning her neck.

"It's a speaker," Bailey whispered.

"No!" Mrs. Chang responded dramatically.

Bailey giggled. "Yes!"

"Does that mean you won't be spirited away after all?" Disappointment dripped from Trina's voice.

Bailey glared at her.

"Anyway," she continued, turning back to her mom, "if we hear the voices again, can we come down here to see if that's where they're coming from?"

"I suppose," Mrs. Chang answered. "But right now I have to go put these packages down. They're about to break my arm!" Mrs. Chang and Trina wrestled their bags to the room.

"Wait a minute," Bailey said to Kate. "We know where the speaker is, but how does it come on? Like, is it on a timer or does it have a motion sensor that sets it off? What trips it to play the sounds?"

"We'll have to look for a hidden switch like Alex said." Kate scratched her head. "That will be our next step."

Kate pulled out her camera-pen and snapped a few pictures of the speaker.

"Now that Mom and Trina are back, let's go see what they're going to do this afternoon," Bailey suggested. "Maybe they would take us into town to do some sightseeing." Bailey raised her eyebrows at Kate.

"That would be fun," Kate agreed. "We haven't had a chance to see the town of Estes Park yet."

"Let's go ask," Bailey said, already hurrying down the hall.

● ─ ● ─ ●

An hour later, Mrs. Chang pulled into a parking place outside a row of shops and Trina, Bailey, and Kate, with Biscuit in tow, climbed out of the car. A gentle breeze blew Bailey's hair into her face. She shaded her eyes from the bright sun.

"Did you see those banners hanging over the street?" Bailey asked.

Trina looked around. "Which ones?"

"One said the Elkfest starts tomorrow, and another one said

something about a film festival!"

"Elkfest?" Trina looked at her sister like she had sprouted antlers.

"I don't know what it is, but that's what the sign said." Bailey pulled out her cotton candy lip balm and generously applied it.

"I read about that on the internet before we left for our trip," Kate said. "It's a celebration of the elk that live here. There are classes, bugling contests, elk tours, entertainment, and all kinds of activities."

"Bugling contests?" Bailey asked.

"That's the sound the elk make," Kate informed her. "I guess the contest is to see which person can sound most like a real elk."

"Now that would be fun to see!" Trina said, laughing. "Maybe we could get Dad to enter."

"I seriously doubt that." Mrs. Chang smiled. "But it would be funny."

"Can we go, Mom?" Bailey pleaded.

"We can pick up some information about it," Mrs. Chang said. "If it works out, I suppose we could."

"Cool." Bailey started down the sidewalk with Kate and Biscuit, while Mrs. Chang and Trina trailed behind. They looked in shop windows, exploring the stores that interested them. Elk and bighorn sheep leisurely roamed the streets, not nearly as hurried as the humans around them.

"Be careful around those animals!" Mrs. Chang yelled ahead to them. "No fast moves that might spook them."

"Okay," Bailey answered, her eyes glued to the window displays.

"Here's a rock store!" Bailey squealed. "Maybe I can find a good one to add to my collection."

Inside, Bailey buried her hands in the barrels of polished stones, letting them trickle through her fingers, cool and slick. She inspected row upon row of shelves that held rocks and gift items. Impressive displays of quartz, geodes, and turquoise glittered from every aisle. Jewelry cases boasted the authenticity of the gems.

"Wo–o–ow!" Bailey said, taking it all in. "This must be heaven!"

"If you can't find something for your rock collection here, you never will," Kate said.

Bailey gasped. "Look at this!" She held a shimmering rock in her hand. "Gold!"

"That can't be real gold," Kate said. "They wouldn't have it in an old barrel."

"But it looks just like gold," Bailey said. "Even the sign says it's gold."

"Yeah, fool's gold," Trina said from nearby.

Bailey whirled around to face her. "Gold is gold."

"And a fool is a fool," Trina muttered.

"Girls," Mrs. Chang warned.

"Bailey, check out this poster." Kate stood by a large wooden pillar on which a poster had been stapled. ESTES PARK FILM FESTIVAL, A WEEKEND OF STARS.

"Stars? Here?" Bailey's knees nearly buckled.

"That's what it says," Kate replied.

"We've got to keep our eyes open!" Bailey exclaimed. "This could be my big break!"

"Or heartbreak," Trina mumbled.

"I've got to look my best at all times, just in case!" Bailey looked down at her sweatshirt and jeans with holes in the knees. "This will never do!" Her voice rose ever higher, approaching the panic level.

"Deep breath, Bailey, deep breath," Kate coached her. She picked up a brochure from a rack of tourist information and fanned her friend. "Do you need your inhaler?"

"What's wrong?" Mrs. Chang asked, rounding the corner.

"Bailey just found out there's a film festival here this weekend and the streets will be swarming with stars." Kate smiled sweetly and pushed up her glasses.

Mrs. Chang put her arm around Bailey. "I hate to break this to you, but we're going home on Thursday."

"Some of the stars may come early. I've got to be ready," Bailey replied breathlessly. "Kate, will you be my manager?"

"Of course," Kate answered.

Bailey eyed her friend's mismatched outfit. "But we may need to work on your wardrobe."

Kate smoothed her clothes out with her hand. "What's wrong with this?" Kate asked.

"Nothing for your everyday girl look," Bailey said. "But if you want to be a Hollywood agent, it doesn't quite cut it."

"*Hollywood* agent?" Kate scrunched up her nose. "You're from Peoria, Illinois, and I'm from Philadelphia, Pennsylvania!"

"But you have to dress for success." Bailey waved her arm with a flair. "You have to act the part of who you *want* to be, not just who you are."

Biscuit yawned loudly.

"Hmm. Maybe I'm not ready for this Hollywood agent thing."

"Of course you are!" Bailey patted Kate on the back. "You just have to believe in yourself."

Suddenly, a commotion outside drew Bailey and Kate to the store window. People scattered from the streets, revealing two enormous elk standing on their hind legs pawing at each other as if they were boxing. When Mrs. Chang and Trina hurried over to see what was going on, Mrs. Chang put her arms protectively around the girls.

"Must be two males fighting over a female," Bailey overheard a man say.

"But they usually do that in the hills, not right here in the middle of town!" said another.

"I see Justin and Joe out there!" Bailey yelled and pulled away from her mother.

"Bailey! Don't go out there!" Mrs. Chang screamed.

Biscuit barked wildly, each bark almost lifting him off his feet.

Bailey flung open the door and as she did, the elk bolted toward the hills, leaving only dust to prove their presence. Coughing, Bailey tried to spot Justin and Joe. Kate, Mom, and Trina appeared at her side.

"I don't see them!" Bailey wailed, beginning to wheeze. She pulled her inhaler from her pocket and breathed in the asthma medication.

As the dust settled, people began talking excitedly. No one had been hurt, just shaken. Bailey, from the corner of her eye, saw two figures running down the street.

"There they go!" she said. "Justin! Joe!" she called. But the two kept on running.

"Guess they're in a hurry to get out of here," Kate said.

"I can't blame them," Trina replied. "Are we ready to move on? I looked at all the rocks I can stand."

"I guess." Bailey gave a longing glance back at the rock shop. "I didn't get anything for my collection, but I'm not exactly in the mood anymore. I think I'm ready to go back to the hotel."

"I'm more than ready," Mrs. Chang said with a shiver. "Too many elk around here for my taste."

"Look at this," Kate said. "This sign says there's a free shuttle a few blocks down the street that can take us back."

"Mom, can Kate and I take the shuttle back?" Bailey begged.

"I suppose," Mrs. Chang answered. "Just stay on the sidewalk and keep your eyes open for running elk."

"I doubt there will be any more since those two just went through," Bailey said. "But we'll be careful."

Mrs. Chang and Trina went back to their car and the girls walked to the shuttle stop.

"I wonder what made the elk come into town like that?" Bailey thought aloud.

"Me too."

"I hate to say it, but it almost seemed like Justin and Joe were ahead of the elk, like they were leading them here." Bailey grimaced at the thought.

"That doesn't seem likely," Kate said. "They were probably just at that end of the street when it all began."

"Yeah, you're probably right."

When the girls neared the shuttle stop, Bailey stuck her arm out in front of Kate to stop her. "Look!" Bailey pointed to the bench at the shuttle stop. "It's them!"

"Let's go!" Kate took off running.

The boys didn't see the girls until Bailey poked Justin's arm.

"What'ja do that for?" Justin snarled.

"We wanted to surprise you." Bailey flashed her sweetest smile.

"Are you guys okay?" Kate asked. "We saw you running from the elk."

"Yeah, we're okay." Justin studied his tennis shoes.

"How was your hike?" Bailey asked.

"Hike?" Joe said.

"I thought you hiked here," Bailey said.

"Oh yeah, we did," Joe said. "But we're taking the shuttle back."

"Where's your hiking stick?" Kate noticed Justin's jacket was unzipped all the way down and hanging open.

"Hiking stick?" Justin's eyebrows descended like dark clouds on a mountain, confusion filling his eyes.

"Yeah, you said the long thing you were carrying in your coat at the hotel was your hiking stick." Bailey crossed her arms and waited for an answer.

"Oh, that!" Justin laughed as if he'd just been told the world's funniest joke. "We left it on our way down from the hill. Got tired of carrying it."

"Hmm," Bailey said, hardly convinced. "Here comes the shuttle."

Back at the room, Bailey sat on the floor with her suitcase and sorted through her clothes looking for just the right outfit for her "Hollywood Moment." A pile of rejected items surrounded her as she pulled out another shirt. "Mom, would you let Kate and me go hiking on one of the trails by ourselves?"

Trina strolled by her and rolled her eyes but held her tongue.

"Only if you promise to stay on the trail," Mrs. Chang replied.

"We will, won't we, Kate?" Bailey tossed a tie-dyed shirt on the floor.

Kate nodded her approval. "And Biscuit could be our guide dog."

"Let's try it tomorrow!" Bailey said, suddenly feeling she'd just been set free.

"Tomorrow's the Elkfest," Kate reminded her. "We'll have to go the next day."

"Shucks," Bailey whispered, her voice registering her dismay. "I wanted to look for that 'hiking stick' Justin left behind."

"Exactly what I was thinking," Kate said with a nod. "We'll just have to pray it's still there when we go."

"There!" Bailey said, holding up a red, long-sleeved T-shirt with rhinestones that spelled "sweet," and a pair of new jeans with flowered embroidery down the leg. "I have my Hollywood outfit figured out for wearing to the Elkfest tomorrow. You never know, there may be a talent scout there for the film festival too!"

That night, Bailey could hardly wait for lights-out in their room. "Hurry up, Trina!" she ordered. "How long can it take for you to brush your teeth and wash your face?"

Trina stuck her head out from the bathroom, growling with her foamy, white mouth.

"Patience, Bales, patience," Mr. Chang said calmly from behind a business report.

"We never hear the children of the night until the lights are out and everyone's quiet," Bailey tried to explain. "We need to get to bed so we can listen."

Kate was already beneath the covers, which she'd tucked snugly under her chin. Biscuit puttered around her feet, making his bed just right. He plopped down with a giant sigh just as Trina finally emerged fresh-faced and ready for bed.

"Okay, lights out!" Bailey said. Mrs. Chang flipped the switch and the room went dark. Silence flooded the room like billowing smoke, filling every corner until Bailey could hardly breathe. "I don't hear anything, do you?" she whispered to Kate.

"Uh-uh."

"Maybe no one's out there to trip the switch." Sweat beaded on Bailey's upper lip. A door in the hallway creaked then slammed. Bailey raised her head to listen even harder, if that was possible.

"We'll just have to wait it out," Kate whispered.

Bailey nodded in the dark and lay perfectly still. Then she heard it.

Elkfest!

A muffled, high-pitched giggle seeped into the room. Bailey and Kate sprang from their bed like jack-in-the-boxes.

"We'll be back in a few," Bailey said breathlessly. She grabbed her robe, then her cell phone for light. Biscuit let out a yip but then settled back into his cozy blanket.

"He must be getting used to us jumping out of bed," Kate said softly.

When Bailey opened the door, Trina groaned and pulled the covers over her eyes as the wedge of light poured in from the hall. Kate followed Bailey to the door but then took the lead once it closed behind them. They hurried to the speaker they'd seen in the hall earlier and waited. Nothing.

"Something has to be tripping this thing to set it off." Kate looked around.

A ding alerted the girls that someone was about to get off the elevator. The doors opened, and a middle-aged couple emerged and went to their room at the far end of the hall in the opposite direction from the girls. Their door closed with a bang.

"Hee-hee-heeeeee!"

Bailey saw Kate's eyes widen and a grin spread across her friend's face. The laugh had come from the speaker above them. The two jogged down the hall. Bailey looked in all the potted plants in the hallway for a switch of some kind that the couple might have brushed against. Kate got on all fours and felt the carpet from the elevator to the couple's room.

"I found something!" she said in a loud whisper. "Feel right here."

Bailey joined Kate on her hands and knees and ran her hand along the carpet. "A bump!" she said.

"I think it's the switch that turns on the ghost children's laughter. It comes on when someone steps on it."

"Let's try it." Bailey scrunched up her shoulders. "I can't wait to tell Alex about this since she's the one who told us to look for a switch." She stood and stepped on the bump.

Almost a full minute of silence passed. "It didn't work!" Bailey moaned. *"Hee-hee-heeeeee!"*

"It's on a delay!"

"Kate! You're a genius!" Bailey hugged her friend.

"They must have delayed the ghost recording so when people hear the children laughing and look out into the hall, whoever tripped the switch would have had enough time to get to their room."

"Yeah, so no one would be there when they checked!" Bailey gave Kate a high five.

"Well, that solves that one!" Kate said.

"Now if we can just figure out why the elk are going nuts."

"Yeah, that's a tougher one to pin down."

Bailey scratched her head. "Maybe Sydney will have discovered some information about elk behavior that will help us. Let's call her tomorrow."

"We'd better get back," Kate said.

They returned to their room, the sound of *Hee-hee-heeeeee!* echoing in their heads.

●—●—●

The next morning, Bailey awoke to a deep, reverberating sound that rose quickly to a high-pitched squeal and was followed by a series of low grunts. Biscuit sat up, ears twitching. Bailey rubbed her eyes. "What was *that*?" Mr. and Mrs. Chang were already up and dressed. Trina obviously slept through anything.

"Not another ghost, I hope," Mrs. Chang said with a smirk.

"Sounds like a wounded elephant," Kate said, stretching.

"I think it's coming from outside." Bailey went to the window to investigate. "There's a guy out here blowing some kind of horn."

"I know what it is," Mr. Chang said. "I read about it in the newspaper this morning. Today is the start of the Elkfest, and he's bugling like an elk to begin the festivities."

"Oh yeah!" Bailey said. "We saw a poster about that in town yesterday and we picked up a flyer that told all about it. We thought you should enter the bugling contest, Dad." She cast a mischievous look his way.

"Sure thing. I'll get right on that," Mr. Chang teased back. "It would be fun to watch some of it, though," he admitted.

"Do you have meetings today?" Kate asked.

"Just one. After that, I'm free." Mr. Chang looked at his watch. "I'd better get going. I hope to be back around ten. We can go into town then if you'd like."

"Yeah, if Trina ever gets up!" Bailey yelled, hoping to wake her sister.

Mrs. Chang gave her a look. "You didn't make it any too easy for her to sleep last night with your ghost capers," she said. "Did you figure anything out?"

Bailey and Kate filled Mrs. Chang in on how the ghost children's voices were activated. "Pretty smart of you to figure all that out," Mrs. Chang said. "I'm impressed."

"We need to send an email to the other CCGs to let them know." Bailey turned on the laptop. "Hopefully, they'll have some elk info for us."

Bailey opened her email and found a note from Sydney. Kate read over her shoulder.

Hi. An elk's #1 defense is his sense of smell. He can spook at the scent of a human as far as a mile away. Hunters have to keep checking the wind to make sure it isn't blowing their scent toward where the elk gather.

Elk also have excellent hearing and can be spooked by a car or an ATV miles away. Of course I'm talking about wild elk. Sounds like the elk in Estes Park are used to people and vehicles, unless they possibly feel threatened by someone and remember their scent.

"That's interesting," Bailey said. "Maybe the elk are catching the scent of someone who's been mean to them and that's what's making them charge."

"Maybe," Kate replied. "Anyway, it gives us something to start with. If there's another incident, we'll have to keep our eyes open for any similar circumstances."

●—●—●

Bailey stepped out of the car at the Elkfest in her favorite jeans with flowers embroidered down the sides of each leg and sequins in the centers of each flower. Her long-sleeved, red, rhinestoned T-shirt had thumbholes at the end of each cuff. Large white sunglasses and shiny pink lip gloss completed her Hollywood outfit. Kate, unaffected by Bailey's pleas that she dress like an agent, wore green plaid pants and a Hawaiian print shirt.

Bailey felt the same excitement when she looked around at the Elkfest as she did her first time at the circus. The sweet aroma of hot Indian fry bread mingled with corn dogs and cotton candy. Elk roamed freely among the crowd, eating the food people dropped. Live country-western music filled the air and a festive mood settled over the town.

"When's the bugling contest?" Bailey asked, looking for movie stars.

Mr. Chang looked at a schedule he'd picked up. "At one o'clock."

Bailey looked at her watch. "It's only eleven thirty now."

"Maybe we should get some lunch, then head over that way so we get good seats," Mr. Chang suggested.

"Hey, there are the Perkinses!" Mrs. Chang said. She waved to the family.

"Hi, Dory," Mrs. Perkins said to Mrs. Chang. "What do you think of the Elkfest?"

"It's terrific! We're interested in the bugling contest, but we see it isn't until one o'clock," Mr. Chang told them.

"Yeah, they always have it in the afternoon," Mr. Perkins said. "My dad is in the competition again this year." He motioned to Justin and Joe's grandpa. "He won it a couple years ago."

"No kidding!" Mr. Chang said.

"Now we'll have someone to cheer for." Bailey wished she could turn a flip like Alex could. She would have done one on the spot.

"We'll see if I'm worth cheering for in a couple hours, won't we?" Grandpa Perkins winked at Bailey. "I appreciate your enthusiasm and support."

Bailey turned to Justin and Joe. "You must be excited to see your grandpa in the contest, huh?"

"Sure," Joe said. "He'll win, I just know it." He smiled at his grandpa, and Bailey thought it was the happiest she'd ever seen Joe. Justin shrugged and kicked a rock in the dirt.

"We were just getting ready to eat a bite of lunch," Mrs. Chang said. "Would you like to join us?"

"We can't eat until after Grandpa's contest is over," Justin glowered at the Changs. "He can't bugle on a full stomach."

"Oh, I see," Mrs. Chang said, hesitation marking her words as she looked uncertainly at Justin.

"Actually, we had a late breakfast so we could eat lunch later after Dad's big performance." Mr. Perkins's face seemed a bit redder than usual. "But thanks anyway."

"Good luck on the contest!" Bailey said as the families parted. "We'll be rooting for you!"

"Thanks!" Grandpa Perkins replied. "I'll need all the help I can get!"

The Changs found a hot dog stand and ordered five hot dogs and drinks. The aroma had tempted Bailey since they arrived. She loaded her dog with ketchup, mustard, and relish.

While they ate, they watched Native American dancers perform. Bailey was enthralled by the unusual dance style—the silent tap, tap, tapping of their moccasin-clad feet and the leaning and swaying of their bodies. They moved to the beat of a tom-tom drum, its leather top being struck hard, then soft, to make different rhythms and sounds.

A medium-skinned man with a long ponytail of black hair streaked with gray sang in his Native American language. The young dancers especially impressed Bailey. Some of them looked much younger than her. She clapped hard when their performance ended.

"Trina and I are going to run to the restroom before going to the bugling contest," Mrs. Chang told the girls. "Do you want to come?"

"I'm okay," Bailey said.

"Me too," Kate agreed.

"That sounds like a good idea," Mr. Chang added. "You girls stay right here until we get back."

Kate grabbed Bailey's arm when the family left. "Look!"

The Perkins family was down the street, and Justin and Joe appeared to be telling their parents something. Then the boys ran toward one of the hills surrounding the town.

"Looks like they're going to do some hill climbing." Bailey frowned. "I wonder if they picked up their 'walking stick' from the area they hiked yesterday."

"You mean *gun*?" Kate snorted. "Those guys are either avid hikers or they are up to something. What time is it?"

Bailey checked her watch. "Twelve fifteen."

"Their hike will have to be short, or they'll miss their grandpa's bugling performance."

"And Joe seemed excited about seeing it." Bailey remembered Joe's unexpected smile. "I don't think he'd want to miss it."

"Justin, however, is another matter." Kate pushed her glasses up. She dug in her pocket and pulled out her camera-pen. Holding it horizontally, she twisted the pointed end to zoom in as close as possible. Justin and Joe's image got larger on the metal clip. She quickly clicked the end. Bailey joined in with her camera-watch.

"Between the two of us, we should have some good shots to share with the Camp Club Girls." Kate returned her pen to her pocket.

"Are we ready?" Mr. Chang said when the family met up again.

"Ready!" the girls shouted in unison.

"Let's go cheer Grandpa Perkins on!"

The Changs sat in the grass near the front and sipped on their sodas. A magician entertained the crowd gathering for the bugling contest.

"I need a volunteer," the magician said. "Who will help me?"

Bailey's hand was up like a rocket.

"You, there, in the red sparkly shirt." The magician pointed to Bailey.

"He's pointing at you, Bailey!" Kate pushed her friend to her feet. "If there are talent scouts out there, they'll all see you on stage. It could be your big break!"

Bailey ran up to the stage, her family applauding her all the way.

The magician asked Bailey her name and age. Then he looked confused. "Hmm. That's unusual," he said.

"What?" Bailey asked.

"You seem to have something on the back of your shirt."

"I do?" Bailey twisted to see.

The magician reached behind her and pulled out a bouquet of flowers. "Oh, I'm sorry. I hope I didn't spoil the surprise you were hiding for your mother."

Bailey squealed and clapped.

The magician handed the flowers to Mrs. Chang. "Let's hear it for my lovely assistant, Bailey! Thank you for your help, miss."

Bailey curtsied grandly and took her seat. "Do you think anyone famous saw me?" she asked Kate.

"If they were here, they totally saw you," she replied.

Soon, the contest began. A panel of judges sat in front of the stage and took notes on each contestant's bugling ability. Bailey scanned the crowd a short time later and spotted the Perkins family, including Justin and Joe, sitting on the other side of the bugling area.

"I guess they made it back in time," Bailey whispered to Kate. She nodded in the boys' direction.

"Guess so," Kate said. "And Justin actually looks almost happy."

"Amazing!" Bailey joked.

Grandpa Perkins's name was announced, and he went to the

microphone. "I've been in this bugling contest five years running and only won once, two years ago. But this is the first time I've ever had two cheering sections." He waved his arm toward his family and then the Changs. They all yelled their loudest. Grandpa gave them an informal salute then cleared his throat and got down to business. He let out two low, resonant tones that quickly rose to a high-pitched squeal, followed by three deep grunts. He sounded just like one of the elk!

The crowd went wild. Even the elk in the park stopped and looked. Grandpa bowed before waving and taking his seat on the stage with the other contestants.

Bailey clapped wildly. "Grandpa Perkins was fantastic!"

Kate nodded. "I bet he wins the grand prize."

The bugling contest continued, but after about the fifth person, Bailey thought she felt a slight tremor. She looked at Kate, who looked back at her, questions in her eyes. The shaking increased and soon people were on their feet running and yelling, "Stampede!"

Elk ran through the crowd on their long, knobby legs, more elk than Bailey had ever seen at one time before. Dust flew and parents snatched small children to safety. When the rumbling and shaking ended, Bailey noticed some people lying on the ground injured.

"The Perkinses! Where are they?" Bailey wondered aloud. As much as she didn't like Justin and Joe, she didn't want any of them to get hurt. The dust cleared and she caught sight of them. "There they are! By the stage."

Mr. Perkins was helping a shaken Grandpa Perkins off the stage. "They look like they're okay," Kate said. "We're lucky we weren't hurt."

Bailey listened to conversations around her.

"What do you think caused the elk to run through town this time?"

"I bet it was the bugling contest. Probably drew them right in."

"They've never done that before."

"Had some mighty good buglers this year."

"They're probably nervous with all these people around."

"They're trying to protect their young."

"Protect their young? They were born in May, five months ago."

"I think they're aggressive because it's mating season."

"Could be. Peak mating is September and October."

"But they've never been this aggressive in mating season before. Something got them stirred up."

"Seems like they show up only to charge lately. They don't roam around as freely as they once did."

"True enough. And they seem to come out more in the evenings than they used to."

"Where did they come from?"

"From that hill," one said, pointing to where Bailey and Kate had seen Justin and Joe hiking.

"That's the opposite direction from when they came out of the woods last time."

Bailey looked at Kate as they took in all the talk. "What do you think, Kate?"

"I don't know," she said thoughtfully. "I think we need to talk to the other girls. Seems when we work together, things come together faster."

"Two heads—or six—are better than one!" Bailey agreed.

As the people gathered, leaders announced that the bugling contest would resume in an hour and the winner would be declared shortly after that. The Changs walked over to where the Perkins family stood.

"Everyone all right here?" Mr. Chang asked.

"Yes, a bit shaken, but not injured," Mr. Perkins answered. "Your family okay?"

"We're fine too," Mr. Chang replied.

"Mr. Perkins," Bailey said to Grandpa, "you were awesome!"

"Yeah, you sounded like a real elk!" Kate agreed.

"I bet you're going to win." Bailey grinned as if she'd just won a prize herself.

"Of course he'll win," Justin said, surprising Bailey. "No *tourist* should win the local contest."

"Well, now, I wouldn't say that," Grandpa said, patting his grandson's back. "The best bugler should win, wherever he's from."

"A tourist doesn't know the elk bugle as well as the locals," Justin maintained. "They should just give up and go home."

Bailey almost laughed until she saw how serious Justin was. No hint of a smile crossed his face, no look of pride in his grandpa. Just the usual anger. Was it her imagination or was that jab at tourists targeted at her and her family?

"Come on, Bailey," Kate said, hooking her arm through her friend's. "I'm so sure Grandpa Perkins is going to win, we may as well go see some more of the Elkfest."

Bailey glanced at her mother. "Is it okay, Mom?"

"Sure, go have fun," Mrs. Chang replied.

CHAPTER 6

Target Practice

When Bailey and Kate returned from the Elkfest that evening, they made a conference call to the other Camp Club Girls. Leaving Trina to watch TV in the hotel room, the two friends sat on an overstuffed couch in the lobby. Biscuit, on his leash, sat quietly between them. After all the girls were on the line, Bailey explained the children of the night mystery. Kate supplemented the story with technical details.

"You were right about the hidden switch, Alex," Bailey told her. "Kate found it under the hallway carpet."

"But what we hadn't counted on," Kate added, "was that it was on a timer, so it didn't go off immediately when stepped on."

"Wow! You guys are awesome!" Alex exclaimed. Bailey imagined her doing a backflip with her typical cheerleader enthusiasm. "Scooby Doo would be proud. Next thing you know they'll be asking you to be on their show!"

McKenzie giggled. "Now *that* I'd like to see! Bailey and Kate as cartoon characters!"

"Anything to report on the elk research, Syd?" Bailey asked.

"Yeah. Hold on. I've found out a few things."

Bailey heard papers rustling, and then Sydney continued.

"The elk in the Estes Park Rocky Mountain area are called wapiti elk. *Wapiti* means 'white rump' in the Shawnee Indian language."

Bailey laughed. "Yep. That's them, all right."

"Like I mentioned before, adult elk have an awesome sense of smell, but they also have excellent hearing and can run up to thirty-five miles an hour. They're well equipped to avoid the cougars and bears that prey on them. Strong animals like elk don't need much cover except during extreme weather, to avoid hunters, or when they're harassed."

"Harassed?" McKenzie asked.

"You know, if people or other animals bother them," Sydney explained. "They're very social animals and live in herds most of the year. They're mostly active at dawn and dusk, but when it gets hot or when they're harassed, elk may become more active at night. When they're not being hunted, elk get along well with humans so lawns and golf courses become some of their favorite restaurants."

The girls giggled and Biscuit joined in with happy barks.

Sydney continued reading. "September and October are good months to observe them because the boy elk—or bulls, as they're called—are battling over the girl elk, so they aren't as worried about being seen. You'll hear the bull's bugle usually near dusk or dawn. You should be careful around the male elk during mating season, especially in areas where they're used to being around people, because they tend to be more aggressive."

"So maybe it *is* because of mating season that the elk have been acting so strange," Kate said. "We heard someone say that at the Elkfest today."

"But from hearing the townspeople talk, it seems they're more aggressive than usual this year." Bailey sighed.

"Sydney said they become more active at night if they're harassed," Elizabeth added.

"Good point," Bailey said. "We overheard someone mention that after the elk stampede today."

"But who or what is harassing them?" McKenzie asked.

"That's the question." Kate stroked Biscuit, her face thoughtful.

Silence filled the phone line for a moment.

"Not to change the subject, but have you seen those boys anymore?" Alex asked.

"Yeah, we've seen them a couple of times," Bailey answered. "They went on a hike yesterday."

"With a very unusual walking stick," Kate added, concern clouding her face.

"Oh yeah." Bailey's eyes sought Kate's. "We didn't get a good look at it, but Justin, the older boy, had something hidden in his coat. When we asked him about it, he said it was his walking stick."

"But it looked like it was made out of metal," Kate chimed in, "and though it *was* sort of long, it was still too short to be a walking stick."

"Then we saw them out the window as they left the hotel and walked to a wooded area. Justin's walking stick was in plain view by then and it turns out. . ." Bailey paused dramatically, ". . .it was a gun!"

The other girls gasped in unison.

"What kind of gun?" Elizabeth asked.

"It looked like an air pellet gun or whatever those are called," Kate said.

"It's called an airsoft gun," Sydney said. "My older brother has one. It's kind of like a BB gun, but smaller, and the pellets can sting but not do serious damage."

"But get this," Bailey's voice rose in excitement. "When they came back, they didn't have it with them. When we asked them about it, they said they got tired of carrying it and left it behind."

"Well, they said they left their walking stick behind, since they just claimed they had a walking stick," Kate said.

"Yeah, right!" McKenzie said. "That doesn't seem likely."

"Bailey, you and Kate have to be careful around those two," Elizabeth warned. "Avoid them if you can. First Corinthians 15:33 says, 'Do not be misled: Bad company corrupts good character.' Don't take any unnecessary chances."

"We won't," Kate assured her.

Bailey stood and stretched. "We'd better get to bed. But if any of you think of anything that could help us, let us know. And Sydney, thanks for the great info on elk. Keep up the good work."

●—●—●

The next morning, Bailey and Kate started out on their hike with Biscuit, taking their secret cameras, water, cell phones, binoculars, and some trail mix. Both girls wore hoodies to ward off the early morning chill.

Rather than taking the free shuttle, Bailey and Kate decided to hike into town. They passed the rock shop and lots of cute restaurants they hoped Bailey's parents would take them to before their vacation ended. The girls lingered outside the fudge and ice cream shop, their mouths watering. They enjoyed seeing the sleepy town wake up, its stores just opening.

"Hey, look! A miniature golf course!" Kate pushed her glasses up.

"Want to play a round before we head up the hill?" Bailey asked.

"Sure!" Kate reached down and picked up her dog. "Reminds me of the day we found Biscuit at Camp Discovery!"

The two grinned and rubbed the wiggling fur ball.

"You were so cute," Kate cooed to him.

"And dirty and stinky!" Bailey plugged her nose at the memory.

Kate covered the dog's ears. "Don't you listen to her. You've always been a prince." She set Biscuit back down.

Bailey paid the man at the counter for the round of golf and they chose clubs that were just their sizes.

"What do you think Justin and Joe are up to today?" Bailey asked.

"Probably still sleeping." Kate stepped up to the first hole and teed off.

Bailey looked at her watch. "I guess it *is* only nine o'clock." She took her turn.

"Look at that huge elk!" Kate pointed to the street. Biscuit barked and pranced around Kate's feet.

Just as Bailey turned to look, the elk raised his head and let out a shrill bugle.

"Wow! He sounds just like Grandpa Perkins!" Bailey said seriously and then laughed at how it must have sounded. "From what we just heard, I bet he won that bugling contest yesterday. We'll have to find out today."

Bailey and Kate moved to the next hole, a miniature Rocky Mountain peak with tunnels for the ball to go through in the middle of the base, and one on either side.

Kate stuck out her neck and squinted through her glasses.

"What are you looking at?" Bailey asked when she realized her friend was looking into the distance rather than at the golf tunnels.

"I think I'm looking at Justin and Joe," Kate replied, pointing toward the hill they hoped to hike later. She pushed her glasses up and squinted to get a better look.

Bailey's head swung in the direction Kate's finger pointed. She snatched the binoculars out of their case and peered through them. Focusing in, she found the boys. "That's them all right, and it looks like they got to the 'walking stick' before we did."

"Really?" Kate sounded disappointed, but then her voice perked up. "Can you see the 'walking stick' clearly?"

"*Very* clearly, and we were right—that's no walking stick."

Kate grabbed the binoculars from her friend and looked. "No, it isn't. That is definitely a gun, and it looks like they're doing some target practice."

"What are they shooting at?" Now it was Bailey's turn to squint.

"Looks like they have empty soda cans lined up on a tree stump," Kate said. "It's hard to tell since the trees are so thick there." Kate lowered the binoculars.

"So we were right," Bailey repeated, her hands on her hips.

Kate nodded. "They were lying, just as we thought."

"Maybe we're jumping to conclusions," Bailey said solemnly. "Just because they're shooting a gun doesn't make them bad people. As long as they're being careful and shooting at things like cans. And it's probably an airsoft gun like Sydney told us about—the kind that just shoots little plastic pellets."

"But why would they try to cover it up by lying?" Kate pointed her golf club at Bailey. "That's what makes it suspicious."

Bailey sighed. "I suppose you're right. Although many people don't approve of kids using even plastic pellet guns."

"Let's hurry up and finish this golf game and get over to that hill," Kate said. "Maybe we'll see what they're up to."

"Yeah," Bailey agreed. "It's your turn."

Bailey and Kate finished their round of golf and hurried to the hill, where elk and bighorn sheep roamed around its base. Biscuit ran ahead of them, causing the big animals to scatter. The air smelled crisp and fall-like, red and gold leaves crunching under their feet as they walked.

"It smells so good out here!" Kate said as she stared at a towering pine.

"If nothing else, maybe we can learn some more about the elk's behavior while we're out here," Bailey said. She moved close to a pine tree and sniffed the bark.

"What are you doing?" Kate looked at her friend like she'd gone crazy.

"Smelling the bark," Bailey answered matter-of-factly.

"Well, I can see that. But why?"

"Come see for yourself." Bailey motioned her over. "Sniff."

Kate looked around then put her nose close to the tree and inhaled. Biscuit came back and sniffed all around the tree too.

"Well?" Bailey asked.

"Smells like vanilla!" Kate cried.

"See? Aren't you glad you tried?" Bailey took another sniff. "Sometimes I can't decide if it smells like vanilla or butterscotch, but either way it smells good."

"Where'd you learn that?" Kate asked.

"Sydney, of course," Bailey answered. "She showed me at camp the first day she and I went out hiking."

"I should have guessed Syd would have taught you that."

The two walked on. Biscuit trotted alongside the trail just a few feet ahead.

"What's that?" Bailey took a few steps off the trail and stopped by a bathtub-size, shallow hole in the ground.

"I don't know, but it smells awful!" Kate covered her nose and mouth with her hands. Biscuit scampered into the sunken earth, sniffing furiously.

Bailey took a few steps closer. "It's so muddy I can hardly get any closer."

"Biscuit's going to be a mess!"

"He already is." Bailey bent down and looked at the huge indentation. "There are light brown hairs in the mud. And look at all these tracks around it."

Kate stooped to look at the four-inch footprints that looked like a long heart shape cut down the middle. "Do you think these are elk tracks?"

Bailey shrugged. "We'll have to check on the internet."

"Or ask Sydney."

"Let's get some pictures of it and we can send them to her to see." Bailey aimed her camera-watch at the indentation and Kate pulled out her camera-pen.

"These hairs sure look the same color as elk fur," Kate said.

"Come on. Let's keep going." Bailey stood and walked back to the trail, trying not to sink into the mud. "Must be so muddy because of that pond over there."

The girls looked at a small pool of water almost hidden by reeds. It sat just yards beyond the smelly indentation.

"Let's go, boy," Kate called to Biscuit. The mud-covered dog plodded his way out of the bog to her side.

"I guess today we'll find out who won the bugling contest." Bailey kicked some fall leaves that covered the trail.

"If anyone can bugle better than Grandpa Perkins, he's probably part elk!"

Bailey suddenly stopped and listened.

"Wha—?" Kate began, but Bailey held her hand up to stop her and put her finger to her lips.

Bailey tiptoed to the right of the trail and hid behind a tree, motioning Kate to join her. When Kate reached her, she whispered, "I think I hear Justin's and Joe's voices."

Kate nodded silently. She picked up Biscuit and reattached his leash, his muddy feet leaving marks all over her light pink hoodie. She didn't dare complain or make a sound.

The girls stayed still as stones but heard nothing more.

"Apparently they've moved farther up the hill from when we saw them earlier. Let's keep going," Bailey whispered. "But stay off to the side of the trail so if they come down this way, they won't see us."

"We told your mom we'd stay on the trail," Kate reminded her.

"We'll be right beside it," Bailey said. "We'll keep it in sight. She just didn't want us wandering and getting lost."

The girls crept silently, like spies, hopping from behind one tree to the next. The boys' voices grew louder.

"Look over there," Bailey exclaimed.

Kate nodded. Justin and Joe had moved their target practice off the trail.

"I can barely hear them," Kate said. "And I don't have a clear view of them."

Bailey scurried to the next tree, which took her several feet closer to the boys. Kate followed carefully. She pulled out her camera-pen and snapped a few pictures of the boys. Bailey did the same with her camera-watch, just for good measure. Biscuit caught sight of what the girls were looking at and a low growl rumbled in his throat.

"*Shhhh,*" Kate said softly as she scratched the dog's head to try to calm him.

Justin stopped mid-aim and looked around as if he'd heard something. Then he refocused his aim at the pop cans lined on a tree stump.

Bailey strained to hear what they said.

"We'll show them," Justin said to his younger brother. "We'll have them so scared they never come back!" With that, he pulled his trigger and a loud pop rang out.

Biscuit barked and leaped from Kate's arms. He ran in the boys' direction, leash dragging behind him.

"What in the wo—" Justin turned and saw Biscuit flying at him, barking wildly.

"It's those girls' dog!" Joe yelled. He spun in circles, eyes searching the woods.

"Biscuit!" Kate jumped from behind the tree and raced after the dog, with Bailey close behind.

"Get that dog away from me!" shouted Justin.

"Biscuit! Come here!" Kate screamed.

The girls reached the boys just as Justin raised his airsoft gun and pointed it at Biscuit.

Lost!

"NOOO!" Kate shrieked.

The gun went off. Biscuit yelped and darted into the woods.

"Biscuit!" Kate rushed through the trees after her dog.

Bailey strode squarely to confront Justin, whose gun hung limp in his hand. "Why did you do that?" she demanded, tears stinging her eyes.

"He was going to attack me!" Justin yelled.

"He was barking around your feet! If he wanted to attack you, he would have jumped at you."

"Well, I wasn't going to wait to find out." Justin ran his hand through his short hair, his face flushed. "It would have been too late to do anything by then." He looked at his younger brother, who stood dazed nearby. "You okay, Joe?"

"I—I think so," he stammered.

"Let's get out of here before that dog comes back and attacks us again." Justin set his gun on the safety setting and stuffed it into his jacket as Joe gathered their targets and supplies.

Bailey wanted to grab the gun and knock both boys senseless with it. Instead she turned and dashed into the woods. "Kate?" she called. The wind in the trees was her only reply. "Kate!" Nothing.

Bailey looked back and realized she could no longer see the trail they'd been on. She stood for a few minutes, trying to push down her fear. *What should I do?* All she could think of was Kate and Biscuit, but she didn't know how to find them. In the shadows of the towering pines, the air felt chilly, even with her hoodie on.

Which way should I go? Bailey looked around her again. *I can't think!*

"Kate!" Still no reply.

Bailey sucked in a deep breath and let it out slowly. *Help me think, God.*

Show me what to do. She tucked her icy hands into her hoodie pockets and fingered her cell phone. *That's it! Thanks, God!* Snatching it out, she dialed Kate. Thank heavens she could pick up a signal. One ring. Two rings.

"Hello?"

"Kate! Thank goodness! Where are you?"

"I'm not sure."

Bailey heard Kate's voice tremble. "Did you find Biscuit?"

"Yeah, he's here with me."

"Is he okay?"

"I think so. I looked over him and didn't see any injuries. I guess he was just spooked by the noise of the gun."

Bailey closed her eyes and sighed. "I about let Justin have it when you and Biscuit disappeared into the woods. He claimed Biscuit was about to attack him. I nearly decked him, even if he is bigger than me."

Kate laughed. "Well, I'm glad you held yourself back. That's all we need is for him to say Biscuit attacked him and then you assaulted him."

The girls grew silent. "Bailey, we have to find each other and get back to the trail."

"I don't know which way to go." Bailey's voice rose, fear once again curling within.

"Hang on a second."

Bailey could hear rustling, as if Kate were looking for something. "Here it is."

"What?"

"My mini-GPS. It's a trial product my dad brought home from work one day. What better time to try it out than now?"

"Trial product? GPS units have been around awhile."

"But this one is tiny. It fits into the palm of my hand. I can clip it onto my belt if I want."

"That's fantastic!"

"Let's see, I'll put in Estes Park, Colorado, and see what it brings up." Kate punched in the city and state. "It worked! Now I just have to zoom in to find that street we were on."

"I'm glad you're the one trying to figure this out," Bailey said. "I'm directionally challenged."

"Here we go," Kate said. "Looks like we walked north to get to this hill from town. The sun was to our right, so that must be east since it rose only a few hours earlier, right?"

Bailey relaxed. "You're starting to sound like Sydney!"

"So to get back we need to go south, so the sun is to our left."

Bailey looked up and shielded her eyes from the sun. "I'll hang up and yell for you. Hopefully, you'll hear me as you get closer. Then we can look for the trail together from here."

"Okay," Kate said, "but if I don't hear you soon, I'm calling you back."

"Deal." Bailey stuffed her phone back in her pocket and yelled, "Kate! Kate, I'm over here!"

She yelled for what seemed like a full minute, stopping only to listen briefly for an answer. A cool breeze swirled dry leaves around her feet, and she zipped her mud-splotched hoodie clear to the neck.

"Kate!" Leaves crunched behind her and Bailey swung around. "Kate?" No answer, but the crunching drew closer. "Kate, if that's you, you'd better answer me!" Silence. "Kate, this isn't funny!"

From behind a clump of trees, a huge elk with enormous antlers stuck out his head and looked at Bailey. She froze, not sure if the elk would charge or if he was as afraid as she was. They stood, eyes locked, neither one moving a muscle. Finally, the elk seemed satisfied that the girl meant no harm and munched on a nearby shrub. Bailey exhaled a breath she didn't realize she'd been holding and inched forward to get a better view of the elk.

Suddenly Bailey was startled by her cell phone ringing. "Kate? I'm watching a big elk eat. You should see him!"

"You're supposed to be calling for me, remember?"

"I did, but then the elk scared me and I was afraid to make much noise."

Bailey heard rustling again and turned to look. The elk turned his head too, ears twitching. "Kate! Over here!"

At the sound of Bailey's voice, the elk turned toward her and narrowed his eyes. He lowered his head, those gigantic antlers pointing in her direction, then took a few steps toward. Hardly daring to take a breath, Bailey froze. Images of charging elk filled her mind.

Biscuit sniffed the air and leaped out of Kate's arms, barking wildly. The tiny dog ran at the towering elk, who seemed momentarily confused by all the excitement. He tried to keep his eye on the dog prancing at his feet, one minute in front of him and the next behind. In apparent exasperation, the elk turned and lumbered off into the woods.

Kate came through the trees. "Bailey! I was so afraid for you." She hugged her friend. "Are you all right?"

"I'm fine. But my legs felt like noodles for a minute there."

Biscuit scampered up to Bailey and jumped to get her attention.

"I see you! Thanks for scaring that elk away. You really are a wonder dog!" She gave the dog a friendly rub. "But you scared us when you ran off into the woods!" Bailey slipped her lip balm from her pocket and applied some. "Now all we have to do is find the trail."

"Shouldn't be too hard with this GPS."

"Let's see that thing." Kate placed the tiny device in Bailey's palm. "I've never seen one this small."

"Dad says it still has a few glitches, but it works well for the most part." Kate took the GPS back. "See? It shows where we are. It looks like this squiggly line might be a trail."

"So we need to turn around and go to our right to find it. Let's try it."

Kate started off in the direction the GPS indicated. Bailey and Biscuit followed close behind. She kept her eye on the device and could see the distance between them and the trail diminishing. "We're almost there!"

"I think I see it!" Bailey went running, Biscuit barking excitedly beside her.

"I was thinking," Kate said when they were back on the trail. "I wonder if Justin and Joe know something about the elk being so agitated."

"Maybe. They sure are angry themselves."

"Maybe Justin is giving anger lessons to the elk."

Seeing the twinkle in Kate's eyes, Bailey laughed. "Yeah, they were probably just waiting for their class to gather when we snuck up on them."

"They seem to spend a lot of time on this hill."

"Yeah. And with that 'walking stick' that looked just like the gun they were shooting pop cans with today."

Just then the ground trembled.

"Did you feel that?" Kate asked.

Before Bailey could answer, the trembling became stronger. "Don't tell me it's another—"

The girls heard loud rustling and soon Bailey spotted a herd of elk running through the forest toward them. "Stampede!"

Kate snatched up Biscuit, grabbed Bailey's arm, and pulled her behind a tree. About twenty elk thundered by so close Bailey thought she could stick out her hand and touch them as they passed. She saw what looked like fear in their eyes and heard their snorts and panting. When the last one was out of sight, the fading rhythm of hooves was all that remained, followed by an eerie quiet. Bailey and Kate cautiously stepped out from behind the protection of the tree and looked around.

A cloud of dust marked the path the elk had taken.

"I hope they don't run clear into town." Kate's eyes registered her concern.

"Something back there in the woods scared them. Why else would they run like that?"

"I don't know, but I think you're right."

"Y—you don't think it was a wild animal, do you?" Bailey forced the words from her mouth, barely daring to speak them.

Kate turned to her friend, eyes wide. "Let's get out of here!"

The girls ran down the trail until they could see the town. "We're almost there," panted Bailey.

"Are you okay? Do you need your inhaler?"

Bailey shook her head. "I'm okay. Just winded."

They slowed down and walked the rest of the way to town. When they got on Main Street, they heard people talking about the elk.

"I can't believe they came through here again!"

"This is the worst it's ever been."

"What are we going to do about them?"

"The elk are becoming too dangerous."

"Something has to be done."

Bailey pulled Kate aside where no one would hear them. "Do you think we should tell them what happened on our hike?"

"You mean our encounter with the elk, the elk stampede, getting separated and lost, or seeing Justin and Joe target practicing?"

Bailey giggled. "I guess we did have a lot going on, didn't we? Should we tell any of it?"

"I'm not sure. It might not have anything to do with the stampede through town."

"Then again it might." Bailey let out a giant sigh. "Maybe we should just go back to the hotel."

"Yeah. We need to gather more evidence before we point fingers at people."

"Let's take the shuttle back. I'm tired of walking."

"Me too." Kate hooked Biscuit's leash on him and set him down. "It's a wonder you didn't get trampled by that huge elk or the stampeding herd," she said in his pointy little ear. "You are so brave!"

"It's amazing none of us did," Bailey added. "God must be working overtime keeping an eye out for us."

"As usual."

The girls joined a couple of people who were waiting at the shuttle stop.

Kate plopped down on the bench. "We should get in touch with the other Camp Club Girls when we get back."

"Yeah, they'll want to hear about our adventure."

A voice interrupted their conversation, and Justin and Joe's grandma joined them under the shelter. "Oh, hi, girls!"

"Mrs. Perkins! What are you doing here?"

"I've been doing a little shopping this morning." She held up her bags as proof. The shuttle pulled to the curb and the group boarded. Bailey and Kate sat across the aisle from Grandma Perkins and her shopping bags. Biscuit sniffed them curiously.

"What have you girls been up to?" Grandma Perkins asked.

"We went for a hike this morning and now we're heading back to the hotel."

"Justin and Joe were hiking today too!"

Bailey bit her lower lip. "Yes, we saw them."

"My stomach is growling." Kate put her hand on her tummy.

Bailey, relieved at the change of subject, looked at her watch. "That's because it's lunchtime. It's almost twelve o'clock."

"Guess we timed that right."

When the shuttle parked in front of the hotel, Bailey, Kate, Biscuit, and Grandma Perkins got off.

"Oh Mrs. Perkins! Did Mr. Perkins win the bugling contest?" Kate asked.

"No, someone else won," Grandma Perkins replied.

Bailey could hardly believe her ears. "That's impossible! He was the best one there!"

"Well, I'm glad you thought so, but the judges didn't agree." Grandma Perkins's voice was kind. "It's all right. He just did it for fun. He didn't care if he won."

"I bet Justin and Joe were really disappointed," Bailey said quietly as they walked down the hotel sidewalk.

"Yes, they were." Mrs. Perkins shook her head. "Especially Justin."

Bailey suddenly stopped and gasped.

"What's the matter?" Kate's eyes followed Bailey's line of vision toward the old historic building.

"I thought I saw a ghost in that window."

"Bailey! You know better than that!" Kate laughed but then paused. "You're as white as a sheet!"

"Which window?" Grandma Perkins asked.

"The fourth floor, four windows over from the right."

"Ah, yes. The famous room 408. And what did this ghost look like?"

"Like a cowboy. He had a cowboy hat and a mustache and he just stared out the window then faded off to the left."

"That must be the old cowboy ghost we read about in the brochure!" Kate kept her eyes on the window.

"Legend has it that a guest thought he saw the same thing years back," Grandma Perkins explained. "But the front desk confirmed that the room was vacant. They said no one could have stood in that window because it was over the bathroom sink, and he couldn't have faded to the left because it would have taken him through the wall. That was the first reported sighting of the cowboy ghost. Many people have seen him since then, but only at this time of the year."

"Are you telling me I saw a real ghost?" Bailey's voice trembled.

"Bailey! You're not going to fall for that, are you?"

"All I'm saying is that you're not the first to have seen it—whatever it is." Grandma Perkins patted Bailey on the back. "You want me to walk you to your room?"

"That's okay. We don't believe in ghosts, do we, Bailey?"

"N–no. We don't."

"Okay then. I'll see you later." Mrs. Perkins left with a friendly wave.

Bailey and Kate stood in the hotel yard, still trying to absorb what had just happened.

"Do you believe that? I mean, really. Who would believe in cowboy ghosts?" Kate snickered as she looked up at the fourth floor window again.

Bailey stood silent beside her, but then she noticed Kate's face grow pale. Bailey followed Kate's eyes and this time they both saw the cowboy. "There he is! I told you it was real!" Bailey's voice quivered.

Kate reached for Bailey's hand. Her mouth moved, but no words came.

Now it was Bailey's turn to reassure Kate. "It has to be special effects, don't you think, Kate? Remember, there are no such things as ghosts."

No sooner had she said those words than the cowboy faded away to the left of the window just as he had done before.

"That is definitely a special effect. It's identical to the movement I saw before!" Bailey squeezed Kate's hand. "Come on. We've got another mystery to figure out. Hopefully, it will be as easy as finding out where the ghost children's laughter came from."

Kate nodded mutely as Bailey led her to the hotel entrance.

Mystery Music

Back in the hotel room, Bailey and Kate bathed Biscuit in the sink. Water sprayed everywhere when he shook himself. The girls screamed with laughter and wrapped the dog in a hotel towel.

"There you go!" Kate dried him off. "Nice and clean."

While the girls fixed sandwiches from food the Changs had put in the mini-fridge, they told Mrs. Chang about their hike and the beautiful scenery. They left out the parts about Justin and Joe, getting lost, and how close they were to the elk stampede.

"When we got back to town, the elk had just stampeded again and everyone was talking about it," Bailey told her.

"Oh no! Not again." Mrs. Chang shook her head. "Was anyone hurt?"

"I don't think so." Kate's green eyes were serious behind her dark-rimmed glasses. "They say it's the worst it's ever been and that they're going to have to do something about it because it's getting too dangerous."

Mrs. Chang nodded as she straightened up their room. "I can believe that. They can't just let the elk run wild in town."

Bailey plugged in the charger for her laptop. "I still think there has to be a reason they're acting so crazy this year. We just have to uncover it."

"Sounds like you had a nice morning, in spite of the stampede," Mrs. Chang said.

"We did!" Bailey replied enthusiastically. "Grandma Perkins rode home on the shuttle with us."

"And when we got to the hotel, we saw the cowboy ghost of room 408!" Kate squealed.

"Cowboy ghost?" Mrs. Chang got that you've-got-to-be-kidding-me look on her face.

Bailey nodded. "We know he's not real, Mom. We just want to figure out how they do the special effect."

"Yeah, like the ghost children. We figured *that* one out." Kate reached for her laptop.

"Well, I guess there's no harm in that." Mrs. Chang glanced at her watch. "Oh, it's time for me to pick up Trina. She and a girl she met here at the hotel went to a movie. Will you be all right for a little while?"

"Yeah. We're going to get online and chat with the other Camp Club Girls."

"Okay. See you later." Mrs. Chang dropped a kiss on Bailey's nose and left.

"Let's download the pictures we took to send the other girls before we chat with them," Kate suggested. "Then they'll have them to look at while we talk."

Bailey and Kate each downloaded their photos and then logged into the CCG website chat room.

Bailey: *Hi! Anybody there?*

McKenzie: *I'm here.*

Sydney: *Me too.*

Kate: *Hang on. I'll call the others to get them to log on.*

Elizabeth: *I'm here now.*

Alex: *Me too.*

Bailey: *We found something weird on the hike we went on this morning.*

Elizabeth: *What was it?*

Kate: *We don't know. But we're hoping some of you might help us figure it out. We sent you some pictures of it.*

Bailey: *We hiked up a trail and found this weird, huge indentation in the ground. It was about the size of a bathtub. It had what looked like elk hair and tracks around it and it smelled awful. Sydney, we were hoping you could tell us if the tracks look like they belong to an elk. You'll see them in the pictures too.*

Sydney: *I'll look and see. And I bet I know what that indentation was too.*

Kate: *What?*

Sydney: *Hang on. I'll look at the picture to be sure. There it is. Yep. Was there any water nearby?*

Bailey: *Yeah, we saw a scummy pond with grass growing in it a few feet away.*

Sydney: *It was probably an elk wallow. And those are definitely elk tracks in the picture. My uncle hunts elk and he told me about them. Usually the male elk, the bulls, roll in wallows to cover their bodies with the scent of urine and droppings so they'll attract the female elk.*

Elizabeth: *Gross! What nasty cologne!*

Sydney: *You think that's bad? The female elk then roll in the wallow to get the same scent on them and let the bull know they're interested.*

Alex: *I'd rather pass notes.*

Sydney: *One thing's for sure. If you have wallows, you have elk.*

Bailey: *Anyway, back to the hike. We caught Justin and Joe shooting airsoft guns at some empty pop cans. We sent you a few shots of that too, no pun intended! Just look at the pictures. They're a little blurry. The noise from the gun scared Biscuit to death!*

Kate: *Yeah, he flew out of my arms and ran at them, barking his head off.*

Bailey: *Justin, or should I say Oscar the Grouch, was so scared he aimed his gun right at poor little Biscuit and shot!*

McKenzie: *Oh no! Is he okay?*

Kate: *Yeah, he wasn't hurt. Apparently our wonder dog is faster than a speeding bullet or else Oscar the Grouch is a lousy shot. Biscuit must have just been freaked out over the sound of the gun because he ran into the woods and I ran after him.*

Bailey: *And I stayed to give those boys a piece of my mind!*

Sydney: *LOL. Careful. You might need that piece of your mind later.*

Elizabeth: *Guess you forgot the Bible says, "A gentle answer turns away wrath, but a harsh word stirs up anger."*

Bailey giggled.

Bailey: *Guess I did.*

Kate: *I found Biscuit after calling for him awhile. But then I realized I had wandered off the path and didn't know how to get back.*

Bailey: *In the meantime, I had gone to find Kate and Biscuit and I realized I was lost too. But I asked God to help me. Then He gave me the idea to call Kate on her cell.*

Kate: *Boy, was I glad to hear from her. We remembered what Sydney taught us about using the position of the sun to figure out what direction we needed to go.*

Sydney: *Wow! I'm impressed!*

Kate: *So when we got back together, we used my dad's mini-GPS I had in my pocket to find the trail so we could get back to the town.*

Sydney: *Wait a minute. Back up. What do you mean "caught" the boys shooting their airsoft gun at the pop cans? They weren't really doing anything wrong.*

Bailey: *No, but they sure acted like they got caught at something.*

Kate: *They were defensive and angry.*

Elizabeth: *Maybe they didn't like being spied on.*

Kate: *Or maybe they're up to no good since they act that way no matter when we see them or what they're doing.*

Bailey: *Wait! I just remembered something I heard Justin say to Joe before he knew we were there. He said something like "We'll make them sorry they ever came here."*

McKenzie: *Who do you think they were talking about?*

Bailey suddenly felt like a rock dropped to the bottom of her stomach.

Bailey: *I hope he wasn't talking about Kate and me, but he sure seems to hate us.*

Kate: *But why?*

McKenzie: *You must be a threat to them in some way.*

Bailey: *How can we be a threat to them when they don't even know us?*

McKenzie: *They're obviously insecure. You just have to figure out why.*

For just a second, Bailey felt sorry for the boys, especially Justin. She remembered her mom saying maybe they had problems at home or something. Maybe they just needed someone to care about them.

Bailey's loud sigh drew Kate's eyes from her computer.

> Bailey: *Maybe we just need to keep being nice to them. Find out what they're interested in and stuff like that. They could be going through a rough time or something and that's what makes them so grouchy.*
>
> Elizabeth: *That's a good idea. I'm proud of you, Bailey.*
>
> Bailey: *I'm not saying it'll be easy. But I'll try.*
>
> Kate: *Guess what?*
>
> Alex: *I'll bite. What?*
>
> Kate: *Bailey and I saw a new ghost at the hotel today.*
>
> Sydney: *No way!*
>
> Bailey: *Room 408. The room with the cowboy ghost.*
>
> Kate: *Of course it has to be another special effect. It moves exactly the same every time it's seen. We're going to figure out how they do it.*
>
> Bailey: *Yeah. He shows up in the window and stares out a minute then fades away to the left. The only problem is that if he was a real person, he'd plow into a wall if he turned that way.*
>
> Alex: *Didn't they use some sort of projection system to make it look like there were ghosts in the movie* Casper? *They could be using one in that room too. Or once I saw a movie where an image was etched onto a window and the sun shining on it made it come to life. Maybe you should look more closely at the window.*
>
> Kate: *We'll do that. Bailey and I need to take a tour of that room to see if we spot anything unusual. Anyway, we just wanted to update you. Let us know if you have any more ideas about how ghosts could be created or any new information about elk.*

Bailey logged off and closed her laptop.

"All right." Kate exited the chat room and brought up a blank document. "Let's see what we have so far in the elk mystery. One. We know the elk are spooked but don't know why." She typed the entry into the blank document.

Bailey jumped in. "Two. We know Justin and Joe have an airsoft gun and were in the woods today before the stampede."

Kate typed the second entry. "But then again, so were we."

"Three. Justin has a grouchy attitude all the time."

"Four. They visit their grandparents here every year." Kate continued typing but stopped. "We don't even know if any of this has anything to do with the elk problem."

"No, but a good sleuth follows hunches," Bailey said. "And I have a hunch it does."

"I hope we're not going down the wrong path." Kate looked thoughtful. "What about what we know about elk?"

"Well, we know they make wallows during mating season," Bailey offered.

"And we know they are more aggressive during that time as well."

"But not usually this much."

"We know they have a great sense of smell and can run really fast," Kate said as she typed.

"Boy, do we know that!" Bailey laughed. "We learned they're usually most active in the early morning and later in the evening, unless they're being harassed."

"That may be a key to this mystery."

"We know the male elk are the ones with that shrill bugle." Bailey did her best impersonation of an elk bugle, starting with the low grunts and ending with a high shriek.

Biscuit sat up and howled while Kate covered her ears and laughed. "You aren't quite ready for that bugling contest yet!"

"I still can't believe Grandpa Perkins didn't win that."

"I can't either. I wonder if that's why Justin was so grouchy today."

"Maybe. Something must be making him mad." Bailey felt a little sad inside, like when she knew a friend was going to do something wrong but she couldn't talk her out of it. She turned at the sound of the key card sliding in the door.

"Hey!" Mrs. Chang gave her standard greeting. "What are you two up to?"

"We just finished chatting with the other Camp Club Girls," Bailey said. "How was your movie, Trina?"

"Not bad." The teenager flipped on the TV.

"We told the other girls all about our hike and seeing the cowboy ghost," Kate told Mrs. Chang.

"Sounds like you had fun. By the way, Bailey, Dad and I are going out to a business dinner tonight."

"What about us?" Bailey stuck out her lower lip.

"Adults only, I'm afraid." Mom's eyes brightened. "But how about a pizza party? We can have it delivered to our room."

"Yeah!" Bailey and Kate gave each other a high five.

"How 'bout it, Trina?" Bailey asked.

"Fabulous." Trina said in a monotone, still channel surfing.

"It'll be fun!" Bailey informed her sister brightly.

"Whatever." Trina gave up on finding something to watch and turned off the TV. She flopped on the bed and started listening to her iPod.

"I'm going to get cleaned up and then I'll call in the pizza." Mrs. Chang headed for the shower.

Awhile later, Bailey whistled when her mom emerged looking fresh and pretty in her black dress, dangly earrings, and strappy heels. The familiar smell of her mom's perfume made Bailey want to snuggle in her lap like she did when she was a little girl.

"What kind of pizza do you want?"

"Pepperoni!" Bailey shouted.

"With black olives?" Kate asked.

"Sure, I like olives and so does Trina."

"Pepperoni and black olives it is." Mrs. Chang phoned in the order.

While they were waiting for the pizza, Mr. Chang came home and spruced up too.

"You guys look great!" Bailey said.

A knock at the door signaled the beginning of the pizza party. Mr. Chang paid for the food and set it on the small table. Then he tapped Trina on the shoulder and she took out her earphones.

"We should be home between nine and ten," he told her. "You're in charge while we're gone. You hear that, Bales?"

Bailey and Kate both nodded.

The Changs blew the girls a kiss goodbye and told them to call on the cell phone if anything came up.

"We can handle this, Mom," Trina said.

"Good. I know you can. Have fun."

As soon as the door closed, the trio playfully shoved their way to the pizza. Trina lifted the lid. "Mmmm. Smell that."

They each took a slice and chatted and giggled as they ate. Kate fed Biscuit a couple of pieces of pepperoni.

"Trina, did you leave your iPod on?" Bailey asked.

"No. Why?"

Bailey cocked her head to listen. "I thought I heard piano music."

Trina put one earphone in. "Nope. It's not this."

"Listen. There it is again." Bailey craned her neck forward.

"I hear it too." Kate said. "It's very soft, though."

"Sounds like old-fashioned music to me." Bailey went to the window to see if anyone was playing music outside but saw only people quietly strolling in the courtyard.

The music became louder.

"I hear it now." Trina joined Bailey at the window.

"It's not coming from outside." Kate put her ear to the air vent on the floor. "It sounds like it's coming through the vent!"

"It sounds. . .spooky." Kate shivered.

"Let's just turn on the TV and forget about it," Trina suggested.

The girls all sprawled out on the beds as Trina flipped through the channels.

A romantic comedy came on. "Oooo. This looks good." Trina fluffed her pillow and put it behind her back against the headboard.

"Didn't our hotel brochure say that F. O. Stanley's wife played the piano and sometimes guests still hear her music?"

"I think you're right! But would we be able to hear it clear up here?"

The eerie music continued.

Finally Bailey couldn't stand it anymore. "I don't know, but I'm going to find out where that music is coming from!"

"I'll come with you!" Kate announced.

"Fine with me," Trina said, still glazed over by the TV. "Just don't leave the building."

"Deal." Bailey grabbed another slice of pizza to munch on while they investigated.

Grabbing Biscuit, they walked down the hallway. The music seemed to get louder. Reaching the elevator, they pressed the DOWN button. When they reached the hotel lobby, the music was much louder.

Bailey marched to the front desk. "Excuse me."

Barbara, the surly hotel clerk, scowled at Biscuit.

"Can you tell me where that music is coming from?" Bailey smiled sweetly.

"From the Music Room, to your right." Barbara pointed to the room at the end of the lobby.

"The Music Room. Of course. Thank you." With a polite nod, Bailey turned to leave.

"And keep that dog under control."

"I will." Kate gave the woman a thumbs-up and raised Biscuit's paw in a wave.

Bailey and Kate walked on the lobby's shiny wooden floor to the doorway of the Music Room, the piano music growing ever louder. Stopping at the door, they peeked inside and saw that the room was unfurnished except for a grand piano at the far end. It sat in a raised alcove, almost a small, rounded room in itself. Its lid was propped open to allow the beautiful music to flow unhindered. A huge fireplace with white columns upholding the mantel took up most of the left wall. A giant mirror hung above it. Arched windows lined the other walls, with square-paned ones in the piano alcove. The piano sat sideways, but Bailey could clearly see the keys moving up and down from the door, though no one appeared to be playing it.

Bailey swallowed hard and looked at Kate, who had just used her free hand to remove her glasses and rub her eyes. She put them back on, steadying herself against the doorframe. She and Bailey nodded pale-faced at each other. A ghost!

Trampled!

Kate, carrying Biscuit, followed Bailey cautiously across the threshold onto the glossy wood Music Room floor. Immediately, the music stopped. Bailey grabbed Kate's arm. They tiptoed toward the piano, as if they were sneaking up on the ghost.

"Maybe whoever was playing will appear," Bailey whispered.

"I doubt it. But maybe we'll be able to see how they're doing the special effect."

"Yeah. I have to keep reminding myself it isn't real."

The girls stepped up into the alcove and inspected the piano.

"I wish I'd brought Biscuit's leash." Kate shifted the dog to her other arm and looked closer. "Aha! Just as I thought. It's a player piano."

"Huh?"

"A player piano. You know, the kind that has songs programmed into it so it plays by itself."

"Oh, I've seen those in stores. But doesn't someone have to start and stop it?"

"Usually." Kate continued checking all angles of the piano. She wrestled with Biscuit who was getting wiggly. "I bet this one has an automatic switch or sensor somewhere that turns it on and off."

Bailey helped her search for a switch, even crawling underneath for a look. "I don't see anything."

Kate studied the strings and hammers for each key inside the piano. "There's so much stuff in here it's hard to tell what doesn't belong. But I think I may see something. Come over on this side for a better look."

Bailey was next to her in a flash.

"See that switch close to the hinge where the piano lid opens?"

"Yeah, I see it."

"I think it may be the culprit. And I think that box next to it is a timer that makes the music play only every so often."

"But how does it stop when someone comes in the room?"

Kate cocked her head and squinted her eyes. Bailey could practically see the wheels turning in her brain. "Maybe a motion sensor that's set to turn it off when someone comes through the door?"

"But we have to find it to be sure." Bailey's eyes started scanning the room. "There!"

Kate followed Bailey's finger to a small device mounted in the ceiling corner of the room. It was pointed directly at the doorway. "Yep, I bet that's our motion sensor."

"Let's go back out to the lobby and try it out." Bailey and Kate walked out to the lobby. They passed the time by looking at the Stanley Steamer car as they waited for the music to begin again.

Soon the melodious sound of the piano wafted into the lobby.

"There it goes!" Bailey made a beeline for the Music Room and stopped abruptly outside the door.

"Okay. Ready?"

"Ready." Kate grabbed Bailey's hand and together they walked into the room. The music stopped. "I'm sure the motion detector saw us."

"I wonder how sensitive it is," Bailey said. "Like, I mean, do we have to enter the room or just move in the doorway?"

"Interesting. Let's find out." Kate, Biscuit, and Bailey filed back out to the lobby so the piano could reset.

Soon the music began again.

"Let's go!"

Bailey and Kate stopped in front of the doorway. "Let's try just kicking our foot through the doorway, but not actually going in," Bailey suggested.

Kate giggled and locked arms with Bailey in chorus line fashion. "Okay. On three. One. . .two. . .three!"

Kate and Bailey each kicked one foot out. Once again, the music stopped.

"Wow! Pretty sensitive!" Bailey grinned from ear to ear.

"Guess we've pretty much solved this mystery. Might as well go back to the room."

"Hey, there goes Justin and Joe across the yard." Bailey pointed toward the window. The floodlights shining on the yard spotlighted the two boys as they walked away from the hotel. One turned around as if to see if anyone was following them.

"Is that their gun he's carrying?" Kate asked.

"Couldn't be. It's too dark for target practice."

"Weird."

The boys disappeared into the shadows.

"Know what I was thinking?" Bailey asked.

"What?"

"I wonder if anyone's staying in room 408."

Kate headed for the front desk. "We could check. And if no one is, we could ask if we can go see it tomorrow."

"Exactly what I was thinking." Bailey asked Front Desk Barbara if the room was vacant.

"Hmmm. Let me check." Barbara typed something into her computer and waited. She ran her finger down the screen until she came to the line she wanted. "Yep. Looks like it's vacant."

"Can we go look at it tomorrow?" Kate asked.

"What for?"

"We're curious about Tex." Bailey smiled knowingly at Kate.

"Tex?" Barbara smirked.

"Yeah. You know. The cowboy ghost. We think we saw him this afternoon from the front lawn."

"Well, I'm off tomorrow, so you'll have to check back with whoever's working then."

"Okay. Thanks." Kate gave a friendly wave as they walked off.

Bailey let out a laugh. "I just had a crazy idea."

"Oh no. What?"

"Let's see if Justin and Joe want to see the room with us tomorrow."

"No way!"

Bailey put her hand out. "Aw, come on. We just talked to the other girls today about trying to get to know them better. What if they really are going through something bad and just need a friend?"

"I seriously doubt that."

"Well, so do I. But what's the harm in asking them? They'll probably just say no anyway."

"That's true. All right. Let's do it."

Suddenly, a man burst through the front door of the lobby. "The elk! They're stampeding again, and this time someone's hurt!"

Bailey and Kate hurried outside. Elk ran frantically in front of the hotel, sending some of the guests scrambling for cover on the porch.

Biscuit leaped out of Kate's arms and darted right into the herd.

"Biscuit!" Kate screamed. The dust settled from the stampede, and people ran in all directions. Kate and Bailey sprinted to the yard where Biscuit lay motionless.

Kneeling beside the little dog, Bailey saw blood pooling beneath his right front paw. Ragged breaths puffed from his open mouth, and his tongue hung out one side. His eyes were open, but he didn't appear to see anything. "Oh Biscuit!" Kate cried.

Shivering from the cold, Bailey pulled her cell phone from her pocket and steadied her finger to dial.

"Hello?" Trina said.

"Trina! The elk stampeded and Biscuit got trampled." Bailey choked down a sob. "We're on the front lawn. We need help."

"I'll be there as soon as I call Mom and Dad."

Bailey returned her phone to her pocket and wrapped her arms around herself to ward off the night chill.

Kate gently stroked the injured dog's side. "Hang on, Biscuit. Help's coming."

Bailey heard a siren in the distance. "Sounds like help is on its way for the people who were injured. I don't know if they'll help dogs too or not."

Within minutes, a red-and-white ambulance screeched to a halt at the far side of the lawn where a group of people gathered. Medics knelt on the ground next to their patient, then lifted him onto a stretcher and loaded him through the open back doors of the vehicle. Just as Bailey and Kate turned their attention back to Biscuit, they heard another siren. Looking back, they saw a second, and then a third ambulance arrive and take away two more people. Police cars began to filter in also as well as news reporters.

"Those elk must have really been mad to run right into all those people," Bailey said sadly. "Or scared out of their wits."

"I hope the people who got hurt will be all right." Kate's forehead wrinkled with concern.

"We need to pray for them tonight—and Biscuit."

"Bailey!" Trina ran to them from the porch, carrying sweatshirts for both girls. "Thought you might need these."

"Thanks." Bailey slipped into her hoodie. "Biscuit's hurt bad. We don't know if we should move him or not. We don't want to injure him any more than he already is."

"That was smart of you." Trina put her arm around Kate, who wiped her eyes and nose with the sleeve of her sweatshirt. "I called Mom and Dad," Trina told her. "They heard about the stampede at the restaurant and were on their way home before I called. They'll know what to do."

"I think we need to say a prayer right now for Biscuit." Bailey laid her hand on the injured dog.

Trina took Kate's left hand, leaving her right hand free to continue comforting her dog.

"God, we're scared for Biscuit. Help him to be strong and brave. Help Mom and Dad to get here fast so it's not too late." Bailey's voice broke. She cleared her throat and went on. "Heal whatever is wrong with Biscuit. Help him to be good as new again, fast. Be with Kate. Give her comfort and peace. And help the people who got hurt tonight to be okay. Thank You for being here with us. Amen."

"Thanks, Bailey." Kate hugged her friend. "I just know Biscuit is going to be all right. He has to be."

"Girls!" Mr. and Mrs. Chang rushed up and hugged them. "We came as quickly as we could."

Mr. Chang looked at Biscuit. "I'll take Biscuit to the car so we can get him to the animal hospital. I parked right over there. Trina, you run ahead and open the door." He tossed her the keys.

"Where is the nearest animal hospital?" Bailey asked.

"A man at our dinner tonight recommended a vet that's not too far from here." Mr. Chang gently lifted Biscuit.

"Guess God worked that out for us, huh?" Kate said quietly as she followed Mr. Chang to the car.

"God's like that." Mrs. Chang smiled at Kate then put her arm around her and pulled her into a hug.

The animal hospital wasn't busy, and Biscuit was taken right in. The vet examined him and found he had a few broken ribs and a crushed paw. Wrapping the paw in a neon green bandage with dog bones printed on it, he explained, "I'm going to give Biscuit an injection of pain medicine. It will help him sleep comfortably for a while so he'll have some time to heal. I'll also wrap his body to keep him from moving too much. We don't want those broken ribs to puncture a lung."

Kate asked, lips trembling, "Can we take him home now?"

"We'll need to keep him overnight for observation, but if all goes well, he should be released tomorrow."

Bailey heard Kate sigh with relief. Biscuit was going to be okay!

●—●—●

"So you heard about the stampede, but we didn't get to tell you about the ghosts yet!" Bailey told her family on the way back to the hotel.

"Not again," Trina moaned and dramatically threw her arm over her eyes.

"Well, not real ghosts, of course, but we figured out the secret of how they make them seem real."

Bailey and Kate told the family all about the Music Room and the mysterious piano playing.

"Pretty good!" Trina said when they were finished with their elaborate, don't-leave-out-a-detail explanation.

"And tomorrow, we're going to see if we can get permission to see room 408 to try and learn the tricks they're using to make the cowboy ghost." Bailey rubbed her hands in anticipation.

"We'll have to see how that works out since we need to pick up Biscuit tomorrow," Kate reminded her. "I might need to stay with him."

"That's okay. I won't go without you."

"Or you could just go with Justin and Joe." Kate gave Bailey a playful nudge.

"Like that would ever happen."

Mrs. Chang looked toward the backseat. "What's this about the Perkins boys?"

"We thought we'd see if Justin and Joe wanted to see the haunted room 408 with us. But we figure they'll say no." Bailey felt her face get warm.

"Well, that was nice of you to think of them. I think those boys need some good friends like you." Mrs. Chang reached back between the front seats and patted Bailey's knee.

Mr. Chang pulled into a parking space in front of the hotel. "It's been quite a night. You girls handled the events of the evening very well."

Bailey pulled her hoodie closer around her and huddled against the cold night air as the group hustled into the hotel lobby. Mr. Chang walked directly to the front desk, Bailey and Kate close behind, while Mrs. Chang and Trina waited by the elevator.

"Do you have any information about the condition of the people who were injured in the stampede this evening?" he asked Front Desk Barbara.

"Only what the news has been reporting." Barbara pointed to the small TV in the corner of the reception desk. "They say three people were taken to the hospital. A man is in serious condition and the other two were treated and released."

"Something is going to have to be done to make sure this doesn't happen again."

"I heard the news reporter saying there's talk of putting up a fence along the wooded areas at the base of the hills to try to keep the elk from coming into town so easily."

Mr. Chang nodded and turned to leave. "Thanks for the information."

"What'd she say?" Trina asked when Mr. Chang joined them at the elevator.

The elevator dinged and the doors opened for them to get on. Bailey pushed the button for the fourth floor.

"Three people were hurt, but only one is still in the hospital. He's in serious condition."

"Wonder who it was." Bailey felt the elevator whisk them up to their floor.

The doors opened on the fourth floor and there stood Grandma Perkins.

"Mrs. Perkins! Good to see you again," Mr. Chang said.

"It's nice to see you too." Grandma Perkins seemed to be in a hurry to get on the elevator and leave. Bailey noticed her eyes looked teary.

"Is everything all right?" Mrs. Chang asked her.

Grandma Perkins shook her head and turned her eyes away. "It's Glen. He was hurt in the elk stampede tonight. We thought it would be fun to surprise our grandsons with their favorite ice cream before they went to bed. When we got out of the car and were walking across the lawn, the elk charged through. Glen pushed me out of the way, but he got trampled. He's still in the hospital." Tears brimmed in her eyes.

"Grandpa Perkins was one of the people who got hurt?" Bailey cried.

Grandma Perkins nodded and wiped her eyes.

"I'm so sorry to hear that," Mrs. Chang said. "We heard someone was seriously hurt, but we didn't know it was him. We'll be praying for his quick recovery."

"Thank you." The older woman had a faraway look. "I just wish we could figure out what's causing those elk to act like this."

"I hope they come up with a solution before anyone else gets hurt," Mr. Chang said.

"I'd better get home. I'm about worn out from being at the hospital and from all the stress. I got a few bumps and bruises myself. My son sent me home and promised he'd stay with Glen tonight. Janice offered to drive me home, but I told her I was fine."

Mrs. Chang took Grandma Perkins's hands in hers. "Of course. Please let us know if we can do anything to help you or your family."

"Thank you so much." She pushed the button and the doors closed.

●—●—●

"I can't believe it." Bailey shook her head as they entered their room. "Grandpa Perkins is such a nice man. I wish he hadn't gotten hurt."

"We have lots of things to pray about tonight, don't we?" Mrs. Chang said. "Including thanking God that none of us were injured. You girls were pretty close to the action. I'm glad you're all right." She kissed all three girls on the head.

"Mom, do you think we could go see Grandpa Perkins at the hospital tomorrow?" Bailey asked.

"That would be nice, if they let kids in. I'll have to check the hospital rules first. We wouldn't stay long. He needs his rest to get better."

"I feel sorry for Justin and Joe. They must be really sad." Kate pulled out her pajamas and headed for the bathroom to change.

Bailey's eyes met Kate's. She suddenly thought, *I hope they weren't responsible for that elk stampede!*

CHAPTER 10

The Cowboy Ghost

The next morning, through a fog of sleepiness, Bailey heard her dad leave for one of his meetings. She had an uneasy feeling but couldn't put her finger on what it was. Then it came to her—the stampede the night before. Biscuit was hurt and so was Grandpa Perkins. It seemed like a bad dream.

Kate rolled over and stretched. "Biscuit?" Still half-asleep, she felt around the bed for him.

"Kate, Biscuit's not here, remember?" Bailey whispered, not wanting to wake the others.

Kate sat up, worry lines creasing her forehead. She rubbed her eyes, blew her nose, and put on her glasses. Her shoulders slumped like she held the weight of the world on them. "Oh yeah. I forgot."

"I was thinking," Bailey said softly, looking to see if her mom and Trina were still asleep. "The elk stampeded shortly after we saw Justin and Joe walking toward the hills last night."

"I know. I thought the same thing."

"I think they've been shooting at the elk and making them charge into town."

Kate thought on that a moment. "The elk are being harassed and it's making them more aggressive, just like Sydney said."

"I bet if Justin and Joe caused the stampede, they're sorry for it now that their grandpa got hurt."

"If it's them, I hope they've learned their lesson." Kate's eyes blazed fiercely.

"But why would they want to make the elk stampede in the first place? I don't get it."

"I don't know either. I have a feeling there's a whole other piece of this mystery that we haven't begun to figure out yet."

"I'm starting to think they're really messed up. They seem to have a nice family, so I don't think that's the problem." Bailey propped herself up on her elbow.

"No, it must be something else. McKenzie mentioned that they might feel threatened in some way. Maybe we need to think about what it could be."

"I know," Bailey replied. "I wish there was some way she could talk to Justin and Joe. She's so good at figuring people out."

"Guess for now we'll just have to rely on her suggestions and figure it out ourselves."

"I think we need to pray for them," Bailey said. "And we need to ask God to show us if there's some way we can help them."

"Maybe if we invite them to see room 408 with us today, we'll have a chance to learn more about them." Kate put her hand over her mouth and sneezed, waking Trina and Mom. She smiled sheepishly. "Sorry."

"Good morning to you too," Trina mumbled then buried her head under her pillow.

"Do you know when we can go get Biscuit?" Kate asked Mrs. Chang.

"I'll call to find out." She looked at the clock. "They're probably just opening." She picked up the vet's business card and dialed the number. "Yes, this is Dory Chang and I was wondering how our dog, Biscuit, is doing and when we might pick him up." Mrs. Chang covered the mouthpiece of the phone and whispered to Kate, "They're checking."

Kate nodded.

Mrs. Chang directed her attention back to the person on the phone. "Okay. Thank you. We'll see you later. Bye."

"What'd they say?" Bailey asked.

"They said Biscuit is doing fine and we can pick him up this afternoon. They need to change his bandage this morning and check his vital signs. If something doesn't check out, they'll give us a call. Otherwise, he's good to go."

"Good. I can't wait to have him back," Kate said, beaming.

"Let's get dressed so we can ask the front desk if we can see room 408 before we get Biscuit." Bailey hopped off the bed and grabbed some clothes.

"Good idea. You think the boys will want to come after what happened last night?" Kate asked.

"Hard to say. But it could be a nice distraction for them." Bailey slipped into her jeans and T-shirt. "I'm ready."

"Wait just a minute, missy," Mrs. Chang said in her mom voice. "You need to eat something and brush your teeth and hair before you go anywhere."

"Aw, Mom. We have ghosts to chase down." Bailey smirked at her mom.

"Then you'll need all the energy you can get from breakfast. Have a seat." Mrs. Chang set the box of cereal in front of her daughter and grabbed a carton of milk from the mini-fridge.

Kate quickly dressed and joined Bailey at the table. "Did the vet say anything else about Biscuit?"

"No, I'm afraid not."

"I can't wait to see him."

"We should turn on the morning news to see if there are any new developments about the stampede." Mrs. Chang grabbed the remote and pushed POWER.

"Witnesses say they observed some young men with guns just before the stampede. . . ," the newscaster said.

Bailey froze, her spoon halfway between her open mouth and her bowl. Kate choked on the bite she'd just taken. Coughing, she snatched a napkin from the table.

"Are you okay?" Mrs. Chang asked her.

"Y–yes. I'm fine."

Bailey glimpsed her friend's worried eyes. They finished breakfast, brushed their teeth and hair, and were out the door to go see if Justin and Joe wanted to go ghost hunting with them. Kate grabbed a small pad of paper and a pen in case they needed to take notes.

"I can't believe our suspicions about Justin and Joe were on the news!" Bailey said as they walked down the hall.

"I hope they didn't do anything." Kate knocked on the Perkinses's door.

A moment later, Mrs. Perkins answered. Bailey told them why they were there.

"Well, how thoughtful. Just a minute, I'll ask them."

A moment later she returned. "Thank you, girls, for thinking of them, but with all that's happened, they think they'll pass this time. We're going to go to the hospital to see their grandpa later. He was hurt in the stampede last night."

"Yes, we heard. I'm sorry." Bailey shifted her weight from one foot to the other. "Mrs. Perkins, do you know if they'd let us see Grandpa Perkins if we went? If children are allowed in the hospital?"

"Yes, I saw children visiting other patients last night."

Kate brightened up. "That would be great. We'd like to go visit him."

"That would be lovely. I know he'll be glad to see you."

"Okay. Well, tell Justin and Joe hi and that we're sorry about their grandpa."

"I'll do that." Mrs. Perkins closed the door.

Standing on tiptoe a short time later, Bailey leaned against the tall front desk. "Excuse me. We were wondering if we could see room 408, please."

The man at the counter smiled. "Barbara told me some young gals might be coming to ask about that."

Bailey looked at Kate, eyebrows high with surprise.

"Let me see. Yes, it's vacant, though I can't let you in without an adult. Would you like me to get a bellhop to take you?"

"Yes, please!" Bailey could hardly contain her excitement. They were going to get to see the haunted room!

"And what are your names?" the front desk clerk asked.

"I'm Bailey Chang, and this is Kate Oliver."

"Very good. I'll get someone to take you up."

"Thank you."

"Now remember," Kate said, pulling Bailey aside while they waited for the bellhop. "We need to look for anything that could be used to make it look like the cowboy appears in the window then fades to the left."

"Got it." Bailey turned at the sound of footsteps. A young man Bailey guessed to be in his twenties approached them.

"You must be Bailey and Kate." He stuck out his hand and shook Bailey's hand first, then Kate's. "I'm Lance. Nice to meet you. So you're interested in the cowboy ghost of room 408, huh?" he asked as they walked to the elevator.

Kate nodded. "We saw him from the front yard yesterday."

"What time of day was it?" The elevator doors opened and they stepped in.

"Around noon. Why?"

"Seems like that's the time most people see him these days."

Kate looked at Bailey, who widened her eyes.

"Why do you suppose that is?" Bailey asked, fishing for more information.

"It has something to do with the lighting. You know, the sun being directly overhead and all."

"Interesting." Kate pulled her pen and paper from her pocket and jotted down the lighting clue. The elevator doors opened, and Lance led them down the hall to room 408. He slid his key card through the slot and they heard it unlock, the tiny green light flashing. "Here we are! I'll wait here by the door for you. Take your time looking around."

Bailey gazed at the room that looked remarkably like their own room down the hall. Nothing special or haunted about it.

Kate walked slowly around the room, inspecting every wall and corner. Bailey followed her as she went to the window over the bathroom sink. It overlooked the front yard where they'd been standing yesterday when they saw the ghost.

"If the ghost looked like it faded to the left from out there," she said to Bailey, "then it would have to move to the right from in here, since it faced the window." Sure enough, the bathroom wall was right there, making it impossible to move in that direction.

"Alex thought we should feel the glass, remember?" Bailey asked.

Kate leaned closer to the window and ran her fingers over the glass. "There are definitely scratches or etching or something. I can feel them." She moved her open hand along the window's surface.

Bailey felt it too. "Maybe people tried to claw their way out of here to escape the ghosts!"

Kate laughed. "I doubt that. I think Alex may be right. It's some kind of etching."

"Sometimes they put etched glass or thick blocks of glass in bathroom windows so no one can see in." Bailey scratched her head. "But who could see in way up here on the fourth floor?"

"We did! Or we thought we saw the cowboy ghost, anyway."

"Let's go out on the lawn at noon again today so we can check it out. We'll see if we see that cowboy ghost again. Maybe Lance will even bring us back up here then so we can see what it looks like from the inside."

Kate high-fived Bailey. "Let's go ask him."

Lance was leaning against the doorframe listening to his iPod. He snatched the earphones from his ears when he saw the girls. "All done?"

"For now," Bailey replied. "But we were wondering if there's any chance you could bring us back up here around noon. We want to see what the room looks like at the time of day we saw the cowboy."

"If I'm not busy with any other guests, I'll be glad to."

"Great! Thanks!"

"I'll walk you back down to the lobby." Lance extended his arm to show the way.

"Oh, thank you," Kate said, "but we're going back to our room now. It's just down this hall. Thanks for letting us in."

"No problem. I'll try to meet you in the lobby around noon."

Bailey followed Kate to their room. "Why did you want to go back to our room? There's not much to do there."

"We need to tell the other girls what happened last night." Kate's eyes grew serious.

"Oh yeah. I almost forgot they don't know about Biscuit or Grandpa Perkins yet."

"Or that we're pretty sure Justin and Joe were involved in the stampede and that the news talked about boys with guns going into the hills just before the stampede."

"We do have a lot to cover with them!" Bailey slid her key card in the door.

"We're back," Bailey announced when they entered the room.

"I was just getting ready to call you." Mrs. Chang bustled around tidying up and then grabbed her purse. "Trina and I are going shopping. Do you want to go?"

Bailey looked at Kate to see if she wanted to go. She detected the slight shake of her head. "No. I don't think so. We were just there yesterday when we went hiking."

"Okay. You'll be all right here?"

Bailey nodded. "We're going to call the Camp Club Girls to tell them about last night's stampede and that Biscuit got hurt."

Mrs. Chang kissed Bailey on the cheek. "Sounds good. We'll probably be back around one o'clock or so. There are sandwich makings in the fridge if you get hungry. We'll go get Biscuit after Trina and I get home."

"Okay. See you later. Have fun!"

Kate dialed Elizabeth then conferenced in all the other girls, including Bailey.

"Everyone there?" Each one confirmed they were there and could hear each other.

"Good. We have a lot to tell you about since yesterday," Bailey said.

"Really? How much could have happened in less than twenty-four hours?" Alex asked.

"A lot! We'll start at the beginning. We heard creepy ghost music last night and went to investigate," Kate began. "Legend says it's the ghost of F. O. Stanley's wife, Flora, playing the piano. Turns out the ghost music came from the Music Room where she always played, but it's really just a piano player on a timer. If anyone comes into the room when it's playing, the music stops."

Bailey picked up the story. "We discovered it's on a motion sensor that's tied into the timer. So if the detector senses motion in the doorway, it turns off the timer and player piano, stopping the music."

"Awesome! You guys are getting good at this!" Sydney exclaimed.

Bailey laughed. "But that's not all! While we were still in the lobby, there was another stampede in front of the hotel."

"I was carrying Biscuit because I'd forgotten his leash," Kate added. "He heard the noise and bolted from my arms and ran outside."

"No!" Alex said.

"We chased after him, but it was too late." Kate's voice shook as she relived the horrible evening. "He'd been trampled by the elk and was lying in the grass with a bloody paw."

"It was terrible!" Bailey wailed. "Poor Biscuit could hardly breathe he hurt so bad."

"What did you do?" Elizabeth asked.

"We had to take him to the hospital," Kate said.

"And get this," Bailey said. "Someone had just told my parents where the closest one was and which vet to ask for!"

"Wow," Elizabeth said. "That sounds like a real God-thing!"

"Totally." Kate cleared her throat. "And the hospital was pretty close too!"

"You did the right thing by not picking Biscuit up to comfort him," McKenzie said. "A loving touch is all anyone really needs as they wait for help in a time like that. So how is he now?"

"Well, the doctor checked him over," Kate told her. "He had a crushed paw and some broken ribs. They wrapped his paw up in a big bandage and gave him some pain medicine to make him sleep so he could heal easier. We had to leave him at the hospital overnight, but we're going to get him this afternoon." Kate grinned triumphantly.

Sydney sighed. "That's a relief."

"Give the puppy a hug for me when he gets home," Alex said.

"And an extra treat from me!" McKenzie added.

"I'm glad he's going to be okay," Elizabeth said. "I'll be sure to remember him in my prayers. You know, in Proverbs, the Bible tells us a righteous man cares for the needs of his animals. I'd say you've done exactly that."

"Thanks, Lizzy." Kate smiled shyly at Bailey.

"But that's not the worst of it!" Bailey continued. "Three people were hurt in that stampede too!"

"Oh no!" Sydney cried.

"Here's the sad part—the one hurt the most was Justin and Joe's Grandpa Perkins." Bailey couldn't bring herself to call Justin "Oscar the

Grouch" under the circumstances.

"That is sad," McKenzie said. "How are they taking it?"

"We don't really know." Bailey shrugged, even though the others couldn't see it through the phone.

"We haven't actually talked to them ourselves yet."

"But here's the creepy part," Bailey continued. "We saw Justin and Joe walking toward the hills the night of the stampede."

"And it was only a few minutes later that the stampede happened." Kate bit her lower lip.

"We think they had their gun with them even though it was way too dark for them to do any target practice."

"Not only that," Kate added, "the news station this morning reported that witnesses had seen two young men with guns before the stampede. So we weren't the only ones who noticed."

"Man," Sydney said. "Those boys are going to have some explaining to do."

"You're telling me." Bailey pulled her lip balm out of her pocket and smoothed some on.

"We want to try to get to know them better to see if we can help them in any way," Kate said.

"They must be really afraid and lonely right now. Not to mention sad about their grandpa," McKenzie added. "They really do need some good friends like you."

Bailey and Kate then briefly told the Camp Club Girls about their trip to room 408 that morning.

"So we're hoping to go back up to see it around noon," Kate said.

"And we want to look at that window from the lawn at that time to see if the cowboy ghost shows up."

"Keep us posted," Alex said. "That sounds like an awesome hotel!"

"We will!" Bailey said. "And in the meantime, we have to figure out what the boys are so angry about."

"Maybe you'll remember something they said that will give you a clue," McKenzie said.

"Yeah, we'll have to think back about our conversations with them," Kate agreed.

Someone knocked at Bailey and Kate's hotel door, ending the conference call. Bailey made sure the chain was latched on the door before opening it the three inches it allowed. She inhaled sharply when she saw who stood on the other side.

Confession

Kate came to the door and peered out over Bailey's head to see Justin and Joe.

"Justin! Joe! What are you doing here?" Bailey unhooked the chain and opened the door.

"W—we just wanted to see if you want to go to the hospital with our family." Justin inspected his black-and-red Nikes as he spoke. "My mom said you wanted to visit my grandpa."

"Yes, we do," Kate said. "We're sorry he was hurt."

"The only problem is that my parents aren't here for me to ask permission right now." Bailey frowned.

"Can you call them?" Joe asked.

"Yeah. Sure." Bailey was so surprised by this unexpected invitation she could hardly get her words out. "When are you leaving?"

"Later this afternoon," Justin replied. "We just wanted to give you a heads-up in case you wanted to come along."

"I'll call my mom right now." Bailey grabbed her phone from her pocket and speed-dialed. "Mom? Can we go with the Perkinses to the hospital later today to see their grandpa? Okay. That should work. Thanks. Love you too."

"Well?" Justin asked.

"She said yes. She'll pick us up at the hospital when she and my sister are done shopping, and then we'll pick up Kate's dog from the vet. Plus, she also wants to see your grandpa."

"Why's your dog at the vet?" Joe asked.

"He got trampled in the stampede too," Kate said.

"He did? Is he all right?" Justin seemed genuinely concerned about the little dog.

"He broke some ribs, and his paw got messed up." Kate grimaced. "He had to spend the night there, but he's getting out today."

"He might not be quite as fast as he was when he saw you in the hills yesterday," Bailey teased the boys.

"Thank goodness for that!" Justin cracked a shy smile, the first Bailey had ever seen on his face. It was a nice smile, she decided, looking at his straight white teeth. He was cute.

"Thanks for inviting us to go with you," Kate said.

"We'll knock on your door when we're ready to leave." Joe seemed more relaxed than Bailey remembered him being before, maybe because Justin wasn't so irritable.

"Wait!" Bailey called. "We're going to check out room 408 where the cowboy ghost is always seen today at noon. You wanna come?"

Justin looked at Joe and shrugged. "Sure."

"We're meeting the bellhop, Lance, in the lobby then if you want to meet us there too."

"Okay, we'll see you in the lobby at twelve o'clock," Joe said.

"Great. See you then." Kate shut the door and latched the chain.

"Can you believe that?" Bailey exploded.

"They're like different people today!"

"Well, they can't help but be changed by what happened to their grandpa." Bailey shook her head. "But I never dreamed the change would be this dramatic."

"Let's tell the girls we're going so they can pray that we have an opportunity to share our faith with the boys," Kate suggested. "This could be just the chance we've been waiting for."

Bailey snatched her laptop from the bed, and Kate grabbed hers off the nightstand. "We'll just have to tell whoever's online since we don't have time to get everyone together before they pick us up." Bailey logged on.

Bailey: *Anyone out there?*
Elizabeth: *Hi! I'm here.*
McKenzie: *Me too.*
Kate: *Of course, I'm here.*

Bailey looked from her computer to Kate and they traded grins.

Bailey: *You'll never guess who was just here.*

McKenzie: *The ghost of Christmas past?*

Kate: *LOL. No, but a very good guess considering where we are.*

Bailey: *It was Justin and Joe!*

McKenzie: *No way! What'd they want?*

Kate: *They invited us to go with them to the hospital to see their grandpa.*

Elizabeth: *That's a miracle!*

Bailey: *That's what we thought. And they were actually nice to us, not grouchy at all.*

Kate: *We told them about Biscuit getting hurt and Justin asked if he was going to be okay.*

Bailey: *And he smiled a really nice smile when I teased him.*

McKenzie: *LOL. You're funny.*

Kate: *Anyway, we wanted you to be praying for us.*

Bailey: *Those boys really need Jesus in their hearts so they'll be happier.*

McKenzie: *And they'll need good friends to support them if they were involved in the stampedes.*

Elizabeth: *You can show them God's unconditional love. I'll be praying.*

Kate: *Thanks. We knew we could count on you.*

Bailey: *Plus, we invited them to go with us to check out the cowboy ghost and they said yes!*

McKenzie: *You're kidding!*

Kate: *I know. We can hardly believe it.*

Bailey: *We have to eat before then, so we'd better go. But maybe you can get the word out to the other girls so they can pray too.*

Elizabeth: *Okay. We'll try. But about these ghosts you're chasing—just remember that Hebrews 9:27 says that man is destined to die once, and after that to face judgment.*

Bailey: *What's that supposed to mean?*

Elizabeth: *It means ghosts aren't real. Once we die, we're dead. We don't come back to haunt people as ghosts.*

Kate: *We know they're not real, Elizabeth, but thanks for the reminder.*

Bailey: *Yeah, thanks. It's easy to get carried away with this stuff sometimes. We'll keep you posted. See ya.*

Bailey logged off and closed her laptop. Kate got out the bread and started making a peanut butter and jelly sandwich.

"Something Justin said at the Elkfest just came to me," Bailey said.

Kate spread the peanut butter on her bread. "What was it?"

"I think it may be what McKenzie was talking about when she said the boys must feel threatened somehow. Remember how Justin was so mad when we said we hoped Grandpa Perkins would win the bugling contest?" Bailey grabbed the peanut butter jar. "He said something about how the tourists shouldn't be able to win and should just go home."

"I thought he was just kidding," Kate said around a bite of sandwich.

"So did I until I looked at him. He was mad and dead serious." Bailey finished making her sandwich and poured a glass of milk.

"That could be it, Bailey!"

"Justin and Joe used to visit their grandparents here before all the tourists started coming. Maybe Estes Park has changed so much from all the tourists that Justin wants them to leave."

"He could be angry that their quiet vacation spot is now crowded and busy." Kate took another bite. "I bet the tourists don't take care of the place like the locals either."

"I know I've seen some of the tourists littering and leaving messes behind," Bailey said.

"That would explain why Justin didn't like us at first. If he feels threatened by tourists, he'd feel threatened by us since we're tourists!"

Bailey stopped eating. "Maybe he's using that gun to scare the elk into town so they'll scare the tourists away."

"But how did he always know where to find the elk?" Kate asked.

Bailey bit into her sandwich and thought a second. Then her eyes lit up. "Sydney said one thing's for sure. If you have wallows, you have elk."

"That's it!" Kate yelled. "The wallows! The boys are finding the elk by finding the wallows. Bailey, I think we may have just figured out our mystery."

"Now we just have to prove it."

"Come on, we have to get down to the lobby. It's almost noon!"

As they exited the elevator, they saw Lance waiting for them. The Perkins boys showed up moments later.

"Everyone ready to check out room 408?" Lance asked.

"Can we start by looking at it from the courtyard first to see if we can see the cowboy ghost?" Bailey asked.

"Sure," Lance said. "I'll wait here for you."

The foursome went to the front yard and looked up to the fourth floor window.

"There he is!" Kate pointed at the image.

"Cool!" Justin said. "I've never actually seen him before."

"We've always heard about this, but never saw it for ourselves!" Joe added.

"Okay, so we know he's showing up right now," Bailey said. "Let's go to the room to see if we can figure out how it's happening."

Lance escorted them to the fourth floor and unlocked the door. The room was bright, flooded with sunlight.

"Look at the etching on the glass now," Bailey said. "You can see a lot more of it with the sun shining directly on it."

"Yeah," Kate agreed. "I can see the whole image of the cowboy now."

"Why couldn't we see it before?" Bailey asked Lance.

He smiled. "You were right about the etching on the glass. When the sunlight shines directly on it, you can see all of it. But some of the etching is done so lightly that it only shows up under bright light. That's why you couldn't see the whole image this morning."

"Look!" Joe said. "A shadow is starting to move across the window."

Bailey and Kate looked at each other, eyes wide. "That must be what makes it look like the cowboy's turning toward the wall before he disappears!"

"Exactly," Lance said. "You guys are pretty smart."

"But wait a minute," Kate said. "If it depends on the sunlight to make it appear, then wouldn't it show up at different times of day depending on the time of year? You know, with the rotation of the earth and all."

Lance laughed. "Now you're really thinking! And you're right. You just happen to be here when the sun shines on it around noon. Other times of the year it's earlier or later in the day." He leaned toward Bailey and said in a mock whisper, "That makes it more mysterious."

"Wow." Bailey walked to the window and ran her hand over the etching. "I can't believe we figured that out."

"Well, we might not have if it weren't for Alex's help about the etchings," Kate reminded her.

Lance looked at his watch. "I'd better get back to work."

"Thanks for showing us all this and confirming our theory," Kate said as they all left the room.

Closing the door behind him, Lance said, "My pleasure!"

Bailey turned to the boys. "I think we'll go out on the porch for a while. If we're not in our room when you're ready to go to the hospital, you can find us down there."

Joe nodded. "Okay, see you this afternoon."

●—●—●

At the hospital, everyone grew quiet. They'd chatted all during the ride, but when they turned into the parking lot, Justin and Joe were back to their usual grouchy faces. Justin's eyebrows made a sharp V-shape over his eyes.

Bailey and Kate walked in silence with the boys' family. When they came to Grandpa Perkins's room, Bailey could hardly believe it was him in the bed. Tubes snaked from his arms and nose. His face was bruised and swollen. His silver hair stuck out in odd places and lay too flat in others.

Grandma Perkins was sitting in a chair by the bed but stood when they entered the room. She motioned for Justin and Joe's dad to take her seat. The others sat on chairs that were brought in and put around the room. Bailey and Kate sat on the far side of the room while Justin and Joe parked themselves close to the door. Their mother stood on one side of Grandpa's bed and Mr. Perkins, now in Grandma's chair, took his father's hand.

"Hi, Dad. We're all here—Janice, Justin, Joe, and even our friends, Bailey Chang and Kate Oliver from down the hall at our hotel. Remember? They cheered you on during the bugling contest at the Elkfest."

Grandpa Perkins's eyelids fluttered then opened slightly. A faint smile crossed his lips.

"You don't have to say anything, Dad. Save your strength for getting better."

Bailey heard a chair scrape and saw Justin leave the room, followed by Joe. She looked at Kate, wondering if they should go. Kate nodded and they went into the hallway where they found Justin and Joe arguing in loud whispers.

"We can't tell!" Justin snapped.

"We have to," Joe said. "They'll find out sooner or later and it would be better if they heard it from us."

"Justin? Joe?" Bailey said.

The brothers' heads jerked toward them in surprise, their eyes blazing.

"Look, we don't mean to intrude, but maybe we can help." Bailey walked closer to Justin and Joe.

"What do you know about anything?" Justin barked.

Kate spoke gently. "We know you seem to be in trouble and we'd like to help."

"No one can help us," Joe said, tears filling his eyes.

"That's not true. If we can't help, we know who can." Bailey's voice was strong and confident.

"But first you have to tell us the problem." Kate stood waiting for their reply.

The boys remained silent.

Justin drew in a deep breath and blew it out slowly. He eyed Joe, who nodded. Justin looked at Bailey and she noticed his chin quiver. Tears pooled in his eyes. "It's our fault. My fault, really. Joe tried to talk me out of it," he finally whispered.

"What's your fault?" Bailey thought she knew, but she figured it was important for Justin to say it himself.

"The stampede. All of them. And Grandpa's injuries."

"How is it your fault? What did you do?" Kate asked.

"We—I—scared the elk. I shot around them with my airsoft gun to spook them. I never shot directly at the elk. Only in the trees and bushes around them. Joe came along because I pressured him. He didn't want to be involved."

"Why did you want to scare the elk? Didn't you see how it made them stampede?"

"Yeah, I saw," Justin replied. "That was the point. I remember when Joe and I were little and we'd come here to visit my grandparents. This place was awesome. It was so beautiful. But over the years the tourists began coming and it started to change. They didn't care about taking care of this place since they'd be going home in a week or two. They acted like they owned the place just because they threw their money around in all these shops.

"The Elkfest used to be just for the locals," he continued, "but now all these fancy tourists were joining it. It made me sick. I wanted Estes Park to be peaceful like it used to be. It was our special place with our grandparents until those tourists ruined it. So I hoped the elk would scare them away."

"How did you know where to find the elk? It seems like you always knew where they were."

"I just looked for a wallow and knew they'd be close by."

"Just as we thought," Bailey said.

"Where there are wallows, there are elk." Justin smiled, but his eyes were sad. "Wait a minute. You *knew* that? Did you know what we were doing too?"

Bailey nodded. She turned to Justin and put her hand on his arm. "It's okay, Justin. We're still your friends. We'll explain later. But you need to tell your parents."

Justin shook his head. "I can't."

"Sure you can. We'll go with you," Kate said. "And God will give you the strength to do what you need to do."

"You talk about God like He's standing right here with us," Justin said.

Bailey laughed. "That's because He is!"

"I wish I had faith like that," Joe said.

"You can!" Kate assured him. "You just have to ask God for it. He loves to help people believe."

Justin shook his head. "Seems like God wouldn't want anything to do with someone like me."

"That's the cool thing about God," Kate said. "He's not like people who only love popular, nice-looking people, or those who never mess up. He especially loves those who need help and who have done things they shouldn't."

"When you really think about it, that includes all of us." Bailey could hardly believe they were having this conversation. She knew the Camp Club Girls' prayers were giving her and Kate the courage to tell the boys about God.

Justin looked at them. "Maybe you're right." He looked toward the hospital room door. "I guess it's time to tell them."

Bailey and Kate followed Justin and Joe back into Grandpa Perkins's room.

"I—I have something I need to say," Justin began. "I owe you a huge apology. I don't know if you'll be able to forgive me."

"Forgive you for what?" Mrs. Perkins looked surprised.

"For causing all this trouble."

"This isn't your fault, son," Mr. Perkins said. "No one could have stopped those elk."

"That's where you're wrong." Justin told the story to his parents and grandparents. "So if I hadn't been so stupid and wanted everything the way it used to be, I wouldn't have shot at the trees and bushes around the elk to spook them and this never would have happened. Grandpa's hurt because of me, and I'm so sorry."

Mr. Perkins's forehead creased with worry, but his words were gentle. "I'm disappointed in what you did, Justin. I always taught you to be responsible with guns and never to use them for harm. You used your airsoft gun inappropriately, and there will be consequences." Mr. Perkins put his arm around his son's shoulder. "But it takes a strong man to admit when he's wrong. I'm glad you told the truth."

"You know you could never do anything to make us stop loving you," his mother said. "Not even this."

"I know." Justin's face relaxed. "You guys are the best."

Mr. Perkins turned to his younger son. "And Joe. I'm proud of you for not taking part in this. Even though you went with him, you did try to talk him out of it."

Joe ran to his father's arms and hugged him.

"However," Mr. Perkins added, "even if you couldn't stop Justin, you should have come to Mom or me. You should always speak up and tell an adult if you know someone is involved in dangerous activities. Maybe none of this would have happened." Justin's face was white, and Joe's ears went red. "You will both have consequences."

A tap at the door shifted their attention in that direction. "Hello?"

"Mom!" Bailey cried, glad to have the tension broken.

Mrs. Chang and Trina entered.

"How is he doing?" she asked.

"The doctor says he's making progress," Mr. Perkins said. "His vital signs are good. It's just a matter of time and healing now."

"He certainly is in our prayers," Mrs. Chang said.

"We appreciate that," Mrs. Perkins replied.

Mrs. Chang turned to the girls. "Kate, are you ready to go get Biscuit?"

"I'm more than ready!" Kate replied. "I can't wait to see him."

"Where is that cute little dog?" Mrs. Perkins asked. "On a playdate?"

"Oh no," Kate said seriously. "He's at the animal hospital. He was hurt in the stampede."

"No!" Mrs. Perkins went to Kate and took her hands in hers. "You were kind to come see Grandpa Perkins when Biscuit had an injury to be concerned about. I'm sorry I didn't know about it sooner."

"At least Biscuit is recuperating." Kate looked at Grandpa Perkins. "I wish Grandpa could go home today too."

"He'll be home before we know it," Grandma Perkins piped in. "And stirring up trouble, no doubt."

"We'd better go," Mrs. Chang said. "You girls ready?"

"Yeah," Bailey said. Then turning to Justin and Joe, she said, "We'll be around if you want to talk or anything."

Justin smiled. "Thanks. We just might."

●━━━●━━━●

On the way to the vet, Bailey and Kate told Mrs. Chang and Trina what they'd learned.

"You're kidding!" Mrs. Chang said.

"Nope. And here's the cool part," Bailey said. "We got a chance to tell them about God and how He loves them no matter what they've done." Bailey's smile was as big as a watermelon slice.

"That is cool," Trina said.

"What did they say?" Mrs. Chang asked.

"Joe said he always wanted to have faith like that," Bailey said.

"And I told him God would help him believe if he just asked Him."

"You girls amaze me." Mrs. Chang looked at them in her rearview mirror. "I'm proud of you. And I bet God's smiling pretty big right now too."

"I hope so," Bailey said. "We told them we would be around if they wanted to talk or anything."

"You've done what you can for now," Mrs. Chang said. "Now God will do His part and help them sort it all out." She pulled the car into a parking space in front of the animal hospital.

Bailey and Kate jumped out of the car and ran to the door. Mrs. Chang and Trina met them inside.

"The nurse is getting Biscuit," Kate said. "We already gave them our name."

Soon, the nurse came out with Biscuit on a leash. He limped on his bandaged paw, but when he saw Kate he hobbled on three legs to her, straining the leash.

"Hey buddy!" Kate knelt so Biscuit could lick her face. "I missed you!"

"Looks like he missed you too!" the nurse said. "As you can see, we've bandaged his middle so his ribs will heal faster. Since the bandage only sticks to itself, you can remove it in a week or two. Just try to keep him as calm as possible for the next couple of weeks. No jumping up or down onto furniture."

"What about his paw?" Bailey asked. "Do we need to know anything about that?"

"We had to stitch it up. Remove the bandage tomorrow and see how it looks. If the wound isn't oozy or bleeding, you don't need to rebandage it. But if it is, go ahead and bandage it up for another day. I'll send an extra one home with you." The nurse handed the bandage to Kate. "Just wrap it with the gauze and tape it so it's secure."

"Thank you for taking such good care of Biscuit," Kate said.

"We were happy to do it," the nurse replied. "If you have any questions about caring for his injuries, give us a call."

"We will," Kate said.

Mrs. Chang went to the counter and paid the bill while the girls headed to the car with Biscuit.

"I can't believe all that's happened this week." Bailey petted Biscuit, who laid his head on Kate's arm as she held him. "Do we have some things to tell the Camp Club Girls tonight!"

CHAPTER 12

Solutions

Back at the hotel, Kate made Biscuit a little bed of blankets on the floor and gently laid him on it. "I'm so glad to have you back, Biscuit," she cooed as she stroked his head. "You be a good boy and stay here while Bailey and I call the girls. We won't be long."

"Mom, Kate and I are going to sit in the lobby to call the Camp Club Girls."

"Okay," Mrs. Chang said and waved them out.

Bailey pulled her phone from her pocket and conferenced everyone in. "We've had quite a day," she told them.

"What's going on?" Sydney asked.

"Oh, nothing," Kate answered casually. "We came up with a solution to the elk mystery we've been working on all week."

Four girls screamed, and Bailey held the phone away from her ear and laughed.

"How'd you do it?" McKenzie asked.

"Actually, we figured it out earlier, but we still had to prove we were right," Bailey said.

Kate laughed and jumped into storytelling mode. "We went to the hospital to see Justin and Joe's grandpa. Just after we got to his room, the boys went into the hall."

"We decided to follow them to make sure they were okay," Bailey said. "You know, in case they were upset by seeing their grandpa or something."

"We found them in the hall," Kate said. "We overheard Joe telling Justin that they had to tell what happened."

"We didn't know what to do at first." Bailey took up the story. "But pretty soon we asked if we could do something to help."

"We got them to tell us what the problem was." Kate looked at Bailey.

"So? What was it?" Alex asked.

"Justin admitted he'd been shooting at the elk to scare them into stampeding," Bailey blabbed.

"No way! Oscar the Grouch confessed?" Alex screeched.

"You were right all along!" Elizabeth said.

"I feel bad about calling him Oscar now," Bailey said. "He's really not so bad after you get to know him."

"What about his brother?" McKenzie asked.

"Joe tried to talk Justin out of doing it, and went with him," Kate said. "So he was involved, but not really."

"Except by association," Elizabeth said. "Proverbs says a person is known by the company he or she keeps."

"Yeah, but when it's your brother, it's hard to stay away from him." Bailey felt sorry Joe had gotten mixed up in his brother's mess.

"I wonder how they knew where to find the elk," Sydney said.

"Remember the smelly wallow we told you about that we found on our hike?" Bailey pulled her lip balm from her pocket and put some on. "We realized the boys must be using them to find the elk."

"But here's the good part," Kate said. "We encouraged Justin to tell his parents and told him we'd even go with him. He was afraid to. But then I told him God would give him the strength."

"So did he do it?" Sydney asked.

"Yep," Kate replied. "He walked right in there and told them everything."

"How'd they take it?" Alex asked.

"Pretty well, considering," Bailey said. "But they'll both have some kind of consequences."

"Guess that's to be expected," Elizabeth said.

"Wow," Sydney said. "You guys *have* had quite a day."

Bailey shifted her phone to the other ear. "We got Biscuit back."

"Already?" McKenzie asked. "How is he?"

"He's bandaged to keep him from moving too much," Kate answered. "That will give his ribs a chance to heal. We're supposed to keep him quiet. We can take the bandage off in a week."

"What about his foot?" Sydney asked.

"It's still wrapped up," Kate replied. "But we're supposed to look at it tomorrow to see if we can leave the bandage off."

"Wow, God really answered our prayers that he would heal fast,"

Elizabeth said. "I'm still surprised he wasn't killed in that stampede. God sure watched out for him."

Kate inhaled deeply. "I've thought the same thing. It's a relief to have him back home. I must have told God thank You a bazillion times already!"

The girls laughed.

"Now we'll just pray that God keeps working on Justin and Joe," Elizabeth said.

"Funny how we were so afraid of them before and now we're hoping they'll come to talk," Bailey said. "God sure turns things upside down."

"I've got to go," Sydney said. "But keep me posted."

"We should get going too," Bailey said. "We'll let you know if anything more happens."

Bailey and Kate went back into their hotel room. Biscuit slept on the little bed Kate made him on the floor and hadn't moved at all. He lifted his shaggy head when they came through the door.

Mrs. Chang was lost in a book and Trina was looking out the window. "Hey, the Perkinses are coming back from the hospital," she said.

Bailey and Kate went to the window and saw the family walk up to the main entrance.

"Hey, maybe we can introduce Justin and Joe to the ghost in the Music Room tomorrow," Kate said.

"Mom, can we go ask when they get up here?"

"I think that would be a nice gesture," Mrs. Perkins said, "just so they don't wonder if we think less of them after what happened."

Bailey and Kate waited until they heard the Perkinses' voices in the hall before going out to greet them.

"We were wondering if Justin and Joe would like to come to the Music Room with us tomorrow," Bailey said. "There's a ghost who lives there!"

The Perkins family laughed.

"That would be fun, but we can't," Justin said. Then he looked at his parents and gave a sheepish grin. "We're pretty much grounded for the rest of our lives."

"Ohhh," Kate said. "We hadn't thought about that. Sorry."

"It's okay." Joe elbowed his older brother. "He's grounded longer than I am. Maybe if you come back again next year about this time I'll be free to go with you. But Justin probably can't for a few more years."

Justin playfully punched Joe in the arm.

"But we told our parents that you talked to us about your faith," Justin said. "They said we could have you over to talk to us again if you wouldn't mind."

"Mind?" Bailey said, her eyes growing to the size of tennis balls. "We'd love to!"

—●—●—●—

"So that pretty much covers it," Bailey told the Camp Club Girls. "We're going over to talk to them tomorrow afternoon, and our parents might even come too."

"That is so cool," Elizabeth said. "You really let your light shine. Knowing Jesus and living a life of faith will be the best solution for their lives."

"For sure," Kate agreed. "And thanks to all of us working together, we have a solution to our mysteries."

Bailey giggled. "I can't wait to see what our next one will be!"

Camp Club Girls:
Bailey's
Peoria Problem

CHAPTER 1

Almost Rammed!

"Look out!"

Alexis turned to see a huge ram lower his head and charge.

"Ahhhhhhh!" Alexis screamed. She sprinted through the herd of sheep toward the fence.

Baaa! Baaaaah! The sheep complained as they tripped out of her way.

Thud-thud-thud-thud! Alex could hear the angry ram close behind.

Chaotic baaing continued as more sheep were disrupted from their peaceful grazing.

Fwap! Alexis smacked into the fence. She frantically hopped up the first rung, swung her leg over the top rung, and fell to the ground below. Safe! She was out of the sheep pen in record time.

Pumph! The angry ram smacked his horns into the fence then darted off to the other side of the pasture.

"Are you okay?" Nine-year-old Bailey helped her friend stand up. As Alexis got up, she couldn't quite hide the fear in her eyes.

"I—I think so." Alex brushed off her jeans, and Bailey noticed her friend's hands tremble. "Did I do something to make him mad?"

Bailey shook her head, her silky black hair swinging around her face. "Uncle Nathan said that one—Brutus—is just plain mean. Sometimes he even keeps Brutus in a different pen."

"Wish I'd known that before I went in there," Alex said.

Bailey put her arm around Alex. "I'm sorry. I should have been more careful about seeing which sheep were in there first. I know you're not used to being around farm animals."

"I'm hardly used to being around city animals! I've never even had a pet—unless you count my brothers."

Bailey laughed. "Well, I'll try to remember to check the pen next time."

"Who said anything about a next time?" Alex gave Bailey a playful nudge. "Anyway, it's not your fault. I should have kept my eyes open and noticed that ram."

"What's all the commotion over here?" Bailey's uncle Nathan strode up behind them, the gravel crunching beneath his heavy work boots. Shy, his Australian shepherd, pranced at his side. Nathan's stocky, muscular build told of his hard work on Curly Q Ranch, which he had bought seven years earlier. His straight black hair was just long enough on top to ripple in the soft breeze.

"Brutus charged Alex," Bailey explained in a nutshell.

Uncle Nathan frowned as he looked at Alex. "Are you hurt?"

"No. I'm fine. Though I've never been so scared in all my twelve years."

"I'm sorry. I should have moved him to another pen before letting you girls come out here."

Bailey giggled. "You should have seen her move and jump over this fence! It was pretty funny now that I think about it."

Alex laughed too. "Guess that cheerleading camp trained me pretty well! I never dreamed it would help me be limber enough to scale fences!"

"I'm just glad you're okay," Uncle Nathan said. "I put your suitcases in the upstairs room next to Brian's. Are you ready for the grand tour of Curly Q?"

Shy, a medium-sized white dog with black and gray splotches of color, sniffed Bailey's hand. Scratching her behind the ears, Bailey answered the uncle she adored. "You bet! But what about Brian? Is he coming?" She never grew tired of spending time with her older cousin, in spite of his friendly teasing and practical jokes.

"I don't think so. He got a call from a friend just as I walked out." Her uncle cupped one leathery hand around his mouth and muttered into Bailey's ear, "Probably some pretty girl. You know how teenagers are!" He winked. "Come on. I'll show you the pasture where most of the sheep are grazing today."

Bailey and Alex followed Uncle Nathan to a lush green field of clover. As they approached, the musky smell of sheep greeted them and the sheep's bleating grew increasingly louder.

"Here they are." Uncle Nathan leaned on the fence, watching his herd as he had no doubt done every day for the past seven years.

"Wow." Alex's mouth gaped as she scanned the herd. "I've never seen so many sheep. How many are there?"

"Three hundred twenty-three," he answered confidently.

"Are you sure? How do you know one hasn't run off or something?"

Nathan chuckled. "A good shepherd knows his flock. He keeps count of them and watches their behavior. If one is missing, he knows it."

"Like Jesus," Bailey piped in. "He knows us and watches us too. He's the Good Shepherd."

"Hey, yeah," Alex said. "I read that in my Bible, but it makes more sense now, seeing these poor helpless sheep. They really do need someone to take care of them, don't they—except for Brutus."

"Absolutely." Nathan rubbed the woolly head of a sheep that had wandered over to the fence. "They rely completely on their shepherd to care for them."

"Listen." Bailey cocked her head. "I love how they have different voices just like people. Some are low and others are higher."

"And they have different personalities like people do too," Uncle Nathan added. "You really do get to know them after a while."

"Look at that baby!" Alex giggled as she pointed.

"Let's name her," Bailey suggested. "She's so cute. Look how she bounces around when she plays—like she has springs in her feet!" Bailey put her hands to the ground and sprang up and down imitating the lamb.

"How 'bout we call her Snowball?" Alex rubbed the lamb's woolly white head when it came close.

"Or Marshmallow," Bailey offered.

"I know!" Alex pulled the stretchy red hair bow from her ponytail, causing her dark brown curls to fall to her shoulders. She put the bright hair tie around the lamb's neck. "Let's call her Bow!"

"Bow it is." Bailey caressed the lamb's face. "You look beautiful, Bow!"

"Will you start shearing the sheep today?" Alex looked at Uncle Nathan.

He checked his watch. "We can probably get some done this afternoon before suppertime. I'll show you how, and then you can have a go at it."

"Do you do it right out there in the field?"

Nathan laughed. "Naw, we'll take them over to the barn. We shear on a nice clean floor so the wool doesn't get dirty when it falls. Also, the sheep getting sheared in the barn won't upset the others waiting their turn in the field."

"They don't like getting sheared?"

"It doesn't hurt them, but they don't like being held still. They can make an awful racket."

Alex grimaced. "I don't think sheep shearing will be my thing."

"I hope you'll try it. I think you'd do fine," Bailey assured her. "But you do have to be strong and determined to do it. They need to know you're in charge."

"That's right." Uncle Nathan patted Alex on the back. "You city girls can do more than you think. You'll see. Now, why don't you and Bailey go change into your grubbies, grab us some bottles of water from the kitchen, and meet me in the barn. We're bound to get thirsty as we work. In the meantime, I'll bring out a couple of ewes and show you how it's done."

Bailey and Alex raced back to the house. The screen door slammed behind them, and they nearly collided with sixteen-year-old Brian in the kitchen.

"Hey! Slow down! I was just coming out to see you." Brian's bear hug lifted his younger cousin off her feet.

Bailey laughed as he returned her to the floor. "Brian, this is my friend Alexis Howell. Alex for short."

"Nice to meet you." Brian extended his hand.

Alex smiled and pumped Brian's hand. Her cheeks turned rosy as she studied his handsome features—thick, wavy black hair that hung loosely around his face and ears, and a brilliant smile that showed off his ridiculously white teeth. His almond-shaped eyes danced almost as playfully as Bailey's. He had his dad's strong build and was already as tall as his father.

"We're after some water, and then Uncle Nathan is going to show Alex how to shear," Bailey told him.

"Looks like you're not wasting any time getting down to business. I'll go with you."

As Bailey turned to the refrigerator for the water bottles, her eyes caught the *Peoria Daily News* on the kitchen table. Its primary front-page headline—MISSING MILLIONAIRE TO BE DECLARED LEGALLY DEAD?—aroused her curiosity, and she quickly scanned the article.

"Check this out," Bailey said to her friend.

"What?"

"This newspaper says an eccentric millionaire named Marshall Gonzalez has been missing for more than seven years. He lived around here. Distant relatives living in California want him to be declared legally dead so they can inherit his fortune. It says he has no near relatives and had few friends. Look. Here's his picture."

Alex came closer to inspect the photo. A plump Mexican man with a mustache and thick black eyebrows stared back at her. He wore a dark suit and tie. "I wonder where they live in California. Maybe it's close to Sacramento where I live." Alex wrapped a strand of curly dark hair around her finger.

"Maybe we can find out more from Uncle Nathan and Aunt Darcy at supper. We'd better change. I'm so glad your parents let you come to spend spring break with me!"

"Me too!"

Minutes later, Bailey and Alex, dressed in worn jeans and old T-shirts, met Uncle Nathan in the barn. Alex pulled her hair back into a ponytail again at Bailey's advice. "It'll keep it out of your eyes while you work. I'd wear mine in a ponytail too if it was long enough." They spotted Brian in the pasture tending the sheep.

"Ready to get started?" Uncle Nathan asked.

Bailey looked at Alex and saw the color drain from her face. "I'm ready," she said, "but I think maybe Alex would rather watch this first time."

"You got that right. I'm not excited about getting too close to those animals after that last encounter."

"No problem. We'll take it slow, and you can just watch for now." Uncle Nathan patted the two ewes with thick, curly fleece that stood near him. Thin legs poked out the bottom of their fleece, reminding Bailey of cartoon sheep. Though she'd seen sheep many times over the years, she still giggled at how funny they looked.

"Nowadays most ranchers use electric shears like this." Uncle Nathan held up the shears so Alex could see. They hung from the end of a long cable leading to an electric motor attached to the barn ceiling. In a flash, he lifted the struggling sheep's chin and brought the animal to a sitting position on its rump, while holding the ewe between his strong legs. In this position, the ewe's struggling ceased, and Uncle Nathan began shearing. He ran long strokes down the length of the sheep's body before flipping it over and doing the other side. Uncle Nathan then sheared the sheep's belly and legs. In a matter of minutes, the once fat, roundish animal looked years younger and not so wise.

"That's amazing!" Alex said. "How'd you do that so fast?"

"Years of practice," Uncle Nathan answered. "But speed isn't the important thing. If you rush, you might accidentally nick the sheep, and the next time you try to shear them, you'll have a mighty fight on your hands. My sheep trust me. They know I'm careful with them. But I try to get it done as quickly and carefully as possible so they don't have to be held still for too long."

"Can I try it now? I'll probably be a bit rusty." Bailey looked at her uncle expectantly.

"After we sweep up this wool. Remember, we have to separate the belly wool from the rest of the fleece so we can bag it separately. Then we need to skirt, bag, and label all of it."

"Skirt? What's that?" asked Alex.

"It's how we roll the fleece to get it ready for market," Bailey answered, proud that she knew the answer.

Uncle Nathan showed Alex how to skirt the fleece, and together they placed it in a plastic garbage bag. "We get more money at market if we have the different wools separated and labeled properly," he explained.

"Now?" Bailey asked, bobbing up and down on her toes. Her hand held the shears.

"Sure thing. I'll be right here in case you need my help."

Bailey flipped on the shears and used her legs to hold the old ewe. She ran the tool deftly across the sheep's skin, the wool dropping on the cleanly swept, concrete barn floor.

Alex stepped forward to watch more closely. It took Bailey twice as long as it had Uncle Nathan, but she got the job done.

"There!" Bailey smiled with satisfaction as she wiped sweat from her forehead.

"You were magnificent!" Alex exclaimed. "I can't believe you could handle the sheep like that!"

"You want to try?" Bailey asked her friend.

Alex hesitated. "I think I'll watch awhile longer. I'm not sure I'm ready yet."

"Good call," Uncle Nathan said. "You can learn a lot from watching. Maybe you'll want to try it yourself in a day or two."

The wheels of a car crunched on the gravel driveway, drawing their attention.

"Aunt Darcy!" Bailey took off running, black hair flying.

Aunt Darcy scrambled out of the car and caught her niece in a giant hug. "It's so good to see you! Let me see how tall you are."

Bailey stood stick straight as her aunt, still dressed in her nurse's uniform, used her hand to measure from the top of Bailey's head to herself. "You're up to my chin! You must have grown three inches since I saw you last!" Darcy spotted Alex standing a polite distance away. "This must be Alex. Welcome to the Curly Q! I'm so glad you could come with Bailey this year."

"Thanks for having me," Alex said as she edged closer. "I'm already learning so much!"

Alex stuck out her hand, and Aunt Darcy took it and pulled her into a hug. "I have plenty of those to go around," she said midhug. "I picked up some fried chicken, corn, and mashed potatoes on my way home from work. Anybody hungry?"

"Always!" Brian ambled in from the pasture and overheard the question. "Let's eat!"

"Go wash up, all of you," Darcy instructed. "Looks like you could use it!"

"Race you to the house," Brian challenged.

Bailey and Alex were off like lightning, but Brian's long legs soon overtook them.

After everyone had washed up and changed into clean clothes, they sat around the table and joined hands. Uncle Nathan offered thanks to the Lord for the food and passed the bucket of chicken.

"Did you see the headline in the newspaper today about the missing millionaire?" Bailey ventured.

"Yes. That case has been in the news off and on for years." Uncle Nathan buttered a roll.

"Do you think he's really dead?" asked Alex.

"Hard to say. No one's seen or heard from him for seven years," Aunt Darcy said.

"That doesn't mean he's dead," Bailey countered.

"No, but it sure leaves a lot of unanswered questions," said Brian around a mouthful of food.

"What do you know about him, Uncle Nathan?" Bailey bit into a chicken leg.

"Not much. He kept to himself, just like the paper said. He didn't have any friends to speak of. Never married, no children."

"So you knew him?" Alex asked.

"No. Just that his name was Marshall Gonzalez," Uncle Nathan said. "I bought this ranch the year he disappeared. I never met him, but I've heard talk of him. People thought he was a bit strange 'cause he was such a loner, but you know how folks like to make up stories about others who are different. Pass the corn, please."

Bailey passed the bowl and asked, "Do you know where he lived?"

"Why all this interest in Mr. Gonzalez?"

"Just curious." Bailey glanced at Alex, who was trying to tame a smile.

●—●—●

Bailey and Alexis headed up to their room at nine o'clock that night.

"This used to be my cousin Jennifer's room," Bailey told Alex. "But she moved out when she went to college last year."

"Which bed do you want?" Alex asked.

Twin beds flanked either side of a window that was much taller than it was wide. Matching rose-covered bedspreads adorned the beds, and a nightstand sat beside each one. A soft, pink beanbag chair slouched against the wall adjacent to the beds and window. Two walls were papered pastel pink with tiny white dots. It reminded Bailey of the dotted swiss material her mother would try to talk her into for making her Easter dresses. It was fine for wallpaper, but Bailey wouldn't want to wear it—or any dress for that matter.

"I usually sleep in that one." Bailey pointed to the bed closest to the adjoining bathroom.

"Okay." Alexis plopped her suitcase on the other bed and started unpacking.

"I don't know about you, but something about this Marshall Gonzalez case seems weird." Bailey moved clothes from her suitcase to the top two dresser drawers, leaving the bottom two for Alex. "Why would distant relatives care about this guy now after seven years? Did they just find out about his disappearance?"

"I know what you mean," Alex agreed. "Maybe he's still alive." She dug in her suitcase for her toothbrush. "I'm going to take a quick shower."

"Okay. I'll take one when you're done. But let's think some more about this case."

●—●—●

After her shower, Bailey slipped into her silky, pink capri pajamas with soft, gray kitties on the pants.

Alex, already in her nightgown, grabbed her toothbrush and toothpaste and entered the steamy bathroom, leaving the door open. "Now about this Gonzalez case. We could make a list of what we know so far and what we still need to find out." Alex started brushing her teeth.

"Good idea. We'll need to work quickly on this since we only have a week until we have to go home." Bailey parked her empty rolling suitcase in the corner. She pulled back the sheets on her twin bed and put her traveling companion, a sandy-brown stuffed dog named Ginger, on her pillow.

Alex spit out her toothpaste. "How will we be able to get away to investigate with all the sheep to shear?"

Bailey took a notebook from her backpack. "Tomorrow's Sunday, silly. Uncle Nathan doesn't believe in working on the Sabbath. We'll go to church in the morning and just relax in the afternoon. Even on the other days we'll probably only shear in the morning. He knows kids need time to play. Usually after lunch we're free to do whatever we want. And believe me, after that long, you'll feel like you've worked all day!" Bailey began scribbling in the notebook.

"What do we have so far?" Alex asked, knowing Bailey was writing down clues.

"Not much, really. Just Marshall's name, and that he's a millionaire with distant relatives in California who want to declare him legally dead so they can inherit his money. He has no close relatives and very few friends. He's been missing for over seven years."

"It may not be much, but it's a start." Alex wiped her face with a cleansing pad, the antiseptic smell filling the room. "Obviously, the motive for wanting him to be declared dead is money."

"Right." Bailey took her turn in the bathroom now, toothbrush in hand.

"For starters, we should find out where Gonzalez lived, don't you think?"

Bailey nodded, her mouth foaming white. She spit and wiped her mouth on a towel. "I wonder how he got so rich."

"Good question. We'll check that out too." Alex yawned.

"I think I'm gonna sleep good tonight. It's been a busy day." Bailey crawled into bed.

"Me too, but I can't wait for tomorrow. We've got more than sheep shearing to do while we're here this week."

"Yeah! We've got a mystery to solve!"

The Mystery Man and the Mystery House

Sunday morning dawned bright but cool, as Bailey and Alex dressed for church.

"Maybe we can find out more about Marshall Gonzalez today," Bailey said, hairbrush in hand. She grimaced with the pull of every tangle in her fine hair.

"Probably won't be until later if we do. I doubt the sermon will be about Marshall," Alex joked.

After church, Bailey and Alex chowed down on burgers at the local Steak 'n Shake with Uncle Nathan, Aunt Darcy, and George and Helen Jones, a couple from their church. Brian took off to eat with his friends from the youth group.

"What do you make of the headlines these days?" asked Mr. Jones.

Uncle Nathan stuffed a crispy fry into his mouth. "Which ones?"

"This business about Marshall Gonzalez." Mr. Jones sipped his soda. "You think he's really dead?"

Bailey and Alex shot excited glances at each other but kept eating while they listened.

"Hard to know for sure," Uncle Nathan said. "But nobody's seen anything of him for a lot of years, so I guess he could be dead."

"Never found a body, though," Mr. Jones added.

"This is hardly mealtime conversation, George." Mrs. Jones reached for the salt.

"Just talking about the news, dear," Mr. Jones said, patting his wife's hand.

"I heard Marshall lived not too far from here," Aunt Darcy added.

"That's a fact. Somewhere east of here is what I heard, though I don't know exactly where." Mr. Jones dipped his french fry in ketchup before popping it into his sizable mouth.

"I suppose if we'd bought the Curly Q a year earlier, we probably would've met him." Uncle Nathan sipped his soda.

"Very likely," Mr. Jones said. "We only moved here five years ago, so we didn't know him either. But they say he kept to himself, which is part of the problem of them not knowing what happened to him."

"Good heavens." Mrs. Jones pressed her napkin to her mouth.

Bailey nudged Alex and suppressed a giggle.

Alex nudged her back and disguised her smile with a cough.

"Are you okay, dear?" asked Mrs. Jones.

Alex took a giant gulp of water. "Yes, I'm fine."

"Well," Uncle Nathan continued, "you'd think someone would have befriended him."

"Maybe," Mr. Jones answered. "But a person can be pretty scarce if he wants to be."

"Was he really a millionaire?" asked Bailey.

"That's what they say." Uncle Nathan bit into his burger, juice dripping from its sides. He quickly grabbed a napkin to mop up the mess.

"How'd he get so rich?" Alex wondered aloud.

"He inherited his money," Mr. Jones responded. "From what I've heard, he didn't have the personality to be much of a businessman. He basically just let his fortune earn interest at the bank and spent his time doing whatever he pleased."

"Inherited his money," Bailey said under her breath. "Just like his relatives are hoping to do." She bit her bottom lip as she thought that over.

"About all anyone knows for sure is that he pretty much closed his house in Peoria and released all the people who worked for him, except for a caretaker." Uncle Nathan took a drink of his pop. "Some say he mentioned something about trying sheepherding before he took off, and had even attended a sheep expo at the state fair in Springfield."

"Then he must have had a sheep farm somewhere." Alex looked at Bailey.

"Only if he acted on what he was thinking about," Bailey said.

"So if he was hardly ever seen, even by his neighbors, how does anyone know when he disappeared?" asked Alex.

"Hmm." Uncle Nathan rubbed his chin. "That's a good question."

"Maybe he had secret business associates who reported him missing when they didn't hear from him," suggested Bailey.

"Or maybe his bank noticed he wasn't using any of his money," added Alex.

Mr. Jones raised his eyebrows and looked at Bailey and Alex. "You guys are good!"

"I've read a lot of Nancy Drew mysteries," Alex explained.

"And I'm just a natural detective." Bailey took a long draw on her straw, trying to get a taste of her thick chocolate milkshake.

"Naturally nosy is more like it," Uncle Nathan teased.

"Nathan!" Aunt Darcy scolded her husband.

Uncle Nathan mussed Bailey's hair playfully. "Aw, she knows I love her."

Bailey's black-brown eyes sparkled at her uncle as she beamed and nodded.

The waitress soon brought the checks. Nathan and Mr. Jones stood and shook hands goodbye while the women exchanged hugs.

"Nice meeting you little ladies," Mr. Jones said to Bailey and Alex.

"Nice meeting you too," Bailey answered.

"Let us know when you crack the Gonzalez case," Mr. Jones added, smiling broadly. "That'd show those authorities, wouldn't it? To have two girls figure it out when they've been working on it for years!" He laughed and smacked Uncle Nathan on the back.

Back at the Curly Q, Bailey and Alex changed out of their church clothes.

"What do you want to do?" Alex asked.

"It's a beautiful day now that the sun has warmed things up." Bailey's eyes twinkled. "I think we should take a walk."

"Ooh, good idea!"

"We probably won't even need our sweatshirts now, it's so nice out."

"Let's go!" Alex started for the bedroom door.

"Whoa, girl!" Bailey slowed her friend with an outstretched arm. "We need to gather some supplies first."

"Supplies? What for?"

"In case we happen to stumble on some clues for the Gonzalez case. I'll bring my notepad and my camera-watch." Bailey rifled through her backpack.

"You have a camera-watch?" Alex's eyes grew to the size of a CD.

"Yeah." Bailey nodded like a bobblehead. "Kate told me about them at camp last summer, so I checked them out online and added it to my birthday wish list. I got it from my dad when I turned nine in January but haven't had much chance to try it out yet."

"You're awesome!" Alex hugged Bailey. "Speaking of Kate, we really should call the other Camp Club Girls to let them in on our latest mystery."

"They may have ideas we haven't even thought of yet," Bailey agreed. "I'll call Kate and Sydney, and you call Elizabeth and McKenzie. With all of us working together, we'll have this mystery solved by the end of the week!"

The girls sat on their beds and flipped open their cell phones.

"I'm so glad my parents finally got me a new cell phone before we came to Uncle Nathan's." Bailey bit her lip as she found Kate's number and pushed TALK. "Kate? It's Bailey!"

Alex, sitting cross-legged on her bed, chatted away to Elizabeth while Bailey filled Kate in on the details they already knew from the Gonzalez case. Then each one called the next girl they were assigned. A half hour later, Bailey and Alex had hung up.

"Did Kate have any ideas about this case?" Alex pushed her phone back into her jeans pocket.

"She's going to check the internet for all the newspaper articles and public records she can find on Gonzalez," Bailey said. "And she's going to see if she can find an older online map of the area that might show exactly where his ranch was."

Alex did a cartwheel between the two beds, her cheerleading skills bursting to the surface. "Good work! That Kate is a genius!"

"How 'bout you? Did Elizabeth or McKenzie have any ideas?"

"Elizabeth will give it some thought and, of course, prayer. In the meantime, she said for us to be careful and not to get in over our heads."

Bailey laughed, knowing Elizabeth's tendency to worry, then added, "I know she really will take the praying part seriously. That's bound to help us!"

"Yeah," agreed Alex. "And McKenzie asked why Gonzalez was such a loner. She wondered if he had bad relations with his family or maybe never even knew his distant relatives. As she put it, there must be some reason he was so withdrawn."

"Hmm." Bailey's eyebrows wrinkled in thought. "I never thought of that. But she's right. It's not natural to avoid all other human contact. There must be more to his story."

"What about Sydney? Did she say anything?" Alex asked.

"Not much. She'll have to think it over. She said to call her as we get more to go on."

Alex nodded. "I told Elizabeth and McKenzie that we'd keep our phones charged, on, and with us at all times in case they need to contact us."

"Good." Bailey laughed. "Oh, and I forgot to tell you—Biscuit says hi!"

Alex burst out laughing. Biscuit was the dog they all found last summer at camp, but with Kate's parents' consent, it became Kate's dog after camp, since the two of them had grown especially close. Biscuit had even helped the Camp Club Girls solve their first mystery and had become known as the Wonder Dog.

"Good ol' Biscuit," Alex said, grinning broadly.

"I think we're ready for our walk now." Bailey patted her pockets. "I've got everything we need—notepad, pen, cell phone, and camera-watch."

"Let's go then!"

At the bottom of the stairs, Bailey called into the living room, "We're going for a walk! We'll be back in a little while!"

"Okay," Aunt Darcy answered.

"We have our cell phones," Alex offered.

"Good thinking. See you later."

The girls walked down the country road past huge oak trees that provided a cool canopy of shade. Small splashes of sunshine shone between the leaves. The sheep pasture was soon on their right, and the girls could hardly talk over the loud bleating. Alex covered her nose and mouth with her hand to block out the smell.

"Hey, look over there!" Bailey pointed beyond the pasture.

"What is it?" Alex squinted her eyes to see.

"I'm not sure yet. We'll have to get closer."

Alex and Bailey were almost jogging as they moved nearer to a run-down house.

"Boy, does that need a fresh coat of paint!" Bailey said. She was glad the noisy sheep would keep her voice from being heard by anyone but Alex.

"It's so far back from the road, it's still hard to tell, but it sure does look like it needs work," Alex agreed.

"Do you think anyone lives there?" Bailey asked.

Alex shook her head. "Who could live in a place like that?"

Both girls returned their gazes to the dilapidated house. Moving closer, but still a safe distance away, they studied the place. Shutters hung crookedly from the front windows. A huge oak tree reached over the side of the house, scraping the sagging roof with every gust of wind.

Some of the shingles were missing, and those still attached curled up like the front end of a toboggan. A porch wrapped around two sides of the house, but several posts were missing from the railing.

"Wow," Bailey finally said.

"Look at those weeds in the yard," Alex added. "I bet they're as tall as you are!"

"It looks haunted." Bailey pointed her watch toward the house and snapped a few pictures. "But it does make an interesting photo subject." They moved, and she took some from another angle.

"Aaaaack!" Brian jumped out from behind a tree.

The girls screamed and grabbed each other.

Brian doubled with laughter until he was red in the face. "You. . . should have. . .seen your faces!" he gasped then laughed some more.

"That was *not* funny!" Bailey's hands were in fists on her hips.

"It sure was from this angle." Brian wiped his eyes. "What are you guys doing anyway?"

"None of your business," Alex answered, eyes shooting daggers at him.

"We're just exploring, that's all," Bailey sputtered.

"Sounds fascinating." Brian rolled his eyes and turned toward home. "See ya later. Sorry if I freaked you out. Feel free to send me your therapy bill." He laughed again as he turned toward home.

Bailey looked at Alex, her heart still pounding. "You okay?"

"Yeah." Alex tucked her curly hair behind her ears. "Guess we probably did look kind of funny." A smile overtook her fair-skinned face.

Bailey sighed. "I was afraid that would make you hate Brian."

"No. He really is pretty fun." Alex inhaled deeply to calm her nerves and then looked back to the old house. "All right. Now that we can breathe again, what next?"

"Maybe we should head back home."

"We could check our email to see if the Camp Club Girls have sent us any updates," Alex suggested.

"Good idea." Bailey snapped one more picture.

"It'll be fun to see if the other girls turn up anything else."

Just then a muscular brown dog shot toward them from the house, teeth bared, barking and growling.

"Run!"

Bailey and Alex sprinted to the road. Bailey glanced over her shoulder and saw that the dog had stopped at the spot where they'd been taking pictures, though he continued to bark. She shivered at the thought of those teeth tearing through flesh and bone. The girls jogged the rest of the way home, Bailey wheezing with each breath.

When they reached their room, Bailey grabbed her inhaler. She breathed in as she squeezed the puff of medicine into her mouth and held her breath for ten seconds as it took effect.

"You okay?" Alex asked.

Bailey nodded, still holding her breath.

"That asthma must be such a pain."

Bailey exhaled loudly. "It's not that bad. You just have to learn to manage it, like having your inhaler handy all the time. I should have taken it with me. But it's no big deal."

"Good." Alex gave Bailey one more worried look. "Then let's check our email." She pulled out her laptop and booted it up.

"Right. And we could download these pictures too." Bailey took off her watch. She pressed a button, and a tiny memory stick popped out. "I'll just slide this into the computer and. . ."

Photos popped up on Alex's laptop before Bailey even finished her sentence.

"Guess I need to get better at using this thing," Bailey said, glancing at her camera-watch. The pictures, some blurry, others clear, passed by in a slide show on the computer screen.

"Wait a minute!" Alex whisper-yelled. "Go back to that last one!"

Bailey went back to a somewhat blurry picture of the front of the house. "What?" she asked.

"Look closely at that window on the left side."

Bailey looked at the picture then at Alex. "What?"

"I know it's not clear, but it almost looks like there's someone in the window."

Bailey peered closer at the fuzzy picture. "Maybe. . ."

"The person isn't right up close to the window, but it looks like someone may be inside that house," Alex insisted.

"Could be, but it's too hard to tell from this shot. Let's keep looking and then go back and take another look at all of them."

Alex nodded.

Though none of the photos were crystal clear, after reviewing them again, some did seem to show a shadowy image in the house.

"I still can't imagine that anyone would live in that place. It's such a mess!" Alex examined the picture more closely.

"Who knows? This image in the window may not even be a human."

Bailey's voice dripped with disappointment. "It may just be a reflection of light or something."

"Or then again, it might not be!" Alex encouraged. "We just have to keep trying to get better pictures. It was your first try with your new gadget. You'll get better at it."

Bailey gave a tiny smile. "Do you think the other girls would be interested in seeing these just for fun?"

"The ones of the front of the house will at least give them a good idea of what it looks like. Even if the house doesn't have anything to do with our case, it's still interesting."

"Okay. I'll send them off." Bailey attached the best photos to an email and hit SEND. "They'll see what they're missing by not being here with us!"

"We may have two mysteries on our hands. One about Gonzalez and one about the haunted house!" Alex laughed.

"Yeah, but we definitely have to go back and get better shots." Bailey crossed her arms and frowned.

"Do we have time to go now before supper?" Alex asked.

Bailey looked at the clock on the wall. "Maybe if we hurry. It's almost five o'clock."

"Let's go!" Alex jumped up from the bed.

"Wait!" Bailey put her camera-watch back on and dug for something in her backpack.

"What are you doing?"

"We need to take something to keep that dog away." Victoriously, Bailey held up a snack pack of cookies and then stuffed them in her pocket.

"Good thinking!"

They hurried down the stairs and through the kitchen.

"We're going back outside for a while," Bailey called as they passed Aunt Darcy.

Her aunt laughed. "I'll call you when it's suppertime."

The girls ran down the road back toward the old house. Suddenly Alex put her arm out in front of Bailey like a barricade and stopped abruptly. "Look!"

From about a quarter of a mile away, something—or someone—moved through the tall weeds in the front yard.

Dude, Rude, and Yeller

"Did you see that?" Alex asked, struggling to keep her voice from trembling.

"I saw it, but I don't know what it was." Bailey squinted her eyes.

"It was either that mean dog jumping or someone standing and then crouching so we wouldn't see him."

"Are you sure?" Bailey's voice quivered.

"Not entirely, but that's what it looked like to me. One second it was tall, and the next it was gone."

"We need to find a place where we can watch but not be seen." Bailey looked around. "I've got it!"

Alex's full attention was on her younger friend.

"Uncle Nathan's sheep pasture backs right up to the run-down house's empty field. And that field is right next to the yard with the tall weeds. If we pretend we're tending the sheep in the pasture, we should be able to keep a watch on the yard without being too obvious."

"I don't know," Alex said. "We may be too far away to see much from there."

"Their field isn't very big, and if we stay toward the back of the pasture, I think we'll have a pretty good view." Bailey pointed her index finger in the air dramatically. "*And* it will be safe. A creek separates our pasture from the empty field, as well as a fence."

"A creek? I never saw that!"

"It runs through a big culvert under the road, so you may not have seen it." Bailey grinned mischievously. "Besides the fact that we were running pretty fast on our way back!"

"You can say that again! I bet I could have beat Sydney in that race with the growling dog chasing us!" Alex laughed, thinking about their athletic friend who competed in the Junior Olympics in track and field.

"Well, shall we try watching from the pasture?" Bailey asked.

"Guess we could see what the view is like from there." Alex picked at a hangnail on her left thumb. "Uh, Bailey?"

"Yeah?"

"I haven't spent much time around sheep. Anything I should know?"

Bailey smiled reassuringly. "Just watch where you step."

Alex burst out laughing. "Thanks for the tip."

"Seriously, sheep are gentle. Why else would the Bible talk about them so much?"

"I guess. . ."

"Think about it." Bailey took hold of Alex's hand and swung it. "Jesus told his disciples He was sending them out like sheep among wolves. It's a comparison—a gentle animal compared to a wild animal."

"I never thought of it like that."

The two walked back to the pasture and entered through the gate, being careful to close it behind them. They made their way through the flock of sheep, the smell almost knocking them over. Their favorite lamb, Bow, sprang over to them in excited leaps. The red bow Alex had put around her neck was still there, though not quite as bright and pretty as it had been. They bent down to pet the baby sheep, but the smell was too much.

"Can't we wear masks or something while we're in here?" Alex gagged, her hand over her mouth and nose.

"After you're around the smell awhile you don't notice it as much. But I think Uncle Nathan has some masks in the barn. We'll have to look for them next time we're in there."

As they neared the far end of the pasture, Bailey heard a faint cry. "Did you hear that?"

"I only hear sheep bleating."

They walked several steps further, and the sound came again, only louder.

"That's no sheep! Look!" Bailey pointed toward the haunted house.

Alex turned in the same direction and saw a man waving wildly to get their attention.

"Hey!" The man yelled, his arms high above his head.

Bailey looked at Alex, unsure what to do.

"I think he needs help!" Bailey said.

"We have to be careful," Alex reminded her. "We don't know that guy."

Bailey inched toward the man with Alex following close behind.

"We'll have to climb over the fence when we get to it," Bailey said.

The girls heard another yell and saw two more men appear in the distance, one wearing a cowboy hat. Bailey and Alex ducked behind two smelly sheep, peeking out just enough to see.

The two men grabbed the first man roughly and shoved him back toward the house. The first man's yelling stopped, but now the other two men hollered at him, though Bailey couldn't make out what they said. She saw the first man look over his shoulder in their direction one last time before being pushed through the front door.

Alex let out a breath she didn't know she'd been holding. "Guess we now know for sure someone is living there."

"As if Fang the dog wasn't enough to tell us that!" Bailey stood up slowly.

"Come on. We'd better go back home." Alex took Bailey's arm and turned to leave. "It's probably almost suppertime."

"We can't go now!" Bailey jerked away. "That guy needs our help!"

"Bailey, we can't go charging over there." Alex stood planted, hands on her hips. "You saw how rough those guys were. It's not safe!"

"Well, we have to do something! What if he's in danger?"

"Maybe we should tell your aunt and uncle," Alex suggested.

"I don't know." Bailey shook her head. "They might try to make us give up our sleuthing on the Gonzalez case."

"Look," Alex said, resting her hand on Bailey's shoulder. "How about if we pray about this and trust that God will show us the right thing to do?"

Bailey nodded. "I just hope He doesn't make us wait too long to show us."

Alex laughed. "I know. But remember, God loves that man just as much as He loves us. He'll protect him until we can figure out what to do."

"I guess you're right."

Bailey and Alex moved between the sheep, making their way back to the gate. Once out of the pasture, Bailey asked, "Why do you think those two men were so mean to the other guy?"

"Maybe he's supposed to be working for them and they thought he was out there goofing off," Alex suggested.

"Maybe." Bailey scratched her head. "Or maybe he was trying to get help for someone who's hurt inside the house and the other two guys don't want people to know about it. Maybe they're the ones who hurt him!"

Alex laughed. "You have a good imagination."

"Or what if they've kidnapped someone and are hiding him there, and the guy yelling was trying to help him!"

"Wow! You really should write books or something."

This time Bailey laughed. "I'd rather act. I love drama."

Alex's eyes flew open wide. "I didn't know that!"

"I've been in a school play, and I'd love to be in community theater."

"Why don't you?"

Bailey shrugged. "Just haven't gotten around to it yet. I'm only nine!"

Alex squeezed Bailey around the shoulders. "Someday you'll be a star."

"Not if I stay in Peoria, Illinois." Bailey's eyebrows wrinkled. "I need to get out of this town and go to Los Angeles or New York or somewhere big to do that. That's my plan anyway."

"Sounds like a good plan, but you can at least get started in Peoria."

"I guess." Bailey sighed and then smiled. "In the meantime, we need to figure out this Gonzalez mystery."

The girls reached their yard and smelled supper cooking.

"Mmm." Bailey put her nose in the air and sniffed. "Smells like spaghetti!"

"Yeah," Alex agreed as she opened the screen door, "and garlic bread!"

"Right on both counts." Aunt Darcy pulled the garlic bread out of the oven. "You're just in time to wash up and eat."

"Perfect timing," Bailey said as she and Alex headed to the bathroom to wash their hands.

After supper, Bailey and Alex went to their bedroom to check their email.

Alex flopped stomach down onto her bed, opened the laptop in front of her, and waited for it to boot.

"I hope one of the other girls has already sent us some information on Gonzo." Bailey hopped onto the bed beside Alex to see.

"Gonzo?" Alex questioned.

"Yeah. Marshall Gonzalez," Bailey explained.

Alex laughed and gave Bailey a playful shove. "I should have known it was only a matter of time until you gave him a nickname."

"I was thinking those guys we saw today should have names too."

Bailey closed her eyes for a moment. "How about Yeller for the first guy 'cause he yells so much, and Dude and Rude for the other two, since the one wore a hat like an old cowboy dude and they both treated Yeller rudely?"

Alex rolled to her back and laughed. "Dude and Rude it is," she said. "And Yeller!"

"Hey look! We got something from Kate!" Bailey pointed at the computer screen.

"And it has an attachment." Alex opened the email, and Kate's short note appeared:

> *Still checking on the Gonzalez stuff. He was good at staying out of the public eye. Will let you know when I find anything. In the meantime, here's a picture of Biscuit doing his latest trick— dancing with me on his hind legs.*

Alex clicked on the YouTube link, and a healthy and happy Biscuit appeared standing on his back legs, front paws in Kate's hands. The girls laughed at the photo.

"He should be on *Pet Stars!*" Alex pirouetted around the room like a ballerina.

"Wow! Look how big he got!" Bailey leaned in to get a closer look at the small light brown-and-white mutt with fur hanging over his big brown eyes. "He's twice the size he was at camp last summer."

"Yeah, but he still only comes to Kate's waist when he's stretched out dancing." Alex's eyes softened. "Aww. He's so cute!"

"And so clean!" Bailey added. "Remember how dirty and matted he was when we found him?" The two girls sat quietly for a moment.

"But no news on Gonzo yet," Bailey said, getting back to business.

"Well at least she's working on it." Alex closed her laptop.

"Oh man!" Bailey slapped her leg in disgust.

"What?"

"I should have taken pictures of Yeller, Dude, and Rude with my camera-watch!"

"O–o–h yeah." Alex snapped her fingers. "But you couldn't have done that without being seen. It's probably best you didn't."

"But then we'd have pictures to examine and to send to the other Camp Club Girls. Maybe Kate could even match it with someone on the internet."

"That would have been helpful, for sure."

"Maybe we'll see them again sometime."

"Even if we do, safety comes first." Alex looked firmly at Bailey. "No pictures if it will put us in danger."

Bailey stared her down.

"Deal?" Alex pushed.

Bailey dropped her gaze and sighed. "Deal," she said.

"Now, what's our schedule for tomorrow?" Alex asked, trying to lighten the mood.

"Well, tomorrow's Monday, so I guess we'll start early with sheep shearing." Bailey perked up at that thought.

"I guess it will be time for me to give it a try, huh?" Alex started picking her nails.

"Uncle Nathan and I can each do one while you watch. Then you can have a turn. You'll do great."

"I'm kind of excited and kind of nervous all at the same time."

Bailey's eyes sparkled with mischief. "If you don't mind me saying, you're looking a bit sheepish."

Alex groaned. "That was a *baaa*d joke!"

"You even sound like a sheep! Sorry, I couldn't resist." Bailey tucked her hair behind her ear. "Really, don't worry. I felt nervous too when I was learning. But you'll see it's not that hard."

"I hope so."

"And remember you don't have to do it fast like Uncle Nathan. He just does it that way 'cause he's had so much practice."

"I know. I'll take my time."

"I read once that a professional can shear a sheep in less than two minutes," Bailey said.

Alex's jaw dropped. "Two minutes! That's fast!"

"And not only that, he removes the fleece all in one piece!" Bailey held up one finger.

"You've got to be kidding. How is that possible?"

"I don't know, but that's what the magazine said."

Alex giggled. "Something tells me I won't master that this week."

"Me neither!" Bailey rolled her eyes dramatically.

"We need to update the other Camp Club Girls on those men we saw," Alex said.

"This time I'll call Elizabeth and Sydney," Bailey said as she flipped open her phone, "and you call Kate and McKenzie."

Chatter and laughter filled the room as Bailey and Alex told the others about Yeller, Dude, and Rude.

"Yeah, funny, huh?" Alex said to McKenzie. "Bailey just comes up with these crazy names for people. It's a hoot!"

"Of course we'll be careful, Elizabeth," Bailey said. "We won't get close to those men. But I might take a few pictures with my watch."

"I'm going to learn to shear sheep tomorrow!" Alex smiled as she spoke to Kate.

"You should have seen us run when that dog was chasing us, Sydney," Bailey told her athletic friend. "You would have been proud!"

Soon both girls finished their conversations and reported back to each other.

"I told Kate we loved the picture of her and Biscuit," Alex said.

"Sydney said to keep up the good running, and maybe we can be in the Olympics with her someday." Bailey giggled.

"McKenzie wondered why those men even have a dog." Alex yawned. "She said maybe they aren't as mean as we thought."

"They sure acted mean, and so did their dog," Bailey said. "I didn't see anything nice about any of them—except Yeller didn't seem to be all that threatening."

"How's Elizabeth doing?"

"Good. She doesn't want us approaching those men. Too dangerous."

"Well, duh!" Alex said. "That's what I said earlier."

"I still plan to get some pictures of them, though," Bailey said.

"If you can do it safely, I'm all for it."

"They sure would be handy in trying to identify Yeller, Dude, and Rude to see if they have anything to do with Gonzo's case."

"You can say that again." Alex saw Bailey's black-brown eyes twinkle and a smile play at her mouth. "But don't."

"You know me too well." Bailey grinned then yawned. "I'm getting sleepy."

"It's been a big day."

"And tomorrow should be even bigger with all the shearing." Bailey pulled her pajamas out of the dresser drawer.

"We'd better get to bed early so we'll be rested and ready for it."

"I plan to get some photos of those guys tomorrow after we're done shearing."

"If they're outside again," Alex added. "Seems like Dude and Rude like to keep Yeller in the house and out of sight."

"Yeah, it does," Bailey agreed, squeezing toothpaste onto her toothbrush. "But maybe we'll get lucky. Yeller may come up with a way to go out since he saw us."

The girls brushed their teeth and crawled into bed. Bailey took care to remove her camera-watch and set it on the dresser; then she switched off the light.

"I just hope he's okay until we can figure out a way to help." Alex pulled the blanket up to her chin. "Don't forget to pray for him."

"And don't forget to pray for *us* to know the right thing to do," Bailey added. She turned onto her side and snuggled into her pillow.

Outside, Shy barked from the sheep pasture. "Silly Shy," Bailey murmured.

Alex giggled, but the barking continued.

There was a sudden rustling outside the bedroom window, then a yell.

The girls bolted upright in bed, eyes wide.

A Strange Place for a Message

Bailey and Alex held their breath, too afraid to speak. They sat still as stones waiting for whatever would happen next. Only their eyes moved as their gaze shifted alternately from each other to the window that sat squarely between their twin beds. Finally, Alex put her index finger to her lips and motioned Bailey out of bed. Trembling, Bailey crouched on the floor by Alex, and then they crawled to the window. Alex peeked over the second-story sill, which was only three feet from the floor. The moon shone brightly, washing the huge oak tree just outside the window with pale blue light.

Bolstering her courage, Bailey also poked her head cautiously over the sill so she could see into the dimly lit yard. "Look!" She pointed toward a grove of trees at the far side of the yard where a man limped toward the thicket.

"That's Yeller!" Alex whisper-yelled.

The injured man disappeared into the woods. Wide-eyed, Bailey stared at Alex.

"The yell we heard must have been Yeller, but what was the rustling just before that?" Bailey asked.

Alex put her face to the window again. "Look under the tree."

Bailey's eyes followed Alex's finger. A broken branch and fallen leaves littered the yard. "He climbed the tree and then fell out!"

"What do you think he was doing here?" Bailey licked her lips nervously.

"Maybe he was trying to get a message to us," Alex suggested, trying for an explanation that wouldn't give her nightmares.

Hoping to chase away her fear, Bailey flipped the light back on and sat on Alex's bed to sort out what had just happened. "But how did he know which window was ours?"

"Good question." Alex picked a hangnail on her left thumb.

"He had to have been watching the house, don't you think?"

Alex nodded, her eyes fearful.

"Maybe he's desperate to talk to us about helping him."

"I think we may need to tell someone about this," Alex said.

"No!" Bailey grabbed Alex's hand. "We can't! We'll never be able to solve the Gonzo case if we tell. They'll think it's too dangerous."

"Well, maybe it is!" Alex's nose turned red as if she were about to cry.

"Come on, Alex. You know how careful we are. We won't take any unnecessary risks."

Alex remained silent, head down.

"Please?" Bailey pleaded. "With cherries on top?"

A faint smile played at the edges of Alex's mouth.

"Come on. . .I see that smile," Bailey teased. "You want to say yes, don't you?"

Finally, Alex broke down and laughed. "You are too much!" She tickled Bailey. "You know I want to solve this mystery as much as you do, but it's pretty scary right now."

"That's half the fun of it!" Bailey's eyes gleamed.

"I guess you're right. I may be older than you, but I'm not braver!"

"You're brave enough. You were the first one to look out the window, remember?" Bailey yawned. "Wow. It's already ten o'clock. We're going to be beat in the morning."

"Yeah. We'd better try to get some sleep, though I'm wide awake after that scare." Alex shivered. "Morning will be here before we know it."

Shoulders drooping, Bailey dragged herself to the light switch, flipped it back off, and staggered back to bed. "I'm half asleep already." She stretched and snuggled back into her pillow.

"Good night, Bailey," Alex said.

"Good night."

●—●—●

The alarm blared a loud country love song at six o'clock, and the girls dragged themselves out of bed. They put on jeans and pulled sweatshirts over their T-shirts. After scarfing down breakfast, they met Uncle Nathan in the barn for a morning of sheep shearing.

"Morning!" Uncle Nathan greeted them over the noisy baaing of the sheep. "A nice crisp morning for shearing, huh?"

"It sure is!" Bailey rubbed her hands together. "But it will warm up nice by this afternoon."

"Guess what I heard on the local news last night?" Uncle Nathan and Shy had already brought several sheep from the pasture and penned them up in the barn.

"What?" Bailey asked.

"The annual sheep-shearing contest for kids is this Saturday at the state fairgrounds."

"Cool!" Bailey gave a thumbs-up.

"Yep. It's here in the newspaper this morning too." Uncle Nathan snatched a rolled-up paper from his back pocket. "Says here there will be three age categories: nine to eleven years old, twelve to fourteen, and sixteen to eighteen."

"Will Brian be in it?" Bailey asked.

"Maybe," Uncle Nathan answered. "But I was thinking you might be interested in trying the nine- to eleven-year-old category. What do you say?"

"Me? Could I?" Bailey's dark eyes danced.

"I don't see why not. You've had a few summers to practice, and you can still work at it all week." Uncle Nathan patted her back. "I'd be proud to have you participate as part of my family."

"Wow! I'd love to!"

Alex grabbed Bailey's hands, and they both jumped up and down. "I'm so excited for you! It'll be fun to see how fast you can get this week."

"I just have to remember not to rush 'cause I don't want to hurt the sheep." Bailey petted the ewe Uncle Nathan just brought from the pen. "Right, girl?"

"I'll do this one; then you do the next." Uncle Nathan reached for the shears.

"And Alex wants to have a try after that," Bailey added.

Uncle Nathan nodded and smiled at Alex. "Good girl. You can't let your fears get the best of you." He flipped the sheep onto its rump, its front legs up in the air, so it wouldn't struggle with him. Then he turned on the shears, running them along the sheep's body. Fleece dropped, and Uncle Nathan was done in no time.

Bailey giggled at the naked sheep.

"Now it's your turn, Bailey." Uncle Nathan returned the first sheep to its pen and came back with another. "Wait a minute. I need to get something." He handed Bailey the rope lead that circled the sheep's neck while he went to the house.

Uncle Nathan returned holding a stopwatch. "I'll help you turn the sheep onto its backside. Then we'll time you so we can have a record of your first training-day time and see how you improve by Saturday. Take your time. You don't have to rush. You'll just naturally get faster the more you do it."

"Okay. Tell me when to start." Bailey held the sheep firmly with one hand and the shears in the other.

"Ready. . .go!" Uncle Nathan watched his niece shear, his eyes moving back and forth from her to the watch.

"You're doing great, Bailey!" Alex encouraged over the buzz of the shears. "Keep it up!"

Bailey kept working intently. "Done!" she finally yelled.

Uncle Nathan stopped the watch. "Twenty-two minutes, forty-three seconds."

"That's awesome!" Alex hugged her friend.

"What's the time that won last year?" Bailey asked.

Uncle Nathan reached for the newspaper in his back pocket again and scanned the article. "In your age bracket, the winning time was twelve minutes, twenty seconds."

Bailey's face dropped. "You mean I have to cut my time almost in half?"

"Only if you want to win." Uncle Nathan grinned.

"You can do it, Bailey!" Alex's natural cheerleading spirit bubbled to the surface, and she did a backflip.

"With support like that, how can you lose?" Uncle Nathan laughed and put his hand on Bailey's shoulder. "And like I said, don't worry about the time. Just do your best. The time will take care of itself."

"I'll try." Bailey looked at Alex. "Your turn."

The color drained from Alex's face. Then she stomped her foot with determination. "I'm ready! No sheep is going to scare me!"

"Good for you!" Bailey led a sheep toward her friend while her uncle swept up the wool from the sheep she had just sheared.

Uncle Nathan leaned his broom against the barn wall and stepped in to sit the sheep on its rump for Alex.

"Now hold it like this." Bailey demonstrated how to hold the animal between her legs. "And flip this switch when you're ready to start."

Uncle Nathan stood close by. "We'll be right here to answer your questions and help you if you need it."

Alex turned on the shears. The sheep startled at the buzz but immediately calmed when the noise became constant.

Alex ran the shears down the stomach, sides, and back of the sheep. Wool fell like a blanket onto the cleanly swept floor. Soon she said, "How's that look?"

"Great!" Uncle Nathan answered. "Looks like you'll make a shearer after all!"

"Way to go, Alex! You did it!" Bailey helped her friend turn the sheep back onto its feet.

"I can't believe I just sheared a sheep!" Alex bounced up and down.

"Now, how about if you girls work on shearing the lambs and yearlings over there, and I'll handle the ewes and rams over here?" suggested Uncle Nathan. "I think you'll find shearing the smaller animals easier." He looked at Alex. "I'll turn the stopwatch over to you so you can check Bailey's time again after she's done a few."

Bailey and Alex moved about halfway down the barn where another set of electric shears hung from the ceiling. They decided they'd share the shears until Alex felt confident enough to handle her own shearing station. Then Bailey would move on down to the next set at the end of the barn. There were four shears in all, and Uncle Nathan said Brian would be out soon to help him with the ewes and rams.

Bailey sheared the first young sheep while Alex played with the lambs. Then they swapped places. After two hours, they had finished five lambs, and the morning had warmed up enough for the girls to shed their sweatshirts. Alex checked Bailey's time again and found she'd already taken two minutes off her time. They leaned against the sheep pen and admired their work. The lambs bleated woefully for their mothers.

"That's hard work!" Alex wiped sweat and dirt from her face with the bottom of her T-shirt.

"I know. Even the little ones take a lot of time." Bailey gulped a long drink of water. "I'll take the next one." She led a yearling from the pen and over to the shearing area. Alex stayed in the pen with the ones yet to be sheared.

Bailey began shearing the yearling's belly and was soon running the shears over the side of the young sheep. Strange dark markings appeared on its skin as the fleece fell to the floor. She turned it over to shear the other side. The same strange markings appeared on that side too. They weren't spots like some of the sheep had. They were more like black lines. "Hey Alex!" she yelled over the noise of the shears. "Come take a look at this!"

Bailey shut off the shears. She set the lamb on its feet and asked, "What do you make of these markings?"

Alex walked around the lamb to study them. "Weird!"

"They're on both sides." Bailey turned the sheep for her to see.

"Almost looks like writing," Alex said.

"That's what I thought too."

"Let's walk him out to the sunlight so we can see better."

Bailey led the sheep out of the barn, squinting against the bright sun. The lamb jumped playfully in its warmth. "Hold still now," Bailey cooed as she crouched beside the animal and petted it. "We want to get a good look at you." She held the lamb firmly for Alex to inspect.

Alex stepped back and cocked her head. "Oh my goodness!"

"What?"

"It spells something!"

"What?" Bailey asked, excitement rising in her voice.

"It says, 'Help'!" Alex clapped her hand over her mouth when she checked out the other side. " 'Gonzo'! I think it says, 'Gonzo'!"

"No way!" Bailey said. "How could writing get under a sheep's fleece, much less something about Gonzo, which is a nickname I made up only yesterday!"

"I don't know, but I'm sure that's what it says," Alex insisted. "See for yourself. I'll hold the lamb."

The girls traded places, and Bailey studied the animal. She looked at it standing up, and then knelt. She squinted while she examined the lamb, shielding her eyes from the sun with her hand. "You're right." Bailey stood back up. "It definitely says, 'Help Gonzo.' But that doesn't make sense."

"We need to hide this lamb so no one else sees it." Alex glanced over her shoulder.

"Quick. In the pasture." Bailey led the lamb toward the gate. "Let's put all the sheared lambs back so no one wonders why they aren't all together. You go get a couple others, and I'll be there in a second to help you."

"I'm on it." Alex swung back toward the barn. At the pen, she took the rope leads off a nail on the wall and slid them over the lambs' heads. "Come on, let's go." The lambs resisted, loudly voicing their complaints, and Alex had to drag them a few feet before they gave up and started walking. "There, that's better," she soothed.

Bailey ran back to the barn, so deep in thought that she hardly noticed Alex pass. She carefully examined the remaining sheep to make sure they didn't have markings.

When the last lamb was back in the pasture, Bailey leaned against the fence, watching them caper around playfully, glad to be back home. The young lambs quickly nuzzled their mothers to nurse. "What do you think the message means?" she asked.

"It could read either 'Help Gonzo' or 'Gonzo help.' So it sounds like either Gonzo is asking for help or someone is asking for Gonzo's help. I suppose it makes most sense that it's a cry for help from Gonzo."

"Do you think this Gonzo is Marshall Gonzalez or someone else?" Bailey asked.

"Who knows?" Alex pulled a blade of grass to chew. "I guess we could ask around to see if there's anyone that goes by Gonzo around here."

"The other girls will go nuts when they hear this," Bailey said. "I'll snap a few pictures of our 'talking' lamb to send to them."

"Good idea. Maybe they'll see something we missed."

Bailey took several photos from different angles. "We'd better get back to the barn before Uncle Nathan wonders what happened to us. I still need to sweep up before you start on your next sheep."

The girls worked for two more hours but found no more mysterious writing.

Uncle Nathan turned off his shears and came by to check on their progress. "How you ladies doing?"

"Great! We've done twelve sheep." Bailey stood tall.

"Not bad for the first day." Uncle Nathan said. "You've had a long morning of shearing. Ready to call it a day?"

"As soon as we get these last few back to the pasture and sweep up. We already took the first few out earlier." Bailey looked down at her clothes. "I'm filthy! I need a shower!"

"Just shows you've been working hard, that's all." Uncle Nathan laughed and hugged her. "Good job, girls. You can have the rest of the day off."

Bailey smiled at Alex. "See! I told you he wouldn't make us work the whole day."

Alex laughed. "You'd better be quiet, or he might change his mind."

After the girls finished their work in the barn and showered, Bailey downloaded the pictures she took.

"You're getting better with that camera—watch!" Alex watched the photos pop up on the computer screen. "Only two blurry ones this time—and that might be because the sheep were running around so much."

"Thanks. I held my arm against my body when I took the pictures so I'd be steadier. Maybe that helped."

"You got some pretty clear shots. Let's email the other Camp Club members about this mysterious message."

"Okay," Bailey said. "And we have to tell them about Yeller falling from the tree outside our bedroom window last night."

"Right." Alex typed the note then pressed SEND, and off it went along with the picture attachments.

Elizabeth was quick to email back, reminding them to be careful and that she was praying for them and their safety.

A knock sounded at the bedroom door. "Yes?" Bailey answered.

"It's me, Brian. Can I come in?"

Alex quickly closed her computer and looked at Bailey.

"Yeah, I guess." Bailey got up and opened the door. "What's up?"

"Did you guys see the weird markings on that sheep you sheared?" he asked.

An Unexpected Assistant

Bailey decided to play dumb until she found out what Brian knew. "Weird markings? What are you talking about?"

"You *had* to have seen them!"

"What did they look like?" Alex asked innocently.

"They looked like words!" Brian's voice rose.

"Words?" Bailey's tone indicated she thought her cousin had gone stark raving mad. "What did they say?" She glanced at Alex. Alex had her hand over her mouth, trying to hide a grin.

Brian looked at the floor, seemingly embarrassed at what he was about to say. His thick, wavy black hair hung like a curtain around his face, "It said, uh, well, it said, 'Help Gonzo,' " he finally blurted.

"Gonzo? Who's that?" Bailey asked.

"Yeah, and why does he need help?" Alex added.

"I don't know!" Brian threw his hands up in frustration. "I just figured you had seen the words too, so I came to see what you thought about them!"

Bailey and Alex's eyes met, and they burst out laughing.

"That's it! I'm leaving!" Brian reached for the doorknob.

"No! No!" Bailey gasped, regaining her composure. "We saw the markings. We were just having some fun with you, that's all."

"Yeah," Alex said. "Sorry if we took it too far."

"So you *did* see them. I knew it!" Brian raised a clenched fist. "What did you make of them?"

"I'd say that sheep must have had weird-looking parents." Bailey smirked. She didn't want to give too much information about their investigation until she knew if Brian could be trusted not to tell.

"You are impossible," Brian said to his little cousin through gritted teeth.

"Well, what did *you* make of them?" Bailey countered.

"I already told you what they looked like to me!" Brian growled. " 'Help Gonzo'!"

Alex gave Bailey a cautionary look then turned her eyes back to Brian. "We thought the same thing," she said quietly.

Brian's eyes lit up. "Really?" He stepped away from the door and moved toward the girls.

"Really," Bailey finally admitted.

"So I'm not going crazy!"

"Not today, anyway," Bailey teased.

"Why didn't you tell someone about the markings?" Brian asked.

"Did *you* tell someone?" Alex asked, suddenly wishing she'd kept her big mouth shut.

"Only you," Brian answered.

"You didn't tell your parents?" Bailey questioned.

"No. Why?"

Bailey and Alex exchanged looks and nodded.

Bailey spoke first. "Because we think we know who Gonzo might be, but we don't want anyone else to know until we're sure about what we think we know."

"Huh?" Brian's eyes glazed over a bit.

"Sit down," Alex suggested. "We'll explain."

Brian looked for a chair but only saw a pink beanbag. "I'm not sitting in that."

"Oh, come on. It won't turn you into a girl," Bailey teased.

Brian hesitated. "You'd better keep this quiet." He pulled the feminine chair close to Bailey's bed where both girls sat. The beans whooshed when he plopped down, and Alex laughed out loud. "I'm warning you. . . ," Brian threatened, but Bailey saw a smile sneaking into his snarl.

Bailey and Alex alternately filled Brian in on who they thought Gonzo might be and what they'd discovered so far about the mystery. They left out the part about Yeller, Dude, and Rude, since they didn't know if the men really fit into the Gonzo mystery. Brian's dark eyes grew bigger with every detail.

"I can't believe it! You guys have only been here three days, and you're already working on a mystery the police haven't solved in seven years!" Brian shook his head.

"But you have to promise not to tell." Bailey pointed a menacing finger at Brian.

"I promise," Brian said.

"Cross your heart?" Alex pushed.

"Cross my heart." Brian made an *X* on his chest with his finger then leaned in. "So you'll keep me posted on any other clues you find?"

"Sure, if you want us to." Bailey nodded her head vigorously.

"You can't tell me all this and then leave me in the dark!" Brian's bright white smile lit up his face.

"Okay. We'll keep you posted," Alex promised.

"How do you think the writing got on the sheep?" Bailey asked.

"It isn't a normal brand, that's for sure," Brian said.

"Looked like a marker to me," Alex added.

"But it was so wide. Do they make markers that fat?" Bailey cocked her head. "And it would have to be permanent to withstand the weather."

"They make big permanent markers for writing on outdoor banners," Brian said.

"How big?" Alex asked.

"The biggest I've seen was probably about an inch wide." Brian held his finger and thumb about an inch apart to show them. "The spirit squad used them at school on posters for football games. And our vacation Bible school director at church used one to write on the banner for the church lawn."

"Good information, Brian," Alex said. "Anything else you know about the markers?"

"They smell horrible!" Brian laughed. "When we used them to make posters at school, our classroom smelled toxic for a couple of days!"

"Perfect!" Bailey clapped her hands.

"What do you mean?" Alex asked.

"We can smell the yearling to see if it has any leftover marker smell!"

"I doubt that it would now." Brian shook his head. "Who knows how long ago that message was written? Besides, markers would be bad for the sheep."

"It's still a clue we need to check out," Bailey insisted.

"She's right," Alex agreed. "A good detective leaves no clue unturned."

"Don't you mean 'leaves no rock unturned'?" Now it was Brian's turn to tease.

"Whatever." Alex smiled. "Let's just turn it over, whatever it is!"

"Brian, do you know where those sheep came from?" Bailey asked.

"Hard to know for sure," her cousin answered. "We bought a lot of sheep at auctions last year to stock up our herds. They came from several different ranches in the area."

"Any way we could find out?" Alex asked.

"I think my dad keeps a record book of when sheep are bought and which farms they come from."

Bailey gave him a you've-got-to-be-kidding look. "A record book?"

"I know. Dad's too old-fashioned to use a computer spreadsheet," Brian answered. "Anyway, he also puts tiny tags on each of the sheep's ears to identify them. He may even record how many sheep he gets at each auction." Brian paused. "The problem is, we won't know for sure which ones came from which farm."

"That info sure would help us narrow down the possibilities, though," Bailey said, excitement rising in her voice.

"Brian, do you think you could get a list of auctions and farms your dad bought from in the past year?" Alex asked. "We can check out each one to see if it's tied in any way to Gonzo."

"I'm not sure, but I could try." Brian rubbed his chin. "I'll have to snoop around my dad's office to find his record book. It's a mess in there!"

"Just be careful. Don't get into any trouble." Bailey's eyes narrowed with concern.

"I won't. Don't worry." Brian thought another minute. "You know, Gonzo could be one of the seasonal migrant workers."

"You think so?" Alexis asked.

"Maybe," Brian said. "Gonzalez is a pretty common name among them."

"Why would one of them need help?" Bailey wondered aloud.

"Good question," Brian responded. "Many of them are pretty poor."

"Seems like an odd way to get help with money." Bailey twisted her mouth.

"Especially if you have children to feed," Alex added. "You'd want quicker results than hoping someone saw your message months later during shearing season."

"I still think we shouldn't rule it out," Brian said. "Never leave a clue unturned." He grinned at Alex.

Alex returned the smile. "You're right. You just might make a good detective after all."

"By the way, how'd the shearing go today?" Brian asked.

"Alex was awesome!" Bailey bragged. "She sheared as many sheep as I did!"

"Only because we were trading off," Alex added modestly. "If I'd been shearing at my own station, you would have done lots more."

"I knocked two minutes off my starting time." Bailey held up two fingers.

"So you're definitely going to compete this weekend?" Brian asked.

"I'm pretty sure. We'll see how much faster I can get first."

Brian looked at Alex. "What about you? Are you going to try it?"

"Me?" Alex squeaked. "You've got to be kidding! This was only my first day of shearing in my whole life. I don't think I'm quite ready."

"Are you going to be in the competition, Brian?" Bailey asked.

"I competed the last few years. I'm not sure if I'll enter again this year." Brian flexed his muscles. "Although I've been training and am a lot stronger now. These guns could really handle those sheep this year!" He patted his right bicep, and all three of them laughed.

"Brian!" Uncle Nathan's voice boomed up the stairs.

"I'm coming, Dad!" Brian jumped up from the beanbag chair. "I've got to get back to work or Dad will get suspicious. Must be nice having the rest of the afternoon off!" he teased. Then he added, "I'll let you know if I find anything about the auctions in his records."

"Thanks, Brian!" Bailey pushed the beanbag back to the wall as her cousin left the room, then sat back on her bed again.

"He could be a huge help with this case," Bailey said.

"I just hope we didn't give him too much information too soon."

"I think we can trust Brian. He seemed excited to be included in the secret, don't you think?"

"Yeah, he seemed excited," Alex agreed. "I just hope he is excited for the right reasons."

"What do you mean?"

"He might just want to use the information to get us in trouble or something. Don't forget, he's a boy!"

Bailey shook her head. "I doubt it. Brian's not like that."

"He did seem pretty sincere, didn't he?"

"Yeah, and if he can get those records of Uncle Nathan's, that will be worth a lot even if he doesn't do another thing!"

Bailey's cell phone rang, startling the girls. She looked at the display window before flipping it open. "Hi, Kate!"

Alex watched her friend intently as she talked.

"Uh-huh. . . . Really? You're kidding!" Bailey's eyes widened.

"What?" Alex whispered impatiently, unable to contain her curiosity.

Bailey held up her index finger to Alex and listened. She scribbled some notes on a pad of paper on her nightstand and said, "Great work, Kate. Let us know if you find out anything else. Okay. Yeah, I'll tell her. Bye."

"What? What'd she find out?" Alex's questions exploded out of her like lava from an active volcano.

"First of all, she said to tell you hi." Bailey smiled sweetly, not rushing into the information Alex was dying to hear.

"Hi, already! Now tell me what she said!"

"Okay. She did some internet research, which she said was pretty tough because there were a gazillion listings for people named Gonzalez. But there weren't many with the first name of Marshall. She was able to narrow it down and found out that our Marshall Gonzalez was born in Sinoloa, Mexico. He grew up the son of a poor shrimp fisherman. However, his grandpa raised sugar cane and was very wealthy."

"Wait a minute, if his grandpa was wealthy, why was his dad so poor?" Alex asked.

"Good question. We'll have to look into that."

"What else?" Alex prompted.

"When Grandpa Sugar Cane died, he left his fortune to his only grandson, Marshall Gonzalez."

"Aha! So that's who he inherited his money from. Go on."

"That's as far as she's gotten so far," Bailey said with a sigh.

"Man! She really knows how to leave a girl hanging, doesn't she?" Alex laughed. "She did great getting that much information to us already. I know she'll dig up more."

"Hey, I've got an idea!" Bailey sat up straight. "Let's conference call the Camp Club Girls and give them all the updates. We can get their takes on this new info Kate just gave us."

"Great idea!" Alex scooted right next to Bailey so she'd be closer to the phone.

Bailey called each girl individually then conferenced them in together. She put the phone on speaker so she and Alex could both hear.

"Syd, can you hear me?" she asked.

"I can hear you," Sydney answered.

"Elizabeth, are you there?"

"I'm right here," she replied.

"How about you, McKenzie?"

"I read you loud and clear!" McKenzie giggled.

"Kate, can you hear us?"

"Biscuit and I are all ears." Kate's voice gave away her smile.

"Alex and I are on my speakerphone, so we're both here too." Bailey held the phone between her and Alex. "Kate, why don't you tell the others the information you've found out so far about Gonzo."

The other girls laughed at the nickname Bailey had come up with for Marshall Gonzalez.

Kate repeated what she'd already told Bailey and Alex.

"Sounds like jealousy may be a motive for this case, since Gonzalez is the only heir to his grandfather's money," McKenzie said.

"Do we know if other grandchildren were left out of Grandpa's will?" asked Alex.

"Not yet," Kate said. "He was the only grandson, but there could have been granddaughters. I'll check that out, and also try to find out if Gonzo's father was still living when his father died. He could have been pretty mad to have been left out of the will too."

"Jealousy can cause people to do things they wouldn't do otherwise," Elizabeth piped in. "Proverbs 6:34 says, 'For jealousy arouses a husband's fury, and he will show no mercy when he takes revenge.' I'd say the same is true for anyone, not just husbands. Gonzo's family could have been very angry as well as jealous, and taken revenge, which could be why we have a missing man!"

"Good point, Elizabeth," Sydney said. "I think I'll research the sugar cane and shrimping industry to see if I can learn any helpful clues from that."

"Good thinking, Syd," Alex said. "Hey, guess what, you guys? We have someone else helping us with the case now." Alex told them about Brian and that he was investigating the Curly Q's purchasing records for them.

"You're sure we can trust him?" Elizabeth asked.

"I'm sure," Bailey answered. "Let's talk again in two days to see what new information has come to light. If we have any big breaks, we can always talk sooner."

"Like if Bailey learns to shear a sheep in two minutes or less and sets a new world record!" Alex laughed and explained to the others that their youngest friend was going to be in a shearing competition this Saturday.

"That'll be awesome!" McKenzie said. "I wonder if Biscuit would make a good sheepdog."

"I wish we could all come to watch." Elizabeth's gentle voice conveyed her remorse.

"We'll let you know how it goes," Bailey assured them. "In the meantime, let's keep working on the case, and we'll talk again in a couple days."

"Sounds good to me," McKenzie said.

"Me too!" added Kate.

Woof! Biscuit barked in the background, and the girls all laughed.

"Guess we have Biscuit's approval too," Kate said.

"And remember, we only have four more days until Alex and I go back home," Bailey reminded them.

"I wish I was as fast at solving mysteries as I am on the track!" Sydney joked.

The girls said their goodbyes and hung up.

"Come on," Bailey said. "Let's get out of here for a while. It's a beautiful day!"

Alex was off the bed in a flash. They opened the bedroom door and immediately heard voices downstairs. They stopped to listen before going down.

Uncle Nathan's voice rose. "Brian! What are you doing in my office?"

CHAPTER

6

Another Message

Bailey clapped her hand over her mouth. How could Brian be so careless after she had trusted him with their investigation secrets?

"Dad!" Brian's voice cracked.

"What are you doing in here?" Uncle Nathan repeated.

Bailey crept silently down the stairs with Alex close behind. They stopped three steps from the bottom where they could see into the office. They sat to watch the unfolding horror show.

"I was looking for something," Brian hedged.

"I gathered that." Uncle Nathan paused. "Are you going to tell me what it is you're looking for?"

Brian lowered his eyes. "I was trying to remember which farms we bought sheep from at the last few auctions. I couldn't remember, so I was going to look it up."

Uncle Nathan gazed at his son without a smile. Brian met his father's eyes squarely, holding a stare for a second before Uncle Nathan's face softened. He put a hand on his son's shoulder. "So you're taking an interest in the family business, huh?"

"Yeah, I guess," Brian replied, relief flooding his features.

"I've always hoped you'd want to learn more about the business side of sheep farming, rather than just the animal care." Uncle Nathan opened a desk drawer and pulled out a spiral-bound black book.

"This is my ledger," he explained to Brian. "In it I keep records of which auctions I attend, which farms I buy sheep from, and what I pay." He handed the book to his son. "I know I should put all this in the computer, but I just haven't made the switch yet. Maybe I'm just too old-fashioned."

Brian held the softcover book, flipping through its lined pages of columns and rows. "It has a lot of writing in it. How long have you been keeping track of all this?"

"Since I bought the farm. About seven years."

"Wow. Can I borrow this to do some research?"

"What are you researching?"

Alex inhaled sharply. Bailey grabbed her friend's hand and squeezed as they waited for Brian's reply.

"I want to try to figure out which sheep came from which farms so I can see if their markings are similar. You know, to see if sheep have any family resemblances like people do."

Uncle Nathan's eyebrows shot up, and he grinned. "Oh, I see. Like a genetic engineer!" He smacked his son on the back. "Sure! Look all you want. I'd better start saving my money for your high-priced education!"

The proud father strutted toward the office door but then stopped and turned back to Brian. "But son, next time you need something, please ask me for it instead of snooping. It doesn't look good when you do that."

Brian laughed. "Sure, Dad. Sorry. Hey, maybe I could enter this stuff into a spreadsheet on the computer for you. It would take some time, but I know how to do it."

Uncle Nathan's face lit up. "Sure! That would be a tremendous help. Thanks!"

Bailey and Alex heard the screen door slam as Uncle Nathan went back outside. They hurried into the office.

"That was too close for comfort!" Bailey searched Brian's face for any hint of remorse.

"You said you were going to be careful," Alex accused.

"I *was* careful! I got out of the mess, didn't I? And I even got permission to look through the record book." Brian held up the ledger.

Bailey sighed. "Yeah, you did. Sorry. I was just scared, that's all."

"Don't be such a worrywart." Brian scowled. "You're worse than my mom."

"Well, this is our investigation, and we've worked hard on it already!" Bailey crossed her arms dramatically and frowned. "We just don't want it getting messed up by one careless move—or person!"

"It's okay, Bailey." Alex patted her friend on the back. "Brian didn't mean to upset you, did you, Brian?" She looked pointedly at him.

"No, of course not."

"I'm sure he'll be more careful in the future. And he did a fabulous job getting the book quickly so we have lots of time to look it over."

"We? I never said you could see it," Brian said.

Now Alex stood straight, glaring at Brian. "What did you say?"

"I told my dad *I* wanted to look at it. I never said *you* could look at it. It's private business."

"Brian Chang, you give me that book!" Bailey charged at him.

Brian laughed and held it up higher than her reach. "I'll look at it and then tell you what I find out. That way we can keep everyone happy. If my dad asks me if I showed it to anyone, I can honestly say no."

Bailey growled, her eyes flaming, then collapsed in a chair. "Fair enough. We don't want Uncle Nathan to get mad at you."

"But you have to promise to tell us everything you find that might relate to the mystery," Alex said.

"I promise."

"Hope to die?" Bailey prodded.

"Not particularly, but if it will make you feel better, then I guess." Brian grinned.

Bailey opened her mouth to speak but was interrupted by her cousin. "And sure, I'd love to stick a needle in my eye too while I'm at it!"

Bailey laughed. "Okay. I'm happy now. But remember, this is top secret!"

"Like you'd let me forget." Brian playfully shoved Bailey. "I need to get back to the barn. I'll keep you posted."

The next morning, Bailey and Alex arose early for their second day of shearing. Bailey wrapped her arms around herself in the crisp air as the sheep bleated their greetings. She was happy to see that Alex was much more at ease with the animals than the day before. She went right into the pasture to talk to them. Little Bow baaed her greeting to the girls, and Alex bent down and hugged her neck. Bailey joined her and immediately spotted the lamb with the message on it. "Let's see if it smells like marker," she suggested.

"I don't know if we'll be able to smell anything but sheep with all these others around." Alex held her nose.

They pushed their way through the herd to the yearling. Its mother stood between them and her baby.

"It's okay, Mama," Bailey cooed. "We aren't going to hurt your baby." She held out her hand for the sheep to nuzzle while Alex moved around to the other side of the lamb.

Quickly, Alex knelt and sniffed the markings. "All I can smell is sheep. Let's take it further away from the others and try again."

"I don't think his mama will allow that." Bailey tried to distract the ewe, but she moved closer to her lamb.

"You're a good mother," Bailey told her. "We'll let you be."

"You girls ready to get started?" Uncle Nathan called from the barn.

"Coming!" Bailey yelled.

Bailey and Alex took up their work, each at her own shearing station today. Uncle Nathan had put several lambs in pens for them to start on. The girls sheared in silence for about an hour; then Bailey heard Alex yell. She flipped off her shears. "What did you say?"

"Come here!" Alex shouted. Her arm waved Bailey over.

"Just a minute. I've got to finish up here first." Bailey turned the shears back on and quickly completed the job. She led the newly shorn lamb back to its pen and joined Alex.

"What's up?"

"I think we have another message." Alex pointed at the lamb she was shearing, tightening her grip on the rope around its neck. "Look."

Bailey studied the strange black streaks. "I can't read it." She tilted her head to get another angle.

"Let me finish shearing it, and we'll see if the other side says anything," Alex said. "Maybe it will help us figure out what this side says."

Alex ran the shears along the side of the sheep. The thick fleece dropped to the barn floor, uncovering more black streaks. "Yep. There's something here too." Alex turned off the shears and showed Bailey.

"Looks like it starts with a *B*." Bailey examined the lamb closely, running her hand over its marked skin. "Let's take her out to pasture so we can see it in the sunlight. I'll bring another one too to avoid suspicion."

The pair coaxed the noisy lambs out of the barn and into the bright sun. "Come on." Bailey pulled on the rope lead. "You can come out here where Bow is." Bailey put her lamb back in the pasture then tried to read the message on the young sheep Alex held. " 'Bundle'?" Bailey guessed at the word. " 'Bridle'? I'm not sure. You try."

She and Alex traded places. Alex stared at the writing, not saying anything. She walked around and looked at it from all angles. " 'Brindle'?" She shrugged her shoulders. "I don't know if that's even a word, but that's what it looks like to me."

"Take a look at the other side now and see what you think." Bailey turned the lamb around.

Alex gazed at its side. " 'Branch.' "

"Are you sure?" Bailey asked.

"Not completely, but it's the best I can come up with."

" 'Brindle Branch.' "

"Or 'Branch Brindle,' " Alex offered.

"Maybe it's not 'branch,' but 'ranch.' "

Alex looked at the writing again. "No, it definitely starts with a *B*."

"I wonder what it could mean."

"I think brindle might be an animal color. Seems like I heard that word when I was watching a dog show on TV. We'll have to look it up when we get back in the house."

"Let's hurry up and finish shearing so we can check this out." Bailey pointed her camera-watch at the lamb bearing the message and snapped a few pictures.

After they finished their last few lambs, they returned all the sheep to the pasture and returned to the barn.

"Uncle Nathan! We're done!" Bailey yelled over the buzz of the shears.

Uncle Nathan stopped his work and smiled. "You're done, huh? You must be getting pretty fast shearing those lambs. I'll have to bring more in for you tomorrow!" He laughed his big, hearty laugh.

"So can we be done working for today?" Bailey smiled and batted her eyes at her uncle.

"How can I say no to those sparkling brown eyes? Go on!" Uncle Nathan shooed them out of the barn with a wave of his hand.

Bailey gave Uncle Nathan a quick peck on the cheek. "You're the best!" She and Alex turned and raced back to the house, eager to investigate the latest message.

Alex opened her laptop and went to her online dictionary. "B-r-i-n-d-l-e." She typed in the word. "Here it is. 'Brindle or brindled: gray or tawny brown with darker streaks, patches, or spots.' "

"I've never seen a branch look like that," Bailey said. "What could 'Brindle Branch' mean?"

"Let's go outside and look at the trees. Maybe one will look more brindled than the others and give us a clue."

As the pair strolled the grounds of the Curly Q, they kept their eyes on the trees but saw nothing unusual.

"Let's go look over by the grove of trees where we saw Yeller disappear the other night," Bailey suggested. "There are more trees to study there."

In the grove, they spied a variety of trees. Some had rough bark, and others were smooth. The colors ranged from dark brown to ruddy red to almost white, but none looked patchy or streaked.

"I can't imagine what kind of tree would look like that," Bailey said.

"We'll just have to keep our eyes open from now on. Maybe we'll spot one that matches the description in the dictionary."

"What are you looking at?"

Bailey jumped, and Alex inhaled sharply.

"Brian! You scared us!" Bailey scolded her cousin. "You pop up in the weirdest places!"

"I could say the same thing about you."

"How'd you find us out here?" Alex asked.

"I saw you pass the barn. Not much out this way but the old grove." Brian looked around. "So what are you doing?"

"Investigating trees." Bailey looked up at the canopy of branches.

"That sounds like a good time." Brian patted his mouth as he yawned dramatically.

"Brian, we found another sheep with a message on it."

Brian's yawn ended abruptly and his eyes widened. "You're joking. What'd it say?"

"Brindle Branch," Alex said.

"Brindle Branch?" Brian repeated.

"Yeah. Any idea what it could mean?" Bailey asked.

"Not really." Brian scratched his head. "Sounds like it would have something to do with a tree."

"That's what we thought."

"I'll have to think about it." Brian looked at the trees around them. "I was just getting ready to drive into town. Want to come?"

Bailey looked at Alex and shrugged. "I guess so. I've never ridden with you since you've been old enough to drive. Maybe we'll spy a brindle tree along the way."

"I'll tell Dad you're going with me." Brian ran to the barn while the girls piled into the car. He returned and climbed in behind the wheel. "Buckle up!"

"All set." Bailey sat in the backseat and Alex in the front.

Brian slowly pulled forward and onto the country road. "I have to pick up a few groceries for my mom. The Historical Society isn't far from there. Want me to drop you off? Maybe you can get some clues to your mystery."

"Yeah!" Alex said. "Maybe we'll find out more about Marshall Gonzalez or his family."

Brian turned onto Washington Street and parked in front of an old building with a sign that read: Peoria Historical Society.

"I'll pick you up in an hour. I've got my cell phone if you need me to come get you sooner."

"Okay, thanks." Bailey climbed out of the backseat, and she and Alex marched up the steps to the main entrance.

"This place looks old," Alex said.

Bailey used all her weight to pull open the oversize wood door.

They each paid the suggested two-dollar donation and then went through a turnstile leading into the museum. The first thing they saw was an old, yellowed map of Peoria hanging on a wall in a glass case. It had brown lettering showing what the area had looked like before it was developed into a bustling town. Farmland covered much of the landscape, which the caption said the Illini Indians originally inhabited.

Bailey looked closely at the map, reading off the names of the rivers and creeks. "Alex! It says, 'Brindle Creek'!"

"No way. Where?"

Bailey pointed to a small creek that ran between acres of farmland.

"Unbelievable!"

"The map's so old I can't tell where the creek's located in relation to where the Curly Q is now."

"Me either," Alex said. "Let's keep looking. Maybe we'll find another clue."

Bailey and Alex split up and looked at two more maps, each more current than the last.

"Here it is!" Bailey called to Alex, who came rushing over. "Brindle Creek runs right between the Curly Q and that run-down house where Yeller, Dude, and Rude live."

"It must be the creek you were telling me about," Alex said. "Didn't you know what it was called?"

"That one's been called Woolly Creek for as long as I can remember, because of all the sheep farms surrounding it."

"Maybe it's not the same one then," Alex said thoughtfully. "But it sure looks like it on the map."

"Or maybe the name changed over the years as sheep farmers moved in."

"Could be."

"Can I help you girls?"

Bailey turned and saw a plump, gray-haired woman with crinkles around her gentle green eyes. Her name tag indicated she was the museum curator.

"Yes," Bailey said. "We were wondering if this Brindle Creek still exists."

"Yes, it does. It runs along the same path, though it is much smaller than it used to be."

"Does it still go by the same name?" Alex asked.

"Oh no. It changed with the times, as most things do. Its name was changed to Woolly Creek about twenty years ago when the sheep industry took off in that area."

Bailey grinned at Alex, who gave her a thumbs-up.

"Thank you," Bailey said. "You've been very helpful."

"If I can answer any other questions, feel free to ask," the curator said warmly.

"Is it okay if I take a few pictures of these maps with my cell phone?" Alex asked.

"Certainly."

Alex snapped a picture of each map showing Brindle Creek. "We can send these to the Camp Club Girls when we get home."

"At least we have more to go on than we did a couple hours ago," Bailey said.

"Yeah," Alex agreed. "We didn't even know what *brindle* meant, and now we have a map showing us where it is!"

"Now if we could only figure out how it might fit into our mystery."

Held Captive?

The next morning, Brian sauntered into the kitchen as Bailey and Alexis ate breakfast. He spread strawberry jam on his two pieces of toast, poured a big glass of milk, and sat down at the table. "Dad's already at the pasture bringing sheep into the barn, and Mom's at work," he said. "Here's what I found out from my dad's record book. We bought sheep from three different farms last year."

"Which ones?" Bailey asked around a mouthful of cereal.

"Hazelwood Sheep Farms, Hollyhock Acres, and Whitestone Ranch."

"Do you know where any of them are?" Alex asked.

"Their addresses were in the record book." Brian smiled proudly.

"Which one is closest?" Bailey wiped her mouth with the sleeve of her sweatshirt.

"It looks like Hazelwood Sheep Farms is closest, but I couldn't be sure from the address."

"Great. We can research it and find out." Alex looked at the clock. "Let's finish eating and get out to the barn."

"Yeah," Bailey agreed. "We need to check my shearing time again today."

"How's that going?" Brian asked.

"Pretty good. I'm down to eighteen minutes, twelve seconds."

"Way to go! You only need to trim five minutes, fifty-two seconds to match last year's winning time."

"And it's only Wednesday." Alex carried her bowl to the sink. "You still have three days to practice before Saturday's competition. If you keep knocking two minutes off each day, you'll beat last year's time easily!"

Brian wiped his mouth with his napkin, tossed it into the trash, and gulped down the last of his milk. "I'll go on out to see if Dad needs any help. See you out there!"

Bailey whipped out her phone. "I'm going to text Sydney to see if she can research Hazelwood Sheep Farms for us."

"Maybe we'll get an answer by the time we're done shearing today."

"That would be great." Bailey texted the message and sent it to Sydney, then put her phone back in her jeans pocket. "We only have three days left to solve this. Do you think we can get it done by Saturday?"

"Of course! We get more information every day!"

Shy scrambled across the yard to greet them. Bailey bent and scratched the dog's head. "I guess Uncle Nathan must have all the sheep already penned, or Shy would still be out there helping round them up."

Bailey took her place at her shearing station. "Let me know if you uncover anything interesting." She winked at Alex.

"You got it!" Alex moved to her spot and started working on a small black lamb.

The shears hummed along with the flies creating a buzzing symphony. Fleece dropped silently to the cement floor. Sheep baaed their complaints. The swish of brooms sweeping wool from the barn floor added rhythm.

Soon Bailey led her fourth lamb to the shearing floor, sat it on its rump, and ran the shears along its body. Black streaky marks appeared with each stroke. Another word! Bailey sheared faster, revealing letter after letter. H-e-l-d. She looked at Alex who was working, head down, on her own yearling. Quickly Bailey turned the sheep and sheared the other side. More letters; these were closer together and harder to read. Bailey again glanced toward Alex and caught her eye. She waved her over.

Alex returned her lamb to its pen and rushed to Bailey's station.

"Look!" Bailey said. "Another message. This side says, 'Held,' but I'm not sure about the other side." She flipped the lamb over for Alex to see.

Alex sounded out the word slowly as she read it. "Cap-tain?"

"Doesn't seem like that would be right." Bailey scrunched up her face. "Try again."

Alex stared at the lamb. "The letters are so close it's hard to tell where one starts and the other stops." She studied the writing again. "C-a-p-t. That much I'm sure of. Maybe the last part is i-v-e."

"C-a-p-t-i-v-e. Captive! Alex, that's it!" Bailey squealed. The lamb squirmed. "Okay, baby. Let's go outside so we can take your picture."

Alex slipped a rope lead around the neck of the lamb Bailey held and got another lead to go on another lamb. She and Bailey led the animals out to pasture after snapping some photos of the mysterious writing.

"This is unbelievable!" Alex said. "I wonder how many other messages we'll find."

"I don't know. But I think we need to put all the words together that we've found so far to see if they say something as a group or if they're only individual messages."

"Yeah, let's do that after we're done. How many more sheep do you have left to shear?" Alex asked.

"Three. How about you?"

"Five."

"How about if you time my next one? Then when I finish my last one, I'll help you finish yours."

"Deal." Alex grabbed the stopwatch off a nail hook and waited for Bailey to get set up.

"Ready. . .set. . .go!" Alex started the clock, and Bailey started shearing. "You're doing great, Bailey! You're going to break your old record at this rate!"

"Done!" Bailey shouted minutes later.

Alex punched the stopwatch. "Fifteen minutes, forty-two seconds!" Alex whooped. "Your best time yet! How did you do that so fast?"

"I pretended I saw a new message under the fleece and hurried to uncover it!"

Alex laughed. "Good strategy."

"I cut more than two minutes off my time!" Bailey hugged the naked lamb.

"You'll win that competition, I just know it," Alex said.

"Then I could get my picture in the newspaper!"

Alex beamed at her friend. "You'll be a star one way or another, even if it's not in theater, though I'm sure you'll make it there too." The girls finished shearing the lambs and returned them to the pasture.

"I've got an idea," Bailey said. "Let's line up the sheep that have messages and take a picture of all three of them together."

"We'll need to take a picture of both sides to get all the words."

The girls gathered the lambs. Bailey tried to get two lambs to stand sideways by the other. "Can you hold all three of the leads and keep them in place while I take the picture?"

"I'll try, but hurry," Alex said. "They won't stay like this for long."

Bailey handed the leads to Alex and rushed in front of the lambs. She snapped pictures from that side and then the other. "They weren't perfectly lined up, but I think I got the words in all the shots."

They returned the sheep to the pasture. The lambs leaped with joy, clearing the ground with all four feet. Bow bleated a welcome to her newly shorn friends, her red bow sagging. Mama sheep baaed wildly and rushed to find their babies.

"Let's go see how they turned out." Alex took off at a run toward the house, with Bailey close behind.

"Wait!" Bailey stopped. "My phone's vibrating. Maybe it's Sydney." Bailey pulled her phone from her pocket and read the text.

HAZELWOOD FARMS IS A HALF MILE AWAY FROM YOU AND ON THE OTHER SIDE OF A CREEK.

Bailey looked at Alex wide-eyed. "Just across the creek? That's where Yeller, Dude, and Rude were!"

"That can't be right." Alex shook her head. "I didn't see any sheep over there."

"Maybe they keep them somewhere else. Or maybe they sold them all."

"Hmm. Interesting." Alex looked toward the old house. "Let's take a walk in that direction this afternoon."

Back at the house, Bailey downloaded her photos onto Alex's computer. "I think I'll write each word of the message on note cards. Then we can rearrange them and see what we get."

"Good idea." Alex dug in her backpack. "I think I have some note cards in here somewhere. Ah. Here they are." She handed the cards to Bailey.

"The first lamb said, 'Help Gonzo.' " Bailey wrote HELP on one card and GONZO on another.

"The second one said, 'Brindle Branch,' " Alex said.

Bailey wrote the words on the cards. "And today's lamb said, 'Held captive.' " After writing the final words, Bailey laid the cards out in front of them. " 'Help Gonzo Brindle Branch Held Captive.' Doesn't make much sense this way."

Alex rearranged the cards. " 'Help Gonzo Held Captive Brindle Branch.' That's better."

"Seems like Gonzo's being held captive at Brindle Branch, wherever that is!"

"Now all we have to do is figure out that piece of the puzzle." Alex wrapped a curl around her finger and bit her lower lip.

"Do you really think this could be Marshall Gonzalez?" Bailey asked.

"Even if it isn't, this Gonzo needs our help."

"True. He must be desperate to send messages on sheep."

"This Gonzo must have been held captive since last shearing season to be able to write his messages on freshly shorn sheep."

"Good point," Bailey agreed. "Many of the farmers shear their sheep twice a year. That must be the case wherever this Gonzo is, because the lambs he wrote them on are only a year old. I doubt that he would have written on a newborn lamb. The mother never would have allowed that."

"So Gonzo probably wrote his messages about six months ago. He's been a hostage for at least six months!"

"How could anyone be held that long without someone knowing about it?" Bailey asked.

"We need to get the other Camp Club Girls in on this. Do you think we should do another conference call?"

"Yes. We have a lot to cover with them since we talked yesterday." Bailey got her phone out and started conferencing in the other girls.

Alex jotted down a few notes to help keep their meeting on track.

"Can you all hear me?" Bailey asked after patching in the last one.

"Kate here. I read you loud and clear."

"This is Sydney. I hear you."

"Me too; it's Elizabeth,"

"McKenzie? You there?" Alex asked.

"I'm here," she answered.

Bailey heard Biscuit bark. "Biscuit hears you too!" Kate said, and they all laughed.

"I'm here too, so I guess we're ready to get started." Bailey cleared her throat. "Alex and I have uncovered some pretty interesting clues since we last talked, but we need your help researching them."

"Bailey and I found two more lambs with messages on them."

Bailey smiled at Alex as they listened to the girls gasp.

"What'd the new messages say?" Sydney asked.

"Alex's message said, 'Brindle Branch.' The letters were written in all capitals like the first message.

"And mine said, 'Held captive,' again in all capitals." Bailey licked her lips.

"We rearranged the words of all three messages today, and we believe they were meant to be read together. We think they should read, 'Help Gonzo held captive at Brindle Branch.' "

"Wow!" McKenzie said. "That's unbelievable."

"So how can we help?" Elizabeth asked.

"We went to the Historical Society yesterday to see if we could find a place called Brindle Branch," Alex said. "The closest we came was finding a Brindle Creek on an old map. It's the same creek that runs right behind the Curly Q, but now it goes by the name Woolly Creek."

"I took pictures of the map and will send those to you electronically," Bailey said. "We're wondering, if it is Gonzalez, how could a grown man be held captive so long without escaping? He had to have written the notes on the lambs at least six months ago when they were last sheared. Apparently he's allowed to go outside by himself."

"That's odd," McKenzie said. "You'd think he could run off if he was alone outside."

"I'll look into that," Kate offered. "I read something recently that may help."

"Great. Thanks, Kate." Alex looked at her notes. "We wonder if Marshall Gonzalez began sheep farming before he disappeared. That would make sense, since the messages are written on sheep. But if he were still in that business, someone else would probably have to be tending his sheep for him if he's being held hostage."

"Not an easy task," Elizabeth said. "Sheep know their shepherd's voice and won't follow anyone else. Their whole existence relies on the shepherd's care. Wait a minute. Let me read you something from my Bible."

Bailey heard the rustling of pages through the phone.

"Here it is, John 10:2–5. Listen to this." Elizabeth cleared her throat. " 'The one who enters by the gate is the shepherd of the sheep. The gatekeeper opens the gate for him, and the sheep listen to his voice. He calls his own sheep by name and leads them out. When he has brought out all his own, he goes on ahead of them, and his sheep follow him because they know his voice. But they will never follow a stranger; in fact, they will run away from him because they do not recognize a stranger's voice.' " Elizabeth paused. Bailey guessed she was setting down her Bible. "That's why I say it wouldn't be easy for someone else to step in and take over the care of someone else's sheep."

"Interesting," McKenzie said slowly. "So if sheep don't take kindly to following strangers, then maybe Gonzo's kidnapping was an inside job, done by someone the sheep already knew."

"I suppose that's possible," Sydney said. "But why would someone kidnap their own friend?"

"That's easy," McKenzie said. "Money."

"She answered that awfully fast, don't you think, girls?" Alex said. "We'd better not get too rich, or she might kidnap *us*!"

Laughter filled the phone lines.

"We also found out," Bailey said, "that Uncle Nathan bought sheep from three different farms at auctions last year—Hazelwood Sheep Farms, Hollyhock Acres, and Whitestone Ranch. We're going to check them out to see if we can come up with any clues about which farm the sheep with messages might have come from. We had Sydney check out the farm locations earlier today, and she found out that Hazelwood is only a half mile from the Curly Q, so we'll start there."

"Good plan," Sydney said.

"Now, just to be fair, we should mention that Brian told us Gonzalez is a common name among the migrant workers in the area. The name Gonzo could refer to one of them." Bailey looked at Alex and shrugged her shoulders.

"Good to know," Elizabeth said. "Anything else you need to update us on?"

"Anyone have anything yet on why the grandpa was so rich while the son was so poor?" Alex asked.

"Not yet," Sydney replied. "I'm still checking into that and the shrimping and sugar cane industries."

"And I'm still researching to see if there were any other grandchildren and if Gonzo's father was living when his father died," Kate added.

"Great." Alex gave Bailey a thumbs-up.

"I think that covers it," Bailey said. "Did we forget anything, Alex?"

"Not that I can think of."

"What about Yeller, Dude, and Rude? Have you seen any more of them?" McKenzie asked.

"No, not since Yeller fell out of the tree outside our window." Alex shivered thinking about it. "But we plan to walk down that way later today. We may see them then."

"How about if I say a little prayer for all of us before we hang up?" Elizabeth asked.

"Sure!" Bailey said. The line grew quiet.

"Dear God, we know You hear us and care about us," Elizabeth began. "Help us solve this mystery about Marshall Gonzalez. Most of all, keep us all safe as we work on it, especially Bailey and Alex. Give us wisdom and insight and help us to honor You in everything we do. Be with Gonzo, wherever he is, and keep him safe too. In Jesus' name, amen."

"Amen!" the other five girls said in unison.

Bailey sighed. "I feel better already."

"Keep us posted on what you find out," Alex said to the girls. "We're keeping a file here of all the details so we can keep track of them."

"Will do," Kate said.

"I think that covers it then." Bailey looked in Alex's direction and saw her nod. "We'll call you with updates." Bailey flipped her phone closed.

"Let's take that walk down toward Yeller's place." Alex got up from the bed.

"We need to take a snack for Fang so he doesn't eat us alive," Bailey said, remembering the growling dog that chased them. She stuffed some cheese crackers in one of her jeans pockets and her inhaler and lip balm in the other. "I think we're ready."

"Have your camera, just in case?"

"Check." Bailey patted her wristwatch.

"I don't know why, but I feel nervous." Alex bit her cuticle.

"I know what you mean. I have a whole flock of butterflies racing around in my stomach." Bailey rubbed her tummy. "We're probably just excited. After all, we're just going for a walk, right?"

The Man Named Gonzo

Bailey and Alex crossed the front yard and ambled down the country road that ran alongside the Curly Q. Shy scampered to catch up with them then ran around them in circles to herd them along.

"Hi, girl," Alex said, rubbing the dog. A gentle breeze blew their hair back as they walked.

"Uh-oh." Bailey grimaced. "We forgot to tell anyone we were going for a walk."

"We'll probably be back before the guys are done shearing anyway, and your Aunt Darcy won't be home from work until after five."

"You're right. It's only one thirty now." Bailey reached for her lip balm. "We have plenty of time."

The girls walked a few paces in silence.

"Let's see if there's a sign by the creek up ahead that tells its history," Alex said. "Since Woolly Creek's name used to be Brindle Creek, maybe we'll learn something that gives us a clue to the 'Brindle Branch' message."

"I don't remember seeing one before, but we can check."

Shy ran on ahead of the girls and disappeared in the brush along the side of the road.

When they reached the creek, they spotted Shy at the edge of the water, helping herself to a drink.

Alex looked around for a sign. "Looks like you were right. No sign with Woolly Creek's history on it."

"We'll just have to keep our eyes and ears open to find out about Brindle Branch." Bailey swatted a fly away. "Let's walk along the creek. I think it's low enough that Yeller, Dude, and Rude won't see us too easily when we pass their property."

The girls climbed down to where Shy was lapping water and

began their creek walk.

"Do you really think their house is the same as Hazelwood Sheep Farms?" Alex asked.

Bailey shrugged. "It sure sounds like the same place Sydney's research turned up."

"Seems weird that it would be so run-down if they were still auctioning sheep just last spring."

Bailey could almost see the wheels turning in her friend's mind.

"Didn't you say Gonzo was getting into sheep farming before he disappeared?" Alex asked.

"Yeah."

"If he lived around here, then there should be some sign of his sheep farm, don't you think?"

"After seven years? I doubt it," Bailey said.

"Yeah, maybe that would be too long." Disappointment filled Alex's voice.

"We can still look for clues to his farm while we investigate Hazelwood Sheep Farms. After all, isn't that the real reason for this walk?"

"I guess," Alex said. "But that means going on Yeller, Dude, and Rude's property. Could be dangerous."

"Well, how else are we going to find out what we need to know?"

"I don't know, but going over there gives me the creeps." Alex shivered.

"What could happen?" Bailey asked.

"For starters, we could be eaten alive by Fang!"

"I brought snacks for him, remember?" Bailey patted her pocket. "Before you know it, we'll be Fang's best friends, and he'll wag his tail every time he sees us."

"I don't know. . ." Alex hesitated. "What if they see us?"

"Maybe we'll get a chance to talk to them. They may hold the answer to this mystery, you know."

"Maybe you're right." Alex looked around nervously.

"We'll let Shy lead the way. Dogs can detect danger before humans. But first we need to get to the other side of the creek."

Alex followed Bailey a short distance to a narrow part of the creek. Stones formed natural steps across the shallow water, and Bailey hopped effortlessly from one to the next. Safely on the other side, she turned around and saw Alex only halfway across. Her arms were stretched out to her sides for balance. She teetered on one stone, and then stepped gingerly to the next.

"Don't worry, they're not slippery!" Bailey yelled above the sound of the creek and the sheep bleating from her uncle's pasture.

Shy waded through the water, circling Alex, trying to herd her along like a stray lamb, but Alex continued on at her own cautious pace. Finally, she drew close enough for Bailey to reach out and take her hand. Alex grabbed it like a lifeline, and Bailey pulled her friend onto the bank.

"You did it!" Bailey hugged Alex.

Shy jumped out of the creek and shook her wet fur, spraying the girls like a sprinkler.

"Shy!" Bailey yelled, wiping off her arms. She looked at Alex and laughed. A drop of water hung from the tip of her friend's nose, and her green cotton T-shirt and gray gym shorts were speckled with wet spots. Tiny rivulets ran down her bare legs.

Alex exploded in laughter. "That dog!"

"Come on," Bailey said, wiping water from her face with her shirt. "Now that we look so nice, let's go visit the neighbors."

Alex giggled. "I needed a good laugh to get over my nerves. I think I'm ready now."

"Lead the way, Shy." Bailey followed the wet dog along the creek bank. "Remember, keep your eyes open for any signs of Gonzo's sheep or Hazelwood Sheep Farms."

"Right," Alex answered. "If we spread out a bit, we can cover more territory." Alex stayed close to the water while Bailey went further ashore. Shy jogged between the two.

The trio marched along, sometimes heads down looking for clues, and other times heads up, keeping nervous watch for any sign of Yeller, Dude, and Rude.

"Look at this!" Bailey stopped and stared at a dry, brown clump.

Alex stepped over rocks at the creek's edge and hurried to Bailey. "What is it?"

"Looks like dry sheep droppings," Bailey said kneeling down.

"Terrific!" Alex said, half smiling. "It can't be from Gonzo's farm, or it would have disintegrated into the soil by now."

"No, but it could be from Hazelwood sheep." Bailey stood and kicked the dry clump with the toe of her tennis shoe. "Let's keep looking."

Alex returned to her place by the water's edge, and they continued their search. Shy sniffed the ground.

"Hey, check this out!" Alex yelled a short time later.

Bailey saw Alex squatting by the water. As she came closer, Alex reached into the creek. "What's up?" Bailey asked her.

"I found something." Alex pulled a small yellow plastic tag with a number on it out of the water. The five-sided tag came to a rounded off point like a triangle at the top, but the sides and bottom were squared, making the whole thing the shape of a tiny house.

"Looks like an ear tag from a sheep." Bailey held out her hand, and Alex dropped the tag into it. "There's a number on both sides. The tags are used for identification, but I don't know how to read them or what they mean."

"Maybe Brian knows!" Alex's hopeful eyes danced.

"We'll ask him when we get home." Bailey handed the tag back to Alex, who slid it into her shirt pocket. "Wow! We're almost past Yeller's house already."

"And no sign of Fang, thank goodness!" Alex added.

"Let's keep looking." Alex and Bailey split up again. Suddenly Shy took off ahead of them.

She's sure in a hurry. Bailey kept walking, eyes to the ground. Her head shot up when she heard Shy bark, though she couldn't see the Australian shepherd.

"I think Shy's found something!" Bailey yelled. She and Alex ran toward the sound, staying low toward the creek until they were safely past Yeller's backyard. They spied Shy by a fenced sheep pasture, barking. The sheep baaed and scattered in confused dismay at this unfamiliar dog making so much noise.

"Sheep!" Bailey shouted at Alex. They reached Shy, out of breath. The dog settled down as soon as the girls reached her side.

"I wonder who they belong to." Alex covered her nose at the foul smell.

"I don't know, but they look—and smell—awful!" Bailey wrinkled her nose and frowned. "Uncle Nathan would have a fit if his flock looked like this." Bailey went closer to inspect the sickly sheep. "Look at this poor, skinny ewe. She has a runny nose, her hooves need trimming, and she has sores on her head. These sheep are half starved. Some of them can barely walk! I bet they have parasites too. Uncle Nathan is always watching his flock for signs of them because they're so common with sheep."

Alex nodded her head. "Poor things."

"Hey! What are you doing?" a gruff voice yelled. A man ran toward Bailey and Alex, a fist raised in the air. Shy barked again.

"We're just out for a walk and stopped to see the sheep," Bailey answered innocently, but the man appeared not to hear her. He stomped closer, his arms swinging madly with each step.

"Bailey!" Alex said. "That's Dude!"

"Or Rude," Bailey added, "since we don't know which is which."

"We'd better go!" Alex grabbed Bailey's hand.

"No! Wait!" Bailey pulled her hand away. "This could be our chance to ask a few questions," she whispered.

"You're on private property!" the wiry man growled. He wore a dirty white T-shirt and grimy jeans. His greasy brown hair looked like he'd just crawled out of bed.

"We're sorry," Alex said. "We didn't know."

"Are these your sheep?" Bailey asked.

"Yeah, they're mine. What of it?" the man answered, his voice low and raspy. The deep lines in his weathered face contorted in anger.

"How long have you been sheep farming?" Bailey tried to sound like a friendly neighbor.

"None of your business."

"I'm Bailey, and this is my friend, Alex." Bailey stuck out her hand for the man to shake. She hoped he didn't notice its tremble. "We're here visiting my uncle. We leave on Saturday."

The man's shoulders relaxed with that bit of news, and he hesitantly shook Bailey's hand. He stared at them, his face clouded with suspicion.

Behind her smile, Bailey gritted her teeth, resisting the urge to wipe her hand on her jeans after shaking the man's dirt-encrusted hand.

"What's your name?" Alex asked, her face a mask of sweet innocence.

Bailey could tell her friend had caught on to her friendly, naive, chatty-girls-asking-questions strategy.

The man didn't respond, and Bailey cringed at his stony glare.

Bailey shrugged, maintaining the naive, chatty-girls plan. "Ever hear of someone named Gonzo?"

The man's small, close-set blue eyes widened slightly, and he squared his shoulders. "Gonzo? That's *my* name!"

Bailey stood up straight. "*You're* Gonzo?"

Shy took a tentative step or two and growled low and throaty.

Alex's mouth hung open. "B–but. . .you're supposed to be dead!"

"Huh?" Gonzo frowned.

Grrrowuf! Just then Fang charged across the yard at them in a snarling mass of teeth and fur. Shy barked back just as fiercely and flew toward the muscular dog.

"Shy! No!" Bailey screamed. She tore after the dog toward the weed-ridden yard of the neglected house.

Alex followed on Bailey's heels. The girls saw Yeller standing by the barn trying to call off the dog. A third man, either Dude or Rude, pulled Yeller out of sight.

"I. . .can't. . .breathe," Bailey gasped, reaching into her pocket for her inhaler. She searched the wrong pocket and found the snack she brought for Fang. Between wheezes, she ripped open the package, and tossed it at him. Then she stuck her hand in the other pocket and grasped her inhaler. Dropping to the ground, she quickly uncapped it, put it in her mouth, and squeezed.

"Keep. . .running toward. . .home!" she told Alex. "Shy will. . .follow you. She's. . .just trying. . .to protect us." Bailey glanced at the pasture where the sick sheep were. Her skin crawled when she spotted Gonzo leaning against the fence.

"I'm not leaving you here!" Alex yelled.

"Go!" Bailey commanded. "I'll be. . .behind you." Her mouth was dry and her palms sweaty as she struggled to stand.

Alex helped her up and then did as she was told. Bailey trailed her as closely as she was able. She heard the snarling and growling of the dogs fighting. The cheese crackers she tossed to Fang apparently hadn't slowed him down. Shy yelped. Moments later the dog limped beside the girls.

"And *stay* away!" Bailey heard one of the men yell. Then he roared with laughter.

"Don't look back," Alex said. As they neared the road, they slowed to a walk. "Are you okay?"

Bailey nodded, still gasping for breath.

"Good thing you had your inhaler along this time."

"Yeah." Bailey crouched down to look at Shy. "You okay, girl?"

The dog nuzzled Bailey's face and licked her.

Bailey wrapped her arms around Shy's neck, breathing deeply to slow her pulse. "That awful dog bit the back of your neck," she said moving Shy's fur aside. "And look at your leg. You got some pretty nasty cuts there. Come on. Let's go see Uncle Nathan."

"How will we explain this?" Alex asked.

"What's to explain?" Bailey replied. "We went for a walk by the creek and a mean dog attacked Shy."

"That's *it*?"

"What more do we need to say?" Bailey asked with her eyebrows raised.

"What about the men? What about Gonzo?"

"What about them?"

"Don't you think we should tell your uncle what happened?" Alex nearly yelled.

"Nothing happened!" Bailey yelled back. "The guy said his name was Gonzo. The dog got loose, and we ran. End of story."

"He warned us not to come back." Alex looked sideways at her friend.

"He didn't warn us," Bailey said. "He just said to stay away."

"Same thing."

"Look. We're closer now than we've ever been to solving this mystery. Please," Bailey pleaded, "let's not mess it up now."

Alex sighed and rolled her eyes. "Oh, all right," she mumbled. "But if anything else happens, we have to tell."

"Deal." Bailey hugged Alex. "Friends?"

Alex laughed. "Of course. Always."

"We need to ask Brian about this sheep tag." Alex patted her shirt pocket. "Oh no, Bailey! It's gone!"

The Old Wooden Sign

"How could it be gone?" Bailey asked. "You put it in your pocket just awhile ago."

"It must have bounced out when we were running." Alex turned, scanning the yard of dirt and tall weeds they had just crossed.

"I bet we could find it if we retraced our steps," Bailey said.

"I'm not going back there!" Alex's jaw clenched. "I just got my heart rate back to normal. Besides, we need to get Shy home."

Looking one last time at the run-down house, Bailey scratched Shy behind the ears. "I guess you're right. Come on, girl. Let's go."

The girls hurried back to the house, Shy limping along beside them.

"Uncle Nathan!" Bailey called as they approached the barn, but the shears drowned out her voice. Her uncle turned them off when he spotted them.

"What are you two up to?" he asked.

"Uncle Nathan, Shy's been hurt," Bailey told him.

Uncle Nathan hurried to them and bent to inspect his sheepdog. Bailey knew Shy was not only a part of the family, but she played an important role in his sheep business. He tenderly lifted the injured leg. "She may need stitches. I'd better get her to Doc Maddox."

"She has a cut on her neck too." Bailey spread Shy's fur to show him.

"That one doesn't look quite as bad." Uncle Nathan picked up Shy like Bailey had often seen him pick up lambs and headed toward his truck. "Tell Brian we're leaving while I load her into the truck."

Bailey did as she was told and was back moments later.

"What happened to her?" Uncle Nathan asked as Bailey climbed into the truck.

"We were taking a walk down by the creek," Alex began.

"And a big, mean dog charged out from that old house across the creek," Bailey finished.

"We think Shy tried to protect us by going after the dog." Alex frowned.

"Shy fought that dog like mad until we were safely past." Bailey sighed sadly. "Then she caught up with us and we came home."

"Were you on our side of the creek?"

Bailey glanced at Alex. "No, we had crossed the creek."

Uncle Nathan looked at Bailey in his rearview mirror. "Why'd you do that?"

Bailey licked her lips. "I. . .I don't know. We found a safe place to cross with stepping-stones and everything. The water wasn't deep."

"The water's never deep," her uncle replied sternly. "But the other side of the creek is someone else's property. You shouldn't go there without permission."

Bailey grew quiet for a moment. "Uncle Nathan, we found out they're keeping sheep over there and aren't taking care of them," she said, not sure if she should tell him. "You should see them. They're skin and bones, their noses are runny, their hooves need trimming. It'd make you sick!" Her voice rose passionately.

Uncle Nathan's eyes darted to his mirror. "Did you see the owners?" he asked.

Bailey and Alex exchanged looks. *The truth.* Bailey knew what was right, and she had to do it. "Yeah, we met one of the owners." Her voice sounded reluctant.

"Bailey. . .what are you not telling me?" Uncle Nathan pressed.

"He said his name was Gonzo. He was filthy, and he didn't even try to help Shy or us when his dog chased us!" Her words spilled out like water over a cliff. Unexpected tears sprang to Bailey's eyes. She wasn't sure if they were from having to admit what they'd done or from the fear she felt as Shy was being attacked.

"We heard him—or one of the other men—laugh as we ran away," Alex added.

"Other men? What other men?" Uncle Nathan asked.

"We saw one man by the barn, and he tried to call off the dog," Bailey explained. "But another man jerked him back into the barn."

Her uncle's temples moved as he ground his teeth. A blue vein bulged on his forehead, but he said nothing. Finally, he blew air from his mouth, like steam being released from a pressurized pot.

"I will have a word with our neighbor," he said in carefully measured words. "That will *never* happen again. These men sound cruel, and I don't want you near them. Stay off their property. You hear?"

"Yes, sir," Bailey said softly.

"We're sorry about all this," Alex said, remorse filling her voice.

"I know you are. It's okay. At least you weren't hurt."

"But Shy was," Bailey said, her voice trembling. She brushed away hot tears.

"Shy'll be fine. Doc Maddox will stitch her, and she'll be good as new in a few days," Uncle Nathan reassured her. "She's used to having to protect the sheep. She's fought off worse than that dog before."

They arrived at the vet's office, and Uncle Nathan carried Shy in.

Bailey's spirits rose at the good report Doc Maddox gave after examining the sheepdog. "She'll be chasing sheep again in no time!"

Turned out Uncle Nathan was right. Doc Maddox sewed Shy up in minutes, and they headed back home.

"Hey, look at that." Uncle Nathan pointed out his window. "A flea market. Should we stop?"

"Yeah!" Bailey yelled.

They pulled into the parking lot, rolled the windows down a little for Shy, and got out. "I'm going to look at the tool booth," Uncle Nathan said.

"Ugh, tools," Bailey teased her uncle. "Can we look around at other stuff? We have our cell phones, so you can call us when you're ready to go."

"You don't want to look at tools with me?" Uncle Nathan grinned and winked. "I guess you can look at something else."

"Thanks! See ya!" Bailey and Alex took off.

The girls fingered hair accessories, stuffed animals, and wind chimes. They tried on hats and laughed at their reflections in the mirror.

"Look at this booth," Alex said. "Everything is carved out of wood."

"Cool!" Bailey picked up a small wooden sign with her name carved in it, then set it back down and continued browsing. "Alex, look!" Her eyes were fixed on a rough sign carved out of old barn wood hanging with other used items.

BRINDLE BRANCH FARM! Alex's mouth fell open as soon as she saw the words.

"May I help you?" An older man, with a face that looked like it too had been hewn from old wood, stood beside them.

"Yes," Alex replied. "We were wondering about that Brindle Branch sign."

"Oh yes, she's a beauty, isn't she?" the man said.

"Do you know anything about its history?" Bailey pointed her watch at the sign and snapped a picture when the man turned his back.

"We got that sign in several weeks ago from a sheep farmer. Said it used to be the name of his property, and the sign hung over the front door of his farmhouse."

"Used to be the name?" Alex asked. "Did he say what the farm's called now?"

"No. Sorry, he didn't."

"What did the man look like?" Bailey asked.

"What did he look like?" The man chuckled softly. "I'm afraid I don't remember." He thought a moment. "Kinda dark, maybe, sort of tall." He waved his hand in dismay. "Aw, I don't know. I get too many people in here to remember what one man looks like."

"Do you know where this Brindle Branch Farm was located?" Alex twisted a curl around her finger.

"Can't say I do. Must not be too far, though, or this fellow probably wouldn't have brought the sign here, I suppose."

"How much does it cost?" Bailey felt for her wallet.

"Twenty dollars."

Bailey looked at Alex. "We'll think about it. Thanks for the information."

"My pleasure." The man turned to help another customer.

"I only have ten dollars with me," Bailey told Alex.

"Let me see how much I have." Alex did a quick count. "Eight dollars and seventy-eight cents."

"Not enough to buy that sign." Bailey sighed.

"Unless he'll let us have it for less." Alex smiled. "They often do that at flea markets!"

"Good idea!" Bailey said. "You want to ask him?"

Alex went up to the old gentleman and cleared her throat. "Excuse me, sir."

"Yes, how can I help you?"

"That Brindle Branch sign. Would you take fifteen dollars for it?"

The man's forehead wrinkled. "Fifteen? Hmm. I don't know. . . ."

"Please, sir," Bailey begged. "It's practically all the money we have with us."

The man eyed them carefully and then melted like butter on a hot biscuit. "Oh, I guess fifteen would be all right. No one else has even looked at it in the time we've had it." His eyes sparkled at the girls as he lifted the sign off its hook and wrapped it in brown paper.

"That'll be sixteen dollars and twenty cents with tax."

"Great!" Bailey smiled at the man and handed him the cash. "You don't know how much this means to us!"

"I don't know why young gals like you would want an old beat-up sign like that, but I'm glad you like it."

The girls walked down the row of booths. "We still have enough money left over to buy a treat from the candy booth." Bailey's mouth watered at the idea.

The girls each chose a treat—Skittles for Bailey and a granola bar for Alex.

Bailey's phone vibrated in her pocket. "Hello?"

"I'm done at the tool booth. Are you girls ready to go?" Uncle Nathan asked.

"Yep. We bought a cool sign and a treat, so we're all ready."

"I'll meet you at the entrance."

"Okay. See you in a minute." Bailey shoved her phone into her pocket. "We're supposed to meet Uncle Nathan at the entrance."

Alex nodded. "Hey, Bailey?"

"Yeah?"

"I'm sorry I was afraid to go retrace our steps to look for the ear tag."

"No biggie. Besides, now we have this sign to investigate."

"Maybe tomorrow I'll feel braver," Alex offered.

"Do you remember anything about the ear tag?"

"It was yellow and shaped like a tiny house. And it was made of plastic."

"Any idea what the numbers on it were?" Bailey pressed.

"Not for sure." Alex paused. "I think one side might have said 'forty-six'. Or maybe it was 'sixty-four.' "

"Great!" Bailey squealed. "I think the other side said 'five-one-two-nine'! At least I'm *pretty* sure those were the numbers. I'm just not positive of their order."

"Now if we can get Brian to tell us what the numbers mean, we're all set." Alex's grin stretched as wide as a slice of watermelon. "Maybe we won't need to look for the tag after all!"

They saw Uncle Nathan waiting. He spotted their bag right away. "Let's see this cool sign you found," he said.

Bailey carefully pulled it from the bag and unwrapped it.

BRINDLE BRANCH FARM, Uncle Nathan read. "Hmm. That sounds familiar."

"It does?" Alex's eyes flew open.

"Do you know where it is?" Bailey asked.

"Can't say that I do, but I've heard of it."

"The sign looks old, don't you think?"

Running a calloused hand over it, her uncle said, "Looks old, all right." He looked at the girls and smiled. "You *did* find a pretty cool sign. It has a lot of character!"

"We're going to research its history and see what we can find out." Bailey rewrapped it in the brown paper before returning it to its bag.

"That should be interesting," Uncle Nathan said. "I'd be curious to know what you find out."

"We'll let you know," Alex said.

Uncle Nathan unlocked the truck, and Shy sat up, yawned, and looked around.

"Looks like someone's been taking a nap," Uncle Nathan said. "Must be tuckered out from such an adventurous afternoon."

When Shy saw them, she stood up on the backseat, her tail wagging like it was attached to a spring. Her mouth parted in a dog smile, her tongue dangling out the side.

Bailey opened the door. "Hi, girl!" She climbed in and was greeted with a face full of wet kisses. "Are you feeling better?"

"Sure looks like it!" Alex said, laughing.

"Uncle Nathan, did you know that Woolly Creek behind your house used to be called Brindle Creek?" Bailey asked.

"Brindle Creek? No, I didn't." Uncle Nathan made a funny face. "How'd you know that?"

"We saw it at the Historical Society a couple days ago." Bailey buckled her seat belt.

"Well, I'll be!"

"So maybe Brindle Branch Farm is along that creek somewhere," Alex said.

"Could be," Uncle Nathan said. "Sounds like you're off to a good start already with researching that sign you bought. But remember, no more going onto someone else's property without permission. You could have been hurt today."

"We won't, Uncle Nathan," Bailey assured him.

Minutes later, the truck pulled into the driveway of Uncle Nathan's home. The girls jumped out and headed toward the house.

"I'll see you gals at supper. I have some shearing to finish." Uncle Nathan waved them off and went back to join Brian in the barn.

In their bedroom, Alex sat on the floor, her back against the foot of the bed. She opened the laptop and checked her email.

"Anything interesting?" Bailey asked.

"Not much. My mom sent me a note." Alexis smiled. "She misses me."

"She won't have to miss you much longer," Bailey said. "We'll be home soon."

"I know. I can't believe how fast this week is going."

"Only two more days to solve this mystery. What do you think we should do next?"

Alex cocked her head. "I'm guessing Brindle Branch Farm must be along Brindle Creek, which is now called Woolly Creek."

"Yeah."

"So tomorrow we should take another walk along the creek— making sure we stay on our own side—to see if we can figure out which place is Brindle Branch."

Bailey perked up. "Maybe we could even talk to some of the neighbors. They may know something."

"Great idea!"

"One way or another, we'll solve this mystery of Marshall Gonzalez and Brindle Branch and the marked sheep," Bailey said.

There was a knock on the girls' door.

"Come in!" Bailey called.

Brian stuck his head in the door. "Dad let me off early since there were only a few sheep left when he got back. I heard *you* had an exciting day!"

"Boy, did we ever!" Bailey answered. "Come on in."

Brian plunked down in the pink beanbag. Bailey and Alex retold the events of the day.

"Wow," he finally said. "I'm glad you guys are okay. Wish I'd been along. I'd have made those guys sorry for messing with you." He winked at Alex.

Alex turned beet red and looked down at her feet. A hint of a smile played on her lips.

Puffing out her chest and holding her head up high, Bailey bragged, "We handled it very well ourselves, thank you."

"Oh! We have something to ask you," Alex said, her color returning to normal.

"Oh yeah! I almost forgot," Bailey added. "Do you know anything about ear tags?"

"Sure. What about them?" Brian sat up straighter.

"What do the numbers mean?" Bailey asked.

"Each farm is given an identification number by the Department of Agriculture. They require that every sheep be given a premise identification ear tag before leaving the farm where it was born. They call it their premise ID. That number goes on one side of the tag." Brian looked from girl to girl. "Care to guess what the number on the other side of the tag is?"

"The sheep's number!" Alex yelled.

Brian pointed at her. "You got it!" He leaned over to Bailey and muttered loud enough for Alex to hear, "I knew she was a smart one."

Bailey laughed.

"Each sheep is given a number when it's purchased," Brian explained. "Often the first number shows the animal's birth year, and the rest of the number is sequential. That number goes on the other side of the tag."

"Do the colors of the tags mean anything?" Alex asked.

"They can, but that's up to the farmer. He may color code them according to age, breed types, or owners."

"So a yellow tag may mean something different depending on the farm?" Bailey asked.

"Exactly. Why do you ask?"

"I found an ear tag in the creek before we were charged by Fang."

"Well, let's see it! Maybe I can tell you whose it is!" Brian said, stretching out his hand.

"I can't. It fell out of my pocket when we were running away from the dog." Alex's voice sounded disappointed.

"No way!" Brian said, a smile tugging the corners of his mouth.

Bailey nodded.

"But we think we remember the numbers," Alex said, her voice hopeful. "I think one side was 'forty-six'—or 'sixty-four.' "

"And the other side said 'five-one-two-nine,' but not necessarily in that order," Bailey added.

"I think I can help you," Brian said, jumping up from the beanbag. "I'll be right back."

CHAPTER 10

The List of Clues

Brian rushed out the door before Bailey and Alex could speak.

The girls looked at each other. Bailey shrugged and said, "I guess he has an idea."

Alex laughed. "Obviously!"

Brian flew back in minutes later, Uncle Nathan's ledger tucked under his arm. He closed the door behind him and flopped onto the beanbag. "I remember seeing a chart of farms and their IDs listed in here." Brian flipped through the pages. "Ah! Here it is."

He ran his finger down a column, all the while mumbling, "Forty-six. . .forty-six." His finger stopped on the second page, and he looked up with a grin.

"Well, did you find it?" Bailey asked.

"Yep, I've got it right here." His fingers tapped the open page.

"So which farm is it?" Alex urged. She craned her neck, trying to get a look at the book.

"What'll you give me for telling you?" Brian teased.

"I'll give you another day to live! Now tell us which farm it is!" Bailey snapped.

Brian laughed. "You're so fun to mess with. All right. I'll tell you. It's Hazelwood Farms."

"That's what we figured." Alex slumped against the foot of the bed. "We're pretty sure that's the name of the farm on the other side of the creek where those terrible men live."

"Then why were you so cranked up to find out?"

"We just wanted to be sure, that's all." Bailey sighed.

"Anything else you want to know before I put the book back?"

"Does it say anything else about how they identify their sheep?"

Alex asked.

"What do you mean?" Brian's forehead wrinkled.

"Like, do they only use ear tags, or do they use other things?"

"Hmm. I'll look." Brian thumbed through a few pages and then stopped. "It says they sometimes use paint sticks to temporarily mark sheep before selling them."

"Paint sticks? That's it!" Bailey jumped up from the bed.

"That's what?" Brian asked.

"I bet that's what the words on the lambs were written with!" Bailey reached down and gave Alex's raised hand a high five.

"You're probably right." Brian nodded. "Permanent markers probably wouldn't be good for the sheep."

"But paint sticks wouldn't hurt them?" Alex asked.

"No. They're specially made to be nontoxic."

"How long does it last?" Bailey wondered.

"Usually several months," Brian replied.

"Over six months?" Bailey pressed, knowing the sheep were only sheared that often.

"Yeah. Often a farmer will paint-brand their ewes when they're pregnant and then give the same number to their babies once they're born and until they're given their own number. It makes it easier to match the mothers and babies."

"Why didn't you tell us about paint-branding before?" Bailey asked. "We were trying to sniff those marked sheep to see if they smelled like permanent marker!"

Brian laughed. "You *would* do something crazy like that." He shrugged. "I don't know. I guess I just didn't think about it."

"That brings us one step closer to solving this mystery," Alex said.

"Speaking of clues to the mystery," Bailey said, "do you want to see the sign we got at the flea market today?"

"Sure," Brian said.

Bailey unwrapped it and showed the sign to her cousin.

"Sweet!" Brian took the sign in his hands. He studied the words carved into the front and then turned it over. "Hey, look at this. The carver's initials."

"Huh?" Bailey was at Brian's side in an instant. Alex flanked his other side.

"See? 'M.G.' " Brian pointed at small letters in the lower left corner.

"Marshall Gonzalez!" Bailey whooped.

"Could be," Alex agreed.

"Why would you automatically think it was Marshall Gonzalez?" Brian looked wary. "Could be Matthew Gardner or Mike Green."

"I guess you're right," Alex conceded. "We just have Marshall on the brain."

"We have to solve this mystery in two days, so we need to stay focused," Bailey reminded her cousin.

Brian nodded. "Well, you're certainly doing that."

"We need to research Brindle Branch Farm," Bailey said.

"I'll Google it." Alex set her computer in her lap.

"It's as good a place to start as any." Bailey stretched out on her stomach, her head at the foot of the bed, to look over Alex's shoulder.

Five entries came up. Alex clicked on the first one. Up popped an article about adopting brindle greyhound dogs. She quickly clicked out and went to the next one. *Brindle Branch Farm, located in Peoria, Illinois. . .*

"Alex! That's it!" Bailey squealed.

"Read it out loud," Brian said from the pink beanbag.

Alex cleared her throat. "Brindle Branch Farm, located in Peoria, Illinois, is a historic sheep farm once known for its high-quality wool production. It stopped wool operation in 2000, but its old house and farm buildings still stand. In 2002 the farm's name was changed to Hazelwood Sheep Farms."

"So Brindle Branch Farm is Hazelwood Sheep Farms, just as we suspected!" Bailey gave a victorious fist pump.

"Okay. Let's review what we know so far. Maybe it will help us connect the dots." Alex pulled out her notebook that listed the facts and clues they had accumulated. "First, Marshall Gonzalez disappeared seven years ago, and his relatives want him declared legally dead so they can claim his fortune."

"Two," Bailey piped in, reading over Alex's shoulder from the bed, "Marshall was a recluse. He didn't have many friends or close relatives."

"Three," Alex resumed, "investigators never found a body, so Marshall could be alive. Four, he lived around here somewhere and started sheep farming before his disappearance."

"Correction." Bailey cleared her throat. "Uncle Nathan said he *supposedly* mentioned going into sheep farming and even attended a sheep expo, but we don't know for sure if he started up a sheep farm."

"Point taken." Alex erased part of point four and wrote in the correction.

Bailey continued reading aloud. "Five, Marshall shut down his Peoria house and released all workers except for a caretaker. Six, three men and a mean dog live in that ramshackle house across the creek. We call them Yeller, Dude, Rude, and Fang. Dude and Rude try to keep Yeller from being seen or heard."

"Seven," Alex read on, "Yeller tried to get our attention. He was even ready to climb the tree outside our window at night."

"What?" Brian bolted upright, his eyes flashing.

Alex frowned at Bailey. "Oops."

"He climbed the tree outside your bedroom window?" Brian pressed.

Bailey's head drooped. "Only once. He fell out and limped away."

"Good! Maybe that will teach him not to slink around girls' bedroom windows! Why didn't you tell me or Dad?"

"Because we were afraid you'd make us stop investigating!" Bailey finally met Brian's eyes.

"You got that right! This could be some weirdo who could hurt you!" Brian stood and paced the room like a caged tiger.

"But he isn't!" Bailey wailed. "He just wants to tell us something. Something important!"

"How do you know?"

"Because the first time we saw him he waved at us and yelled. He was trying to get our attention."

"Yeah, then the other two hauled him back to the house." Alex nodded.

"And these are the same guys whose dog attacked Shy, and they didn't help you? They sound like real charmers to me." Brian rolled his eyes.

"Yeller tried to help, but the other guy wouldn't let him," Bailey said.

"It's true," Alex added. "The other guy pulled him into the barn."

Brian raked his hand through his dark curls. "We need to tell my dad."

"Brian, it's history! Over!" Bailey stood and planted herself in his face, her hands on her hips.

"You don't know that." Brian took a deep breath and let it out slowly. "He could come back tonight for all you know."

"But I honestly don't think he's trying to hurt us. He would have already come back and tried. After all, that happened on Monday, and it's Friday now. He just wants to tell us something." Bailey sat back down.

Brian looked at Alex. "Do you agree?"

Alex nodded. "I thought we should tell at first. But now I don't think Yeller would hurt us. Like Bailey said, he's had all week to try again. The other guys might be dangerous, but not Yeller."

"I think he needs help," Bailey said.

Brian kept pacing, his eyebrows forming a V. Bailey watched him until he stopped in front of them.

"I'll make you a deal," he said. "You promise to call me on my cell phone the second anything *potentially* happens with these guys. Even if they look at you cross-eyed! And I won't tell Dad."

Alex quietly nodded. Bailey sighed with relief. "I promise, Brian." She wrapped her arms around his waist, laying her head on his chest. "Thanks."

Brian patted Bailey on the back. "Now, where were you on that list of clues?" he said.

Alex laughed. "Let's see, I think we were on number eight." She looked to the notebook. "Yes. Eight. We have three messages written on lambs. Together they read, 'Help Gonzo held captive Brindle Branch.' Number nine, Kate dug up that Gonzalez was from Sinoloa, Mexico. He's the son of a poor shrimp fisherman, but his grandpa was a rich sugar cane farmer. Grandpa left Gonzalez his fortune when he died. So jealousy could be a motive for his relatives wanting him declared dead."

"Number ten," Bailey jumped in. "Woolly Creek behind the Curly Q used to be called Brindle Creek. The name was changed twenty years ago."

"Eleven," Alex said. "Curly Q sheep were bought at auctions from three farms: Hazelwood Sheep Farms, Hollyhock Acres, and White-stone Ranch. Hazelwood is the closest, just across the creek. Twelve, the kidnapping may have been done by someone Gonzalez knew. The kidnapper would have to care for Gonzo's sheep, and they only follow their own shepherd's voice. Thirteen, I found an ear tag with the number forty-six on one side and five-one-two-nine on the other."

"Fourteen," Bailey said. "There are sick sheep living in the pasture behind the house. They're not being cared for properly."

"Fifteen," Alex stated. "The man at the sheep pasture said his name is Gonzo, but he doesn't look like the newspaper photo of Marshall Gonzalez. He's taller and thinner."

"And dirtier!" Bailey added with a laugh. "Sixteen. Brindle Branch Farm was a sheep farm. The sign that bears its name was carved by someone with the initials M.G."

"Seventeen," Alex said. "Brindle Branch Farm was probably located on Brindle Creek, which is now Woolly Creek."

"Last but not least, number forty-six from the ear tag Alex found belongs to Hazelwood Sheep Farms, which used to be called Brindle Branch Farm. They probably use paint sticks to temporarily brand their sheep when new babies are born.

"And," Bailey added, "those paint sticks might be what the messages on the lambs were written with."

"Wow." Brian shook his head appreciatively. "You guys have dug up a lot of information in only a few days."

"We had to! We only have a few days to figure this whole thing out!"

"Wait a minute!" Alex's eyes blazed. "We missed an obvious step!"

Bailey's forehead creased. "We did? What?"

"The ear tags! We know Hazelwood Farms' ID is forty-six. Now we need to see if the lambs with the messages have the same ID!"

Bailey clapped her hands. "You're right! How could we have missed that?"

"Good thing we reviewed our notebook. It really did help us connect some ideas!"

"So what are we waiting for?" Brian asked. "Let's go check some ear tags."

All three were out the door in the shake of a lamb's tail. They ran into Aunt Darcy in the kitchen.

"Supper will be ready soon. Don't go too far."

"We won't," Brian answered. "We're just going out to see some of the lambs." He winked at the girls.

The three ran across the yard to the pasture, slowing as they approached so as not to scare the sheep. Shy limped along in the chase. Opening the gate, they pushed their way through the flock. Bow nuzzled their hands for some attention.

Bailey absently stroked the lamb's head. "I don't see them." Her head turned to look first one way, then another.

"Me neither," Brian said.

"They've got to be here somewhere," Alex encouraged. "We just need to keep looking."

They split up, and each took a section to search, but they couldn't find the marked sheep.

"Where could they be?" Bailey asked.

Brian looked stricken.

"Brian, what is it?" Bailey eyed her cousin.

"Sometimes Dad separates the animals that are going to be sold."

"Sold? He can't sell those lambs! It would be like selling Charlotte in *Charlotte's Web!*" Alex wailed.

"Yeah, they're communicating with us just like she did in her spider-web," Bailey agreed.

"I remember hearing Dad say some men were coming this after-noon to look over some of our young sheep. Some of them might be the ones with the weird markings."

"Now we'll never find out which ranch the sheep came from!" Bailey felt like throwing herself on the ground. Disappointment curled through her like a giant wave from her stomach to her eyes, threatening tears. She took a deep breath and let it back out.

"I didn't say they'd been sold already, but he may have separated them from the others," Brian said gently.

"So where are they?" Bailey demanded.

"Could be a number of places—in a different pasture, in the barn, or maybe at another farm already."

"We've got to find them." Bailey looked around. "Which place should we check first?"

"The barn's the closest. Let's go there," Alex suggested.

Without a word, they worked back through the flock of milling sheep and out the gate to the barn. Shy trotted with them, happy and uncon-cerned. Bow baaed her dismay when they walked away. Bailey knew before they ever set foot in the barn that the lambs weren't there. It was too quiet. But the trio walked through the building checking each stall.

"Maybe they're just sleeping in a pen somewhere," Alex said hopefully.

"They're not here," Bailey said.

"Where do we look next, Brian?" Alex asked.

"The other pasture," Brian said. "But it's too far to go to before supper."

"It'll be getting dark after that!" Bailey moaned.

"If they're in the far pasture, they'll still be there in the morning," Brian said matter-of-factly. "And if they're not, we probably won't find them anyway."

Bailey thought she might cry but bit her lip hard to hold back the tears. Their best clue. Gone!

CHAPTER 11

The Lost Sheep

Bailey and Alex trudged back to the house while Brian secured the gates and made sure everything was closed tight.

"Those marked lambs were our best clue!" Frustration filled Bailey's voice.

"I know," Alex said. "It seems the odds are against us solving this mystery. But we have lots of other clues to work with. And we have pictures of the lambs' messages."

"Yeah, I guess. I just hope if the police get involved, they won't think we marked the sheep ourselves and then took pictures of our funny little joke. We have absolutely no proof."

"We didn't have proof even when we had the sheep."

They entered the kitchen, slamming the screen door behind them.

"Supper's ready as soon as you wash up," called Aunt Darcy, carrying a steaming casserole to the table and setting it on a trivet.

Bailey and Alex shared the bathroom sink as they washed their hands. "We'll have to ask Uncle Nathan about the lambs," Bailey suggested as she handed the towel to Alex.

"Just don't give away the investigation in the process," Alex warned.

Brian came in just as they returned to the kitchen. Bailey threw him a questioning look, but he shook his head on his way to wash up.

They all sat down, and Uncle Nathan asked God to bless the food.

"What is it?" Brian asked his mom as he lifted the casserole lid.

"Tuna casserole with peas." She uncovered a plate of warm, freshly made whole wheat bread and passed it to Bailey, along with the tub of butter.

"Mmm! This bread smells delicious!" Bailey gushed. She quickly spread a heap of butter on a slice and bit into it.

"How was your afternoon?" Uncle Nathan asked the girls. "I assume you didn't get chased by a dog."

Bailey laughed as she finished chewing the bread in her mouth. "No, nothing that exciting this afternoon."

"I can't believe all that happened only this morning." Alex shook her head, eyes wide. "Seems like days ago!"

"Time flies when you're having fun." Brian flashed a smile at Alex.

She quickly looked away, red creeping into her face.

"Uncle Nathan, did you move some lambs today?" Bailey tried to sound casual in her question, casting a glance at Alex.

"A few. They showed signs of getting hoof rot, so I had to quarantine them from the rest of the flock."

"Hoof rot?" Bailey passed the butter on to Alex.

"It's a fungal infection of the hoof that can lead to lameness if it isn't treated."

"How do they get it?" Alex asked.

"It usually happens when sheep spend long hours on wet grounds. That's why it's important to keep their bedding clean and dry."

"But we do that," Brian said and took a bite. After swallowing, he added, "We take good care of our sheep."

"Of course we do, but these are some sheep we bought at the last auction. They may have been infected before they came to us and just didn't show the symptoms until now."

Bailey kicked Alex. Alex jumped at the sharp jab and shot Bailey a dirty look. Bailey opened her eyes as wide as possible as if to give her friend a clue that she had an idea. Alex nodded. They'd talk later.

"We've had sheep with hoof rot before," Aunt Darcy said.

"Will they get better?" Bailey's voice came out high, registering her concern and her tender heart.

"Oh yes," Uncle Nathan assured her. "We'll soak their feet in Epsom salts and put medicine on them. And keep their bedding extra clean and dry until they are ready to join the rest of the flock again."

"So where are the lambs now?" Brian asked. "We didn't see any in the barn."

"They're isolated in the old henhouse." Uncle Nathan spooned a mountain of casserole on his plate and dusted it with pepper.

Bailey looked at Brian and Alex. All three raised their eyebrows and exchanged smiles.

In their room that night, Alex checked her email while Bailey got ready for bed. "Here's something from Sydney. I'll read it out loud."

"Hi, Bailey and Alex! I found out Gonzo's grandpa, Pedro, disowned Gonzo's dad, Jaime, when he was a rebellious teenager. However, when Pedro learned he had a grandson, he started a relationship with him against Jaime's wishes, continuing their bad relationship. Pedro eventually cut his son completely out of his will and put Gonzo in instead."

Alex looked wide-eyed at Bailey. "Sounds like that could be the motive in our mystery."

"Yes!" Bailey then shared the idea that prompted the kick under the table. "Remember those sheep we saw at Hazelwood Farms?"

"Yeah, they smelled worse than Uncle Nathan's sheep!"

"But remember how sick they seemed? Some could barely walk!"

"Yeah, I remember." Alex looked blankly at Bailey.

"I bet they had hoof rot, and the sheep with the messages came from that flock."

Alex's eyes lit up like twin candles. "You're a genius!" She grabbed Bailey's hands, and they danced around the room in their pajamas. They finally collapsed on the floor in laughter.

"But wait a minute," Alex said breathlessly. "The message said Gonzo was being held captive at Brindle Branch."

"Yeah. . ."

"But we met Gonzo at Hazelwood. It's the wrong farm, and he didn't seem like he was being held against his will anyway."

Bailey's eyebrows came together. "Hmm. You're right." She paused. "I don't have an answer to that right now, and I'm too tired to think it through." Bailey yawned and stretched. "How 'bout if we sleep on it, and maybe something will come to us tomorrow."

"Okay." Alex flipped off the light. "We also need to take a walk down the creek to see if we can learn any more about Brindle Branch Farm."

"And I need to spend extra time shearing to get my time down. It'll be my last day to practice before the big competition. Looks like we have a busy day ahead of us." Bailey yawned again. She heard Alex breathe heavy, no doubt counting sheep.

—•—•—

Friday morning dawned bright and warmer. After a quick breakfast, Bailey and Alex hurried to the barn to start shearing. Alex timed Bailey partway through their morning's work and found she had trimmed off another minute.

"Still not enough to win tomorrow's contest." Bailey's forehead wrinkled.

"Just keep at it. We'll time you again at the end of the morning." Alex smiled and gave Bailey an encouraging pat on the back. "I just *know* you can do this."

Before long, Bailey was guiding her last sheep to the shearing station. She waved Alex down. "Will you time me once more? I'm on my last sheep."

"Sure." Alex set her shears down and came to Bailey's station. "Let me know when you're ready." Alex's finger was poised to push the stopwatch button at Bailey's word. "Remember—just pretend you're uncovering another message on the sheep."

"All right. Ready!" Bailey said.

Alex started the stopwatch, and the shearing began. Fleece fell to the clean barn floor in thick, curly bunches.

Minutes later, Bailey called, "Done!"

Alex punched the button on the stopwatch and checked the time. "Thirteen minutes, thirty-nine seconds. Bailey, you dropped almost two minutes today!"

"Yeah, but it still isn't enough to beat last year's record of twelve minutes, twenty seconds. I'm out of days to practice."

"I still think you have a chance to win. Every time you shear you get faster. When you compete, I bet you'll have your fastest time ever."

"I hope so." Bailey looked to Alex's workstation. "Are you finished with your lambs?"

"I only have two more; then I'm done."

"I'll take one and you do the other. Then we'll be through," Bailey offered. "That will give me a little more practice, and we can get to our detective work sooner."

"Sounds good to me."

After the last lambs were sheared, Bailey asked, "What should we do first?"

"Let's peek at the lambs in the henhouse."

"I'm glad we still have a chance to check their ear tags." Bailey started toward the building the hens had once occupied.

"Me too!"

Bailey and Alex ran toward the henhouse. They heard the lambs bleating. Bailey pulled the weathered door open and stepped into the shadowy building. Sun poured through glassless windows and spaces between the old wooden wall slats, striping the henhouse in light. A rotten stink permeated the air.

The lambs weren't penned up. They roamed freely in the building, though there wasn't much room. Most limped, their hooves infected.

"Here you are!" Bailey said as she moved closer to the lambs. Then she stopped short. "Alex!"

Alex was just entering through the door.

"It's not them!"

"What?"

"These aren't the lambs with the messages!"

Alex joined Bailey, and the two looked closely at each sheep. No messages adorned any of them.

"Where could they be?" Alex bit the cuticle on her thumb.

"We need Brian to show us where that other pasture is he told us about yesterday."

"What if they're not there either?"

"Then we need to tell Uncle Nathan that someone stole his sheep." Bailey looked at her watch. "Brian won't be done shearing for another couple of hours. In the meantime, maybe we should take that walk down the creek to see if we can learn anything about Brindle Branch Farm."

"We promised Uncle Nathan we'd stay on this side of the creek."

"There are farms on this side of it too. We might be able to talk to some of those neighbors." Bailey pulled out her lip balm and smeared on a generous layer.

"Good point," Alex said. "Let's go."

At the first farmhouse they reached, a slender woman wearing blue capris and a floral, button-down sleeveless shirt was weeding a strawberry bed.

"Excuse me," Bailey called.

The woman looked up from her plants. "Yes?"

"I'm Bailey Chang, and this is my friend Alexis. We're visiting my uncle Nathan who lives just across the pasture."

"Oh yes," the woman replied. "We know Nathan. It's a pleasure to meet you, Bailey." She extended a hand to each of the girls, one at a time.

"And you too, Alexis. I'm Trudy Myers."

"We're doing a bit of research about the area and wondered if you could help us fill in some gaps." Bailey pulled out her notepad.

"I'd be glad to help if I can," Ms. Myers said.

"We found out the name of this creek used to be Brindle Creek," Alex informed her. "But we found an old sign at the flea market that said Brindle Branch Farm, and now we're curious about that."

"Brindle Branch Farm?" Ms. Myers pulled another weed. "Yes, I've heard of that."

"You have?" Bailey felt like hugging the woman.

"I haven't lived here so many years that I can say I *remember* it, but I do recall hearing people talk of it."

"What did they say?" Alex asked.

"Not much, just that the men who lived there weren't nice. Didn't take care of their farm, I guess."

"Anything else?" Bailey asked.

"No, not that I can think of."

"About those men," Alex questioned. "Do you know their names or how many of them there were?"

"Heavens! I haven't the foggiest notion of their names, but I think I heard there were two men." Ms. Myers eyed Bailey and Alex and smiled. "What are you girls up to anyway?"

"Just research, that's all," Bailey answered. "Do you know where their farm was?"

"Sorry, no," Ms. Myers said.

"Thanks for your help," Alex said.

"Yeah, we've learned a lot already!" Bailey flipped her notepad closed.

"Anytime," Ms. Myers answered, bending over to pull another handful of weeds. "Good luck!"

Bailey and Alex went on to the next farm, where an elderly man was scattering grain for his chickens.

"Hello!" Bailey greeted him with a smile and wave.

The man looked up from his chores. "Hello yourself!" His wrinkled face crinkled in a crooked grin. Gray hair poked out on all sides beneath his straw hat. "What can I do ya for?"

Above the clucking of the chickens, Bailey introduced herself and Alex. Then she told him they were doing research of the area.

"Research, huh? Sounds important! Oh, by the way, the name's Don."

The girls shook his leathery hand.

"Now let's hear more about this research you're doin'."

"We're trying to learn about a place called Brindle Branch Farm. We found a sign at the flea market with that name carved in it." Alex kept a close eye on the speckled hens pecking and scratching the ground around her. A huge red rooster eyed them from a distance.

Don rubbed his gray, whiskery chin. "Brindle Branch Farm. . .yes, I remember that. Its name changed a few years back."

"It did?" Bailey's neck jutted forward, and her eyes popped.

"Yes, ma'am. Changed ownership about the same time too." Don tossed another handful of grain from the cloth bag hanging over his shoulder, and the chickens ran to peck it up, clucking away.

"What did the name change to?" Alex asked.

"One of those new flavors of coffee creamers, as I remember."

"Huh?" Bailey wondered if the man was a taco short of a combo plate.

"You know—Irish cream, French vanilla, hazelnut, something like that."

"Hazelwood maybe?" Alex asked, her eyes gleaming.

"Hazelwood! That's it!" Don clapped his hand against his lean thigh. "It's just over there on the other side of the creek." He pointed a crooked finger in the direction of Yeller, Dude, and Rude's house.

"Did you ever meet the owners?" Bailey asked.

"Knew the first owners." Don's eyes dulled and his voice grew husky. "Good people."

"I'm sorry," Alex said softly.

"How about the new owners?" Bailey gently pushed. "Do you know them too?"

"Tried to, but they keep to themselves. They let the place go to pot."

Alex twirled a curl around her finger. "We heard that only men live there. No wife or children."

"True enough," Don agreed. "Just three men who don't care two hoots about taking care of their property or their animals."

"Three men?" Bailey asked. "You sure about that?"

"Sure as my name's Don Jeffers! There are three men, but two of them do most of the work, what little work they do. The other one stays pretty much out of sight. The two told me once that their brother isn't right in the head. They said I shouldn't pay any attention if he hollers or waves his arms around. Said he's kind of crazy."

Bailey nodded. "We can't thank you enough for the information. You've been a great help to our research."

"My pleasure," Don said. "You come on back anytime."

Bailey and Alex walked back toward the creek. "Incredible!" Bailey said as soon as they were out of Don's earshot.

"No kidding!" Alex turned a cartwheel on the soft, cool grass. "Hazelwood and Brindle Branch are the same place!"

"That's weird what he said about the third guy. Do you really think he's their brother? Or that he has all those problems they say he has?"

"Who knows?" Alex pushed her curly hair behind her ears. "Guess it could be a family business, but they don't seem very friendly like brothers should."

Bailey checked the time. "It's still a little early, but Brian may be almost done with his shearing. Let's start back home."

The girls turned back the way they'd come, chatting as they walked. Soon they were across the creek from the pasture of sick sheep they'd seen yesterday.

"There are those poor sheep again." Alex plugged her nose.

"Wait a minute!" Bailey stopped and squinted her eyes as she stared at them.

"What?"

"I think some of those sheep have writing on them!"

The Mystery at Hazelwood

"See? Look at that little one in the corner." Bailey leaned in and pointed so Alex's eye could follow her finger.

"Yeah! I'm sure those are our sheep!"

Bailey chewed her lower lip. "What should we do?"

"Tell Uncle Nathan someone's stolen some of his lambs."

Bailey stood silent for a moment. Finally, she nodded. "I guess we'll have to. I don't know what else to do."

Both girls were surprised when Bailey's phone rang.

"Hello? Oh, hi, Kate. . . . You did?"

Alex put her ear close to the phone.

"Hang on, Kate. I'm going to put you on speaker." Bailey pressed the button. "Okay, go."

"I found out how someone could be held captive so long," Kate repeated. "Especially if he's allowed outside, as apparently Yeller is."

"Great!" Alex said. "What's the secret?"

"They could have Yeller hooked up with a house arrest bracelet that tells them if he leaves the property."

"How's it work?" Bailey asked.

"It's equipped with a GPS system that shows the person's location on a monitor."

"Impressive," Alex said.

"But wouldn't they have known if Yeller was off the property?" Bailey asked.

"They should have seen it on the monitor," Kate confirmed. "And an alarm is supposed to sound when a breach occurs."

"Something doesn't add up." Alex picked a hangnail from her finger. "Anything else we should know?"

"That's about it."

"Good work, Kate." Bailey wished she could hug her friend. "Thanks."

"No problem-o," Kate said.

"Give Biscuit a scratch behind the ears for me," Alex said.

Kate squealed. "Biscuit! Get down! I think he heard that. He's trying to lick the phone!"

The girls laughed and updated her on the stolen lambs.

"Unbelievable!"

"We're on our way home to tell Uncle Nathan now." Bailey's shoulders slumped.

"Good luck," Kate said. "I'll be praying for you!"

At home, Uncle Nathan strolled from the barn toward the house.

"Uncle Nathan!" Bailey called.

Her uncle stopped and turned. "What's up?"

"We need to talk to you about some of your lambs."

"I'm all ears," he said.

"We think some have been stolen." Bailey watched her uncle closely.

He screwed up his face. "Stolen? Why do you think that?"

"Because some of the lambs we sheared had messages written on them, and now they're gone!" Alex spilled.

"At first we thought they were the ones you separated because of hoof rot, but they weren't," Bailey explained.

"And we saw some marked sheep at the ranch across the creek that looked just like the ones we sheared," Alex added.

"We didn't go over there!" Bailey assured him. "We saw them from *our* side of the creek."

Uncle Nathan held up his hand. "Whoa!" he said. "Back up. Messages on sheep?"

"Yeah," Bailey answered.

"What kind of messages?"

"They said, 'Help Gonzo held captive Brindle Branch.'" Bailey grinned. It felt good to finally tell an adult what they'd uncovered.

"Anyone else know about this?" Uncle Nathan asked.

"Only Brian," Bailey answered.

"And the Camp Club Girls," Alex added.

Uncle Nathan's eyebrows raised in question.

"They're our friends from camp who help us solve mysteries," Bailey said.

"And you have a mystery to solve?" Uncle Nathan prodded.

"We think so." Bailey shrugged. "Why else would there be messages on sheep?"

"Good point." Uncle Nathan exhaled. "So you think the neighbors stole the sheep with the messages."

"Right." Bailey nodded.

Uncle Nathan looked toward the neighbors' ranch. "Can you show me?"

"Sure!" Alex's eyes sparkled. "You'll need binoculars if you want a good look."

Uncle Nathan went inside, returning with a pair of binoculars around his neck. "All set. Lead the way."

Bailey and Alex took off toward the dilapidated house. When they got to the creek, they walked along its bank a short distance and then pointed to the pasture on the other side.

"See?" Bailey said. "They're over there behind the fence."

Uncle Nathan looked through the binoculars.

"Do you see some young sheep with strange black markings?" Bailey asked.

"Sure do," he answered. "My binoculars aren't strong enough to read the ear tag though."

"May I look?" Bailey reached out her hand.

Uncle Nathan took the binoculars from around his neck and handed them to her.

Bailey scanned the pasture, looking for the marked sheep. "There's one!" she announced.

"Which one is it?" Alex asked.

"Brindle Branch."

Alex nodded. "Yep. Those are your sheep, Uncle Nathan."

"How many had messages?" he asked.

"Three. I bet they stole all three so no one would see their messages." Bailey kicked a rock into the creek.

"All right, girls." Uncle Nathan hung the binoculars back around his neck. "Let's go call the sheriff."

Twenty minutes later, two deputies came to the house. "I'm Officer Cahill," said the dark-haired one, "and this is my partner, Officer Hamilton."

"Come in," Uncle Nathan said. He introduced Bailey and Alex. "They're the ones who brought this to my attention. They spotted the sheep from across the creek. Here, have a seat." Uncle Nathan waved his hand toward the living room. The officers settled into the easy chairs across from the couch where Bailey and Alex sat. Uncle Nathan grabbed a kitchen chair for himself.

"Tell us what you saw." Officer Cahill spoke gently to the girls and listened attentively.

"Wait a minute," he interrupted their story. "You say these sheep had messages written on them?"

"Yes, sir." Bailey nodded solemnly.

"What did they say?"

Alex told him and explained how the message was spread between three sheep.

"Interesting." Officer Cahill rubbed his chin.

Bailey looked at Alex with questioning eyes and received a nod of approval.

"Sir, there's more."

"More?" the officer asked.

"We think we may have figured out the Marshall Gonzalez case."

"What?" Uncle Nathan jumped up as if he'd sat on a tack. "I'm sorry, officers. I don't know anything about this."

"Tell me what you know." Officer Hamilton knelt so he was eye-to-eye with Bailey sitting on the couch.

Bailey licked her lips and looked around nervously.

"It's all right. Don't be afraid."

Bailey and Alex told them everything—from the marked sheep, to the nighttime visit from Yeller, to discovering the original names of the ranch and creek.

Officer Cahill took notes furiously as the girls spoke. When they finally slowed down, so did his pen. He looked at his partner with a grin and a nod.

"I am very impressed with your detective work, girls," Officer Hamilton said. "We'll check this out and get back to you."

"Will you go to Hazelwood Ranch?" Bailey asked.

"Yes, we'll pay them a visit. Hopefully, they'll cooperate and you'll have your sheep back within a few hours. But it may take us longer to piece together all you've told us about the Marshall Gonzalez case."

"Don't take too long getting back to us!" Bailey blurted. "We have to leave tomorrow evening!"

Officer Cahill laughed. "We'll try to work fast!"

After dinner the policemen were back at their door.

"Mr. Chang?" Officer Cahill held a clipboard. "We have some sheep to deliver."

Uncle Nathan clapped his hands. "Hot dog!" he said. "So they *were* my sheep!"

"They were indeed. The ear tags showed your ID on them, so there wasn't much the thieves could say."

"Did you haul them off to jail?" Brian appeared over his dad's shoulder, excitement blazing in his eyes.

"They're being booked."

"What about the Gonzalez case?" Bailey asked.

"We're still working on that." Officer Cahill smiled at Bailey. "But we're pretty sure you're on to something."

Bailey and Alex grinned. Their hard work was paying off.

"I'll help you unload those sheep." Uncle Nathan followed the officer to a livestock trailer. The sun was setting, and the men worked quickly to get the lambs back into the pasture with their mothers. The ewes nuzzled their babies, and the lambs baaed their dismay at having been away.

"Alex, wake up! It's Saturday!"

Alex rolled over and rubbed her sleepy eyes. "Huh?"

"Wake up! Today's the sheep-shearing competition. And we'll find out about our investigation!"

Alex's feet hit the floor running. She jumped into her clothes and shoes. "I'm ready. Let's go!"

The aroma of bacon and eggs greeted the girls as they charged down the stairs.

"Good morning, sleepyheads!" Aunt Darcy called over her shoulder as she flipped the eggs.

"Mornin', Aunt Darcy!"

Uncle Nathan entered from outside. "Well, look who's up!" He planted a kiss on top of Bailey's head and ruffled Alex's hair. "Sleep good?"

Bailey and Alex both nodded.

"The police already called this morning," Aunt Darcy said. "They're on their way over."

"Now?" Bailey asked. "What'd they say?"

"Just that they'd talk to us when they get here." Aunt Darcy set a plate full of bacon on the table and slid a fried egg onto each plate. "So I suggest we eat fast."

Uncle Nathan blessed the food then passed the bacon to Alex. Aunt Darcy poured milk while Bailey and Alex ate their eggs. They'd started clearing the table when someone knocked. Uncle Nathan went to answer it.

"Good morning, Officer Cahill, Officer Hamilton." Uncle Nathan waved them inside. A third, shorter man appeared from behind the two policemen.

"Mr. Chang, it gives me great pleasure to introduce to you Marshall Gonzalez."

"Wha—*The* Marshall Gonzalez?" Uncle Nathan stammered.

"Marshall Gonzalez?" Bailey pushed past Uncle Nathan, with Alex behind her. A cleaned-up Yeller stood before them, grinning from ear to ear. "Yeller!"

"Yeller?" Officer Cahill looked from Gonzo to Bailey.

"That's just the nickname Bailey gave him 'cause he yelled to us the first time we saw him," Alex explained.

"Come in, come in," Aunt Darcy said, her manners edging out her astonishment. She bustled past her husband and pulled the men inside. "Have a seat. I'll make some fresh coffee."

"But that other guy told us *he* was Gonzo!" Bailey cried.

"He confessed to that lie," Officer Hamilton said. "Said he was trying to confuse you about Marshall's identity in case you were nosing around and knew anything."

Alex laughed. "He doesn't know us very well, does he, Bailey?"

"We'd never quit that easily!" Bailey giggled. "So if you're the real Gonzo, the other two men must have been your captors, as we suspected."

Gonzo nodded. "They were hired by my own father who wanted my money. They kidnapped me and made me wear that house arrest bracelet for seven years! That's why I don't look much like that newspaper photo. I'm thinner and older now."

"Why did you only try to contact the girls?" Suspicion tinged Uncle Nathan's voice. "Why didn't you try to tell an adult?"

"My kidnappers told everyone I was their crazy brother and not to pay any attention to what I said or did." Marshall's head drooped. "When I saw these girls, I thought maybe they'd believe me since they were new around here and probably hadn't heard about the crazy brother."

Uncle Nathan nodded. "I do remember hearing the gossip about you, now that I think back. Guess I just took it for truth."

Bailey cocked her head. "But if you wore a house arrest bracelet, how did you sneak out that night you came over here?"

"My captors drank so much alcohol they passed out." Marshall looked at Bailey, his eyes serious. "That's when I came over here. I'm sorry if I scared you. I was desperate for someone to know I wasn't dead!"

"But when they woke up, didn't their monitor show you'd been gone?" Alex's eyebrows furrowed.

"Yep. They woke up while I was gone and came looking for me. I heard them yell at me while I was up in your tree. When I turned to look, I lost my balance and fell."

Brian stumbled into the kitchen bleary-eyed. He looked more confused than ever as he saw the strangers. The girls brought him up to speed on what was going on.

"So you wrote those messages on the sheep with a paint stick?" Brian asked.

"I did," Gonzo replied rather proudly.

"So what's next for you, Marshall?" Uncle Nathan asked.

"Well, thanks to these gals, my relatives will not get my fortune!" He looked with gratitude at Bailey and Alex. "I feel the whole world has opened up to me. I used to be an unhappy, lonely man. But after what I've been through, I'd like a chance to start over right here in Peoria. I hope to fix up my ranch and be the good shepherd my sheep deserve."

"Looks like *the* Good Shepherd watched out for you in spite of all your troubles," Bailey said softly.

"Indeed He has," Marshall replied. "I hope to get to know Him better in the future."

"We'd better let these good people get on with their day." Officer Cahill stood to leave. "We knew the girls would be anxious to find out how their super sleuthing turned out. You did a great job figuring out this mystery, girls. We owe you a hearty thanks."

"You don't need to thank us. We love sleuthing!" Alex beamed at the officer.

"We're just glad Mr. Gonzalez is safe again. Thanks for coming by so we could meet you." Bailey stuck out her hand for him to shake.

Gonzo took her hand and pulled her into a big hug. Tears welled in his eyes. "I can never thank you enough!"

While Uncle Nathan walked the officers and Gonzo to their car, Aunt Darcy picked up empty coffee cups and set them in the sink. She leaned against the counter, eyeing Bailey and Alex with a smile. "It's amazing what you girls accomplished in only six days."

When Uncle Nathan returned, he noticed the time. "Are you ready to go to the big shearing competition?"

"I almost forgot!" Bailey replied. "But I'm ready."

"Then let's load up!" her uncle said.

As they pulled up to the fairgrounds, the smells of popcorn and hot dogs filled the air. The hum of people, mingled with the baaing of sheep, made a chaotic, festive atmosphere.

They sat in the stands watching kids in Bailey's age group compete. The first, a nine-year-old girl like Bailey, worked slowly, with an ending time of twenty-two minutes, thirteen seconds. Then a ten-year-old boy gave it his best shot, finishing at twelve minutes, forty-three seconds.

Bailey felt a hand on her elbow. "Come on, it's almost your turn." Uncle Nathan helped her stand. Her legs suddenly felt like jelly. *What if I can't handle the sheep? Maybe I'll embarrass myself and Uncle Nathan too.*

Alex grabbed Bailey's hand. "I'll be here cheering and praying for you like mad. Your last practice time of twelve minutes, twenty seconds beats everyone we've seen so far!"

Bailey gave a weak smile. How would she ever be a famous actress if she let her nerves get to her like this? Inhaling deeply, she let out her breath slowly. "With God's help I'm going to beat all those times!"

"That's the spirit!" Aunt Darcy hugged Bailey. "Remember, we're proud of you no matter what!"

Bailey nodded and followed Uncle Nathan to the competitors' waiting area. By the time they reached it, only one girl was ahead of her. She had the fastest time yet at twelve minutes, five seconds.

"That's fifteen seconds faster than last year's winning time!" Bailey wailed.

Uncle Nathan squatted, took Bailey by the shoulders, and looked directly into her black-brown eyes. "Don't you worry about anybody's time but your own, you hear? Just do your best."

Bailey nodded and swallowed a lump in her throat. Her mouth turned to cotton. She put on another coat of lip balm.

"Bailey Chang!" the announcer called.

Uncle Nathan nudged Bailey toward the arena. Bailey had never felt so small. The crowd cheered, and a woolly sheep was brought to her. A timekeeper stood close by.

Bailey whispered a quick prayer then flipped on the shears. The timekeeper started the stopwatch. Bailey ran the shears up and down the lamb's body, and fleece fell like a soft blanket. She imagined a message appearing beneath the fallen wool and pretended Gonzo's life depended on her uncovering it quickly. Minutes later, she switched off the shears, and the timekeeper punched the stopwatch.

"Eleven minutes, seventeen seconds!" Raising Bailey's hand in the air, he announced, "A new record!"

Uncle Nathan ran to Bailey and scooped her into his arms. "Way to go, Bailey! You were awesome!"

"I didn't win yet, Uncle Nathan," Bailey cautioned. "There's still one more contestant."

"I know." Uncle Nathan let her slide back to the ground. "But I'm so proud of you."

Aunt Darcy raced toward them. "Bailey! I can't believe how fast you were!" She wrapped her in a bear hug and kissed her cheek.

"You were amazing!" Alex said.

"Hey, kid!" Brian sauntered up, cool as ever. "You were almost as good as me!"

"*If* you'd had the nerve to enter the competition!" Bailey teased.

"I didn't want to compete against you! Maybe I'll give it a try next year." Brian messed up Bailey's hair.

The group turned their attention to the last competitor as the announcer's voice echoed through the loudspeaker. "Last year's champion in the nine- to twelve-year-old group, Jackson Pruitt!"

The arena exploded with applause, and the crowd rose to their feet.

The announcer continued. "Jackson set a new record at twelve minutes, twenty seconds last year. Bailey Chang already broke that record today! Will Jackson be able to beat her time and keep his title?"

Jackson and his sheep took their places. The race was on! His arm flew, the shears buzzed, the fleece fell as silently as the crowd had become. Moments later, he turned off the shears.

"Eleven minutes, forty seconds! Bailey Chang is our new champion with her time of eleven minutes, seventeen seconds! Bailey Chang, come on out here!"

Uncle Nathan, Aunt Darcy, Brian, and Alex all walked into the arena with Bailey. The judge draped a "Shearing Master" sash across her shoulder and presented her with a huge trophy. Thunderous applause shook the stands.

Bailey looked around her. All this was for her? She quietly bowed her head. *Thank You, God. You did this for me.* When she raised her head, tears filled her eyes as Marshall Gonzalez came from the crowd and placed an enormous bouquet of yellow roses in her arms.

Gonzo was free and safe, she'd won the shearing competition, and she'd enjoyed a whole week with Alex. This spring break was more than she'd dreamed it would be!

Camp Club Girls:
Bailey and the
Santa Fe Secret

Strangers in a New Land

"What was that?"

Nine-year-old Bailey Chang jumped at the snort she heard behind her and twirled around.

Elizabeth Anderson, her fourteen-year-old friend from Amarillo, Texas, grabbed her hand. Sweat beaded on her pale forehead. "I don't know."

They inched toward a clump of dried bushes in the New Mexico desert. The pungent odor of livestock grew stronger as they approached the bushes. The hot August sun beat down on their sleeveless arms and necks, and a trickle of sweat rolled down Bailey's back.

"Smells like my grandma's farm!" Elizabeth held her nose.

Bailey covered her nose and mouth with her hand. "Maybe even *worse* than a farm." She saw the brown bush move. "Something's in there." Her slight frame trembled like a bowl of jelly.

Suddenly, with a squeal and a grunt, a bristly gray javelina charged stiff-legged at them from behind the bush and ran across the landscape. The girls screamed and bolted in the opposite direction, just as terrified as the wild pig. They didn't stop running until they got to Halona Tse's home, nearly a half-mile away. Halona was a distant cousin to Bailey and her mom.

"Whoa, what's the matter?" Halona said as they burst through the door.

Bailey, her mom, and Elizabeth had come to help Halona with her pottery shop just that morning, and the girls had gone out exploring the barren territory around her house. It was so different from Peoria, Illinois, where Bailey lived, or Amarillo, Texas, where Elizabeth lived.

"We came face to face with a fanged pig!" Wheezing, Bailey pulled her inhaler from her jeans pocket and breathed in the medicine to open her airway.

Halona laughed. "Sounds like you saw a javelina."

"He was so ugly." Elizabeth shuddered. "Gray and black bristly hair, little stiff legs, and an underbite like he needed braces!"

Bailey let out the breath she'd been holding since using her inhaler. "Yeah, he was a real beauty." She giggled. "But boy, could he move fast!"

"I'm just glad he didn't chase us, or I would have freaked out," Elizabeth said.

"You weren't freaked out?" Elan, Halona's thirteen-year-old son, smirked at Elizabeth. His build was small, but he had a handsome face and a winning smile. His long black hair was pulled back into a short ponytail that reached just beyond his shoulders. "You could have fooled me."

"Well, maybe just a little," Elizabeth admitted with a smile.

"We're used to seeing javelinas," Elan's younger sister, Aiyana, said. "We've grown up around them." Her dark eyes sparkled, and her soft, black curls fell like a waterfall down her back. At eight years old, she stood nearly as tall as her brother.

"But you still have to be careful," reminded her mother. "Wild boars are not to be taken lightly any more than rattlesnakes are."

The color drained from Elizabeth's cheeks. "Rattlesnakes? I'm petrified of snakes."

"They're all over the place, but we don't see much of them." Elan acted like it was no big deal. Though he didn't stand much taller than Aiyana, he behaved as if he were ten feet tall. "But they're hiding out there. It's part of their defense mechanism."

Bailey's mom chimed in. "I'm sure you won't see one while we're here, Beth. I've never spotted one yet in all the times I've visited."

"Why don't you live closer to town?" Bailey asked, sitting next to Elizabeth on the couch. "Then you wouldn't have to worry about those things as much."

"We Native Americans have our own land to live on. It's called a reservation. We even have our own government completely separate from the United States. We're a nation of people living among your nation, but our land is our own. We like to live out here where it's peaceful and quiet. Some of us work in town, though. My pottery shop is in Santa Fe."

"I can't wait to see it." Bailey looked around the Tses' small home. It was sparsely furnished and clean. Family pictures hung on the wall, but little else. The green plaid couch reminded Bailey of furniture she'd seen at secondhand stores, but she liked how soft it was and the way she sank down into it when she sat. Pottery lined a display shelf and sat on tables. "You have a lot of pottery here too."

"We've made pottery for generations. It's one of our native crafts."

Elizabeth gazed at a brown pot with black swirls painted around it that sat on the coffee table. "This one is beautiful. Did you make it?"

"No, my mother made that one." Halona's eyes misted, and she smoothed her blue cotton dress. Her long black hair was pulled back into a bun at the back of her head. Streaks of gray made it sparkle like icicles on a Christmas tree. "She was a master at the pottery wheel. The best I've ever seen. I'm trying to keep the shop going now that she's gone, but it's so hard to keep up with everything during the heavy tourist season."

Halona's eyes got a faraway look. "My husband died when Aiyana was just a baby, and I didn't think I could go on. But my mother helped me keep the shop going. With her help, we somehow made it. Then when she passed away, I thought I could never do it alone. We've managed until now, the busy season. I can't thank you enough for coming to help us."

Bailey felt a stab in her heart. *It must be awful to lose your mother, even if you're already grown up*, she thought.

"How long has it been since your mother died?" she asked.

"Six months, though it seems only yesterday." Halona smiled weakly and looked at her children. "But I have good help. Elan is almost a man at thirteen. And my Aiyana does so much for me even though she is only eight. She lives up to the meaning of her name, 'ever blooming.' I never hear a word of complaint from her."

"It's a beautiful name," Elizabeth said.

"Names are very important in the Native American culture," Halona said. "We give great thought to what they mean. Elan's name means 'friendly,' and mine means 'of happy fortune.' I keep reminding myself of that when times are tough and I struggle to pay my bills."

"That's cool," Bailey said. "Mom, what does my name mean?"

Bailey's mom shook her head. "I'm sorry, but I don't know. We just liked the way it sounds."

Bailey sighed. "I'll have to look it up sometime, I guess."

"I know what my name means," Elizabeth said. "I was named after Elizabeth in the Bible, John the Baptist's mother. It means 'God-directed.' But sometimes people call me Beth, for short."

"Wow." Aiyana's eyes shone. "That's a beautiful name too."

"Yes, it is," Bailey's mom said. "Halona, hopefully we can be of some help to you while we're here so it won't be so hard for you to live up to your name."

"So when can we see your shop?" Bailey asked.

Halona laughed. "Right now, if you'd like. We didn't open it up for the day yet since you were coming, but now that you're here, you can help us."

"All right! Let's go!" Bailey jumped up off the couch.

The group piled into Halona's big white Suburban and buckled up. It was an older vehicle, with windows you had to crank up and down. The dark blue backseat upholstery was torn on the passenger side. Aiyana rode in the front seat with Halona and Bailey's mom, and Bailey sat between Elan and Elizabeth in back.

Dust flew as they rode down the dirt road from the reservation to the paved main road. Bailey was awed by the rugged majesty of the Sangre de Cristo Mountains that ran alongside them. Prickly pear cacti dotted the desert as they zoomed toward Santa Fe. Soon they were on the freeway and arrived in Santa Fe minutes later.

"It's amazing how different it is here from on the reservation." Bailey stared at all the specialty shops around her. People roamed the streets popping into the small stores to look at handmade jewelry, pots, and art.

Halona parked in front of a store bearing a terra cotta sign with blue lettering that said EARTH WORKS on it. "Here we are!" she said.

"Earth Works," Bailey said. "I like it!"

"We take clay, which comes from the earth, and make it into pottery," Elan explained.

"But we use much more than clay in our pottery." Halona unlocked the shop door. "We use precious stones and minerals from the mines, and even ropes, which are made from plants. So much of what we use in our work comes from the earth."

The musky aroma of incense greeted the girls as they followed Halona into the store. Elan went to the counter and lit a short incense stick that looked as if it was left over from the day before.

"What kinds of mines do you have in New Mexico?" Elizabeth asked.

"Turquoise, copper, gold, silver—there are all kinds of mines here," Elan said.

"And we own one of the turquoise mines!" Aiyana's dark eyes gleamed. Her red T-shirt and brown corduroy pants could have been a boy's outfit, but looked decidedly feminine on the pretty little girl.

"Well, sort of," Halona corrected. "Legend says our family once owned the Suquosa Mine, which was one of the largest turquoise mines. It is no longer in operation. And the deed to the mine has been lost over the years. We have no proof we own it."

"What if you found the deed?" Bailey asked. "Could you reopen the mine and use the turquoise?"

Elan jumped in. "If we found it, we'd be rich!"

Halona put her hand on her son's shoulder. "We are rich in other ways now. But yes, Bailey, it would help us immensely in our work."

Bailey shot a look at Elizabeth, who smiled and nodded. The two walked around the shop admiring the beautiful pots while Halona took Bailey's mother to the office to show her the bookkeeping system she'd be helping with.

"I've never seen so many kinds of pots," Elizabeth said. "Some have handles, some are tall, and some are short. Others are painted with bright colors and some earth tones."

"And I've never seen pots with gems embedded in them before," Bailey added. "Those are my favorite."

"Do you make the jewelry too?" Elizabeth asked Elan and Aiyana.

"Some of it," Elan replied. "We make all the pots ourselves, but we buy some of the jewelry and blankets from other Native Americans."

"It must take hours and hours to make these things!" Bailey scanned the shop, taking in the variety of items.

"It does," Aiyana said. "That's why we need your help during tourist season."

"Mom feels bad if Aiyana and I have to work too much." Elan shrugged. "But I don't mind. I tell her I am not a kid anymore. I'm the man of the family, and it is my duty."

"What happened to your dad?" Bailey asked gently. "Was he sick?"

"He had cancer and died when Aiyana was only five months old," Elan replied. "So I'm the man of the house."

Bailey nodded. Her heart broke for Elan and Aiyana as an image of her own dad filled her mind. She thought about the way he had tossed her in the air when she was a tiny girl and the way he teased her now that she was older. She couldn't imagine what it would be like to grow up without him.

Elan stepped outside to sweep the front sidewalk, and Elizabeth moved to another shelf full of painted pottery. Bailey followed her until she heard voices yelling outside.

"Look at the boy doing girl's work!"

"Sweep, little girl. Sweep!"

Bailey glanced out the front window and saw some teenaged boys on bikes taunting Elan. He didn't look up at them, but his face reddened as he swept the sidewalk with hard, deliberate strokes.

How can they be so mean? Just because he's smaller than they are doesn't mean they should get away with talking to him like that. Don't they know his dad died and he has to help his mom?

"Beth, come here!" Bailey motioned her to the window.

Elizabeth immediately saw why Bailey had called her over.

"You'll never be man enough to get married!" one boy jeered.

"Good thing your people don't perform the ceremonial rite of passage anymore, or you'd never be declared a man. You'd be a little kid forever!"

That did it. Elan dropped his broom and put his hands on his hips. "You want to come over here and say that?"

"Sure, I'll say it right in your face." One of the bigger boys hopped off his bike, letting it fall by the road. The other boys straddled their bikes, waiting to see what would happen.

"Should we go out there?" Bailey asked.

The big boy reached Elan, and the two stood facing one another, inches separating them, though Elan stood almost a foot shorter.

"What did you say to me, Paco?" Elan said through gritted teeth.

"I said you'll *never* be a man." Paco spat the words slowly and deliberately. Then he shoved Elan.

Bailey burst through the door with Elizabeth and Aiyana close behind. None of the girls spoke, but glared at Paco.

"These your girlfriends, Elan?" Paco teased.

"Bailey's my cousin, if it's any of your business."

"Looks like she's come to do your fighting for you."

"We have not!" Bailey said. "Just leave him alone and get out of here."

"Who's gonna make me?"

"I am!" Elan pushed Paco so hard he staggered backward.

"Elan!" Aiyana yelled.

"Why you—" Paco steadied himself and grabbed Elan's shirt collar, flinging him to the sidewalk.

"Stop it!" Elizabeth stepped forward and stood face-to-face with Paco. She was as tall as he was. Bailey and Aiyana moved to Elan's side and helped him up.

Paco laughed and turned to leave. "Have a nice day—sissy!" He grabbed his bike by the handlebar and hopped on.

"You showed him!" Willy, one of Paco's friends, said.

"Yeah, he's such a shrimp you could have eaten him!" said another.

The boys rode away laughing.

"Are you okay, Elan?" Bailey asked.

"I'm fine." He brushed dirt off his pants.

"Who are those guys?" Elizabeth asked.

"Guys from my tribe who think I'm too small to be of any good." Fury blazed in Elan's dark eyes.

"Guess they don't know the measure of a man is inside him," Elizabeth said. "God judges the heart, not what a person looks like on the outside."

"Try telling that to them," Elan said. "They've been pestering me for years."

"Does your mom know?" Bailey asked.

Elan shrugged. "She did a few years ago. But I haven't told her it's still going on."

"I think we should tell her," Aiyana said.

"No!" Elan shot back. "Mama isn't to know anything about this. She has enough on her mind."

Aiyana lowered her head, her black hair falling around her face like a curtain.

"I'm sorry, Aiyana," Elan said. "I didn't mean to yell at you. But I can handle this on my own. I'm practically a man. One day they'll be sorry they messed with me."

Elizabeth cleared her throat. "The Bible says, 'Do not seek revenge or bear a grudge against one of your people, but love your neighbor as yourself.' It's not easy, but it's the best way to solve a problem with other people."

"That may be the way you do things, but things are different in our Native American culture." Elan frowned.

"Different?" Bailey asked.

"Your Bible also says, 'An eye for an eye and a tooth for a tooth,' doesn't it?" Elan asked.

"Yes, but—" Elizabeth began.

"So that's how we solve things around here. We believe in peace for a time, but if that doesn't work, then it's time to take action." Elan spoke as if no one could ever change his mind.

Bailey nodded. "We'll pray for things to work out."

"Oh, they'll work out," Elan said. "I'll prove to them that I'm a man."

"You don't have to prove anything," Elizabeth said. "They're the ones with the problem."

"Yeah, well I'll show them." Elan turned and stomped back into the store, ending the conversation.

Bailey glanced at Elizabeth and Aiyana. "You don't think he'll do anything crazy, do you?"

"I doubt it," Elizabeth replied. "He's just mad."

"Those boys make him mad all the time," Aiyana added. "He's never done anything about it before."

Bailey inhaled deeply and blew out her breath through her mouth. She hoped Elizabeth and Aiyana were right.

The Mystery of the Mine

Inside Earth Works, Bailey wandered the aisles looking at the pottery, trying to forget what she'd just seen and heard. Her fury at the boys slowly subsided, though a dull ache remained inside her. Soon her eyes were drawn to a pot sitting on a shelf in a hallway toward the back of the store. She slipped toward it to take a closer look.

The pot was round and full at the bottom, but tapered up to a narrow neck and out again to form a wider lip. Standing only about eight inches tall, it was painted in intricate detail. A sunset desert landscape—complete with prickly pear cacti, mountains, and tiny quail—encircled the wide, round pot belly. The painted sunset blazed in brilliant orange, yellow, and pink just behind the rugged mountain. The pot took Bailey's breath away. She reached out and touched it. Then she picked it up.

"No!" Aiyana yelled.

Bailey jumped, almost dropping the pot. She quickly set it back on the shelf.

"You can't touch that." Aiyana flew to her side, taking Bailey's hand to pull her an arm's reach away from the pot.

"I–I'm sorry." Bailey felt the weight of disappointment descend on her like a heavy Native American blanket. How she wanted to hold that gorgeous pot and examine every inch of its painted picture. "I—I didn't know."

Elizabeth went to Bailey. "Is it some kind of special pot?"

"It is a pot that has been handed down from generation to generation in our family."

"It's beautiful!" Elizabeth exclaimed.

"We keep it back here so no one bothers it."

"I could still see it from the main store area," Bailey said. "You might want to hide it better so no customers try to buy it."

"We would never sell it even if someone offered us a fortune for it." Aiyana's black-brown eyes became serious.

"Even if they offered you a million dollars?" Bailey teased.

Aiyana shook her head. "Not even a trillion."

"Wow. I guess some things are worth more than all the money in the world." Elizabeth smiled at Aiyana.

Aiyana looked down, studying her small, nervous hands.

"Aiyana? Are you all right?" Bailey asked.

The girl nodded, still not looking at Bailey and Beth.

"You sure?" Elizabeth asked. "Did we say something we shouldn't have?"

Suddenly Aiyana looked up at the girls, a determined fire in her eyes. "If I tell you a secret, do you promise not to tell anyone?"

Bailey and Elizabeth leaned in to hear what Aiyana would say. "Of course we'll keep your secret," Bailey said. "What is it?"

Aiyana stepped closer and said softly, "My grandmother used to say that this old pot held the key to riches."

"Riches?" Elizabeth sounded surprised. "Do you know what she meant by that?"

"I'm not really sure." Aiyana scrunched up her face in apology. "Maybe she meant it would remind us of our rich family background." She paused and scratched her head like she'd never thought about this so much before. "But Mama said *her* grandma always told her that behind the sunset our treasure awaits."

"Was she talking about this pot?" Bailey asked.

Aiyana nodded.

" 'Behind the sunset our treasure awaits,' " Elizabeth repeated. "I don't know what that means."

"Me neither," Aiyana said.

"That's totally mysterious. Sort of reminds me of the pot of gold at the end of a rainbow. Maybe they used to keep their money hidden in it." Bailey looked closely at the pot, being careful not to touch it. She saw more detail every time she studied it. "Is that turquoise going around the bottom rim?"

"Yes," Aiyana said. "Mama said they were really careful to cut the stones to the perfect diamond shape and size, and they polished them to make them shine. Then they set the turquoise in melted silver and let it harden. When it cooled, they pressed the silver and turquoise band into the clay while it was still soft—or at least that's what she's been told. Of course the pot was made before she was born."

"It's gorgeous," Elizabeth said. "Your family does awesome work."

"I'm just learning to embed stones in the pots I make, but I've been making pottery without stones for a few years now."

"Do you still cut and polish the stones yourself?"

"We don't, but there are people in our pueblo who do it for us."

"Is turquoise the most popular stone to use?" Bailey asked.

"It is around here." Aiyana nodded. "Around here Native Americans like my family are practically famous for their turquoise work because our ancestors lived near turquoise mines. But a long time ago, there was no rain for almost two years, and they had to move closer to the cities."

"Wow," Bailey said. "Two years with no rain is hard to imagine. We hardly go a week without rain in Illinois!"

"The drought was hard on my family back then. They were experts at using turquoise in their jewelry and pottery, but they had to move away from the mines. They just couldn't survive out there without water." Aiyana looked around to be sure no one else was listening. "Remember that mine I told you my family owned?"

Bailey and Elizabeth nodded.

"It had the most turquoise of any mine in the area. And they say the turquoise was more beautiful than the stones in all the other mines."

Bailey shook her head. "Too bad the deed got lost over the years."

"That's for sure." Aiyana said sadly. "We'd have the biggest and best turquoise mine around."

Elizabeth's face brightened. "Maybe we can help you find it while we're here."

"How could you do that?" Aiyana asked. "It's been lost for hundreds of years."

"I don't know how we'll do it, but I promise we'll try." Elizabeth patted the girl's hand.

"Elizabeth and I are great at solving mysteries," Bailey told her. "We're even in a mystery-solving club called Camp Club Girls."

"You are?" Aiyana's eyes widened. "Have you solved any mysteries yet?"

Bailey laughed. "We've solved lots of them! We were all in the same cabin at Camp Discovery, and we solved our first one at the camp. We found lost treasure. Since then we've solved more than a dozen mysteries together!"

"Then maybe you'll be able to solve this one too!" Aiyana's smile was filled with hope. "It would help my family so much if we could prove we own the old mine. We could reopen it and not have to pay other people for their turquoise. We'd get stones from our own mine and use them for free!"

"That would sure save your mom a lot of money," Elizabeth agreed. "Plus, she could sell turquoise to other people to use in their crafts too."

"Aiyana, would you mind if we told the other Camp Club Girls the secret about the pot so they could help us solve the mystery?"

Aiyana hesitated. "I guess that would be okay. We don't tell many people, because we are afraid someone may try to steal the ancient pot from us. But I know you wouldn't do that."

"That's for sure," Beth said. "And neither would our friends. Besides, they don't even live in New Mexico."

"Do you know where the mine was located?" Bailey asked.

Aiyana's face fell, and she shook her head. "That's the other problem. We don't even know for sure which land is supposed to be ours, much less where the mine is."

"Hmm." Elizabeth screwed her mouth up. "That is a problem."

"Well, we'll do our best to try to figure it out and find out if there's really a mine on it. Hopefully we'll find the deed to prove your family owns it too." Bailey crossed her arms and nodded as if that settled the matter.

That afternoon, Bailey and Elizabeth went into their bedroom at Halona's house and used their cell phones to conference call the other Camp Club Girls. Bailey sat at the head of the bed and Elizabeth at the foot.

"Hey girls, everybody there?"

"We're here!" everyone shouted together.

"Guess what? Beth and I are in Santa Fe, New Mexico!" Bailey announced.

"Santa Fe! How'd that happen?" McKenzie asked. McKenzie Phillips was a fourteen-year-old from Montana who was good at seeing people's motives behind their behavior, and loved to ride horses.

"My mom's distant cousin, Halona, is a Native American who lives here," Bailey explained. "Her mother died and she needed help to keep their pottery store going during the busy tourist season."

Elizabeth jumped in. "Bailey asked if I could come and help too. I'm only out of school for another week, but we decided it would be a fun ending to the summer. Plus, since I want to be a missionary someday, my folks thought it would be good training for me to see the Native American culture up close and personal."

"Do you want to be a missionary to the Native Americans?" McKenzie asked.

"I don't know yet," Elizabeth replied. "But learning any new culture is good training."

"Sounds interesting," said Alexis Howell, a twelve-year-old from Sacramento, California, who was also known as Alex. "Met any cute boys?"

Bailey rolled her eyes at Beth and smiled. "No, but we've met some not-so-cute ones."

Elizabeth laughed. "Some boys were really mean to Bailey's cousin, Elan."

"Why were they mean to him?" Sydney asked. Sydney was the athletic girl of the bunch, a twelve-year-old from Washington, DC.

Bailey shook her head, the frustration of the encounter washing over her again. "Because he's small for his age and was sweeping the sidewalk in front of the pottery shop. They said he was doing girls' work. Can you believe that?"

"Sounds like they're living in a time warp," Kate said. Kate was the whiz kid of the group, even though she was only eleven. She specialized in gadgets galore at her home in Philadelphia. "Men do all kinds of different things these days, just like women do. How old is Elan?"

"He's thirteen, but is not too much taller than his eight-year-old sister."

"I think those boys must not feel very good about themselves, or they wouldn't bother someone else over something so ridiculous," McKenzie said. "My mom says people often mirror their own fears in what they say to other people."

"I never thought of that," Bailey said. "But whatever the reason, they were sure mean. Poor Elan tried to stand up to them, but the biggest boy, Paco, pushed him down."

"Do his parents know they're picking on Elan?" Sydney asked.

"His mom knew at one time, but doesn't know it's still going on. And his dad died when he was very young."

"His little sister, Aiyana, wanted to tell her mom, but Elan wouldn't let her." Elizabeth pushed back her blond, wavy hair.

"Anyway, that's not the real reason we called." Bailey sat up straight on the bed. "We have a mystery to solve."

"All right! What is it?" Alex asked.

Bailey and Elizabeth told the girls all about the pot that was handed down from generation to generation.

"It's so beautiful!" Elizabeth said. "You should see it!"

"Yeah, it has a desert landscape painted on it," Bailey told them. "It has cacti and even little quail walking in a line. And a bright sun setting behind a mountain fills the sky with all kinds of colors. It's so cool!"

"Why don't you email us a picture?" Kate suggested.

"We will," Bailey said. "I hope we can get a good shot of it. We aren't supposed to touch it. I found that out the hard way."

"Well, don't break any rules or anything, but do the best you can." Kate suddenly giggled. "Biscuit, stop!" More giggling. "I think Biscuit says hi. He's licking the phone. It's disgusting!"

Even Biscuit was part of the sleuthing team! The girls had found him at Discovery Lake, and though Kate kept him most of the time, he still found ways to help the girls solve mysteries.

"Sounds like nothing has changed much with Biscuit!" Alex said. "So Bailey, what's the mystery about? Does it have something to do with the pot?"

"Halona's family used to own land that had a huge turquoise mine on it," Bailey explained. "The problem is that the deed has been lost for hundreds of years."

"Not only that," Elizabeth added, "but they don't even know where the land is or if there really is a mine on it. Our job is to try to determine the location of both and find the lost deed that proves it's theirs."

"Man, that's gonna be hard!" McKenzie wailed. "I'm not sure we can do that."

"Hold it!" Elizabeth said with a smile. "Don't forget that with God, anything is possible."

"True enough," Alex said. "What's your cousins' last name? Maybe I could research public records on the web."

"Their last name is Tse." Bailey spelled it for her.

"Oh! We almost forgot to tell you an important clue to the mystery!" Elizabeth banged her forehead with the heel of her hand. "Elan and Aiyana's grandmother used to tell them that the pot held the key to riches. And their great-grandmother always said that 'behind the sunset our treasure awaits.' "

"Weird!" Sydney said. "That sounds like some kind of code."

"Could be." Bailey tucked her feet under her legs in crisscross style.

Kate piped in. "I remember learning in history that some Native Americans were code talkers in World War II."

"Oh yeah!" McKenzie said. "I learned that too!"

"Well, maybe this is some kind of code too." Sydney cleared her throat. "I'll research that angle."

"Great!" Elizabeth said. "I think we've got a good start."

"How long will you be in Santa Fe?" Alex asked.

Bailey licked her lips. "Today is Saturday, and we leave on Thursday, so almost a week."

"That doesn't give us much time," Sydney said. "We'd better get busy."

"Okay," Elizabeth said. "Stay in touch with anything you come up with, even if you're not sure it really applies to the case."

"Right," Bailey agreed. "That's what the police always say about tiny bits of evidence. If you know anything or saw anything that could possibly have something to do with a case, call. We'll try to put the pieces together later."

"Okay," Kate said. "Have fun in Santa Fe!"

"We will!" Bailey hung up and high-fived Beth.

The mystery solving had begun.

Becoming a Man

Monday morning, the Tses, Bailey, her mom, and Elizabeth went to open up the shop at eight o'clock. Bailey removed the black velvet coverings off the jewelry cases, and Beth dusted the pottery. Aiyana swept the floor while Elan turned on soft Native American music. Bailey's mom retreated to the back office with a steaming cup of coffee to work on the bookkeeping records that were weeks behind.

"When you're done dusting, let's look at that pot again," Bailey suggested to Elizabeth.

"I don't know, Bales," Elizabeth replied. "Maybe we should just leave it alone."

"We won't pick it up," Bailey said. "But it can't hurt to look at it. We told the girls we'd get pictures of it to send them."

"Okay, but we have to be careful." Beth tickled a pot with her feather duster. She finished dusting the row of merchandise and returned the duster to the closet. "I'm done. Are you?"

"Yeah, I'm done too." Bailey hopped off a high stool behind the counter, and the two walked to the back of the store.

"Let's get those pictures taken and then get away from here." Elizabeth pulled out her phone and held it close to the ancient pot. "I hope the lighting is good enough."

"Guess we'll find out," Bailey said.

Elizabeth clicked the picture and then showed Bailey. "What do you think?"

"It's a little dark, but I'm sure they can still see it," Bailey said. "It only shows part of the painted picture, though. I'll turn it one quarter of the way around so they can see the continuation of it."

"Bailey," Elizabeth said in a warning voice. "We shouldn't touch—"

But it was too late. Bailey had already reached out and turned the pot.

"See? I was careful," Bailey assured her friend.

Elizabeth snapped a shot of the pot in its new position, and Bailey gave it another one quarter turn. Soon they had four pictures that showed the entire desert landscape to send the other girls.

"I'm glad that's done." Elizabeth wiped imaginary sweat from her forehead.

"You worry too much," Bailey said. "How could I break it when I wasn't even picking it up?"

"I know, but I hate to take chances." Beth blew a strand of hair from her face. "Anyway, it's done, and nothing happened. I'm praising God for that!"

The two laughed.

"Hey, what's this?" Bailey looked into a room across from the office where her mother was entering data on a computer spreadsheet.

Halona and Aiyana came to the back of the store just as she asked.

"That's our studio," Halona said. "I teach pottery classes in there."

Bailey's dark almond eyes widened. "You do?"

Halona nodded. "Pottery making has been in my family for generations, so it comes naturally to me. We even follow pueblo tradition of making our own dyes from plants and other parts of nature."

"Wow. That's amazing," Bailey said. "Who do you teach it to?"

"Anyone who wants to learn." Halona smiled broadly.

"Could you teach me?" Bailey asked.

"I could *start* teaching you," Halona replied. "There's a lot to learn in the short time you'll be here."

"That's okay," Bailey answered. "I'll learn as much as I can, and then maybe I could take more lessons at home. Do you want to do it too, Beth?"

"Sure!" Elizabeth shrugged. "Sounds like fun."

"When can we start?" Bailey asked.

Halona peeked down the short hallway and into the shop. "Well, it looks like we don't have any customers yet, so how about now?"

"All right!" Bailey raced into the studio and took a seat at the table.

"Before you get too comfortable, put on a smock," Halona said.

"Yeah!" Aiyana said. "Pottery making can get pretty messy."

"Elizabeth, do you have a tie so you can keep your hair out of the way while you work?" Halona asked.

Elizabeth pulled an elastic band from around her wrist. "I always keep these handy." She quickly smoothed her long, medium-blond waves into a ponytail.

"You'd hate to have to do that after you've started, or you'd have wet clay stuck in your hair." Aiyana laughed and finger-brushed her own dark curls back and secured them in a scrunchy. "Believe me, I know!"

"See?" Bailey tucked her chin-length, silky black hair behind her ears. "We're learning things already!"

Elan appeared at the door and peered in. "What's up?"

"We're going to take pottery lessons from your mom." Bailey spoke as proudly as if she'd just gotten an Olympic gold medal.

"This I've got to see." Elan flipped a chair backward and straddled it, his tan arms resting on the back. His black hair hung loose today, and he flashed a grin at Elizabeth, causing her to blush. Bailey had to admit her cousin really did look good in his blue jeans and brown T-shirt. He chuckled. "Let the show begin."

"First, we need to lay out this canvas so your clay doesn't stick to the table." Halona whooshed the fabric out over the table like a clean sheet over a bed. "And now you each need a chunk of clay."

Halona retrieved a block of gray clay and removed the plastic wrapping that surrounded it. She sliced a hunk off for Bailey and one for Elizabeth, plopping them down in front of the girls with a dull thud.

"Now, roll and press the clay to change its shape from a rectangle into a ball," Halona instructed. "This will also help soften it and make it easier to work with."

Bailey pressed and rolled the clay. "This is so much stiffer than the modeling clay I used to play with when I was little."

"No kidding." Elizabeth stood to put her full weight on her glob of clay. "We're going to get strong doing this!"

"Yes, it takes strong arms and hands to be a potter." Halona watched the girls' progress, giving tips as they worked to soften the clay.

"This makes me think of where the Bible talks about God being the Potter and us being the clay." Elizabeth rolled her clay on the table. "I wonder if I'm ever as stubborn as this clay is."

"My mom says I have a strong will." Bailey worked her clay. "It can be bad, like if I'm stubborn and want to do things my way instead of God's way. Or it can be good, like when I'm strong enough to say no to a group of kids who want me to do something I shouldn't."

Elizabeth nodded, and Bailey continued. "Like once some of my friends thought it would be funny to place an order at a fast food drive-through window and then run the other way before the workers had time to see us. I told them it wasn't funny to play jokes like that and we could get into trouble. It's like stealing people's time, and you can't give that back. Then I just walked away."

"What'd they do?" Elizabeth turned her clay over.

"Most of them went ahead and did it anyway, but one other girl walked away with me. She seemed glad to have someone to help her stay out of trouble."

"You did the right thing. I guess the main thing is that we're soft and moldable so God can make us into who He wants us to be." Elizabeth flipped her ponytail back, and then shoved the heel of her hand deeper into the clay.

Bailey stood back and looked at her clump of clay with a smile.

"What?" Elizabeth asked.

"I was just thinking. What if my pot said, 'I don't want to be a bowl? I want to be a vase.' And it wouldn't let me make it into what it was meant to be?" Bailey laughed at her own idea. "I guess sometimes I say that to God."

Elizabeth laughed. "I'm sure we have lots of learning to do about being moldable clay for God to use and about making actual pots from clay. I want to be a useful vessel for God, not just a hunk of unmanageable clay!"

The girls kept working their clay until, finally, their rectangular pieces were smooth, round balls.

"Good," Halona said. "Now push your fingers into the middle of the ball to make a nice indentation. This will be the start of your bowl."

The bell on the front door dinged, announcing Earth Works' first customer of the day. "I must tend to the customers. Elan, you stay here and help the girls."

"No problem." Elan stood and laced his fingers, then stretched his arms out, cracking his knuckles. A smile played on his lips as he pulled a narrow strip of leather from his pants pocket and tied his hair back. "I'll teach 'em how it's done."

Aiyana rolled her eyes. "Puh-lease."

Under Elan's direction, Bailey and Elizabeth molded their clay balls into dishes, dipping their fingers in a small bowl of water to smooth the rough spots.

"That's neat that your family makes their own dyes," Bailey said.

"And it's earth friendly too."

"Native Americans have always been earth friendly," Elan replied. "The rest of the nation could learn a lot from our ways."

Beth smoothed the side of her pot. "Seems like you have a lot of cool traditions you still practice."

"Yes, we do," Elan said. "But we also have some that have fallen by the wayside."

"Like what?" Bailey asked.

"Well, for instance, we used to have a rite of passage for boys when they turned thirteen."

"Rite of passage?" Bailey gave him a look. "What's that?"

"It's when you're declared an official adult of the tribe." Elan thought for a moment. "It means you're not a little kid anymore, and you have adult responsibilities."

"I've heard of other cultures that do that too," Elizabeth said.

"Do you have to get a job and not go to school anymore?" Bailey asked.

"No, not like that," Elan said. "The boys had to prove themselves."

"Prove what?" Bailey looked at Elan like he was slightly crazy.

"Prove that you're ready for manhood."

"How?" Bailey asked.

"The boys used to have to climb the rock face by the Puye Cliff dwellings by hand—no ropes or tools allowed."

"That sounds dangerous!" Beth said.

"That's part of the reason they don't do it anymore." Elan's face dropped a bit, and Bailey sensed his disappointment. "It's a sheer cliff, straight up and down, with only a few hand- and toeholds for men to pull themselves up with. The whole tribe would come to watch and cheer on the boys. Now they just have a special ceremony for us and perform a rite of passage dance to say you've become a man."

"Did anyone ever fall from the cliff?" Elizabeth's eyebrows lowered over her hazel-green eyes.

"Sometimes," Elan said. "But then that gave them the chance to show their bravery through injury. It still proved their manhood. No one ever died."

"Did you already have your rite of passage ceremony?" Bailey dipped her fingers in the water and back to her clay.

"Yeah, they did it a few months ago."

"So you're officially a man now?" Beth asked, color rising to her cheeks.

"I guess," Elan said. "I don't feel any different."

"Well, I'd say you're a man whether you feel like it or not." Bailey looked up from her project. "You had your rite of passage, and you already have a job."

"Yeah." Elizabeth nodded, her color returning to normal. "You even help take care of your mom and sister. You definitely have adult responsibilities."

"I wish the boys at school could see it that way." Elan's voice was soft and low.

"What difference does it make?" Bailey said. "What they think doesn't decide who you are."

Elan paused and seemed to think about what Bailey said. "I still wish I'd had the chance to prove myself on that cliff. That would settle it once and for all."

"Unless you fell and cracked your head open," Bailey said. "Then you'd be sorry you took the chance."

"I'd show them I could take it like a man." Elan sat up tall and puffed out his chest. "Maybe one day I still will."

"Now you're talking crazy." Aiyana was much further ahead in shaping her bowl than Bailey and Elizabeth were.

"What's so crazy about it?" Elan asked his sister. "Hundreds, maybe even thousands, of boys have scaled the Puye Cliff dwellings. People used to live in them!"

Aiyana eyed him smartly. "Yeah, but they're closed to the public now because it's too dangerous."

"They're closed to the public because people were damaging the old cliff dwellings," Elan corrected. "They want to preserve them for history."

"*And* because it's too dangerous," Aiyana countered. "Mama says people were afraid they'd get taken to court if someone climbed up there and fell."

"Sounds like there were several reasons to close the cliff dwellings to the public," Elizabeth put in. "I'm sure you're both right."

Bailey breathed a sigh of relief that Elizabeth was stepping into the brother and sister squabble. She knew her friend was a great peacemaker, a quality she hoped she'd learn someday. But for now, she usually found herself inwardly cringing on the sidelines when people argued.

"Maybe you can take us to see the Puye Cliff dwellings sometime," Elizabeth said. "I've never seen ancient rock houses before."

"Sure, we can go there. But they have most of it fenced off now, so we can't get as close as we used to." Elan checked Elizabeth's bowl. "This is looking pretty good. But you don't want to make that side too thick," he warned. "It will crack in the kiln if it's thicker than the rest, because it won't dry evenly."

Elizabeth smiled. "Okay, thanks."

"So what do we do next now that we have our bowls shaped?" Bailey asked.

Aiyana jumped in before Elan could answer. "We take them outside and set them in the sun until they're bone dry."

"Do we get to paint them?" Bailey asked.

"Eventually," Aiyana replied. "After they're dry we'll glaze them. That's what the paint's called."

"How long does it take them to dry outside?" Elizabeth asked.

"Usually a day or two." Aiyana looked at the bright sun beaming through the window. "When it's this warm outside, probably only a day."

The door dinged again, and Elan stood. "I'd better go help Mother with the customers."

"Thanks for helping us get this far." Bailey waved as he left.

After the boy had left the room, Elizabeth asked, "What do you think about what Elan said?"

"What do you mean?" Aiyana tilted her head.

"Do you really think he'd try scaling the Puye Cliff dwellings?" Elizabeth's eyes were clouded with concern.

"No." Aiyana sounded sure of her answer. "He's talked of doing that plenty of times before. He'd never do it. It's way too dangerous."

Bailey picked up her bowl and followed Aiyana toward the back door.

"Do you think we should say anything to your mom about it just in case?" Elizabeth scooped her dish up and went with them.

"No, I'm sure he's just talking big." Aiyana held the door for the girls. "We've got nothing to worry about."

Elizabeth didn't look so sure. "I hope you're right."

CHAPTER 4

Desert Wanderings

Back at the Tses' house that afternoon, Bailey flopped onto the bed and opened her laptop. Elizabeth sprawled out next to her. They sent the photos of the ancient pot from Elizabeth's phone to the other Camp Club Girls. It wasn't long before Bailey's phone rang. "Hello?"

"Hi, Bailey. It's Kate."

"Hi, Kate. Did you get the pictures?"

"Yes! You were right. That *is* a gorgeous pot. I love all the colors in the sunset!"

"Me too. Hang on a second. I'll put you on speakerphone so Beth can hear too." Bailey pushed the speaker button.

"Hi, Kate! It's Elizabeth."

"Hi, Beth."

"Anyway, back to the subject," Bailey said. "The sunset's my favorite part too."

"I'm going to print the pictures out so I can research them. Biscuit!"

Elizabeth giggled when she heard Biscuit panting over the line. "Hi, Biscuit!"

"He's going nuts!" Kate laughed. "Get down, boy. Anyway, I'm hoping I'll spot a clue somewhere in the picture that you didn't pick up on."

"That would be great," Bailey said. "Let us know if you find anything."

"Okay. Will do."

"Okay. Bye." Bailey flipped her phone closed.

A knock on the bedroom door made Bailey sit up. "Come in!"

"Hey!" Elan said. " 'S up?"

"Not much. We just got off the phone with one of our friends from camp," Elizabeth said. "What about you?"

"I wondered if you wanted to go see the Puye Cliff dwellings." Elan held a floppy, off-white canvas hat, and his eyes flashed with excitement.

"Sure!" Bailey was off the bed in a flash. "Is your mom driving us?"

"No. It's not far. We'll walk."

"Really?" Bailey looked doubtful. "They're that close?"

"Well, it's a good hike, but I've done it plenty of times." Elan sounded so sure. But still, a little worry sat at the edge of Bailey's mind.

"Let us get some water bottles first," Bailey said. "I don't know much about hiking, but I know you should always take plenty of water."

The girls grabbed water bottles from the fridge and handed one to Elan, who put on the wide-brimmed hat he'd been holding. They tucked their cell phones in their pockets and were ready to go.

"Here," Elan said, handing them each a fanny pack. "We usually wear these when we hike so we don't have to carry water bottles. I also put a little bag of trail mix in each one in case we get hungry."

"Thanks." Bailey strapped hers on and slipped her water bottle into the mesh side pouch.

Bailey's mom was reading the newspaper in the kitchen. "Mom, we're going to hike with Elan to the Puye Cliff dwellings," Bailey said. "He says they're not far."

"Okay, be home for supper."

"We will. We have our phones if you need us." Bailey patted the pocket holding her phone.

"Have fun!" Mrs. Chang called.

The screen door slammed behind them as they started out. Every time she went outside, Bailey marveled that her cousin's house was so far in the middle of nowhere. A few other homes spotted the barren landscape, but Bailey noticed there weren't any stores like she was so used to in Peoria, Illinois.

Elan led the way through the dry terrain. "We have to walk this direction awhile, then you'll see the cliff dwellings." A lizard sunning itself on a rock scurried to safety under a creosote bush.

"Is this a desert?" Bailey asked.

"Not really. But it's typical of the southwest with its dry, hard dirt and gravel and tall, dry grass. Lots of scrubby bushes and big rocks too. We have some cacti like prickly pear, but not the tall saguaros with arms you see in some deserts. Southern New Mexico has part of the Chihuahuan Desert in it, but Santa Fe's in the northern part of the state."

"We won't run across any snakes, will we?" Elizabeth asked.

"Probably not." Elan kept walking. "But you never can tell."

Bailey saw Beth's wide hazel-green eyes scanning the desert for any sign of movement.

"If a rattlesnake was around, we'd know before we got too close," Elan said. "That's what the rattler is for—to warn people and tell them to get away."

Bailey saw the worry in Elizabeth's eyes. "Don't worry, Beth. Elan grew up out here. He'll take good care of us."

Elizabeth nodded but kept scanning the area.

"Are we near the cliff dwellings yet?" Bailey asked.

"A little farther," Elan said. "Up around those big rocks, then a little bit past that."

Bailey stopped and sipped her water. The sun was beating down without mercy. Only scraggly bushes and tall desert plants grew here with an occasional desert willow tree, which didn't provide much shade.

"We should have put on sunscreen," Elizabeth said. "I'll be burnt to a crisp."

Elan said, "Here. Why don't you wear my hat? At least that will shade your face." He whipped off his hat and tossed it to Elizabeth.

Beth looked at the floppy hat and laughed. "This will be a new look for me." She shoved it on and struck a pose. "How do I look?"

Bailey laughed. "Like a cross between a fashion model and a desert rat."

"I think you look great!" Elan said. "At least you won't look like a lobster when we get back."

"Not my face anyway." Elizabeth held her arms out and inspected them as they walked. "My arms, maybe. We'll have to try to take cover under some of the trees or tall rock formations."

"What time is it?" Elan asked.

Bailey checked her cell phone. "Three thirty-five."

"At least we're not in the most damaging rays. They're usually the worst between ten and two o'clock."

"Good point," Elizabeth said. "But then again I've heard the hottest part of the day is usually around five or six o'clock, just before the sun goes down."

"Hopefully we can get back before that," Bailey said.

"Yeah, I feel like I'm being barbecued." Elizabeth wiped sweat from her forehead.

Elan stopped and looked around.

"What's wrong?" Bailey scanned the area, looking for signs of trouble.

"Nothing." Elan looked the other way.

"Elaaan," Bailey said, drawing out his name. "Tell me what's the matter."

"Nothing! I just thought the cliff dwellings were right over there, but they're not. We must have gotten turned around when we stopped to take a drink or when I gave Beth my hat."

"How could we have gotten turned around?" Elizabeth said. "We barely even stopped."

"I don't know, but something's not right." Elan walked ahead, and the girls followed. "I think we need to go this way."

"Are you telling me we're lost?" Elizabeth said.

"Not lost," Elan replied. "Just turned around. We need to go toward those rocks over there."

Bailey followed Elan's finger to the rocks and saw them in the distance. "Clear over there? I thought you said the cliff dwellings weren't far?"

"They aren't if you take the direct route!" Elan's voice rose. "But when you're traveling with two complaining girls, it's easy to get turned around." Then he mocked them. "I'm hot. I'm getting sunburned. I need a drink. Are we almost there?" Then back to his own voice. "No wonder it's taking so long!"

"It's not our fault if it's taking longer than usual," Bailey shot back. "We've kept up with you step for step."

Elan stomped toward the distant rocks. Elizabeth and Bailey hurried behind him, determined to keep up with his faster pace. Bailey wiped the sweat from her face with her T-shirt sleeve. Elan was now ten feet ahead of them.

"Elan, slow down!" Elizabeth called.

But he continued, angry, toward his destination.

"Bailey, we'll never be able to keep up this pace." Elizabeth's face was red with heat.

"Let's stop and rest." Bailey sat on a rock and opened her water bottle, gulping the lukewarm water that filled her mouth.

"He'll wait for us when he sees how far behind we are." Elizabeth took a drink and sat beside Bailey. She put both feet on the rock and rested her head on her knees.

Suddenly, the girls heard a rattle. They looked at each other and froze in fear. "A snake!" Bailey whispered.

Elizabeth nodded, her face paling.

"We have to step away from this rock so he knows we won't hurt him," Bailey said. She slowly stood and took a giant step. "Come on, Beth!"

Elizabeth opened her mouth, but nothing came out.

"You can do it, I know you can!"

"I can't move!" Elizabeth finally squeaked.

"Yes, you can." Bailey held her hand out to her friend. "First you have to stand."

"I'm afraid to put my feet on the ground. The snake may strike me!"

Bailey spoke in a calm, soothing voice. "No, he won't. I was sitting next to you when I got up, and he didn't strike me. You can do this."

The snake's rattle continued.

"You know snakes are one of my worst fears, Bales."

Bailey saw tears run down Beth's cheeks. "I know, but you can do everything through Him who gives you strength! We learned that verse at camp, remember? Philippians 4:13. It applies to situations we think are too hard for us. You can do anything with God's help. Even this."

Elizabeth closed her eyes and pointed her face skyward as if praying silently. She wiped the tears from her face, then inched her feet down the rock until her toes touched the ground.

"Good girl!" Bailey cheered quietly. "If that snake wanted to hurt you, he would have already done it. Now stand and take a step toward me."

Beth steadied herself against the rock as she slowly stood. Then she practically ran into Bailey's waiting arms.

"You did it!" Bailey hugged her friend.

"More like God did it," Beth said. "I couldn't have done that without His help."

"You are living proof of the verse we learned."

"That's for sure."

Bailey grew silent, and then she heard the rattle again. She saw the snake's head poke out from behind the rock, its tongue flicking the air. "Let's get out of here!"

Both girls took off running in the direction Elan had gone. They saw he had turned around and was coming back in their direction. When they started running, he ran to meet them.

"What's the matter?" he yelled.

"A rattlesnake!" Bailey screamed.

As they got closer, they slowed to an exhausted trudge.

"Why did you leave us?" Elizabeth scolded when they were close enough to talk. "We were practically bitten by a rattlesnake!"

"Because you were blaming me for getting us lost!" Elan looked away. "I'm sorry. I should have stayed with you. Are you all right?"

"We are now," Bailey said. "But the snake was hiding under the rock where we stopped to rest. Way too close for comfort."

"I've never been so scared in all my life." Beth shuddered.

"I'm sorry." Elan tugged at his ponytail. "I really am. But I do have some good news."

"You do?" Bailey said.

"The Puye Cliff dwellings are right past these boulders. We're practically there!"

"Finally!" Elizabeth said. "I don't know how much farther I could have walked."

"Yeah, we've been walking an hour in this heat already." Bailey lifted her hair off her neck, wishing it were long enough to pull in a ponytail.

"Come on." Elan extended his hand to show them the way. "Follow me. Some trees up here can shade us so it won't be as hot. I promise it's not far."

The trio hiked another ten minutes and, just past the boulders, they saw the cliff dwellings. Some of the ruins were on the ground, remains of an ancient civilization. Handmade stone walls stood only about three feet high, but the three could still see the shape of rooms and buildings that had once stood there.

"Wow!" Bailey said. "This is amazing!"

"The Puye Cliffs were home to around 1500 Pueblo Indians in the late 1100s to around 1580," Elan explained. "Then the drought forced them to move to the Rio Grande River valley."

"Oh yeah. Aiyana told us about the drought," Bailey said. "Are you a Pueblo Indian?" she asked Elan.

"Yes and no. The Pueblo Indians split into eight different pueblos when they had to move. We're known as Santa Clara Pueblo Indians," Elan replied.

"Look up there." Elizabeth pointed to the side of the cliff.

"Cliff dwellings!" Bailey said. "How did they ever build them on such a sheer hill?"

"I'm not sure," Elan said. "It's even more amazing when you realize they didn't have modern equipment to help them."

"It looks like it has two levels." Elizabeth pulled out her phone and took a picture.

"It does," Elan said. "The people used ladders to go from one level to the next."

"It's like an ancient apartment complex!" Bailey laughed.

Elan pointed to the solid rock wall to the right of the cliff dwellings. "During the rite of passage, the boys would climb this side of the cliff without ropes or tools of any kind." He eyed the rock with awe.

Elizabeth shook her head. "I can't imagine how anyone ever did that."

"It wouldn't be that hard," Elan said. "I bet I could do it. You can see the handholds when you get up close."

"You'd do it or die trying," Bailey said. "How could any parent let a kid do that?"

"That's the point," Elan said. "They're not children anymore. They're becoming adults in the rite of passage."

"Seems like a silly tradition to me," Elizabeth said. "No reason to have to grow up overnight, especially by doing something so dangerous."

"Our traditions mean a lot to our people." Elan sounded offended.

"I'm sure you have many traditions that are worth keeping, but I'm glad this one fell by the wayside." Bailey patted Elan on the back. "I'd hate to see my cousin up there!"

Bailey and Elizabeth took more pictures of the ancient dwellings.

"What's that?" Bailey pointed to a mountain area not far from the cliff dwellings.

"That's where some of the old turquoise mines used to be." Elan shaded his eyes with his hand. "They're not open anymore. They were closed when the drought hit too."

"It's sad what a lack of rain can do." Elizabeth looked around again. "Very cool, Elan, but we'd better get back now."

Elan looked at his watch. "Yeah, we've been gone almost two hours. It will be time for supper when we get home."

"I'm already getting hungry from all this walking." Bailey pulled out her bag of trail mix to munch on.

"Hopefully it won't take as long to get home as it did to get here," Elan said. "We'll try to stay on track this time."

"They should build roads to the cliff dwellings," Elizabeth said.

"They have, but they're on the other side going toward Santa Fe. None of them lead back to the reservation." Elan laughed. "I guess they figured Santa Fe tourists wouldn't want to hike all the way out there."

"Probably a good guess. It was far enough coming from your house."

Bailey pulled her cotton candy flavored lip balm out of her pocket and smeared some on her parched lips. "Anyone else need some?"

"I'll take some." Elizabeth applied the lip balm. "Mmm. This makes me think of *food*!"

"Thanks for taking us to see the cliff dwellings, Elan," Bailey said. "They're really neat."

"Yeah, and I even got to meet a rattlesnake!" Elizabeth laughed. "Not that I want to ever do it again!"

"I'm glad you got to see them." Elan gulped down a drink. "I go there fairly often. It doesn't seem that far to me, but I guess it is for people who don't hike that much."

"If I were you, I wouldn't take that hike alone, Elan," Beth said.

"What if something happened?" Bailey added. "You'd be stuck out there with no one to help."

Elan waved the mother hens off with his hand. "I've hiked alone plenty of times. I've even hiked up some of the cliff dwellings."

Bailey stopped and planted her hands on her hips. "Your mom would have a fit if she knew that."

"Well, she doesn't, and if she finds out, I'll know who to blame."

"Well, I hope you won't do it again," Elizabeth said. "That is totally dangerous."

Elan shook his head. "We'll see about that."

Disaster!

"We need to leave!" Halona called to the others the next morning.

"Where's Elan?" Bailey asked as she climbed into the Suburban.

"He's not feeling well," Halona explained. "He's staying home to rest."

"Maybe that hike yesterday was harder on him than he thought," Elizabeth said as she buckled her seat belt.

When they arrived at Earth Works, Bailey took over Elan's job of sweeping the front sidewalk while Elizabeth dusted the shelves and pottery inside. Before long Bailey heard the familiar voices of Paco and the other boys who teased Elan.

"Oh, look!" Paco taunted. "Elan has a girl doing his work for him. Must have been too hard for him."

"It just so happens Elan is sick today." Bailey was immediately sorry she had given them the satisfaction of an answer.

"Aw. Isn't that too bad." Paco used his best baby voice. "Hope the delicate little thing gets better soon so we can pound him into the ground!" The baby voice morphed into a growl.

The other boys laughed. Bailey shot poisonous darts from her eyes. She was steaming mad but didn't say anything else. The boys rode off, still laughing.

As soon as Bailey finished sweeping, she went back into the store and pulled Elizabeth into the back hallway. "I'm going to give that dorko a shocko if he's not careful."

"Huh?" Elizabeth frowned.

"That mean guy, Paco, came back on his bike while I was sweeping."

Elizabeth laughed. "Paco the Dorko? That's pretty funny. Not nice, but funny."

"Well he's not too nice. I can see why he gets Elan mad."

"Just let it go," Elizabeth advised. "They're gone now anyway."

Bailey nodded. "While we're here, we should study that ancient pot again," she said. "I keep thinking after our hike yesterday that maybe some of the landscape on the pot will look familiar."

The girls went to the shelf in the hall to look again.

"I know what you mean." Elizabeth leaned so close to the pot her nose almost touched it. "But there were way more trees and dry, scrubby bushes where we hiked than there are on this pot. It can't possibly be the same area."

"But the place on the pot has to be close," Bailey said. "This is where the Tses' ancestors are from. They didn't move that far away when the drought hit. They only moved closer into town."

"It just looks so different."

"I wonder if Kate found anything else out about the pot since she printed the pictures we sent." Bailey scratched her head.

"I hope so, or I'm afraid we may have run into a dead end." Elizabeth turned when she heard the bell on the front door ring. "Sounds like Halona's got customers."

Bailey looked at the pot on the shelf once more, twisting her neck to see as far around the side of it as she could. "It's no use. I can't see enough of it without picking it up."

"Bailey?" Halona called. "Could you girls please come and wrap these purchases while I ring them up?"

"Sure thing," Bailey answered.

Bailey and Elizabeth joined Halona behind the counter and pulled out a stack of white paper squares from underneath.

"Pastor John, I'd like you to meet my cousin's daughter, Bailey, from Illinois. And this is Elizabeth, Bailey's friend from Texas. Girls, this is John Whitcomb, pastor of the church down the street."

Bailey shook the pastor's hand. "Nice to meet you, sir. This is a beautiful vase you're buying."

"You can call me Pastor John. The vase is a birthday present for my wife, Lelana." Pastor John smiled broadly, but then put his finger to his lips. "So no telling if she comes in here."

"Our lips are sealed." Bailey giggled.

Halona bagged the wrapped vase. "Here you go," she said as she handed the bag to Pastor John.

"Thanks, Halona." Then to the girls, "If you're still in town on Sunday, come on over to the church and visit us. Bible classes are at 9:30, and services start at 10:30."

Bailey's shoulders sagged. "I wish we could come, but we leave on Thursday."

"Well, next time you visit then." Pastor John smiled pleasantly. "It was nice meeting you."

Bailey's phone vibrated as she waved goodbye. She pulled it from her pocket. "Hello?" Bailey strolled to the back of the store, her phone pressed to her ear. "Hi, Kate!"

Elizabeth followed Bailey to the studio where they'd taken their first pottery lesson.

"Okay, we'll hang on." Bailey whispered to Elizabeth, "She's going to conference all the girls in, so get ready to answer your phone."

Elizabeth pulled her phone from her jeans pocket and it rang in her hand seconds later. "Yes, I'm here. Can you hear us?"

"I think we've got everyone," Kate said. "Bailey?"

"Check."

"Alex?"

"Check."

"Sydney?"

"Check."

"McKenzie?"

"I'm here."

"Elizabeth?"

"I'm here too."

"Good," Kate said. "What's going on with you guys? Anything new?"

Bailey sighed. "'Fraid not. We went on a hike yesterday with Elan to the Puye Cliff dwellings. We thought some of the area might resemble the scenery on the ancient pot, but nothing looked familiar."

"We're starting to feel this may be one mystery we aren't going to be able to solve," Elizabeth said.

"Don't give up yet!" Kate said. "I have good news and bad news. Which do you want first?"

"The bad news," Bailey said.

"Okay. Remember I told you I was going to print out the pictures you sent me so I could study them better?"

"Yes." Bailey looked nervously at Elizabeth.

"Well, I did print them out, and they looked great. So I laid them out on the floor to examine them. Biscuit came running into the room and got his muddy paws all over them."

"Oh no!" Alex said. "Are you going to have to reprint them?"

"I'm not sure." Kate cleared her throat. "Here's where the good news comes in. Or at least it may be good news. I'm not sure."

"Let's hear it!" Sydney said.

"Well, the funny thing about the muddy paw prints on the picture is that it almost looks like trees painted onto the scenery."

"I don't see where you're going with this," McKenzie said. "How could that be good news?"

"I think I see where she's going," Sydney said. "Think about it. The Santa Fe landscape had to have changed over the last few hundred years or so since that pot was made."

"Oh, I get what you're saying." Elizabeth's eyes sparkled at Bailey. "Trees and bushes and cactus plants would have grown in since then, so it may look entirely different than the pot's picture."

"Bingo!" Kate said. "And that's exactly what the picture looks like to me with the muddy paw prints on it."

"Why don't you send us photos so we can see them with Biscuit's paw prints? Then we'll get a better idea of what the area might look like now."

"I already did." Kate giggled. "Check your email."

The girls burst out laughing.

"You're really on top of this!" Bailey said.

"Anyone else have anything to report?" Elizabeth asked.

"No, I'm still researching the public records on the Tse family," Alex said. "Haven't turned anything up yet that's of interest."

"Sydney, any news on the Native American code talkers?" McKenzie asked.

"Only that the Navajo Indians were the ones who did the code talking in World War II," Sydney said. "I don't find any connection that would tie them or their code to the Pueblo Indians."

"All right," Bailey said. "Let's keep working on this. Thanks for calling, Kate. Your tip about those photos may crack this case."

Kate laughed. "Just doing my job. Or at least Biscuit was!"

"We're working at the shop right now, but we'll check our email as soon as we have time," Elizabeth said. "We'll let you know if the picture resembles anything we've seen so far."

"Okay," Kate said. "Keep us posted."

Bailey and Elizabeth said goodbye.

"Good thing I brought my laptop along," Bailey said. "I thought we might get bored, so I brought it in case we wanted to play games while my mom worked."

Bailey typed in her username and password, and Kate's email popped up with photo attachments. Elizabeth scooted her chair closer.

"There it is," Bailey said.

"Boy, that's amazing!" Elizabeth leaned in to get a better look. "Those muddy paw prints really do look like trees."

Bailey laughed. "Who knew Biscuit was such an artist!"

"This looks a lot more like the area we hiked yesterday with the 'trees' added," Elizabeth said.

Bailey squinted her eyes and pointed at the mountain to the right in the picture. "I wonder if this could be the mountain beside the Puye Cliff dwellings."

"I'm not sure." Elizabeth shook her head. "It looks more purple than that mountain. I thought it was brown or black."

"Maybe you're right." Bailey had another idea. "Or maybe it was just the lighting at that time of day."

"I'm not sure the shape of the mountain is right." Elizabeth's eyebrows narrowed in thought. "Wasn't the top flatter than this?"

Bailey nodded. "I think you're right. Maybe the painting on the pot isn't where we went hiking after all." She clicked the picture off and closed the laptop.

Halona wandered into the pottery studio. "What are you girls up to?"

"We were checking our email," Bailey said.

"Ready to see how the pots you made yesterday look now that they've dried?"

"Yeah!" Bailey pushed the computer to the end of the table, out of the way, while Halona got the pots from out back and brought them to the table.

"Now we get to paint them?" Bailey stood up and down on her tippy-toes.

"We glaze them," Halona said. "Have you thought about what colors you want to use?"

"I want mine to be like the sunset on your family pot, so I'll choose pink, orange, and yellow."

"I just want blue and green on mine," Elizabeth said. "Those are the colors in my room."

"Blue and green it is," Halona said as she got out big bottles of glaze and poured a little of each color into cups. She pulled paintbrushes from a drawer and laid them on the table by each girl. "What color do you want the inside of your dishes to be?"

"Pink, please," Bailey said.

"I think I'll make mine blue."

Halona poured some pink paint into Bailey's dish. "Pick up your bowl and swirl it around to make the glaze coat the bottom."

Bailey did as she was told.

"Now tip your dish on its side to get the glaze on the sides." Halona watched as Bailey let the pink glaze cover the sides of her dish.

Halona then poured blue glaze into Elizabeth's bowl, and Elizabeth covered the inside in blue.

Bailey dipped her brush into the pink glaze and started working on her sunset. "I wish these colors were brighter." She couldn't disguise her disappointment as she looked at her painting.

"They will be after we fire them in the kiln," Halona replied.

Elizabeth cocked her head. "Guess that's a good thing to remember when we disappoint ourselves with the way we sometimes act. Just like the colors we paint on these dishes, we don't always shine like we should. But we're a work in progress. God isn't finished with us yet."

"You are wiser than your years, Beth," Halona said. "We always have room to grow and improve, don't we?"

"So the next step is firing them?" Bailey asked.

Halona nodded. "Yes. I'll turn on the kiln."

"When Mom and I bake cookies we set the oven at 375 degrees," Bailey said. "What temperature do you set the kiln to cook the pots?"

Halona laughed. "Much hotter than your kitchen oven. The first firing, the bisque, is usually at 900 to 1,000 degrees."

Bailey's eyes widened. "That's hot!"

"Yes it is," Halona agreed. "That's why you must never play around the kiln."

"How long do you bake it?" Elizabeth asked.

"Usually about eighteen hours." Halona set the oven.

Bailey's jaw dropped. "Eighteen hours! Seems like they'd be burnt to a crisp by then."

"If they were cookies they would be!" Halona teased.

"Do you use special potholders to take them out?" Beth asked.

Halona shook her head. "No. We let them cool in the kiln for two to three days before we remove them."

Bailey could hardly believe her ears. "So our pots won't be finished until we have to leave?"

"I'm afraid not," Halona said. "Making pottery is a slow process. There are many steps, and each one takes time."

"Wow. Now I understand why each piece is so special," Elizabeth said. "Especially that beautiful one handed down from generation to generation."

Halona smiled. "We take great pride in our work. For a pot to last hundreds of years as that one has only proves the excellent craftsmanship of my people."

"That's for sure!" Bailey said.

A ding at the door followed by baby cries told them they had customers.

"I'd better get back out to the front of the store," Halona said. "But I thought we should get those pots started so they'll be ready for you to take home with you on Thursday."

"Thanks for helping us," Elizabeth said. "I'm learning a lot."

"Me too!" Bailey said. "Like never try to bake a pot and a batch of cookies in the same oven!"

Halona laughed, her dark eyes twinkling, and hugged Bailey. "It's so good to have you here. You make me laugh in a tough year when laughter is hard to find." She gave Bailey one more squeeze and went to the front of the store.

"I was thinking," Bailey said to Beth. "Maybe we should compare the pictures Kate sent us with the actual pot. We might spot something we missed before."

"I guess it couldn't hurt," Elizabeth said. "Let's log back on."

Bailey opened the laptop and pulled up Kate's email. Soon the pictures appeared on the screen.

"Let's take it to the shelf where the pot is." Elizabeth picked up the computer.

"Okay. I'll turn out the light." Bailey flipped the switch by the door.

The two slipped into the hallway where the shelf containing the pot stood. Beth held the computer beside the pot. "What do you think?" she asked.

"I think the lighting is terrible in this hallway," Bailey said. "And the light from the computer is making the colors on the actual pot look weird."

"Go turn the light back on in the studio and leave the door open to see if that helps," Elizabeth suggested.

Bailey flipped on the light, pushing the door open as far as possible.

"Is that any better?"

"A little," Beth answered. "I wish the shelf was on the other wall. The light shines more on that side." Elizabeth was distracted by the noisy cries of the baby in the store and the sound of its mother trying to comfort him. "Sounds like it's someone's naptime," she told Bailey.

Bailey nodded absently. "I think we should hold the pot in the light," Bailey said. "It'll only be for a minute."

"Bailey!" Elizabeth warned. "Don't you dare even think about picking up that pot."

"Come on, Beth." Bailey faced her friend, hands on her hips. "Don't be such a worrywart."

"I am not a worrywart," Beth said. "I just know right from wrong, and we were told not to touch it."

Bailey reached out and touched the pot with one finger. "See? Nothing happened. You're blowing this thing way out of proportion."

Elizabeth's face was getting red. "Here. You hold the computer. It'll keep your hands busy."

"You're doing a fine job with it." Bailey wouldn't take the laptop from Beth but moved toward the shelf. "I'm just going to take the pot in the light for a second." She put her hand out to grab the pot.

"Bailey! No!" Elizabeth whisper-yelled while moving in Bailey's direction to stop her. Instead, she bumped the computer. Bailey's hand slipped and knocked into the pot, sending it crashing to the floor.

The girls looked at each other, eyes wide with fear.

"Now look what you made me do!" Bailey frantically picked up pieces of pottery from the floor, thankful it had broken into five neat parts rather than shattering into a million pieces.

"Me!" Fury filled Elizabeth's eyes. "This wouldn't have happened if you had just done what you were supposed to!"

"We can glue it back together and no one will ever know," Bailey said desperately.

The bell on the door rang again. More customers.

"Bailey? Elizabeth? Could you come give me a hand?" Halona called.

"S—sure, Halona," Bailey replied. "W—we'll be right there." She looked around wildly, wondering what to do with the broken pottery pieces she held. "Come on!" Bailey hurried back into the studio and stuffed the fragments into a lower cabinet against the wall.

Elizabeth set the laptop on the table and closed it. Taking a deep breath, she followed Bailey to the front of the store.

"Here, will you wrap these like you did earlier?" Halona handed a shallow bowl to Bailey and a narrow vase to Elizabeth. "Are you girls okay? You look a little pale."

Bailey giggled nervously and tried to smile. "Sure. We're fine, aren't we, Beth?"

Elizabeth lowered her head, but nodded. She took the vase from Halona and carefully started wrapping a paper square around it.

Aiyana bounded through the door, a plastic bag swinging from each hand. "I got the supplies you asked for, Mama."

"Thank you, sweetheart," Halona replied. "You can put them in the studio. The clay goes in the lower cabinet."

Bailey followed Aiyana with her eyes, and then wiped her sweaty hands on her jeans before picking up the bowl to wrap it. Her hands shook as she set the bowl in the center of her paper square. She could hear Aiyana singing in the studio. Bailey pulled one corner of the paper up and stuffed it into the center of the bowl, then another.

She stopped, hands in midair, when Aiyana screamed.

CHAPTER
6

The Treacherous Summit

Aiyana's scream from the studio froze all activity in Earth Works. Halona rushed to the back and was met in the hallway by Bailey's mom, who'd raced out of the office. Together, they hurried into the pottery studio where Aiyana stood dazed, holding the broken pottery pieces in her hands. The cabinet door stood open, and the newly bought clay sat on the floor in front of it.

"Aiyana, what is it?" Halona went to her daughter.

Bailey and Elizabeth quietly appeared in the doorway and stood with Bailey's mother.

"The pot! Our key to riches. . .it's broken!" Tears poured down the little girl's face.

"Wha– There must be some mistake." Halona took the pottery shards from Aiyana's hands. She turned the pieces and looked at the painted pictures. "It can't be!"

The bell on the front door rang as it opened.

Paco's friend, Willy, burst into the store looking for Halona. "Come quick! It's Elan! He's in trouble on Puye Cliffs! He's losing his footing, and I think he's going to fall. You've gotta come!"

Halona left the pottery pieces on the countertop and hurried out the front door, not bothering to turn the OPEN sign to CLOSED as she locked the door. She hoisted Willy's bike into the back of her Suburban while he and the others buckled up for the trip to the cliffs.

"He's climbing the side of the cliff like they used to do in the ancient rite of passage," Willy explained when they were on their way. "I think he's trying to prove his manhood by scaling the cliff. Sort of his own personal rite of passage. But he's slipping a lot, and I don't care if he gets mad at me. Someone needs to make him get down."

"He has nothing to prove," Halona said, defiance and fear gripping her voice. "He's more man than most boys his age."

Willy said nothing.

"Is anyone else there?" Bailey asked.

"Paco was there when I left."

Bailey closed her eyes and shook her head. That could only mean trouble.

Halona sped out of Santa Fe and into the desolate area that took them to Puye Cliffs. She swung her car into a parking space on the tourist side of the cliffs, and they ran to the place Elan had showed Bailey and Elizabeth, where the ancient rites of passage used to be held.

Willy looked up and pointed. "Whoa. He's a lot higher now than when I left." Willy walked away to where Paco stood by his bike.

"Elan!" Halona cried when she saw where her son was. "You must come down!"

"I can't!" The tremble in Elan's voice gave away his fear.

Halona snatched out her cell phone and dialed. "Chief Maska. We need your help. Elan is scaling the Puye Cliffs. You've got to talk to him. Yes. . . Thank you."

"Is he coming?" Bailey's mom asked.

"Yes. He'll be here in just a few minutes. He lives nearby."

"Aiyana, did you know he was planning to do this?" Halona asked.

"No," Aiyana replied. "He talked about proving to those boys that he was a man, but I didn't think he'd do something this crazy."

"What boys?" her mother demanded.

Aiyana shrunk back. "He didn't want me to tell," she said.

"You must tell."

"Paco and his friends have been bothering Elan almost every day since school let out. They tell him he's not a man."

Halona's mouth gaped, and tears filled her eyes. She nodded at Aiyana and hugged her. "It's okay. You did the right thing to tell me."

Bailey spoke up. "He told Beth and me about the ancient rite of passage and acted like climbing the cliffs wouldn't be hard to do. We told him we were glad the tribe dropped that tradition so he wouldn't have to do it."

"We even told him we thought he easily qualified as a man since he helps you so much and already has a job," Elizabeth added. "But I guess we didn't convince him."

"No one should have to tell him," Halona said. "He should know inside himself."

"Elan, come down!" Tears pooled in Aiyana's eyes. "We need you to help take care of us!"

"Hang on, Elan! Help is coming!" Bailey called. Even as she spoke, Elan took another step higher.

"He's not giving up," Elizabeth said. "He's determined to do this."

More boys from town had apparently heard about the daredevil rock climbing attempt and gathered at the foot of the cliff to watch. A slight breeze moved the dry, hot air.

"Boy, word sure travels fast," Bailey said to Elizabeth. "Dorko and his pals must have called all their friends."

Elizabeth didn't seem to hear. She was busy looking at the area around them. "Bales, look at this place."

"Yeah, so what? It's the same place we saw yesterday when we came with Elan."

"But think about the pictures Kate sent us," Beth said. "It looks just like this!"

Bailey viewed the landscape with fresh eyes, imagining it without all the trees and bushes. "You're right! This could be the site shown in the sunset painting on the ancient pot!"

The girls' conversation was interrupted when a white pickup truck pulled up. A man in a uniform jumped out. Gazing up at the cliff, he gave Halona a quick hug. "I see he's gone quite a ways up already."

"Yes, he has. Thank you for coming, Chief Maska." Halona wrung her hands as she watched Elan go still higher. "I don't know what to do."

"He's proving his manhood," Chief Maska said. "We can only wait and pray."

"Don't you think we should try to talk him out of it?" Bailey asked.

"Has anyone tried that yet?" the chief asked.

"Yeah, we tried, but he wouldn't listen!" Aiyana wailed.

"Then that is your answer." Chief Maska's eyes stayed on Elan. "We'll let him finish. He's climbed too high to come down safely now."

"But he could fall! Or even die!" Halona's voice rose.

The chief placed his strong hands on Halona's shoulders to calm her and looked into her eyes. "The Great Spirit will show him the way."

Elizabeth spoke up. "I don't know about the Great Spirit, but I know my God was strong enough to protect Daniel in the lion's den, and He opened up the Red Sea like a book to protect the Israelites from the Egyptians who were chasing them. I know He can hold Elan against that cliff and keep him from falling too."

Bailey's mom put her arm around Elizabeth and squeezed her shoulder.

Bailey cupped her hands around her mouth and shouted, "You can do this, Elan! God will help you!"

"You can do everything through Him who gives you strength!" Elizabeth added. "The Bible says so in Philippians 4:13." She winked at Bailey.

"Yeah, Elan! Be strong and courageous," Bailey said. "For the Lord your God is with you wherever you go. Even up the side of a cliff!"

Elan looked down over his shoulder, then up at the rest of the cliff above him. He inched his right hand up the cliff wall until he found a handhold. He did the same with his foot. Over and over, he repeated the motion. Soon he was three-fourths of the way up.

"He looks so small up there." Sweat dripped down Bailey's face, and she wiped it with her sleeve. "I bet he's as high as my dad's four-story office building downtown!"

"If he makes it to the top, how in the world will he get back down?" Elizabeth wondered aloud.

"One step at a time, child," the chief told her.

Bailey noticed Paco and his pals had grown unusually quiet. She nudged Elizabeth and nodded in the boys' direction. "Dorko doesn't have such big things to say now, does he?"

"Nope." Elizabeth smiled. "This stunt has really shut him up. Let's keep praying Elan doesn't fall. And that Paco learns a lesson from this."

Bailey turned at the sound of rocks falling and gasps from the crowd. Her hands flew to her mouth.

"Oh no!" a woman behind her screamed.

Elan had lost his grip and slid about five feet down the side of the cliff. He caught himself on a tree rooted in a crack in the rock wall.

"I can't watch!" Halona wailed. Bailey's mother put her arms around her sobbing cousin.

"Deep breath, Elan," the chief called. "Steady yourself. You're okay."

Elan appeared to listen. Clutching the branch, he searched for a foothold. Then he laid his forehead against the cliff.

A man wearing jeans and a polo shirt hurried to Halona. "I came as soon as I heard."

"Pastor John!" Halona grasped his outstretched hand like a lifeline.

The pastor then shook hands with Chief Maska, who told him Elan was determined to prove his manhood by climbing Puye Cliffs.

"All we can do for him now is pray for his safety," the chief said.

"That I can definitely do," Pastor John replied.

Bailey shook the pastor's hand too. "Elizabeth and I have been trying to give him extra courage and strength by telling him Bible verses that have helped us."

"Yeah," Elizabeth said. "Just like the other day when Elan took us hiking out here and Bailey and I practically tripped over a rattlesnake!"

Pastor John grinned. "I think that's an excellent plan. You can't go wrong with God's Word."

"It has superhero powers in it that transfer to you when you believe," Bailey said seriously.

"That's true, if you're referring to God as the superhero," the pastor said. "I never quite thought of it that way, but I think you're on to something there." He smiled and ruffled Bailey's silky black hair. "So how about if we call on some of that supernatural strength to help Elan now?"

"Let's do it!" Bailey said and high-fived Pastor John.

She, Elizabeth, and Pastor John joined hands in a little circle. Bailey prayed first.

"Dear God, we are afraid for Elan. Protect him. Help him find the right places for his hands and feet as he climbs. Give him strength to hold on. Most of all help him not to fall and to trust in You. Amen."

Elizabeth went next. "God, thanks for being here with us. We know You're helping Elan right now, but he needs to know that You're the only Father he needs to show him how to be a real man. Give him courage to make good choices. Keep him safe. In Jesus' name. Amen."

Pastor John squeezed the girls' hands as approaching sirens wailed in the background. "God, I can't possibly say it any more eloquently than these girls have, but please be everything Elan needs in his life—his Protector, his Father, his Strength, his Confidence. May he turn to You in times of difficulty and uncertainty. May his heart belong to You. Bring him down safely to his mother. In Your Son's strong name. Amen."

Bailey looked into Pastor John's face and saw a tender smile. His eyes were moist, and he hugged them. "Thanks, girls. I know God heard our prayers and is already answering them in the way He knows is best."

"He's almost to the top!" someone yelled.

Bailey saw that in about two more reach-and-step movements, Elan would indeed be to the flat mesa at the top of the cliff. "You're almost there, Elan!" she shouted. "You can do it!"

By now a TV news helicopter hovered overhead. Police cars and fire trucks came next, sirens blaring, standing by in case emergency medical care was needed.

Elan reached one last time, and his arm landed over the top ledge. He pulled himself up and swung his leg onto the landing.

"You did it!" Elizabeth whooped.

Elan stood, his arms raised in victory.

Halona's cell phone rang.

"Mom! I made it! I proved myself a man!" Elan was talking so loud that Bailey could hear him through the phone.

"I am so proud of you, even though you scared me to death," Halona said. "Don't you ever try anything like this again, do you hear me?"

"I won't," Elan promised. "I'm worn out and all scraped up. I'm ready to be brought down."

Chief Maska stood right next to Halona. He tapped her on the shoulder and motioned for her to give him the phone, which she did.

"Elan? It's Chief Maska."

"Did you see me, Chief? I made it!" Elan jumped up and down on the mesa plateau.

"I saw you. You did a remarkable job getting up there."

"I was just telling Mom that I'm tired and all scraped up and ready to be brought down now."

"Brought down?" Chief Maska smiled wryly. "Elan, you've only done the first part of proving your manhood. Being a man means continuing even when you're tired, doing what's right even when you're hurt, and taking responsibility for your actions and choices. You must now come down from the mountain on your own, not expect someone to rescue you."

"What? I can't make it! I'm too tired. I can't do it!"

With that, Bailey saw Elan drop in a heap on top of the mountain.

CHAPTER 7

One Step Closer

"You *can* do it, Elan." Chief Maska spoke gently. "I will show you another way to come down that is easier than the one you took up. Walk to your right until you see a boulder the color of the sunset."

Elan slowly stood and looked around him, cell phone still against his ear. He then followed the chief's directions. "I think I see it."

"Good. Now climb over it and follow the small path that winds to the left."

Step by step, the chief guided Elan down the mountain until finally, a half hour later, he emerged at the bottom, tired and ragged. Halona grabbed him in a hug before the paramedics checked him over.

"Elan!" Bailey rushed to him. "You made it! Are you okay?"

"I think so. Just a little beat up." He raised up his hands, scraped and raw, for her to see. "My knees are bloody too. And I think I have blisters on my feet, but not as bad as if I'd climbed barefoot like many of my ancestors."

Halona hugged him again. "I'm just glad you made it down in one piece."

Paramedics bandaged his wounds and listened to his heart.

"I guess there's no doubt that you're a man now," Bailey said. "We knew it before, but this should take care of any questions anyone may have had about you." Her eyes flitted in Paco's direction, and Elan smiled.

"So no more taking risks like that!" Halona scolded. "You could have been killed, and where would that have left Aiyana and me? We need you."

"I know, Mama," Elan said. "I won't do anything like that again. I know that a real man needs to be responsible, not just brave."

The paramedic helped Elan to his feet. "Okay, son. You're good to go."

"Come on. Let's get you home." Halona wrapped her arm around Elan and led him toward the car.

"Hey, Elan!"

Elan swung around to see Paco, Willy, and several other boys coming toward him. He scowled until Paco extended his hand.

"I was wrong." Paco's smile brightened his usually gloomy face. "You're tougher than I thought."

Elan shook Paco's hand, wincing as his bandaged fingertips met Paco's grip.

Paco let go. "Sorry."

"No problem."

"Well, we'll see you around." Paco and his buddies jumped on their bikes and took off toward town.

"Who was that?" Halona asked.

"Just some guys from school." Elan kept walking toward the car.

"Were they the ones who teased you?"

Elan glared at Aiyana.

"I had to tell!" Aiyana cried.

"Yeah, they're the ones," he admitted. "But it doesn't look like they'll give me any more trouble."

"You should have told me," Halona said. "I'm sure we could have come up with a better solution than you risking your life."

As the Tse family—plus Elizabeth, Bailey, and her mom—piled into the Suburban, a sense of dread filled Bailey. With the excitement over, she suddenly remembered the broken pot.

"Halona, about the broken pot Aiyana found in the cabinet at the store," Bailey began. She figured she may as well come clean with the whole awful truth and face the consequences now.

Halona looked at her in the rearview mirror. "Oh yes! I'd forgotten all about it in my worry over Elan."

"I broke it, and I'm terribly sorry." Bailey felt hot tears prick her eyes.

"What pot?" Elan asked.

"The pot of our ancestors!" Aiyana blurted. "The one that held the key to riches!"

"How'd *that* happen?" The accusation in Elan's voice was unmistakable.

"I—I wanted to look at it in better light. So we could figure out if the painting on the pot was of an area somewhere around here."

Elizabeth spoke up. "It wasn't all Bailey's fault. We both knew we shouldn't touch the pot, but we were equally curious. As she reached for the pot, I accidentally bumped into her and made her knock it over. That's when it fell to the floor and broke. I'm sorry too."

"Bailey!" Mrs. Chang's face meant business. "You girls have gone way over the boundaries with your sleuthing this time!"

"I'm sorry," Bailey said softly. "I'll try to fix it. I think it will glue back together."

"Still, the damage is done. 'Sorry' and a little glue won't fix hundreds of years of history." Mrs. Chang shook her head.

"Bailey," Halona said gently. "It's okay. It's true the pot meant a lot to our family. But I think God put Elan on the side of that cliff today for more reasons than just to prove his manhood."

Bailey looked at the rearview mirror where she could only see Halona's kind eyes looking back.

"I think He put him there just at that time so I could see this situation from a different perspective." Halona paused. "The pot was very important to us, but not as important as our family or the lives we live. Elan's life was on the line today and, by comparison, that pot isn't worth the clay it was made from."

Tears spilled down Bailey's cheeks. She looked at Elizabeth and saw tears in her eyes too.

"I don't know what to say," Bailey whispered. "Thank you."

"Yes, thank you," Elizabeth echoed. "We'll do whatever we can to repay you and repair the damage."

"I know there's really no way to do that." Bailey wiped her tears with the palm of her hand. "But you can bet we'll try our best."

"I know you will," Halona said.

● ● ●

That evening, Bailey sat cross-legged on the floor of the bedroom with her computer in her lap and chatted with the other Camp Club Girls on the CCG chat room.

> Bailey: *It's been one of the most miserable and wonderful days all rolled up into one.*
> McKenzie: *How so?*
> Bailey: *I'm almost embarrassed to tell you.*
> Alex: *Go ahead, Bales. Spill it.*
> Bailey: *I broke the ancient pot.*
> Elizabeth: *With my help.*
> Kate: *Shut up.*
> Sydney: *No you did not!*
> Bailey: *Yes I did, sorry to say.*

Alex: *How'd that happen?*

Bailey: *I wanted to compare Kate's paw print pics to the pot.*

Kate: *And?*

Bailey: *The lighting was bad, so I decided to take it into the light.*

Elizabeth: *But I told her not to, and when she reached for the pot, I accidently bumped her. It fell to the floor.*

Sydney: *Oh no! what happened?*

Bailey: *Halona called us to come help her, so we picked up the pieces and put them in a cabinet.*

Alex: *That doesn't sound good.*

Elizabeth: *Just as we went to help her, a kid came in saying Elan was in trouble.*

Bailey: *Elan was scaling Puye Cliffs without ropes or tools to prove his manhood.*

Sydney: *You're kidding.*

Elizabeth: *His people used to do that as a rite of passage.*

McKenzie: *Did he make it to the top?*

Bailey: *Yes, but it was scary. He slipped a couple of times.*

Elizabeth: *After he climbed down. his fingers and knees were bloody.*

Alex: *Gross! TMI!*

Elizabeth: *Sorry.*

McKenzie: *So what about the pot? Did you get in trouble?*

Bailey: *On the way back from the cliffs, I confessed.*

Elizabeth: *We apologized, though we knew it wouldn't make anything better.*

Sydney: *How'd the family take it?*

Bailey: *Mom was mad. Can't blame her.*

Elizabeth: *Halona was cool.*

Bailey: *She said Elan's climb showed what was important.*

McKenzie: *Amazing.*

Kate: *Any consequences?*

Bailey: *Not too bad. Mom took my phone away. That's why we're chatting instead of calling.*

Elizabeth: *Do you have anything to report?*

Alex: *I found the Tses owned a turquoise mine north of the northern point of New Mexico in the Jemez Mountains.*

Bailey: *I thought the mountains around here were the Sangre de Cristo Mountains.*

Sydney: *Sangre de Cristo. I learned those words in my Spanish class. They mean "Blood of Christ."*

Elizabeth: *Impressive, Syd!*

Alex: *Bales, from what I read, the Sangre de Cristo Mountains are the most important mountain range in New Mexico, but the east side of the Jemez Mountains is where the Puye Cliff dwellings are.*

Bailey: *So that probably explains why I've heard more about Sangre de Cristos.*

Elizabeth: *Alex, did you find out anything about the deed?*

Alex: *It was issued in 1848 to a man named Hakan Kaga.*

Elizabeth wrote the name and date on a paper lying on the nightstand.

Bailey: *Good work, Alex! I'll ask Halona if she's ever heard that name.*

Alex: *Don't bother. I already found out that it was Halona's maiden name.*

Bailey: *Awesome!*

Elizabeth: *Anything else?*

Alex: *That's it for me.*

McKenzie: *I don't have anything.*

Bailey: *OK. If any of you come up with anything, call Beth's phone or email us.*

Sydney: *Will do.*

Kate: *C U l8r.*

Bailey signed off. "We could do a bit of research on the name Hakan Kaga ourselves."

Elizabeth's green eyes twinkled. "Just what I was thinking." She typed the name into her search engine. Most of what popped up was genealogical information, which she scanned. "Looks like Hakan was Halona's great-great-grandfather."

"Nothing about a turquoise mine?" Bailey asked.

"Not on this site. I'll keep looking." Elizabeth scrolled down. "Aha."

"What?"

"It says the Suquosa Mine was mined by the Kaga family from the 1600s. Somehow when people began officially purchasing land, it was bought by someone named Taime Wapi. It was bought again by Hakan Kaga in 1848. He worked the mine and passed it on to his family after his death. He was only fifty-eight when he died."

"That's not very old," Bailey said. "Does it say how he died?"

Elizabeth kept reading. "Hmm. It says he suffered injuries in a mining accident, but doesn't say what the injuries were. But the accident happened the same year he died."

"I bet that's no coincidence."

"No." Elizabeth replied. "It might have caused his death."

"Can you find a death certificate?"

"I'm looking." Beth scanned the listings. "Here. Hakan Kaga. Cause of death: injuries sustained in mining accident."

"So he died, then the mine was passed to his family from generation to generation until now it belongs to Halona and no one can find the deed to prove it." Bailey shook her head. "Can you find out when the mine shut down?"

Elizabeth typed in "Suquosa Mine." She clicked on the first entry that came up. "It gives a brief history of the mine. Let's see here. . . . It says the mine was haunted by the deaths of many workers in the early 1900s and finally shut down due to drought and safety issues in 1925."

"Anything about where it was located?" Bailey leaned forward.

"Not really. Just that it was in the Jemez Mountains in northern New Mexico."

Bailey growled. "I wish they were more specific!"

"Something has to give pretty soon," Elizabeth said. "I feel like we're close to the solution, but somehow just can't see it yet."

"Me too. We have to keep our eyes and ears open even more than ever."

"I think we need to ask God's help," Elizabeth said. "We haven't been the best at seeking Him first."

Bailey was quiet, then nodded. "You're right. We've been trying to do this all on our own and forgot to put God first."

The girls bowed their heads and Elizabeth prayed aloud. "God, we're stuck on this mystery, and we need Your help. If You want us to solve this, would You please show us the pieces to the puzzle that we're missing? It would help Halona and her family so much if we could find that deed to the mine and prove her to be the rightful owner. Thank You for listening to us and helping us. In Jesus' name. Amen."

"There." Bailey said. "Now we're even one step closer to the solution."

CHAPTER 8

The Secret Compartment

Wednesday morning at Earth Works, after their store-opening chores were done, Bailey and Elizabeth pulled out the pottery pieces from the cabinet.

"The pot seems even older now that it's broken." Bailey laid the pieces on the table and brushed off her hands. "I feel like we've just found these old relics on an archaeological dig!"

"Seriously, that's something to think about," Elizabeth said. "As old as this pot is, we should be extremely careful in handling it and studying it, just like the archaeologists would. We'd hate to damage it even further and lose an important clue in the process."

"You're right." Bailey went to the countertop along the wall and opened a drawer. She returned to the table with two small paintbrushes. "These should help us uncover clues without touching the pot too much."

"And what about some gloves, so oils from our skin don't get on the pot when we do have to touch it?" Elizabeth asked. "I think the part that's painted will be protected, but I'm afraid our skin oils could discolor the plain, unpainted clay."

"Good thinking. I'll see what I can find." Bailey scrounged through drawers and cabinets until she found what looked to be Halona's gardening gloves. "These should do the trick."

"Perfect."

Bailey slipped on a pair of gloves and picked up a paintbrush.

"Wait!" Elizabeth said.

"Now what?"

"We should spread out some old newspaper on the table to make our cleanup easier."

Bailey sighed. "Cleanup? You're as bad as my mother." She started to grab a couple sections of newspapers from a pile sitting in the corner, but then reconsidered. "What if the newsprint comes off on the pot?"

"You're right. We shouldn't use that."

"We could use the same paper that we wrap the pots in when someone buys them," Bailey said. "I'll run and get some from under the counter." Bailey hustled out to the front of the store and, after getting Halona's permission, returned with a small stack of the wrapping paper. They spread the sheets out until the tabletop was covered. "Satisfied?"

Elizabeth laughed. "Yep! If we can't keep our mess on all this, then it's a project we probably shouldn't do."

"Let's get started." Bailey gingerly picked up her favorite piece—the one with the sunset painted on it—and set it in front of her. It still had some of the pot's bottom attached to it, so it stood up as if it had never been broken. Bailey dusted off the small painting with her paintbrush, then turned the pot to dust the inside. As she turned it, she noticed a little hole only about a half inch long, exposing what seemed to be a pocket built into the pot near the top, almost like a wall within a wall.

"Check this out!" she told Elizabeth.

"What?"

"This side is hollow." Bailey stood to peer down at it.

"Of course it is," Elizabeth replied. "Pots have to be hollow to hold anything."

"Not like that," Bailey said, irritation creeping into her voice. "The actual side of the pot is hollow, like it has a pocket or a secret hiding place or something. There's a space only about a quarter of an inch wide between the two walls."

Elizabeth raised her eyebrows and stood to look at the piece Bailey was inspecting. "Wow! I see what you mean!"

"Why do you think they made it like that?" Bailey asked.

Elizabeth ventured a guess. "Maybe to hold something important, like today's safety deposit boxes do?"

Bailey had her eye right up to the hole. "I can't see if there's anything in there."

"You need a flashlight or something."

Once again, Bailey rummaged through drawers and cabinets. "It's no use. I can't find one."

"How about if I shine my cell phone light on it while you look in?" Elizabeth suggested.

"It's worth a try."

Elizabeth opened her phone and shone the light just above the hole in the side of the pot, but Bailey's head kept blocking the light. "Your head's in the way," Beth told her.

"That's where it has to be if I'm going to be able to see in," Bailey said. "Why don't you move the light?"

" 'Cause I don't have anywhere else to move it to where it will shine into the hole!"

Bailey thought for a moment. "How about if we stick something in there to see if we feel anything inside?"

"Great idea!" Beth said. "We need something small, but long enough, like a pencil or pen."

"I think we should use a pen so we don't risk making marks on the inside with a pencil."

Elizabeth nodded. "That wouldn't be good."

Bailey stuck a black ballpoint pen down into the hole and moved it around.

"Feel anything?"

"I'm not sure." Bailey moved the pen again. "Maybe."

"Let me try." Bailey stepped aside and Elizabeth pushed the pen into the hole and wiggled it. "I see what you mean. It's hard to say for sure since there's not much wiggle room, but I think something's in there. It sounds different than if the pen were just hitting against the clay pot. Muffled." She pulled the pen out, and powder from the dry surrounding clay came out with it.

"You just made the hole bigger!" Bailey said. She put a gloved finger at the edge of the hole between the two pocket walls and brushed more powdery clay out.

"Do you think we should really break this pot more than we already did just to satisfy our curiosity?" Elizabeth asked. "I mean, isn't that what got us into trouble in the first place?"

Bailey peered into the little hole, not hearing Beth. "Almost there. . ." Another brush with her finger and a couple more with the paintbrush. "I can see it!"

"See what?" Elizabeth squealed. "What is it?"

"I don't know, but there's definitely something in there."

"So now what do we do?" Beth asked.

"We brush away more of the side until we can get it out." Bailey kept working on it, and Elizabeth did her part by blowing the dust out of the way. Finally, Bailey tried to put her index finger and thumb in the hole to pull out whatever was inside, but they wouldn't fit.

"We need some tweezers," Beth said.

"Oh! I saw some in the drawer." Bailey was up in an instant. "I figured they probably used them for adding beads and stones to the pottery." She retrieved the tweezers and twisted them this way and that to try to grab onto the hidden contents. "I think I have it!"

"Be careful," Beth said. "Don't let it go."

Bailey pulled the item to the hole and they saw for the first time that it was something resembling folded dark brown leaves. "What in the world?"

Elizabeth tilted her head to try to determine what it was. "Pull it out."

"I'm not sure I can without ripping it or damaging it somehow," Bailey said. "But I have a feeling this brown part is protecting something inside it. So maybe it doesn't matter if it gets torn."

Beth brushed some more of the side away to enlarge the hole. "There. Try that."

Bailey gently pulled the tweezers and whatever was in their grasp through the hole. The brown wrapping was more pliable than they thought it would be, and only tiny pieces chipped off as it was birthed through the gap in the pot.

Electricity charged between the girls as they looked at the brown leafy package.

"I've heard that people used to use certain kinds of leaves to wrap things to protect them against moisture." Bailey's hands trembled as she gently unfolded the leaves to reveal its contents—a yellowed document with the word "*Deed*" written across the top in fancy curlicue writing. With great care, she lifted the deed out of its protective cocoon. Some of the words were faded, but she could clearly read the words "*Suquosa Mine*" and "*Hakan Kaga.*"

Elizabeth's jaw dropped and she high-fived Bailey. "We found the deed to Halona's mine!"

Bailey couldn't contain the huge grin that stretched across her face. "Should we tell her right away?"

"Maybe we should see if we can find the mine first. What good is the deed if there's no mine anymore?"

"You're right." Bailey nodded. "We don't want to get her hopes up only to disappoint her later."

"We have to find out where that mine is," Elizabeth said. "Surely there must be an old map online somewhere."

"Or in the public records at the county recorder's office," Bailey offered.

"I'd think that if it was on public record, the Tses would have already found it. It can't be that easy." Elizabeth looked at the table with the broken pottery pieces. "We'd better clean this mess up before we start looking for the map."

"What'll we tell Halona about not putting the pot back together?" Bailey asked.

"We'll tell her the truth." Elizabeth gathered the wrapping paper covered with pottery dust. "That we found some information we needed to check out before we can finish. If she presses us, we'll just have to trust God that she won't be too disappointed if we can't find the mine."

Bailey brought the trash can to the table. "Yeah, we sure don't want to glue the pot back together and not be able to show them where we found the deed. I think she'll be happy that we found it even if we don't find the mine right away."

"I do too." Elizabeth carried the broken pottery pieces back to the cabinet, then rolled up the wrapping paper and dumped it into the trash. "But I think she'll be overjoyed if we find both!"

Bailey looked the room over. "We've got everything picked up, but what should we do with the deed?"

"I can put it in my bag," Elizabeth said. "No one will look in there, and it's big enough not to bend it."

She tucked the document into her bag. Then Elizabeth opened her laptop to look for a map of the mine's location. Bailey sat next to her to help her look. They clicked on several old maps and found nothing that showed Suquosa Mine. Then they clicked on one more link and found what they were looking for.

"There it is!" Bailey said, pointing at a tiny black dot.

"I can't believe it," Elizabeth said.

"Looks like it's close to where we were at the Puye Cliffs."

"I don't remember seeing anything that looked like a mine in that area, though Elan did say there used to be some up there." Elizabeth pushed back her blond hair. "I hope this isn't another dead end."

"We won't know until we try to find it," Bailey said. "What are we waiting for?"

"A ride." Elizabeth laughed. "We can't walk there from here. It's too far."

Bailey groaned. "We don't have any time to waste. We leave for home tomorrow! Maybe my mom would take us to Halona's house, and we could walk from there," she suggested. "It's really slow here at the store today. I've only heard the bell ring once or twice all morning."

"It's worth a try. Let's go ask."

"Hi!" Aiyana skipped into the studio. "What are you doing?"

Bailey looked at Elizabeth nervously.

"We're getting ready to see if my mom will take us to your house."

"Why? Are you sick?"

"No," Bailey said. "We have something we need to do."

"What is it?" Aiyana's dark eyes grew.

Elizabeth and Bailey looked at each other, then Beth nodded to Bailey.

Bailey took her little cousin's hands in hers. "Aiyana, remember when you told us a secret about the pot and the things your ancestors said about it?"

Aiyana bobbed her head up and down.

"And you asked if we would keep your secret?"

"Yes." Aiyana's face was somber.

"Would you do the same for us?" Bailey asked her. "Keep a secret?"

A wide grin sliced Aiyana's face, and her eyes snapped. "Sure!"

"Okay then," Elizabeth said. "Bailey and I need to go back to Puye Cliffs to try to find the mine that belongs to your family."

"But you can't tell!" Bailey reminded her.

Aiyana looked ready to burst with excitement. "I won't!"

Elizabeth patted her on the back. "Good girl. That's why we want Bailey's mom to give us a ride to your house—so we can hike to the cliffs from there."

"Oooh. I won't tell, I promise." Aiyana pressed her lips together and pretended to lock them and throw away the key.

"We want it to be a surprise for your mom if we can find it," Bailey added. "Understand?"

Aiyana nodded, lips pursed.

"Okay." Bailey turned to Elizabeth. "Let's go find my mom."

"I'm going to leave my bag in the studio," Elizabeth said. "I'm sure no one will bother anything in it."

She winked at Bailey, who smiled back.

Mrs. Chang was in the office working on the books. Her fingers flew over the keyboard, while she intently stared at the bookkeeping program on the computer.

"Mom, could you run Beth and me back to the house?"

Mrs. Chang looked up. "What on earth for?"

"We have something we need to do that we can't do here."

"Like. . . ?" Mrs. Chang prompted.

"Like. . .something we can't really tell you about yet." Bailey hedged with a smile. "It's sort of a surprise. But I promise it's nothing bad."

"Have you talked to Halona about this?" Mrs. Chang asked. "You're supposed to be helping her."

"Not yet," Elizabeth said. "We thought we'd find out if we even had a ride before we asked her."

"Besides," Bailey added, "the thing we need to do would help her more than us being here at the store."

Mrs. Chang eyed the girls suspiciously, a faint smile playing at the corners of her mouth. "You're up to something."

"We are!" Bailey admitted. "But it's a surprise!"

Mrs. Chang sighed and gave in to that smile. "Oh, all right. If it's okay with Halona."

Bailey hugged her mom and kissed her on the cheek. "Thanks! You're the best."

●—●—●

The second car stopped in front of the Tses' house, Bailey and Elizabeth jumped out.

"I have my cell phone if you need us." Elizabeth held it up for Mrs. Chang to see.

"Part of what we have to do involves a hike, but don't worry," Bailey told her. "We'll take water, sunscreen, and Beth's phone."

Concern flitted across Mrs. Chang's face. "Don't make me sorry I brought you here."

Bailey laughed. "We won't. Thanks for the ride. Love you." She blew a kiss to her mother.

"Now," Elizabeth said as Mrs. Chang drove away, "let's gather our things and get going."

"We need to print out the map first," Bailey reminded her.

"Right. I'll do that while you get the water and sunscreen."

With the sun already hot at ten-thirty in the morning, the girls set out on their hike.

Looking for the Lost Mine

Bailey and Elizabeth chatted easily as they started out.

"The sky here in this big open space is so much bluer than in Peoria," Bailey said.

"I know what you mean." Elizabeth pointed up. "Look at that cloud. It looks like the breeze is just carrying it along, not a care in the world."

"It's a gorgeous day!" Bailey loved the feeling of the warm sun on her skin. She was glad they'd remembered to put on sunscreen.

"Look! A roadrunner!" Elizabeth said. The leggy bird darted this way and that before disappearing behind a rock formation. A hummingbird with its iridescent green head zipped around in the distance.

"It's a regular wildlife preserve around here!" Bailey joked.

"Well, hopefully we won't see any wildlife we *don't* want to see, like coyotes or javelina."

"Or snakes!" Bailey added cheerfully. "Hey, we haven't told the other Camp Club Girls about finding the deed yet!"

"Oh yeah." Elizabeth snatched her phone from her pocket. "I'll call them right now." Once she had them all conferenced, she hit speakerphone so Bailey could hear too.

"Okay," Elizabeth began. "We have some big news to report."

"Let's hear it!" McKenzie said.

"Remember we told you we were going to try to piece the broken pot back together?" Bailey asked.

"Yeah...," Sydney replied.

"We started on it, but had a minor distraction." Bailey winked at Elizabeth.

"Did we ever! Bailey found a hidden compartment in the piece that had the sunset painted on it."

259

"A hidden compartment?" Kate whooped. "You've got to be kidding!"

"Nope," Bailey said. "The side with the sunset was hollow, sort of like a second side hiding behind the one we could see, making a pocket that could hold things."

"Was there anything in it?" Sydney asked.

Bailey and Elizabeth grinned and kept walking.

"As a matter of fact, yes!" Elizabeth said.

"What was it?" some of the girls asked in unison.

Bailey tried to sound casual. "Just a dirty old deed to Halona's turquoise mine."

All four of the girls screamed and talked at once, and Biscuit barked excitedly.

"You're kidding!" Kate said. "I can't believe it—and neither can Biscuit!"

"What did it look like?"

"That's insane!"

"Are you sure it's the real thing?"

"I know. It's almost too good to be true!" Bailey's voice registered her enthusiasm. "But it really was the deed we've been looking for!"

"Unbelievable!" Alex said. "Was Halona thrilled?"

"We haven't exactly told her yet," Elizabeth said.

"Haven't told her? Why not?" McKenzie sounded incredulous.

"We thought it would be best to find the mine first," Bailey explained. "What good is a deed to something if it doesn't exist?"

"I see your point," Kate said. "It would only get her hopes up, and if you can't find it, she would be really disappointed."

"Exactly." Bailey climbed over a rock, then took the phone from Elizabeth so she could do the same.

"So what's the next step?" Alex asked.

"We found an old map online showing where the mine used to be," Bailey said.

"Was the map hard to find?" Sydney asked. "I looked for it a little when I did my research on the code talkers, but didn't find one that showed the old mines in the area."

"It took a bit of searching, but not too bad," Beth said. "We're just glad we found it. We go home tomorrow, you know, so time was getting short."

Bailey kept a steady pace as they talked. "We're on our way to Puye Cliffs now to see if we can find the Suquosa Mine. It's supposed to be close to there."

"I thought you sounded a little winded." Sydney's giggle rippled across the line. "You've got to get in better shape! I'll have to take you running with me next time we're together."

Elizabeth groaned. "I can't wait."

"Anyway, we'll let you know if we find it," Bailey said.

"You have to be careful around mines, you know," Kate said.

"Yeah, we know," Elizabeth said.

"No, seriously," Sydney added. "We had a special speaker come to our school and talk about that. You shouldn't go into them. They can have holes as deep as skyscrapers. Not to mention that animals or snakes may have decided to make their home in them."

Bailey watched the color drain from Elizabeth's face as Sydney continued.

"Plus, miners may have left explosives behind that could go off with the slightest touch." Sydney made a sound like a bomb exploding. "Just like that, you're gone."

Bailey imagined spit flying when Sydney imitated the explosion. "Hey! I think you got me wet with that noise!" The other girls howled with laughter.

"No joke. I saw a movie once where a guy got trapped in a mine and there were poisonous gases and pockets with no air," Alex put in. "Of course he was near death, but then was saved just in the nick of time."

"Good to know," Elizabeth said, her color still off. She gave Bailey a nervous half-smile. "We'll keep all those things in mind."

"We probably won't need to go into the mine anyway," Bailey said. "We just want to find where it is so we can take Halona there." She hoped the girls' stories hadn't scared Elizabeth out of searching for the mine altogether.

Sydney used her best snooty voice, and Bailey could imagine her nose in the air. "All right then. You have our permission to go."

McKenzie giggled. "But call us when you find it. I've never seen a real mine before, and I want to hear all about it."

"You mean *if* we find it," Bailey corrected.

"No, I mean *when* you find it," McKenzie said. "Think about it. If you can find an old deed that's been lost for generations hidden in a secret compartment of an ancient pot, this should be a piece of cake!"

"You do have a map, after all," Kate added. "Don't forget to use it!"

Elizabeth smiled. "I guess you're right. Thanks for the vote of confidence."

"We'll call you *when* we find it," Bailey said. "Bye!"

Elizabeth hung up and tucked her phone back into her pocket.

"Look at that!" Bailey pointed to a lizard doing push-ups on a nearby rock. "It must be time for aerobics!"

"We have lizards in Texas," Beth said. "I've heard they do that to cool off. Which reminds me, we've been walking for almost an hour. Let's take a rest."

Bailey plopped to the ground and gulped a long drink of water. "It seems like we've been walking forever."

Elizabeth pulled her hair up into a ponytail. "I know. But it can't be too much further. I remember when we came with Elan the Puye Cliff dwellings were just beyond those big boulders. I can see them in the distance, so we're probably over halfway there."

Bailey nodded, then shook her head back and forth, back and forth. Her hair swung around her head like fringe.

Elizabeth watched her curiously. "What are you doing?"

"Providing a breeze!" Bailey's swinging hair slapped first one cheek, then the other.

Elizabeth laughed. "You're too much!"

"Can you feel it?" Bailey's head continued to swing.

"Okay, sure. I can feel a slight breeze." Beth put both hands on the sides of Bailey's head to stop her. "All right. Now that you've cooled us off, we'd better get back at it."

"I guess." Bailey smoothed her hair back in place. "We want to get to the mine and back before everyone comes home from Earth Works."

"Besides, if we find the mine, we'll be anxious to tell Halona about it and show her the deed." Elizabeth smeared on some fresh sunscreen while Bailey slathered on some cherry lip balm.

"I can't wait to see the look on her face." Bailey smiled.

The girls walked on, sweat running down their backs and foreheads. Before they knew it, they were to the cliff dwellings.

"If I remember right, Elan said the old mines were over that way." Bailey pointed to the right of the ruins.

"That's what I remember too, so it must be right." Beth looked at the map they'd printed. "Looks like that's where it would be on this map too. Let's go check it out."

The hard earth was cracked from baking in the sun. Tufts of dry grass and spiny bushes miraculously grew from the cracks. A stiff breeze kicked up, and a tumbleweed rolled past Bailey and Elizabeth.

"I feel like we're characters in an old western movie," Bailey teased.

"Hopefully we won't run into any gun-toting outlaws!" Elizabeth pretended to draw guns from her holster and shoot. Then she blew off the tips of her index fingers and returned them to their holsters again.

Bailey giggled. "Pretty good! And I thought *I* was the one who should be an actress!"

Elizabeth hopped onto a good-sized rock and surveyed the area. "Let's start looking over here."

The pair split up and searched for any sign of a mine on the mountain, moving rocks as they went.

"Beth, come here!" Bailey called. "I think I may have found something."

Elizabeth hurried over.

"See? There's some rusted barbed wire around those rocks."

"It must have been put there years ago to keep people away from something," Elizabeth said. "Let's see if we can move it out of the way and get to the rocks behind it."

Bailey took one section of the barbed wire in her hand, and Beth held it about six feet down from her. Taking great care to keep the sharp barbs away from their arms and legs, they tugged and pulled, ripping up old weeds entangled in the wire from their dry roots. After several minutes of yanking at the sharp wire, the fencing was torn away from the rocks, and they stepped on it to bend it toward the ground.

"Ouch!" Bailey looked down at the drop of blood trickling down her calf. "It got me!"

"Shoot!" Elizabeth said. "And we were trying to be so careful. Does it hurt?"

"Not too bad. Do we have any tissues?"

Beth dug in their fanny pack. "No, I don't see anything." She looked around trying to find something to use in its place. "Stay here. I'll find something you can use."

Elizabeth walked a ways along the base of the cliff. Bailey saw her bend down and pick up something, then start back toward her. The stream of blood had almost reached her ankle and was beginning to dry.

"Here," Elizabeth said, handing her a handful of semi-dry leaves. "It was the best I could find."

"Thanks." Bailey took the leaves. "It'll be better than nothing." She sat down and dabbed the wet blood with the softer leaves and scrubbed the dried blood off with the rougher ones. "That worked pretty good," she said when she finished. She stood up and was ready to get to work. "Good to go."

"Now we just need to move some of these rocks." Elizabeth lifted one and tossed it aside.

"I don't want to freak you out, Beth, but remember that snakes, lizards, or bugs may be hiding under them. We should warn them so they can get out without feeling too threatened by us." Bailey threw a stick toward the pile of rocks. A startled lizard zoomed away.

"Anybody else in there?" Elizabeth threw a small rock.

They waited a moment, but there was no more movement.

"I guess if there are any rattlers, we'll know it when we hear them." Bailey stepped forward and lifted a rock. Instantly, the ground beneath it swarmed with bugs. "Ewww!" Bailey chucked the rock away.

"Well, as gross as that was, I'd rather see that than a snake any day." Elizabeth moved another rock and then another. Bailey joined in, and soon they had half the rocks out of the way, and a hole in the mountainside began to emerge. Elizabeth tossed another rock aside, and two grasshoppers flew up at her. "*Aaaaaa!*" she screamed.

Bailey jumped. "What?"

Elizabeth sighed. "Oh, that scared me. Turned out it was just a couple of grasshoppers."

Rock by rock they unstopped the hole until it was almost big enough for them to crawl through.

"We've found the mine!" Bailey squealed.

"I just hope it's the right one."

"Let's make the hole big enough that we can walk into it," Bailey said.

"Hold it right there." Elizabeth stopped working, her hands on her hips. "We are not going into that mine, remember?"

"Oh, I know." Bailey wiped the sweat from her forehead with her sleeve. "But we want to be able to see into it without lying on our stomachs, don't we?"

Elizabeth paused with her lips pursed. "I guess these rocks would be pretty hot to lay on," she said. "Some of them burn my hands just tossing them out of the way."

They returned to their work, moving more rocks though their hands were scraped up. Sweat poured down their red faces.

"Look! I think we've moved enough rocks that we can step into the mouth of the mine," Bailey said. "Let's go!"

Elizabeth hesitated.

Bailey knew what she was thinking. "We won't walk into it, Beth, but it won't hurt to stand at the mouth so we can see inside."

Elizabeth frowned. "I'm not sure that's safe."

"Of course it is," Bailey said. "It's only three feet from where we were just moving rocks."

Beth looked at the rock pile and the hole in the mountain. "Okay. . . but we aren't going to go any farther than that. Got it?"

"Of course." Bailey frowned, annoyed at her friend's overprotective nature. "Believe me, I don't want to get trapped in an abandoned mine any more than you do."

The girls swigged some water. As they stood on the rock pile, Bailey noticed a partially obscured piece of weathered wood poking out toward the bottom of the mine's mouth. She pushed the rocks away to reveal a dilapidated sign that said SUQUOSA.

"Beth! This is it! We've found Halona's mine!"

Elizabeth took Bailey's hands and they danced on the rocks, moving their bodies more than their feet.

"Whoohoo! We did it!" Elizabeth threw a kiss heavenward. "Thank You, God!"

Still holding hands, the girls stepped down off the rocks and into the mine's mouth.

"I can't believe we're standing in what was once known as the best turquoise mine around." Bailey looked all around her. Sunlight lit the mine's opening, but darkness so thick you could almost touch it loomed before them. Cobwebs hung at the sides of the entrance, and tiny bugs exposed to the first light they'd seen in years scurried away.

"The shade feels wonderful," Elizabeth said. "My skin will never be the same after all the sun it's had this week."

"I know what you mean." Bailey rubbed her arm. "Even though I'm not nearly as light-skinned as you, I'm glad to be out of the sun too."

"I wonder if this is how Jonah felt when he looked at the belly of the whale." Elizabeth wrapped her arms around herself.

"It does feel like we're in the open mouth of some kind of a monster." Bailey shivered.

As they stared into the darkness before them, a rumble groaned deep and low. Bailey looked up and saw dust fall from the mine ceiling. In the shadow, she saw a mix of confusion and fear wash over Elizabeth's face. Suddenly, they felt the ground vibrate, and tiny rocks pelted their faces.

"Earthquake!" Bailey screamed.

Earthquake!

Bailey grabbed Beth's hand and dashed toward the opening they'd just unearthed. The ground shook and rolled.

Bailey tilted off balance and tumbled to the ground. Elizabeth toppled over her, pinning her arm to the hard rock. Rocks fell around them, and dust filled Bailey's lungs, making it impossible for her to breathe. She wheezed and gasped, then felt Elizabeth's hand pulling her to her feet.

"Get up! We have to get out of here!" Elizabeth rolled off Bailey.

Bailey frantically searched her pants pocket for her inhaler. She puffed the medication into her mouth. Holding her breath, she pushed to her knees, then tried to get her feet beneath her, but it was no use. The girls stumbled and fell again. An avalanche of falling rock filled the entrance, blocking their way out.

Suddenly they were in total darkness, as if someone had flipped off the light switch.

Bailey blew out the breath she'd been holding, her breath returning.

"We're trapped!" The ground finally stopped moving, but Bailey trembled just the same. "We're trapped!" she said again, taking shallow, panicked gulps of air.

Elizabeth silently wrapped her arms around Bailey.

Bailey coughed, then laid her head on Beth's shoulder. Suddenly the welcoming shade of the mine felt cold and confining. Bailey shivered and lifted her head. "What will we do?" she whispered into the darkness.

"I—I don't know." Elizabeth's voice sounded flat.

"See if we have a phone signal," Bailey said.

Elizabeth pulled out her phone and the light shone. "I'll try calling your mom," she said. But she couldn't get a signal.

Tears pricked Bailey's eyes. "Now what?"

She heard Elizabeth suck in a big breath and blow it out. "We need to pray," Beth replied.

The two girls snuggled closer and squeezed each other's hands.

"God," Elizabeth started, her voice shaky.

Bailey heard her sniff and exhale loudly again.

"God, we're trapped in here." Elizabeth struggled to stay calm. "We're scared and don't know what to do."

Bailey squeezed Beth's hand tighter.

"No one knows we're in here but You." Elizabeth choked down a sob. "But You're the only One who really matters anyway. We believe You have the strength and power to save us, and we ask You to do that. Help us to trust You and not be afraid. Amen."

Bailey patted Beth's hand, and then the two girls dissolved into tears, hugging each other in the dark.

"We'll make it, Bales." Elizabeth sniffed loudly. "You'll see."

Bailey nodded and wiped her eyes. "I know we will."

"At least we told Aiyana we were coming here," Elizabeth said. "If we don't make it back home in time for supper, they'll come looking for us."

"But they don't even know this mine exists," Bailey moaned. "I hope they can find it."

"Maybe they won't have to," Elizabeth said.

Bailey felt Beth stand up. "What are you doing?"

"I'm going to try to get us out of here," Elizabeth said. "If we moved rocks from the outside to get in, maybe we can move rocks inside to get out!"

"Great idea!" Bailey felt her way through the darkness to the rock wall. She tugged on a rock, but it wouldn't budge. "I can't get this rock out. It's wedged in too tight."

"Maybe if we can see the wall we can spot a place to start," Elizabeth said. "You know, kind of like playing Pick-Up Sticks or Jenga. You always try the loose ones first." Elizabeth aimed her phone light toward the wall. "See anything?"

Bailey felt the rocks wherever Beth lit them up. "This one wiggles. I'll try it." Bailey scooted the rock from side to side, and then pulled. "I got it!"

"Good!" Elizabeth reached out through the dark to hug Bailey and whacked her in the head instead.

"Ow!"

"Sorry, that was supposed to be a hug."

Bailey laughed. "That's the roughest hug I've ever had."

"I'll keep my hands to myself," Beth teased. "At least I didn't try to high-five you."

"I'm thinking it wouldn't have felt much different." Bailey smiled in the dark. "Let's work another rock out."

Again, Elizabeth pointed the light while Bailey searched for a loose rock and pulled. One by one, the two girls removed rocks from the entrance to the mine.

"You'd think we'd see some daylight soon," Bailey said.

"I know. I wonder how deep this rock wall is." Elizabeth sat down on the dirt floor. "All those rocks we moved out of the way must have rolled right back into place with the earthquake."

"And then some! Bummer." Bailey plopped down beside her friend. "All that hard work for nothing."

"Well, not for nothing, really," Elizabeth said. "We got into the mine, didn't we?"

"Boy, did we. And now we're stuck here."

"Sydney failed to mention earthquakes as one of the dangers to watch out for in the mine safety talk she gave us."

"Beth?" Bailey's voice quivered. "I'm sorry I said we should come in here. This is my fault."

"Don't be ridiculous," Beth replied. "I would have stopped you if I thought it was really dangerous. We would have been fine if it weren't for that earthquake. Who could have predicted that?"

"I guess," Bailey said.

"Besides, I'm older," Elizabeth added. "I'm supposed to look out for you. If anything, I'm responsible for this mess we're in."

"Remember that comment you made about Jonah when we first stepped into the mine?" Bailey asked.

"Yeah," Beth said. "I remember."

"Well, I bet this is how he felt when he was stuck inside the belly of the big fish," Bailey said. "Nothing to do but to turn to God and beg for Him to help him get out of there."

"You're right." Elizabeth inhaled the damp, earthy smell of the mine. "I bet that fish smelled a lot worse than this mine, though."

"Come on." Bailey stood. "We'd better get back to work. I'll hold the light this time, and you can work on moving the rocks."

Elizabeth handed the phone to Bailey and then began prying at a loose rock.

"I'm praying silently for you while you work," Bailey informed her. "Those rocks don't stand a chance!"

Bailey's hands felt raw from handling so many rocks, and the muscles in her arms were weak from lifting them. She and Elizabeth had traded off holding the cell phone light and moving the rocks, but hadn't made much progress. They were still trapped inside the dark mine.

"I remember hearing about miners who were trapped in a mine and tapped on a pipe until rescuers found them," Elizabeth said while she and Bailey rested.

"Wish we had a pipe to tap on," Bailey said. "We'll have to think of something else."

"We could always yell," Elizabeth said.

"But what if we're running out of air in here?" Bailey asked. "We'll use it up even faster if we yell."

"Better than not doing anything," Beth said.

"Yeah, but maybe there are other options we haven't thought of yet."

They sat in dark silence.

" 'When I am afraid, I put my trust in You.' " Elizabeth spoke quietly, as if to herself.

"Huh?"

Elizabeth spoke louder. " 'When I am afraid, I put my trust in You.' Psalm 56:3."

"Where'd that come from?" Bailey asked.

"My mom used to tell me that when I was only about three years old," Elizabeth said. "I was very afraid of the dark when I was little, and when she tucked me in at night, we'd say that verse together. It was the first verse I ever learned."

"Cool. Are you afraid now?" Bailey asked.

"Yes, but that verse came back to me just when I needed it."

"Mind if I borrow that verse and make it mine too?" Bailey asked.

Elizabeth laughed. "Help yourself!"

More dark silence.

Bailey spoke. "We have to get out of here so we can tell Halona her mine is real. Are there any sticks or something we could use to poke between the rocks?"

Elizabeth walked around, shining her phone close to the mine floor. A thick wire about three feet long was laying about five feet away. "Yes!" She jumped up and grabbed it.

"Now all we have to do is find a place to stick it through," Bailey said.

"I don't know if there is a place," Elizabeth said. "I don't recall seeing any light peeking through those rocks, do you?"

"No, but God just provided us with a wire, so maybe He'll show us a place to put it." Bailey took Elizabeth's hand and they walked to the blocked off entrance. "Put your phone away so there's no extra light in here," Bailey said. "We'll see the light shining through better in complete darkness."

Elizabeth tucked her phone in her pocket. Hand in hand, the girls walked along the rocked-in mouth of the mine.

"I don't see any light anywhere, do you?" Bailey asked.

"Unfortunately, no." Beth sighed.

"I know! Let's back up and look from further away," Bailey suggested. "Maybe we're just too close to it to see it shining through."

The girls linked arms and stepped about ten paces back, then started walking the distance of the wall again. Bailey tried so hard to see something that she started seeing weird colors in front of her eyes.

"There!" Elizabeth said. "I think I see something."

"Where?"

"I'm pointing to it." Elizabeth put Bailey's hand on her arm and had her follow it to her pointing finger. "Put your head by mine and look down my arm."

Bailey did as she was told, her eyes following where she felt Elizabeth's finger pointing. There it was—a tiny pinpoint of light between two rocks.

"I see it!" Bailey squeezed Elizabeth's arm. "Now let's walk toward it, not taking our eyes off it until we're there."

Gingerly, they made their way to the speck of light, wire in hand.

"It's up higher than I thought," Elizabeth said, as they approached. "I hope we'll be able to reach it."

As they got closer, the light disappeared.

"It's up too high!" Bailey said. "We can't even see it when we're this close."

"Okay," Elizabeth said. "We just need to back up and find it again. Then one of us will stay back here and the other will have to go toward it."

"But we can't even see each other!"

"I'll turn on my phone and light up the mine long enough to see which way you need to go, and I'll direct you toward it," Elizabeth said. "We'll see if you can climb up the rock wall and stick the wire through it."

"It's worth a try," Bailey said.

The two backed up to where they could spot the tiny dot of light. "There it is." Elizabeth flipped open her phone and turned it in Bailey's direction. "Now you walk until you get to the rocks."

Bailey followed her friend's instructions, darkness surrounding her as she moved farther from Elizabeth's phone light. Hands outstretched, she soon felt the cool rocks. "I'm there."

"Start climbing. I'll tell you which way to go."

Bailey put the wire in her mouth so she'd have both hands free for climbing. Elizabeth closed her phone for a second to see the pinpoint of light better. Then she opened it again to spot Bailey on the wall. "Move a little to your right. You're almost right underneath it," she instructed. "You'll need to climb up about three feet."

Bailey thought of Elan scaling Puye Cliff. *This should be nothing compared to that.* Placing her foot on a rock she couldn't see, she felt for a place to grab with her right hand. She moved her other foot up to another rock and then reached for a handhold with her left hand. Little by little she moved higher.

Elizabeth shone the phone light. "You're there! It's just above your head. Stick the wire in!"

Holding on to a rock with her left hand, Bailey took the wire from her mouth with her right hand and felt for the hole. She poked over and over, only to feel the wire hit hard rock. "I can't find it, Beth! And I can't hold on much longer."

Suddenly, another low rumble began, and Bailey heard a strange creaking. She climbed down a few feet, then jumped from the wall and ran to where she hoped Elizabeth was. The ground began to shake and roll. Dirt and rocks fell around them, and Bailey heard rocks from the mine entrance shift. Frantically pawing the air to find her friend, she yelled, "Beth!"

"I'm here!" Their hands swept the air until they found one another. Huddling together, they covered their heads with their arms. Seconds later, the trembling stopped and the mine was silent. Bailey and Elizabeth slowly unfolded themselves from their fetal positions.

"I think that was an aftershock," Elizabeth said. "It didn't feel as strong as the first one and didn't last as long."

"I heard a creepy creaking when I was up on the wall, so I jumped down," Bailey said. "I was afraid the whole mine was going to collapse on us!"

Elizabeth looked toward the rock wall where Bailey had been seconds before.

"Oh my goodness! Bailey, look at the entrance!"

CHAPTER 11

Daylight!

Bailey looked, shocked at what she saw. Narrow slivers of light streamed through the rock wall in three places. "God is making a way out for us!" Bailey still quivered from the quake.

"Or at least making it easier to get a signal out to people who can help us," Beth said. "Do you still have the wire?"

"Yeah. I hung on to it when I jumped down."

"Good. Let's see if we can find something to tie on to it. We can use it as a flag to stick through a crack between the rocks."

"Okay," Bailey said, "but don't you think we should try to move more rocks? We might be able to get out now."

"I think we should do both," Elizabeth said. "Let's make a flag to hang out one of the openings first. Then if someone comes looking for us while we're working on the wall, they'll see where we are."

"Good thinking," Bailey said. "That way *it* can be working while *we* work!"

"Exactly." Elizabeth paused. "The brighter the flag, the better."

"I don't know if we have anything bright to use." Bailey tried to see through the blackness. "It's too dark to find anything."

Beth aimed her phone light all about the mine but didn't see anything in the dim light that they could use. "I'm going to shine the light closer to the ground while I walk around to see if I can find something."

Bailey followed behind, and the two walked slowly, painstakingly, looking for any scrap of brightly colored fabric that could be used as a flag, without going further into the mine. "Whoa! Look at this!" Bailey held up a blue rock about the size of a walnut. "Turquoise!"

Elizabeth brushed some dirt off it and held her phone close to look it over. "It's beautiful! Must be plenty of turquoise left in this mine if it's just lying around like that."

"Yeah. Here's another piece!" Bailey felt like cheering. She put the rock in her pants pocket and continued searching. "I don't think we're going to find anything we can use for the flag," Bailey said finally.

"I don't think we are either." Elizabeth started to put her phone away.

"Wait!" Bailey said.

"What? Did you see something?"

"Your shirt! It's red!"

Elizabeth pointed the light on herself and laughed. "I forgot what I wore today!" Beth suddenly grew quiet.

"You won't have to take it off," Bailey said, realizing what was troubling her friend. "Let's just rip off the pocket."

"You've got a deal!" Relief flooded Elizabeth's voice. She put her fingers into her pocket and pulled. The pocket tore halfway off. Another tug and it was in her hand. "I got it!"

"Good job!" Bailey said. "Should we just poke the wire through it or tie it on?"

"I think we should tie it so it doesn't fall off as easily. Hand it to me, and I'll do the tying."

Bailey stuck out her hand, but Elizabeth didn't take it. "Here."

"Where?" The girls searched for each other's hands, and then Elizabeth found the wire. She held it between her knees as she tied the red pocket to the end. "I'll try to tie it from the corner so more of the pocket will hang out."

"Good idea," Bailey said.

"There. I think I got it. Do you want me to climb up to put it in one of the openings, or do you want to?"

"Doesn't matter," Bailey answered. "I guess you can since you already have it."

"Here. You hold the light."

Bailey held up the phone, which dimly lit Beth's path. "I'll direct you like you did for me. Let's just pray the battery doesn't die on us."

"Okay. Let me know if I'm getting off course." Beth started climbing the wall. "At least that one hole isn't quite as high as the others. I'll try for it."

"You're doing good," Bailey encouraged. "A little to your left."

"The trick is going to be squeezing the flag through that slit." Beth climbed a little higher. "I see it. I think I can reach it from here." She took the wire, flag end first, and tried to poke it into the tiny space where the light shone through.

"That's it!" Bailey said.

"It's not going in." Elizabeth pushed it again and felt the wire go through the hole. "It's going!"

"It is, but the flag isn't," Bailey told her. "It's scooting down the wire instead of going through the hole with it."

Elizabeth groaned. "I need to come down. I can't hold on anymore." She started her descent, then jumped when she was close enough to the ground.

"I've got an idea," Bailey said when Elizabeth was down from the wall. She shivered in the cool, damp air. "We could tie the pocket to the wire, then bend the end of the wire back over the flag so it can't slip off."

"Let's try it," Elizabeth said.

Bailey held the phone light while Beth tried to secure the flag with the wire. After she bent the wire over the flag, she twisted it over the remaining wire below the red pocket. "There. That should do it."

"Want me to try taking it up this time to give your arms a rest?"

"Sure." Elizabeth took the phone back.

Once more, Bailey started up the rock wall that blocked the mine exit. "If this doesn't work, I'd say we should start moving rocks and making noise so people will hear us."

"Me too." Elizabeth kept her eyes on Bailey in the dim light. "But I sure hope it works this time."

Hand, foot, hand, foot. Bailey made her way up the wall, wire and flag between her teeth.

"Almost there. Only about one more step and then reach."

A dot of light shone in Bailey's eyes, and she blinked against the unaccustomed brightness. She took the three-foot wire from her mouth. "I found it!"

"Good. I'll be praying down here while you try to stick the flag through."

Bailey pushed the wire flag first into the bright light. It resisted, bending the wire. She continued to twist and push until it suddenly flew through, almost making her lose her balance on her foot- and hand-holds. "I did it! It's through!"

"Awesome! Way to go!" Elizabeth clapped her hands as Bailey made her way back down. "Now, we start tearing down the wall."

"I need to rest a minute," Bailey said. "My arms and legs are shaky from all that climbing."

"That's okay," Elizabeth said. "You rest. I'll get started."

"I'll make noise while you move rocks in case anyone's within earshot."

"Perfect!"

Elizabeth worked on the wall, one rock at a time. Each one took a considerable amount of time as she wiggled and pulled, moving it only fractions of an inch at a time.

Bailey took her noisemaking job seriously. "Help! We're in this mine! Help! Come find us!" Finally, she stopped yelling and listened. Nothing.

"Beth?" Bailey's voice was quiet.

Elizabeth continued working on the wall. "Hmm?"

"What if they don't find us? And what if we can't get the wall moved?"

Elizabeth stopped her work and climbed her way back to Bailey in the dark. "Give me your hand."

Bailey did, and Elizabeth found it after swiping the air with her own. She sat down by her friend. "Listen, Bailey," she said. "We're *going* to get out of here."

"That's what we hope will happen, but what if we're wrong? What if they can't find us?"

"You know they'll look until they do. Nothing will stop them."

Bailey was silent. "What if" thoughts swirled around in her head like a giant whirlpool. "You're a good friend, Beth. The best."

Elizabeth squeezed Bailey around the shoulders. "So are you, Bales."

The girls sat that way for a few minutes, saying nothing.

" 'Surely I am with you always, to the very end of the age.' " Elizabeth quoted the words of Jesus. "Matthew 28:20. We're not in this mine alone."

Bailey wiped at the tears that threatened to fall down her cheeks. "I know. But I'm still scared."

"I think everything's finally catching up to us," Elizabeth said. "The hike, moving rocks, the stress of the earthquake. Maybe we should rest awhile, before starting to work on the wall again."

"My mom always says a girl can cope with things better when she's well rested," Bailey said. "Maybe things won't look so hopeless if we take a short nap."

Elizabeth laughed. "I usually hate taking naps, but that does sound pretty good right about now."

Bailey agreed, and they leaned against each other, Bailey's head on Elizabeth's shoulder. Within minutes, the two fell asleep, backs against the cold wall.

What seemed like only seconds later, Bailey and Elizabeth awoke to the sound of men's voices.

Elizabeth jumped up. "Help! We're trapped in here! Help!"

Bailey scaled the rock wall, making it to their wire flagpole in record time. She wiggled it frantically. "Over here! See the red flag moving? We're behind these rocks!"

The voices grew more distant and then faded away.

"They didn't hear us!" Bailey wailed. "I wiggled the flag! I thought for sure they'd see it."

"I know. So did I," Elizabeth said. "Did you recognize the voices?"

"No, they sounded pretty muffled behind these rocks. Did you?"

"No," Beth said. "At first I thought maybe one was Elan, but it was too deep."

"We've got to move more rocks so they can hear us easier." Bailey started working on one rock and Elizabeth on another.

"We won't give up, Bales," Elizabeth said. "We can do this."

"With God's help, we'll get out of here ourselves if they don't find us first."

"I think that catnap we took helped." Hope filled Elizabeth's voice. "I feel like I have more energy, don't you?"

"A little," Bailey's voice trembled. "I just want out. I'm sick of being in the dark."

"I know what you mean." Elizabeth worked her rock side to side. "I'm starting to crave sunlight."

Bailey pulled on her rock, her fingers burning and raw. "It's weird how cool it is in here when it's so hot out there."

"Yeah, I'm afraid we'll freeze if we don't get out before dark."

"We'll get out." Bailey stood straight. "I have faith!"

Elizabeth laughed. "I'm glad. So do I."

Bailey's rock suddenly came free, and she landed on her backside. She laughed. "I'm glad you couldn't see that, Beth."

"See what?"

Bailey explained what had just happened.

"I missed it," Elizabeth teased. "I could've used a good laugh too!"

With each rock that was pulled out, a bit more light came in, but other rocks fell in, filling the hole they'd just made.

"We can't seem to clear enough space to crawl out!" Bailey wailed.

"Just keep at it," Elizabeth said. "We can't give up!"

"Hello?"

"Anybody there?"

Bailey and Elizabeth stood stock still for a nanosecond. They leaped onto the rock wall.

"Help! We're in here!" Elizabeth shouted.

Bailey reached the wire flagpole first and wiggled it wildly. "Help! Help!"

"We hear you!" the rescuer said. "Hold tight. We'll get you out of there."

Elan yelled into the rocked entrance. "Bailey! Elizabeth! It's Elan! You're going to be okay."

"Elan!" Tears sprung to Bailey's eyes. "I'm so glad to hear your voice."

"Are you hurt?" one of the men asked.

"No," Elizabeth replied. "Just tired and scared."

"Bailey? Is that you? It's Mom!"

"It's me," Bailey answered, her voice shaking. "Don't worry. We're okay now that we know we'll get out of here soon."

The girls caught glimpses of hands until a circular hole at the top of the wall spanned about two feet wide.

"Do you think you can crawl out?" a rescuer yelled into the hole.

"Sure!" Bailey said. "We just have to climb the wall, and I've already been up it plenty of times today!"

She started climbing the wall once more, wincing at the pain from her sore toes and raw fingertips. Elizabeth crawled up behind her, and when Bailey got to the top, the rescuer pulled her out as Elizabeth pushed from behind. The warm sun never felt so good on Bailey's face.

In minutes, both girls were out and hugging Bailey's mom and the Tses.

"Oh Mom, I love you! I've never been so happy to see you in my whole life," Bailey said, as she hugged her mother.

"That goes double for me!" Mrs. Chang hugged Bailey, then held her at arm's length to look her over. "You weren't hurt in the earthquake?"

"No, but that's how we got trapped," Bailey said. "The rocks fell and covered the entrance so we couldn't get back out."

"God was looking out for you, that's for sure," Halona said.

"We knew it all along," Elizabeth said. "He was right there in that mine with us, wasn't He, Bales?"

"Yep, and His Word kept coming to our minds," Bailey added.

"That's why it's so important to hide God's Word in your heart, like you've done," Bailey's mom told them. "Then it's there to draw from when you need it."

"It was pretty cool, the way that worked," Beth admitted.

"Come on," Halona said. "Let's get these girls home. They've had quite a day."

"That's for sure." Bailey turned to her rescuers. "Thank you for finding us and getting us out." She hugged them with all her might.

The four o'clock sun blazed as they started walking toward the tourists' parking lot, when Bailey remembered. "Halona!" she said. "I almost forgot. We have some good news for you!"

The Surprise

Halona swung around toward Bailey. "What good news?"

"Well," Bailey said, "when I tried to fix the pot I broke, I found a secret hiding place inside."

"What?" Halona unlocked the car doors and the group piled inside. "I can't wait to hear *that* story on the way home!"

Once they were in the Suburban, Bailey continued. "I picked up the piece with my favorite part of the painting on it, the sunset." Excitement fizzed in Bailey like carbonation in a soda. "I was going to glue it to another piece, but I noticed that the side where it had broken looked weird."

"How was it weird?" Halona asked.

"It was hollow!" Bailey raised her eyebrows. "It had a hidden wall inside the outer one, making a pocket-like compartment just behind the sunset." Bailey buckled her seat belt, and they were off.

"Was something in it?" Bailey's mom asked.

Bailey nodded. "Yes, but I'm not going to tell you what until we get back to the shop."

Halona looked at Bailey in the rearview mirror. "Well, aren't you the mysterious one?"

"I don't mean to be mysterious," Bailey said. "I just think it will be neater to show it to you instead of just tell you about it. Don't you think so, Beth?"

"Definitely," Elizabeth said. "Believe me, this is worth waiting fifteen minutes to find out."

Soon, the Suburban pulled up in front of Earth Works, and they all climbed out. Halona unlocked the store and stepped inside, where Bailey saw her wince at the sight of the earthquake damage. Her hands flew to her mouth, tears pooling in her dark eyes. The smell of pottery dust hung in the air.

"I'll never be able to afford to replace all this merchandise," she whispered.

"What about your insurance?" Mrs. Chang asked. "Will it cover it?"

"It may cover some of it, but probably not everything." Halona slumped onto a stool behind the counter. "I don't know if we can recover financially from this. We may have to shut down the store."

"Wait." Bailey strode to the studio with Elizabeth close behind and rummaged through the pieces of broken pottery in front of the open cabinet that had held the family heirloom. As she brushed shards aside, she spotted the one with the sunset painted on it and picked it up. Like jigsaw puzzle pieces from different puzzles all mixed together, the ancient pot was beyond repair.

"Where's the deed?" Bailey asked.

"In my bag," Elizabeth replied. "Remember? We put it in there so no one would find it and so it wouldn't get crumpled." Elizabeth retrieved her bag and pulled out the deed.

She handed it to Bailey. "Let's go present this to its rightful owner."

The girls walked down the hall to the store, where everyone was busy picking up broken pottery pieces, baskets, jewelry, and blankets. Elan was putting his broom to good use.

"Seems like something's missing." Bailey looked around the store and spotted the incense holder. "That's it!" She went over and lit a fresh stick of incense. "Now it smells like it should in here. It smells like Earth Works."

"We found what we wanted to show you, Halona," Elizabeth said.

All work stopped, and everyone gathered by the counter.

Bailey cleared her throat. "It is with great pleasure that I present to Halona Tse this deed to the Suquosa Turquoise Mine. It belonged to her ancestors and now belongs to her and her family."

Halona's mouth fell open. Her eyes went from Bailey to Elizabeth, then to Bailey's mom and her own children. "The deed? Is this for real?"

"It's real, all right," Bailey said. "It's what we found inside your pot." Bailey showed her the broken piece of pottery and the pocket where the deed was found.

Aiyana tugged on her mother's hand. "Mama! It's just like what your mother told you, remember? 'Behind the sunset our treasure awaits'!"

"So that's what it meant," Halona said, still stunned. "And my grandma always said the pot held the key to riches. They knew. They knew! But the specifics of it didn't get passed to the next generation."

Halona hugged Bailey and Elizabeth. "You girls have solved an age-old mystery."

Her finger traced the fancy old-fashioned writing that spelled the word *"Deed"* at the top.

"Now we just have to find out if the mine still exists, and if so, where." Halona's eyes clouded with doubt. "It will be a huge undertaking."

"It sure was." Bailey grinned, her eyes crinkling.

"Was?" Elan asked. "What's that mean?"

"It was a huge undertaking," Elizabeth said. "But it's already done."

Confusion danced across Halona's face. "I don't understand."

"That's what we were doing on our hike." Bailey laughed. "We were looking for your mine when the earthquake hit and we were trapped inside."

"But at least we found it!" Elizabeth said.

"How can you be sure it's the right mine, the Suquosa?" Halona asked. "There are many old mines in that area."

"We're sure." Bailey's voice brimmed with confidence. "For starters, we found an old map on the internet that showed its location, so we printed it out and took it along."

"And it led us to the right spot!" Elizabeth said. "But a huge rock pile covered the entrance."

"So we decided to move all those rocks and try to get inside." Bailey saw her mother's frown. "We know mines are no place to play around, but we weren't going to walk back into it or anything. We just wanted to see if it really was behind those rocks."

Elizabeth nodded. "Our hands got scraped up, so we were glad when we uncovered the mine's entrance. We opened it up enough to stand in it."

"And when we did," Bailey put in, "we saw an old wooden sign sticking out from behind some rocks. We moved them too, so we could read the sign."

"What'd it say?" Aiyana asked.

"It said 'Suquosa Mine'. " Bailey folded her arms across her chest and raised her chin proudly.

"It is too much to take in," Halona said. "All of this is so unbelievable."

"This is what we've dreamed of, Mama." Elan took his mother's hands. "We can have our mine back."

"We don't even know if there is still turquoise in the mine," Halona said. "That will be important to learn before we get too excited."

Bailey stuck her hand in her jeans pocket and pulled out two blue stones. "Will this be enough proof to answer your question?" She opened her hand to show the stones to Halona.

Halona inhaled sharply and tears sprung to her eyes. "It is too good to be true!" She grabbed Bailey and Elizabeth and hugged them fiercely. "Thank you! You have no idea how much this means to our family."

●—●—●

Thursday morning, while the Tses went to the county recorder's office to update paperwork on the mine, Bailey and Elizabeth called the other Camp Club Girls.

Elizabeth had her phone on speaker so she and Bailey could both hear as she conferenced in the rest of the girls.

"Mystery solved!" Bailey announced.

"No way!"

"What?"

"How'd that happen so fast?"

"Amazing!"

"Yep," Beth told them. "We followed the old map showing where the mine should be. We couldn't see it at first, but then noticed a big pile of rocks with some old rusted barbed wire around it."

"We started moving the rocks and found the mine entrance," Bailey added.

Bailey and Elizabeth recounted their work getting the mine entrance cleared.

"Wait a minute," Alex said. "You didn't go into the cave, did you?"

"We only stepped in at the edge," Elizabeth said. "We didn't walk back into it."

"But Sydney forgot to mention one thing in the safety talk she gave us," Bailey said.

"I did?" Sydney said. "What?"

"Earthquakes." Bailey waited for a response.

"Huh-uh," Sydney finally said. "You did not have an earthquake while you were in that mine!"

"We sure did," Bailey said. "And we were trapped inside for hours."

"You should have listened to me in the first place and not gone in there!" Sydney scolded.

"I know," Elizabeth said. "You were right. We had no business going in there."

"What'd you do?" Kate asked.

Bailey told them what it was like being stuck in an old abandoned mine, and Elizabeth added information about how they worked to get out and made a flag to help rescuers find them.

"Were you scared?" Alex asked.

"Totally!" Bailey said. "I was more scared than Beth. She kept telling me cool Bible verses to keep me calm. I need to memorize more verses so I'm better prepared for bad situations in the future."

"Bailey was very brave," Elizabeth said. "It was pitch dark in the mine except for when I shined my cell phone light. She did great."

"So did Beth," Bailey said, "especially for a kid who used to be afraid of the dark. We couldn't get a signal for Beth to call for help on her cell phone, but at least the light on it worked."

"We were afraid the battery would die, but we decided to trust that God would get us out safely." Elizabeth winked at Bailey. "We even prayed together in the dark."

"So how did you get out?" McKenzie asked. "Did you move all the rocks?"

Bailey told them about hearing the men's voices and how they were rescued. "We climbed out the hole they cleared, and boy, did that sunlight seem bright when we came out!" Bailey covered her eyes and laughed.

"Was Halona surprised about the deed and the mine?" Kate asked.

"We told her we had a surprise for her, but we didn't tell her what it was until we got back to Earth Works." Bailey scrunched up her shoulders.

Elizabeth continued the story. "Her store had a lot of damage in the earthquake with broken pottery all over the place. As soon as we got back there, she forgot about the surprise. She started talking about how much it was going to cost to replace all the ruined merchandise and how they might have to close the store."

"It was really sad," Bailey said. "But then I thought about the deed and the mine. I went into the studio and found the piece of pottery with the pocket to show Halona."

"And I got the deed from my bag," Elizabeth added.

"Then we presented it to Halona." Bailey couldn't stop grinning.

"She must have had kittens right there on the spot," Kate said.

Elizabeth laughed. "Practically! She could hardly believe it was real."

Bailey went on. "And then she decided she shouldn't get her hopes up too high until they found out if the mine was still around and if it had turquoise in it."

"We informed her that we found the mine and Bailey showed her the turquoise stones she had picked up while trapped inside." Elizabeth shook her head. "She was dumbfounded!"

"I've never been hugged so hard in all my life!" Bailey teased.

"What will they do now that they have the deed?" McKenzie asked.

"They're at the county recorder's office right now updating their claim." Elizabeth smiled proudly at Bailey. "They have the deed, and she has her identification to prove it's hers."

"It didn't look like it would take much work to make it operational again, and it should pay off for them in the long run." Bailey shrugged.

"You guys were amazing!" Sydney said. "I can't believe you found the deed and the mine in only a few days."

"We wouldn't have found the deed if the pot hadn't broken," Bailey admitted. "I'd say God had something to do with that."

"And, of course, you guys helped too!" Elizabeth said. "Biscuit's paw prints showed us that the landscape around Puye Cliffs really did match the pot's painting with trees added."

"Good old Biscuit, the Wonder Dog," Kate said.

"And Sydney eliminated the idea that the things Halona's grandma and mother said about the pot was some sort of code when she researched the Native American code talkers from World War II," Bailey added.

Elizabeth jumped in. "And Alex researched all the public records on the Tse and Kaga families."

"The rest of us prayed for you like crazy!" McKenzie said.

"We know you did!" Bailey said. "We might still be sitting in that dark mine if you hadn't been praying!"

"Anyway, we just wanted to let you know that the mystery is solved, and Halona has her mine back," Bailey said.

"I'm glad you called," Sydney said. "But mostly, I'm glad you weren't hurt in the earthquake or from being trapped in the mine."

"God really was looking out for you," Alex said.

"No doubt about it," Elizabeth said.

"We go home this afternoon, so we'd better hang up so we can pack." Bailey looked at her clothes strewn all over the bedroom.

"Okay," McKenzie said. "Thanks for calling us with the good news. Hopefully, we'll have another mystery to solve soon."

"I hope so!" Bailey said. "Bye!"

Halona hugged Bailey's mom goodbye. "It was so good to see you again."

"I'm glad we could come to help out for a little while," Mrs. Chang said. "I hope you can get things repaired and replaced in Earth Works soon."

"I will," Halona replied. "I spoke with the insurance company this morning, and they're going to pay for more of it than I thought."

Halona's arms went around Bailey, then Elizabeth. "When I invited you all to come give us a hand, I had no idea how helpful you'd be."

"Thanks." Bailey held the finished dish she had made in the studio. "It was fun to learn to make pottery and work in your store. I've never done those things before." She looked at her dish, which had somehow survived the earthquake, and admired the sunset she'd painted on it. "This will remind me of our time together."

Elizabeth hugged Halona. "Thanks for letting me come with the Changs."

"You girls gave me far more than a little help in the store," Halona said. "You gave me a better life for my family. I can't thank you enough."

"We're happy everything turned out so well," Elizabeth said.

"But I still feel a little guilty about breaking your ancient family pot," Bailey said.

"That's okay." Halona smiled at Bailey. "You showed us that sometimes we have to sacrifice something good to get something better. The real treasure wasn't the beautiful pot. It was what was inside, a bright future with my family."

A week later, back home, Bailey called Elizabeth.

"Hey, Beth, guess what?"

"I give up."

"Remember how I said I needed to learn more Bible verses so I'd have them ready in a tough situation?"

"Yeah. . ."

"Well, I've already started." Bailey smiled proudly. "Wanna hear it?"

"Sure!"

Bailey cleared her throat. " 'Store up for yourselves treasures in heaven, where moths and vermin do not destroy, and where thieves do not break in and steal. For where your treasure is, there your heart will be also.' Matthew 6:20 and 21."

Elizabeth cheered. "Way to go, Bales! I'm proud of you!"

"I'm learning the real treasure is knowing God and letting Him be the boss of our lives," Bailey said. "Like when we had to trust Him in that mine."

"Wow, Bailey," Elizabeth said. "That's pretty good!"

"But I didn't really call to brag about learning a new verse," Bailey said.

Elizabeth laughed. "You didn't? Then why did you call?"

"We got a package in the mail today!" Bailey squealed.

"Cool! Who's it from?"

"Halona!"

"Did you open it yet?" Elizabeth asked.

"Not yet. I thought I should wait until I called you so we could sort of open it together, since it's addressed to us both."

"Well, open it!" Elizabeth begged.

Bailey cut through the mailing tape with a pair of scissors and tore off the brown wrapping.

"There are two smaller boxes inside the bigger box," Bailey reported. "One has your name on it, and one has mine."

"Open yours first," Elizabeth said.

"Are you sure?" Bailey asked.

"Yes! Open it!"

Bailey lifted out the box bearing her name and removed the lid. She gasped.

"What is it?" Elizabeth asked.

"It's a beautiful turquoise necklace!" Bailey said. "Wait. There's a note under it." Bailey picked up the note and read:

Thank you for your help at Earth Works last week. Let this necklace serve as a reminder of how much we appreciate and love you. It is made from turquoise taken from the Suquosa Mine, which is now operational again. Thank you!
Love, Halona, Elan, and Aiyana

"Wow!" Bailey fingered the turquoise stone. "Shall I open yours, or do you want me to mail it to you as a surprise?"

Elizabeth giggled. "Open it!"

Bailey lifted the lid and found a similar necklace and note for Elizabeth. "You're going to love it, Beth."

"Thanks for letting me come with you on that trip," Elizabeth said. "It was a real adventure."

Bailey laughed. "You can say that again. I'm just glad we know where our True Treasure lies!"

Camp Club Girls:
Bailey and the Florida
Mermaid Park Mystery

CHAPTER 1

The Breathless Mermaid!

Bailey Chang leaned forward in her seat, mesmerized. Carefully she watched the graceful mermaids in the Underwater Theater at the Mermaid Park in Golden, Florida. Twelve-year-old Sydney Lincoln, her friend from Washington, DC, sat beside her, brown eyes wide. The Underwater Theater was like a large auditorium with a giant aquarium as the stage.

The mermaids in colorful bodysuits of red, green, yellow, and blue dipped and swam in unison through the water.

"Look at the one with the red tail," Bailey whispered. "I wonder why her eyes look so big!"

"Probably just her makeup." Sydney leaned in for a closer look. "But her movements don't match the others' either."

The music the mermaids swam to continued as the girls watched.

"Something's wrong!" Bailey jumped up from her chair.

"Yeah. She looks like she's panicking!" Sydney exclaimed.

The red mermaid frantically kicked her tail. She wildly stroked her arms as the dramatic music grew louder. The mermaid's bodysuit shimmered, sparkles punctuating each move the girl made. The other mermaids glanced at the red mermaid.

Bailey and Sydney noticed a worker standing by the stage chatting with another employee. Bailey ran to him. Sydney followed.

"One of the mermaids is in trouble!" Bailey pointed with a shaky arm.

The man charged through a door marked, AUTHORIZED PERSONNEL ONLY. Within seconds, the show stopped. The red mermaid surfaced, coughing and gasping. The other mermaids followed her to the surface.

The auditorium lights came on and the audience looked around, unsure what to do. Gradually, the place emptied. Bailey and Sydney stood alone in the chlorine-scented auditorium waiting for word of the mermaid's condition.

"What do you think happened?" Bailey's voice trembled.

"I don't know," Sydney replied. "It looked like she couldn't breathe."

Within minutes, the coverall-clad worker returned through the door.

"She's okay," he announced.

"What happened?" Bailey asked.

"Her breathing tube had a kink," he replied. "It's fixed now. We're used to dealing with this stuff."

Sydney lifted her hand and waved weakly as the man sauntered away.

"He sure didn't seem to be upset about that poor mermaid!" Bailey clenched her fists.

The beads on Sydney's cornrows clacked as she shook her head. "No, he didn't." She frowned.

"Bailey? Sydney?" Bailey's grandma Cora poked her head through the auditorium doorway. Bailey and Sydney had come to visit her for two weeks during their summer vacation.

"Hi, Grandma," Bailey said.

"I had a feeling I'd find you here." The older woman with short, light brown curls strode in, her jeans and tee shirt belying her age. Tennis shoes and a Chicago Cubs baseball cap, which she wore backwards, finished her look. "Did you like the mermaids as much as you did when you were a little girl, Bailey?"

"Yeah," she said, "but one had an equipment problem and almost drowned! I've never been so scared in my whole nine years of living!"

"Oh dear." Grandma's forehead creased. "Not again!"

"It's happened before?" Bailey could hardly believe her ears.

"A few times," Grandma said. "It's been on the news. And Mr. and Mrs. Fuller have talked to me about it. They've been working together with the police to figure out what's going on."

"Are those the people who own this place?" Bailey asked.

"Yes," her grandma answered.

"Seems like it shouldn't be that hard to figure out." Sydney's eyebrows scrunched as she frowned. "Either the equipment is defective or it isn't being used right."

Grandma Cora nodded and tucked a loose curl into her cap. "It does seem straightforward doesn't it? But there's often more to a story than what meets the eye."

"That's for sure." Bailey looked at Sydney, remembering all the mysteries they'd worked on together, some with surprising solutions. "We know all about that, don't we, Syd?"

"Come on." Grandma took Bailey's hand. "Let's find the Fullers and tell them what happened."

Grandma Cora's friends, Ed and Lenore Fuller, had owned the Mermaid Park for fifty years. Bailey had known them since she had been a baby. The girls ran ahead of Grandma to the entrance of the park, to Mr. and Mrs. Fuller's office. Actually their office was more like an apartment or small home with a tiny kitchen and a living area with a TV in the corner. The apartment also had a full bathroom and one bedroom just big enough to hold the double bed they used for short rests.

Bailey and Sydney knocked on the door.

"Come on in!" a low voice called.

They entered, followed by Grandma. The smell of coffee greeted them as Ed Fuller, a large man, crossed the living room in just three strides. As he hugged the girls, Bailey grinned at his western attire—a short-sleeved brown-and-green plaid shirt with pearly snaps running down the front and on the pockets. His shirt stretched over his ample belly. And a belt with a huge silver buckle held up his worn blue jeans.

Bailey wondered if Mr. Fuller had been a cowboy in his younger days. She felt like she all but disappeared in his bear hug, and the smell of aftershave remained in her hair long after he released her.

Mrs. Fuller stepped from the kitchen, drying her plump hands on a dish towel.

"If we can ever figure out how to fit a dishwasher in here, I'll have it made!" Her hazel eyes crinkled as she grinned. "Come in, come in," she said moving a newspaper from a chair. "Make yourself at home."

Mrs. Fuller's head barely reached Ed's shoulder. She wore stretchy tan pants with a flowered shirt that gapped slightly between the buttons when she moved.

"Want a cookie?" She shoved the package toward Bailey and Sydney.

The girls each took two chocolate chip cookies and sat on the love seat.

"Thank you," Bailey said.

"The girls just had a bit of excitement at the Underwater Theater," Grandma said.

"You don't say." Mr. Fuller pulled in a chair from the kitchen table. "What happened?"

Bailey leaned forward. "The red mermaid almost drowned!"

"Good heavens!" Mrs. Fuller replied. "Not Jessica!"

"She's been one of our most popular mermaids for five years," Mr. Fuller said. "She knows the routine backward and forward. I'm surprised she had problems."

"We alerted the worker in the auditorium and he went backstage," Sydney said. "When he came back out, he said her breathing tube had a kink in it."

"You had to *alert* him?" Mr. Fuller's voice rose. "He's paid to watch the show in case of any problems! That's why he's called the spotter!"

Mrs. Fuller nodded. "We'll have to check out where we get those tubes," she said. "We've had too many problems with them lately."

"How'd the worker react?" Grandma Cora asked.

"He seemed bored by it," Bailey said.

"What do you mean?" Mr. Fuller asked.

"He seemed like he didn't even care if the mermaid had a life-threatening experience."

"Yeah, he just shrugged it off." Sydney frowned. "I guess he's used to things like that happening."

"Such a shame," Mrs. Fuller said. "People are so indifferent these days. It's like they're afraid to really care."

"Well, at least he helped," Mr. Fuller said. "Of course that's what he's paid to do."

"When we bought this place we had no idea it would still be around fifty-two years later." Mrs. Fuller threw up her hands. "But here we are, still kicking!"

"Yep! Started out as a roadside attraction back in the fifties after people came home from World War II. Traveling by car became popular back then."

Mrs. Fuller laughed. "We were just a small business that featured girls dressed as mermaids performing plays in an underwater theater. We even had a few mermen."

Bailey cocked her head. "Mermen? What are those?"

"Boy mermaids!" Mr. Fuller said. "It's hard to find guys who want to play those parts anymore, but once in a while we get one or two."

"Over the years we added a few other attractions, like the Tunnel of Love, the Jungle Adventure cruise, bird shows, and reptile exhibits."

Mrs. Fuller sat back and crossed her arms, looking satisfied.

"We've had to learn new technologies along the way, but we've done okay." Mr. Fuller winked at Mrs. Fuller.

"That doesn't mean we haven't had hard times," Mrs. Fuller added. "We're barely staying afloat right now."

"Why?" Bailey asked.

"Lots of bigger, flashier attractions are going up all around us," Mr. Fuller said. "It's hard to compete with all their money."

"They use all kinds of special effects and high-powered motors on their rides." Mrs. Fuller twisted her hands. "We still have basic underwater shows and boat rides like the Tunnel of Love and the Jungle Adventure Cruise. But people want speed and amazing effects these days."

Ed ran his rough hand over his balding head. "We can't afford roller coasters and thrill rides, so we just keep doing what's worked for us."

"Well, I like your Mermaid Park," Sydney said.

Mrs. Fuller chuckled. "Thank you, honey. We do too."

"Problem is we still have lots of maintenance, staff, and other things that cost us a ton of money." Mr. Fuller sighed. "And business gets slower and slower as these new theme parks come in."

"Why don't you raise the admission price?" Bailey asked.

"We're charging as much as we can already," Mrs. Fuller replied. "Some people are already complaining it's too much. What we really need is a way to bring in more people."

"That's right," Mr. Fuller said. "If we can't get more business, this may be our last summer at the Mermaid Park."

"You can't close Mermaid Park! It's practically a historical monument!" Bailey exclaimed.

"There must be a solution to this," Grandma Cora said. "And if I know these girls, they'll come up with it." She grinned at Bailey and Sydney.

"We'll do our best, Grandma," Bailey said. "But we don't know much about running a business. We only know about solving mysteries."

"Mysteries?" Mrs. Fuller asked.

"Tell them, Bailey," Grandma Cora said with a grin.

Bailey blushed a big grin. "We're part of the Camp Club Girls," she explained. "Six of us from across the United States met at summer camp. We ran into a mystery there with jewel thieves. Since then, we've all put our heads together to solve mysteries we run across."

Mrs. Fuller looked impressed, "My goodness, that sounds intriguing!"

"One of their mysteries even involved saving the president of the United States from an assassination plot!" Grandma Cora said. She turned to Bailey, "This may not be a mystery, but you have lots of creative ideas.

Maybe one of them will help Ed and Lenore save this park."

"Oh Bailey!" Mrs. Fuller clapped her hands. "I almost forgot to tell you. We started a couple of new programs to try to draw in more people. We're having guest mermaids and junior mermaids who get to practice with our regular performers. Then after a week of rehearsals, they perform with our hired mermaids at a special show."

"Wow!" Bailey exclaimed.

"That's a great idea to attract more people!" Sydney added.

"Ed and I wondered if you girls would like to try out as junior mermaids."

"I'd love to!" Bailey jumped up. "Want to, Syd?"

Sydney hesitated. "I'm not sure. Maybe."

"If being in the spotlight isn't your thing, we have other jobs you could do, Sydney." Mr. Fuller smiled gently at the girl. "We need people to help with the lighting, sound, and scene changes. We also need assistants who help the performers with their costume changes."

Sydney's eyes sparkled. "That's what I'd rather do—help behind the scenes."

"You've got a deal," Mr. Fuller said. "Just report to Jessica at the Underwater Theater this afternoon at three o'clock. Bailey, you'll have to audition for the junior mermaids, but I have a feeling you'll be chosen." He grinned and winked at her.

"Should I wear my swimsuit?" Bailey asked.

"Yes," Mrs. Fuller answered. "They want to be sure the girls they choose are comfortable in water and can swim. They'll teach you the routine and underwater skills."

Bailey rubbed her hands together. "I can't wait!"

At three o'clock sharp, Bailey and Sydney waited outside the door of the Underwater Theater with a small group of girls and young women who had gathered for the auditions. Bailey wore her swimsuit under her T-shirt and shorts. She carried a bag holding her beach towel and a hairbrush.

Sydney strapped her digital camera around her waist. "I hope I can get pictures of your audition," she said. "It could be your big break into show biz!"

Bailey giggled. "I hope you're right. I wore my brightest swimsuit to help me stand out from the other girls."

"You'll do great," Sydney said. "I know you'll get in the show."

"Besides," Bailey added. "I can do fish lips." She sucked her cheeks in and made her lips stick out and move.

Sydney laughed. "Wait. Do it again so I can get a picture."

Bailey posed and Sydney snapped the shot.

The Underwater Theater door opened and a dark-haired young woman with creamy skin and big blue eyes stepped out.

"Hello. Welcome to the guest and junior mermaid auditions. My name is Jessica and I'll walk you through the process," she said.

"Yep, that's the mermaid who almost drowned, just like Mrs. Fuller said," Bailey whispered.

Sydney nodded. "I hardly recognize her without her costume."

The group followed Jessica into the building and backstage. The seven girls in Bailey's group giggled nervously. They ranged in age from about seven to fourteen. The girls sat in a semicircle of chairs while Jessica spoke to them as a group, then with each one individually.

"I'd like to help with the lighting and costumes, instead of being in the water," Sydney said.

"Great!" Jessica patted Sydney's knee. "We hardly ever get that kind of help. I know the crew will be thrilled to have you."

Bailey spoke up. "I'm a strong swimmer and I hope to be a famous actress someday."

"Good for you!" Jessica said. "This will be a great learning experience you can tell your future movie directors about!"

After talking to each girl, Jessica stood and clapped her hands together. "Girls, those of you who would like a part as a junior mermaid, please come over here. We'll get into the water tank for a short swim, just to show you what it's like."

Bailey shed her T-shirt and shorts, showing a shocking pink-and-green one-piece swimsuit. "What do you think?" she asked Sydney.

Sydney stared at her wide-eyed. "That should get their attention, all right." She took Bailey's picture.

"I'm looking for Sydney and GraceAnn," a man said.

Sydney turned and looked at the short man with the friendly voice. "I'm Sydney."

A small, blond-headed girl joined Sydney and the man. "Hi, I'm GraceAnn."

"I'm Zeke, the head of the lighting crew." He shook both girls' hands. "I understand you two are interested in helping us."

"Yes!" Sydney's face lit up.

"Come on, I'll show you our equipment."

Sydney and GraceAnn followed Zeke while Bailey climbed the steps to get into the Underwater Theater tank.

Their first lesson done, Bailey towel-dried her hair and put on her clothes. She and Sydney walked out the door into the bright sunlight.

"That was awesome!" Bailey said.

"No kidding! You should have seen all the buttons and switches I learned about!"

"I think all the girls who auditioned made the cut." Bailey put on her sunglasses. "They said they're shorthanded and need as many as they can get."

"That's great!"

They rounded a corner and were practically run over by a worker driving a golf cart with a huge box of detergent in the back.

"Excuse us!" Sydney said.

"Sorry." The reckless worker wore the usual blue coverall uniform. He looked both ways, then zoomed off to the Underwater Theater and parked outside a back door.

"Did you see the size of that box of detergent?" Bailey asked.

"Must be the janitor getting ready to do some serious cleaning," Sydney responded.

"More like Mr. Bubble, with all that soap," Bailey joked.

Sydney laughed. "I bet if we could have seen his name tag that's what it would have said!"

The girls watched as the worker glanced around, and then hefted the super-sized box to his shoulder. Taking one last look behind him, he snuck into the theater.

Pranked!

"That was weird," Sydney said. "Why would a worker sneak around like that?"

"Maybe he was supposed to meet someone who didn't show up," Bailey said. "He might have taken one last glance around to see if the person was coming."

Sydney looked at Bailey warily. "Right. And I'm a dolphin just leaving the Underwater Theater."

"Just because something looks a little weird doesn't mean we should suspect someone of doing something wrong." Bailey shrugged and walked on. "We're naturally curious—even suspicious—because we're sleuths. But we shouldn't always assume the worst about people."

Sydney sighed. "I guess you're right. He could have been just doing his job. Who knows? Maybe he's had a bad experience that's made him jumpy so now he's always looking over his shoulder."

"There you go!" Bailey beamed at Sydney. "Now you're thinking more positively."

Sydney grinned. "But I still think he's up to something."

Bailey laughed. "You're hopeless! Come on. We'd better get back to Mr. and Mrs. Fuller's office."

"I'll race you," Sydney dared.

Bailey stopped and planted her hands on her hips. "You, the Junior Olympics athlete in track and field, want to race me, a nine-year-old mermaid wannabe?"

"Why not?"

"Okay, but I get a head start."

"It's a deal. I'll give you ten steps and then I'll start. Ready?"

Bailey crouched to a runner's starting stance. "Good thing there aren't many people here. I'd hate to mow anyone down."

"That's for sure. Set?"

Bailey nodded.

"Go!"

Bailey flew down the paved walkway toward the park entrance. She counted her steps. "One, two, three. . ."

At ten, she knew Sydney had taken off, trying to catch up and pass her. She pumped her arms harder, willing her legs to go faster. Her breathing became ragged, then wheezy, but she continued. Footsteps pounded closer and closer.

Soon, Bailey heard steady panting breaths. Mr. and Mrs. Fuller's office was in sight now, and Bailey kept her eyes on it, running with all her might. She could see Sydney's arm swinging from the corner of her eye. Bailey wheezed with each breath.

"Bailey, stop running!" Sydney gasped. "You'll have an asthma attack!"

Bailey kept on, refusing to give up so close to the finish line. *Just a little further.*

She stretched out in her final stride. Her right foot landed on the cement slab outside the office door, just a fraction of a second before Sydney's. Bailey slammed against the door with outstretched hands. She bent over and tried to catch her breath. Then she straightened up. Sweat dripping, she searched her pocket for her inhaler and squeezed the mist into her mouth. Holding her breath, she felt as if her chest would explode.

"You should have stopped." Sydney said, panting. "Your face is as red as Jessica's mermaid costume."

Bailey let go of the air she was holding.

"I'm. . .okay," she said between breaths. Then she raised her fist in triumph and grinned. "I beat you!"

Sydney wagged her finger in Bailey's face. "Only because you had a head start! But you were harder to catch than I thought you'd be. You may make an Olympic athlete yourself someday if you keep that up!"

"No thanks." Bailey waved her off. "I think I'll stick to mermaid swimming. Hey, maybe they'll make *that* an Olympic sport!"

Sydney laughed. "Now that would be interesting. It could be sort of like synchronized swimming except you'd be dressed as a mermaid."

"What's all the commotion out here?" Ed Fuller came through the front door, which narrowly missed Bailey as it opened. "Whoops! Sorry, little lady. Didn't know you were standing so close."

"That's okay. You missed me."

"Guess I'll have to go back in and try again," Mr. Fuller teased.

"Mr. Fuller!" Sydney scolded.

"Guess what?" Bailey said. "We just got back from our first mermaid show lesson."

"How'd it go?"

Mrs. Fuller came to the door with Bailey's grandma.

"Why don't you come in and tell us all about it?" She opened the door and extended her arm like a game show model showing the prizes.

"It was awesome." Bailey was anxious to tell them all about her first experience as a mermaid-in-training. "Jessica talked to all of us first. Then those who wanted to be mermaids went with her and a man took Sydney and another girl to learn about stage lighting."

"His name was Zeke, and he's in charge of the lighting for all the shows." Sydney's dark eyes sparkled.

"I got into the tank where they put on the shows," Bailey said. "It was incredible! I felt like a mermaid just being in there and I didn't even have a costume."

"Did they teach you any special mermaid moves?" Grandma Cora asked.

Bailey laughed. "Not yet, but they will. They just wanted us to get used to swimming in the aquarium. In a regular swimming pool, you can lift yourself above the water at the sides of the pool. But in the mermaid tank, the walls go clear up to the top of the curtain, so you can't do that. You're completely enclosed, except about fifteen feet above you. And there's a plexiglass door above the waterline in the back of the tank with a ladder where we climb in and out. It takes some getting used to."

"I can't believe you didn't tell me about that before," Sydney said. "Was it freaky?"

"A little, at first," Bailey admitted. "But then you get used to it and don't really notice it. Plus, a ledge goes all the way around the tank that you can stand on if you need to rest."

"What about you, Syd?" Mrs. Fuller asked. "What did you do?"

"Zeke showed us the lighting panel. It had tons of switches! But Zeke said we'd only be in charge of certain ones, so we didn't have to learn the whole panel."

"I bet that was a relief," Bailey said.

"When's your next practice?" Mr. Fuller asked.

"Tomorrow morning, nine o'clock sharp." Grinning, Bailey scrunched up her shoulders. "I can't wait!"

The next morning, Bailey and Sydney filed into the Underwater Theater behind the other students.

Jessica led them in. A young woman with puffy blond hair, dark eyeliner, and heavy blue eye shadow stood beside her. Her cheeks were bright pink and her lips were covered with fire truck-red lipstick. Bailey thought she looked like a little kid who'd gotten into her mother's make-up drawer. A thick, red velvet curtain hid the water tank from view.

"It's good to have you all back," Jessica said. "I'll show you some movements you can practice in the water today. My assistant, Shondra, will help us since it's hard for me to get to all of you at once."

Shondra's smile was too sickeningly sweet for Bailey's taste.

Bailey murmured to Sydney. "I hope I get Jessica."

"Why?" Sydney asked.

"She just seems more like me—not all fancy and made up."

Jessica continued talking. "Let's raise the curtain on the Underwater Theater and get started. Are our lighting assistants here?"

Sydney's hand shot up and so did GraceAnn's.

"Wonderful! Zeke's waiting for you backstage. He'll show you how to raise the curtain."

"Have fun!" Bailey squeezed Sydney's hand excitedly before she left.

A moment later, the curtain rose and the mermaids-in-training clapped. Some even whistled. To Bailey, the water looked extra blue and pretty. Special lights came on one by one and Bailey smiled, knowing Sydney was probably working the light panel. But when the curtain rose as high as the waterline, the applause stopped and jaws dropped. Bailey gasped.

The Underwater Theater tank was filled with suds!

"What—?" Jessica sputtered. Her pleasant features clouded. "What happened?" She paused for a moment. "This had to have been done deliberately by someone playing a prank. But who would do something like this? Don't they know how long it will take to clean this up before we can use it again?"

Shondra rolled her eyes and took charge. "Girls, it looks like we'll have to move to another tank to practice. Follow me. Jessica honey, why don't you tell the lighting people to come join us at the Sweetwater Tank?"

Jessica glared at Shondra. "Do we even know if that tank is available?"

"The performers in that show don't have a performance until this evening. I'm sure they won't need the tank until later." She winked at the girls. "Always remember, girls, in show biz you have to be flexible. Right, Jessica?"

Jessica looked like she had choked on a fish. She cleared her throat. "Uh, right. I'll call over there first to check in with the Sweetwater crew. We'll go only if they say it's all right." She pulled out her cell phone and dialed.

Shondra frowned at Jessica, and Bailey swallowed hard, taking in this power struggle. Shondra was obviously trying to take over Jessica's job.

Sydney had now joined the group again. She and Bailey stood close enough to Shondra to hear her mutter something about "the rinky-dink shows in this mom-and-pop park."

"You were right about Shondra," Sydney hissed in Bailey's ear. "She's awful!"

"She's trying to bully Jessica." Bailey shook her head. "I'm glad Jessica's not putting up with it."

Jessica flipped her phone closed.

"The Sweetwater Tank is occupied." Bailey thought she saw a faint smile on Jessica's lips. "We'll have to practice at the Dolphin Pool."

"With dolphins?" one girl asked.

"No, it's just what they call the tank," Jessica replied. "They used to hold dolphin shows in it, but they don't anymore."

Jessica turned to Shondra. "I'll take the girls over there while you make sure the suds get cleaned out of this tank so we can use it tomorrow."

Bailey stifled a laugh and nudged Sydney, who had her hand over her mouth. Shondra's jaw dropped. Flames shot from her eyes as she turned and stomped into the Underwater Theater.

"Sydney and GraceAnn, you can stay here with Zeke and learn more about the lighting. We'll meet you back here in half an hour."

Sydney and GraceAnn stepped out of the group and followed Zeke backstage.

"Okay, girls, follow me." Jessica led them down a curving path to a blue building with jumping dolphins painted on the outside walls. "We won't have much time for practice with all the interruptions we've had this morning, but we'll do what we can."

Bailey changed into her swimsuit and was soon learning to swim like a mermaid.

"Pretend your feet are tied together and kick them as if they're one body part," Jessica instructed.

Bailey kept her legs together and kicked. She found it was much harder to swim this way. She went to the side of the pool to rest a moment. Then she swam mermaid-style to the other side. By the time the lesson ended,

Bailey was worn out. The girls changed back into their clothes and walked back to the Underwater Theater. Bailey waited in the auditorium until Sydney and GraceAnn came out from behind the lighting panel backstage.

"How was it?" Sydney asked.

"Tiring!" Bailey answered. "I never knew it was such hard work to be a mermaid! How was your lesson?"

"Great! Zeke's a good teacher and GraceAnn is really nice."

The two rushed from the theater, and practically mowed down a dark-haired boy just outside the door.

"Oh, sorry," Bailey mumbled before she and Sydney hurried off.

Sydney glanced back at the boy and elbowed Bailey. "Did you see him?"

"Not until we almost ran him over."

"That's not what I mean."

Bailey stopped walking and cocked her head. "What?"

"I mean did you *see* him?"

Bailey looked back. "Yeah, I saw him. What about it?"

"Don't you think he's cute?"

Bailey looked again. "I don't know. I guess he's okay."

Sydney's eyes looked all sparkly and gooey.

"What's the matter with you, Syd?"

Sydney shook her head. "Uh, nothing. I just think he's cute."

No sooner had she spoken than the boy started in their direction.

"Here he comes!" Sydney quickly smoothed her cornrows and slathered on some lip gloss.

"Hi!" The boy looked at them. "You look lost. Can I help you find something?"

Bailey thought Sydney would melt. The lean boy stood a little taller than Sydney, his skin the same color as the toasted honey-wheat bagel Bailey had eaten for breakfast. Shaggy black hair hung down on his forehead and halfway over his ears. Bailey guessed he was probably a couple of years older than Sydney, maybe fourteen. He wore jeans with holes in the knees and a brown T-shirt with a guitar outlined in white.

"We're not lost," Bailey said. "We just got out of practice for the mermaid show."

"You work here?" The boy looked surprised.

"No, not really." Bailey noticed that Sydney seemed to have lost her ability to speak. "We're here visiting my grandma and will be in the guest mermaid show. Sydney's working the lights." Bailey jabbed Sydney with an elbow.

"She is, huh?" The boy smiled, showing off his straight white teeth. "Nice to meet you, Sydney. I'm Stephen Christou."

Sydney smiled, but didn't say a word.

"She's a little shy, but we're glad to meet you, Stephen. I'm Bailey. Do *you* work here?"

"No, but I hang out here a lot. My family owns the Sponge Diving Park next door."

"Sponge diving!" Sydney finally found her voice.

Stephen laughed. "Yeah, you should come see it sometime. I'll show you around."

"That would be awesome!" Sydney blurted out.

"We'd have to check with my grandma first." Bailey gave Sydney a look.

"Of course," Stephen said. "Is she around here somewhere?"

"She's at the office by the entrance. We're friends with Ed and Lenore Fuller who own this mermaid park."

"Sure! I know Mr. and Mrs. Fuller. Maybe you could check with your grandma and see if you could come right now. My dad has a fishing business over there I could show you too—unless you have other plans."

"No!" Sydney replied a little too loudly. "We don't have any other plans, do we, Bales?"

"No, we don't. It sounds like fun! You can come with us to ask my grandma." Bailey started walking toward the office. "She might want to come and learn about the fishing and sponge diving industry too." Bailey joked, "She's not big on us taking off with people we just met."

Stephen laughed. "I don't blame her a bit. I'd love to meet her and she's welcome to join us."

When they reached the office, Bailey entered first. "Gram, we brought a new friend home to meet you."

Grandma Cora looked up from the book she was reading and quickly stood. Mr. Fuller flipped off the TV program he and Mrs. Fuller were watching.

"This is Stephen. His family owns the Sponge Diving Park next door and he offered to show us around. He's free right now and he invited you too."

"How sweet! Nice to meet you, Stephen."

"Stephen! It's good to see you! Look how tall you're getting!" Mrs. Fuller flew to his side. "Why, you're towering over me!"

"It's been awhile, Mrs. Fuller."

"So can we go, Grandma?" Bailey asked.

"I don't see why not," Grandma Cora answered. "I'll just grab my purse and I'll be ready."

"Do you want to come along?" Sydney asked Mr. and Mrs. Fuller.

"No, I think we'll hold down the fort here," Mr. Fuller said. "But thanks. Tell your dad hello for us, Stephen."

"Will do, sir." Stephen held the door open for the girls and led the way to the Sponge Diving Park.

"It's okay, Bob," he said to the man taking tickets at the entrance. "They're with me."

The man waved them in.

"Do you sponge dive?" Bailey asked.

"I'm not allowed to," Stephen said. His voice was filled with disappointment.

"Why not?" Sydney asked.

Stephen sighed. "Long story short, my grandpa died in a diving accident when my dad was ten years old. Now he won't let me dive because he's afraid something will happen to me."

"Too bad," Bailey said softly. "Did he ever let you try it?"

"I did it once and fell in love with it. It was so beautiful down under the water. Like another world—so peaceful and quiet."

The foursome walked a little further. "Our sponge diving boats are over here. Come on. I'll show you."

"Are you sure?" Grandma Cora asked. "I don't want you to get in trouble."

"I won't. It's no big deal. I'll just show you around the boat."

Waves lapped at the side of the docked boat as Grandma Cora, Bailey, and Sydney followed Stephen aboard. Suddenly, they heard a shout.

"Stephen! Get over here!"

CHAPTER 3

Camp Club Girls to Action!

Stephen swung around at the harsh voice. "Dad!"

Bailey's stomach twisted. She'd never heard a father speak so unkindly to his son.

"Get over here!" his dad repeated even louder.

Grandma Cora put her hand on Stephen's shoulder. "You'd better go. We can see this another time."

"I'm sorry," Stephen said. "Come back tomorrow. My dad will be out on a fishing expedition." He took off running to the boat where his father waited, hands on his hips.

"Do you think he'll be okay?" Bailey searched her grandma's eyes.

Grandma Cora stroked her granddaughter's silky black hair. "I think so. But perhaps we need to pray for Stephen and his family."

"Good idea." The raspy voice startled the girls. A rugged old fisherman, skin wrinkled and tanned by the sun, leaned against the boat's rail. "Sorry. Couldn't help overhearin'."

"That's okay." Bailey's grandma eyed the man warily, putting a protective hand on each girl's shoulder.

"Do you know Stephen?" Bailey thought the old man looked like he'd just rolled out of bed. His gray hair hung every which way and his clothes were old and baggy. She wondered if he'd put them on one morning when he was young and strong and had never taken them off as he withered into a thin old man.

The man nodded. "Yup, I know Stephen a little. Know his dad better. But I was best friends with his grandpa. We started this sponge diving operation together years ago."

"You started the Sponge Diving Park?" Sydney's dark eyes widened.

"Not the park." The man chuckled. "We started the sponge diving business. It evolved into the park it is today. I don't care about any of that stuff. I just like teaching people to fish and sponge dive."

"Is Stephen's dad mean to him?" Bailey asked.

"Bailey!" Grandma Cora's face reddened. "I'm sorry, sir."

"No, no harm done." The man waved his hand and shook his head. "Name's Andrew, by the way."

"Should we call you Andrew, or Mr.—" Sydney asked.

"Andrew's fine. Can't even remember my last name—been so long since anyone's used it." The old man's eyes twinkled.

"Nice to meet you, Andrew," Bailey said.

Andrew nodded, then returned to the previous subject. "Cyrus—Stephen's dad—is hurting and it makes him sound angry."

"Hurting?" Sydney said. "Did he get injured?"

"Yes, but not in the way you're probably thinking. His heart was broken when his father died in a sponge diving accident."

"Oh yeah," Bailey said softly. "Stephen mentioned that."

"Cyrus was only ten years old and adored his father. They were from Greece, and he practically thought of his father as one of those Greek gods, I think. He never quite got over it." Andrew glanced at the sun and rolled up his shirtsleeves. "I saw a flicker of light in his eyes when Stephen was born, but in time it burned out. That boy is his father's greatest joy, but Cyrus went back to being sad and angry again. So your prayers are needed."

Bailey nodded. "I'm glad we met you, Andrew."

"Me too," Sydney added. "You can count on us to keep praying for Stephen and his dad."

"Yes, thank you." Grandma Cora extended her hand. "It's been a pleasure."

Andrew shook their hands, tiny blue eyes twinkling again. "Pleasure's mine."

Bailey faintly smelled salt and fish when she shook his sandpaperish hand. She liked the way it squeezed around hers like he really meant it.

The three stepped onto the dock and walked toward the Mermaid Park.

"Hey!" Bailey grabbed Sydney's arm. "We forgot to tell Mr. and Mrs. Fuller about the bubbles in the tank!"

"Bubbles?" Grandma Cora looked confused.

Sydney brought her hands to her cheeks and grinned. "I guess in all the excitement over meeting Stephen we forgot all about it!"

"Bubbles?" Grandma repeated.

"Well, you were more excited about meeting Stephen than I was, Syd," Bailey teased. "You practically turned into a blob of jelly when you saw him. I was afraid I'd have to scrape you up and take you home in a jar!"

"I did not!" Sydney defended herself. But a little smile pulled at the corners of her mouth.

Grandma stepped in front of the girls and faced them. "Is anyone going to tell me about the bubbles in the tank or do I have to tickle it out of you?"

Bailey laughed. "We're almost to the Fullers' apartment now. We may as well wait and tell them at the same time." She started running, dashing past her grandma, with Sydney in full pursuit.

Grandma groaned and chased the girls to the Fullers' door.

Bailey flung the door open wide. The smell of coffee greeted her as she burst into the tiny living room. "We're back!"

"No kidding." Ed Fuller faked surprise.

"That was quick," Mrs. Fuller said. "Did you see the Sponge Diving Park?"

"We started to go on one of the boats," Bailey explained, "but then Stephen's dad called him."

"Stephen said to come back tomorrow and he'd show us around." Sydney's eyes were all gooey again.

"But we met Andrew, one of the sponge fishermen," Bailey added.

"Andrew's a good man," Mr. Fuller said.

"You know him?" Grandma asked.

"He's been around here almost as long as we have. He's pretty crusty, but he's a Christ-follower with a heart as tender as the sponges he dives for."

"Yes, that's the impression I got too," Grandma replied.

"Mr. Fuller, we forgot to tell you earlier about what happened at our practice this morning," Bailey said.

"Oh?" Mr. Fuller settled into a hard-backed chair.

"When we got to the Underwater Theater, GraceAnn and I got to raise the curtain," Sydney said.

"And when it got to the top of the water, we saw the tank was full of suds!" Bailey's eyes popped.

"Suds? Like a bubble bath?" Mrs. Fuller leaned forward in her chair.

"Yep. Only it was more bubbles than I've ever seen in my life! The layer of foam was probably as tall as I am!" Bailey leveled one hand against her forehead. "But they didn't smell flowery like a bubble bath. It was more of a detergent smell."

"What did you do?" Grandma Cora asked. "You couldn't practice in that, could you?"

Sydney shook her head. "They had to go to another tank while GraceAnn and I stayed and learned more about the lighting system."

"Unbelievable!" Mr. Fuller clenched his fists. "It's like someone is trying to undo all our hard work. First, the mermaids' air lines keep getting messed with and now this!"

"Sabotage, that's what it is," Mrs. Fuller said. "As soon as we get things running smoothly, someone pulls stunts like this. If they think we'll give up on this mermaid park, they've got another thing coming!"

"Do you really think someone is trying to sabotage the Mermaid Park?" Sydney asked.

"I don't know, but I *do* know things like this are happening way too often lately." Mr. Fuller stood and stomped around the room. "I hate to think like that, but I don't know what else it could be."

"After all, bubbles don't suddenly appear in tanks on their own," Mrs. Fuller said. "Someone has to put them there."

"Bailey!" Sydney turned to her friend. "Remember the man we saw going into the Underwater Theater after our first practice?"

"I hadn't put the two together!" Bailey exclaimed "I bet he's the one who made the suds!"

"What on earth are you talking about?" Mrs. Fuller asked.

"We saw a worker in blue coveralls driving a golf cart to the Underwater Theater's back door," Bailey told her. "He had a huge box of detergent in his cart."

"We didn't think much of it at the time, though we joked about him and even called him Mr. Bubble," Sydney said. "We figured he was going to do some serious cleaning or something. But he did act sort of suspicious."

"In what way?" Grandma asked.

"He looked over his shoulder a lot, like he was making sure no one saw him." Sydney glanced at Bailey. "Remember?"

"Yeah, I remember." Bailey sighed. "I told Sydney not to be so suspicious of everyone. But maybe she was right."

"What did he look like?" Mr. Fuller asked. "Did you see his name tag?"

"He had brown hair and a big mustache that curled up at the corners of his mouth." Bailey thought a moment. "He was only a few inches taller than Grandma."

Ed started scribbling notes on a pad of paper. "How tall are you, Cora? About five four?"

"Five three," Grandma answered.

"So this guy would be around five seven or eight?" he asked the girls.

"I guess so," Bailey answered.

"We couldn't see his name tag," Sydney said. "Bailey named him Mr. Bubble."

"And he drove a golf cart, huh?" Mr. Fuller mumbled.

"Recklessly," Bailey added. "He almost ran us over, he was going so fast."

"He apologized, but not until after we said 'Excuse me.' " Sydney stretched her long legs. "I think he just wanted to get rid of us."

Ed sat back down. "I'll check this out myself, but we may need to call the police to file a report."

"Do you think you know who the man is?" Grandma asked.

"Not offhand," Mr. Fuller replied. "I don't recall hiring anyone with a big mustache."

Bailey and Sydney exchanged wide-eyed glances.

"Well, let us know if there's anything else we can do to help," Bailey said.

"We will. You've already given us a lot to go on and we appreciate it. If you see any other suspicious activity, come tell us right away."

"Okay." Bailey looked at her grandma. "Can we go now?"

"Sure," Grandma Cora replied. "What are you going to do?"

"I don't know," Bailey said. "Just wander around the park awhile."

"Keep your cell phones handy."

Sydney patted her pocket. "Got mine."

Bailey nodded. "Me too."

The girls jumped up and went outside.

Sydney fiddled with one of her earrings. "I didn't know this was going to turn into a big hairy deal."

"Me either," Bailey replied. "Are you thinking what I'm thinking?"

Sydney's white teeth gleamed as a giant smile emerged. "Mystery!"

The two exchanged a high five.

"We've got to call the other Camp Club Girls."

Bailey pulled her phone from her pocket at the same time Sydney did. Sitting on a park bench, they conferenced the girls in together and confirmed each one could hear.

"I'm glad we caught you when you're all available," Bailey said.

"We've got a mystery to solve but not too many clues yet."

"All right!" McKenzie Phillips shouted over her phone. McKenzie was thirteen years old and from White Sulphur Springs, Montana. Besides riding horses and performing in rodeos, McKenzie tended to look at why people did what they did.

"Someone is trying to sabotage the Mermaid Park here in Florida," Sydney told them. "Remember we told you we were coming here? Now our job is to figure out who is trying to sabotage it and why."

"Sabotage?" Bailey asked, looking at Sydney. "What's that mean?"

"It's when someone does something sneaky to keep you from accomplishing something," Alexis Howell explained. At twelve, Alexis was the media specialist of the group. She loved old movies and TV shows and had her own cable column. "Like in The Parent Trap when the twins kept playing tricks on their dad's girlfriend so she wouldn't marry him. They were sabotaging his relationship with her."

"Ohhh," Bailey said.

"Hold it," Elizabeth Anderson said. Elizabeth was fourteen and lived in Amarillo, Texas. She tended to be the girl in the group who reminded them of God's perspective and involvement. "How do you know someone's trying to sabotage the park?"

"Because the Underwater Theater was filled with soapsuds this morning and that doesn't just happen by accident," Sydney replied.

"Wait, what's the Underwater Theater?" McKenzie asked. "First things first!"

Sydney quickly explained the basic information about the park to the girls. Kate, who'd looked up the park on the internet while Sydney was explaining it, then jumped in to give the girls the web address where they could read about and see pictures of the park.

"We think we may have seen the guy who made the bubbles in the tank," Bailey added. She told them about Mr. Bubble.

"Do you think Mr. Bubble is acting alone or does he have an accomplice?" Alexis asked.

"We don't know," Bailey said. "I hadn't really thought about him having someone helping him, did you, Syd?"

"No, but we didn't see anyone with him."

"That's not much to go on," Kate Oliver said. Bailey heard Biscuit the Wonder Dog, panting into the phone. The girls had found Biscuit during their first mystery together and Kate had taken him home with her to Philadelphia. Kate's dad was a scientist and she'd taken after him with her skills. The girls often used gadgets Kate had created to help with their sleuthing.

"No, but we just wanted you to know what's going on so if anything comes to mind, you can let us know." Bailey held the phone with one hand while she put on some lip balm with the other.

"And if you hear of anything that could get us thinking about this from a different angle, call us," Sydney said. "We're going to need all the help we can get on this."

"Okay," Elizabeth said. "Will do."

"Guess what else?" Bailey said.

"What?" the girls chorused in unison.

"Sydney's got a crush on a boy named Stephen who lives here."

"I do not!" Sydney's cheeks flushed.

"Then what do you call it?" Bailey asked with a smile.

"I call it. . .nothing. He's just cute, that's all."

"Come on, Syd, spill it," Elizabeth said.

"We want to hear all the juicy details." Bailey could imagine Alexis's wide grin.

"There are no juicy details," Sydney said. "He's just a boy we met when we came out of our mermaid class this morning. His family owns the Sponge Diving Park next door and he invited us over to see it. End of story."

"So did you go?" McKenzie asked.

"We went, but his dad yelled at him from the next boat to get over there," Bailey said. "He sounded really mean. But Stephen invited us to go back tomorrow while his dad's out fishing."

"I don't know, guys," Elizabeth said. "You might want to think twice about going over there again. He'll really get in trouble if he does something behind his dad's back."

"Is Stephen a sponge diver?" Kate asked.

"No," Sydney said. "But he'd like to be. His grandpa died in a sponge diving accident when his dad was just a kid. So now his dad won't let him do it because he's afraid of losing Stephen too."

"Bummer," Alex said.

"His dad seems kind of mean to Stephen, or at least he talks rough to him," Bailey said.

"He must be having a hard time letting his son grow up and try things after losing his dad like that," McKenzie offered. "My mom says it's hard to let your kids go sometimes."

"Not to change the subject, but what's Stephen look like?" Alexis asked.

"He's got dark hair that hangs over his ears and onto his forehead," Sydney said. "He's taller than me and he looks like he's about fourteen. He's got beautiful tan skin because he's Greek. And he has a gorgeous smile," Sydney concluded.

"Wow, you've got it bad," Alex said.

"Huh? I do not."

"Oh, yes you do," Alexis challenged. "I can tell from the way your voice goes all dreamy when you talk about him."

"Besides all that," Bailey added, "he has really good manners and held the door open for us and everything."

"Well, we don't have time for romance," Sydney said. "We have a mystery to solve and that's what I intend to do."

"Good girl," Elizabeth said. "Stay focused. There will be plenty of time for boys when we're older."

Kate jumped in. "Biscuit heard that and, being a boy, he's none too happy with you right now, Beth."

The girls laughed.

"We'll let you know if anything else happens around here," Bailey said.

"Sounds like a plan," McKenzie said.

The girls stuffed their phones back in their pockets and walked down the path to the Mermaid Park.

"We need to keep our eyes open for clues," Bailey said.

Sydney pointed at what looked like a rope on the ground several feet in front of them. "What's that?"

As they drew closer, the rope lifted its head and flicked a forked tongue at them.

"A snake!"

Tunnel of Terror!

"Run!" Bailey screamed as the snake darted toward them.

She and Sydney ran down a side path leading to the Tide Pool, where kids could touch starfish, anemones, and purple sea urchins.

The path wound uphill from the main walkway and soon Bailey's legs ached. From the corner of her eye, she saw something slither in the groundcover beside the walkway, so she ran even faster. Sydney passed her. She finally stopped when Bailey glanced over her shoulder, and not seeing the snake anymore, shouted, "It's gone!"

Both girls stood, gulping air. Bailey bent over, hands on her knees, trying to catch her breath. "I thought. . .I'd die. . .running up that hill," she sputtered.

"Where. . .did that thing. . .come from?" Sydney gasped.

Bailey shook her head. "I don't know. . .but I think. . .there was a second one. . .in the bushes." She pulled her inhaler from her pocket and breathed in the medicine.

Sydney took a quick look around her feet. "I only saw one, but that was enough."

Bailey nodded, holding her breath, then exhaled.

"I've never seen snakes here before," she said. "And we've vacationed here plenty of times. Now we see two in one day?"

"More like two in one minute! It doesn't make sense." Sydney played with the end of one of her cornrows.

"Hello, girls!" Shondra said as she approached them from the direction of the Tide Pool.

"Hi, Shondra." Bailey wished she had a tissue to wipe off some of the makeup caking Shondra's face. She'd be prettier without it.

"What are you two up to?" Her bright red lips smiled too big. She held a stack of small papers in her hand.

"We just saw a snake!" Sydney said.

"A snake?" Shondra's eyes widened and she stepped back, scanning the ground. "Where?"

Bailey pointed down the hill. "Actually it was two snakes. Down on the main path."

"I'd better report this to the groundskeeper so he can track them down." Shondra strode off toward the main walkway.

"You're going to go that way?" Sydney asked. "Aren't you afraid you'll run into the snake?"

Shondra froze, then swung around. "You're right. I'll go the long way around." She grinned and brushed past them.

"Will the groundskeeper let the Fullers know about the snakes in their park?"

"Oh, of course. It's SOP."

"SOP?" Sydney asked.

"Standard Operating Procedure. We have one in place for every situation."

"What are those papers you're holding?" Bailey asked.

Shondra looked at her hand like she forgot she was holding anything.

"Oh, these!" She flapped them in the air. "I was handing out fliers to try to get more business in the Tunnel of Love tonight. I'm working a double shift there and wanted to make sure it's worth my time. You want one? Here, take a few in case you have some friends who can use them." Shondra held out a several sheets. "They have a coupon for a half priced ticket."

"Thanks! You work in the Tunnel of Love too?" Sydney asked.

"Just once in a while to fill in for someone who's sick. I'll go over after the mermaid show is done." Shondra waved the fliers at the girls. "I'd better report those snakes. Toodle-oo!"

"Bye." Bailey waved weakly, and then turned to Sydney. "Toodle-oo? Who says that?"

"She creeps me out," Sydney said. "She acts so friendly, but it seems so fake."

"I know what you mean." From her hilltop vantage point, Bailey watched Shondra push her way through clumps of people below. "But why would someone pretend to be nice if they're not?"

"Yeah," Sydney agreed. "If they want to come across as a nice person, why not be nice through and through? Seems like faking it would be exhausting after a while."

"Oh brother." Bailey put her hand over her mouth. "We're doing it again."

"What?"

"Assuming the worst about people."

"Well, we were right about Mr. Bubble," Sydney said.

"Or at least we think we were," Bailey corrected. "We still don't have proof he's the one who caused the suds in the Underwater Theater tank."

"I guess." Sydney sighed. "Being super sleuths is making us super suspicious!"

"Speaking of Mr. Bubble, look over there." Bailey nodded her head toward the bottom of the hilly path.

"That's him!"

Mr. Bubble secured a burlap bag into the back of an official Mermaid Park pickup truck. Then he hopped out of the bed and climbed into the driver's seat.

"Only this time he's driving a truck instead of the golf cart," Bailey said.

Sydney shielded her eyes from the bright sun. "I wonder what's in that bag."

"Maybe it's trash or tree trimmings," Bailey suggested.

"Seems a little small for that," Sydney said. "I wish we'd brought the binoculars so we could see better."

"If it isn't tree trimmings I don't know what it is." Bailey strained to see the bag better. "I've seen landscapers use that kind of bag to gather trimmings when they're done."

Sydney nodded. "But usually there's more than one bag, especially in a place this big."

Mr. Bubble started the engine.

"Come on. Let's follow him and see where he goes." Sydney took off running with Bailey close behind.

"We'll never be able to keep up with a truck!" Bailey huffed.

"We don't have to," Sydney said, each step jarring her words. "We just have to keep it in sight so we see where it goes. Besides, it won't be able to go very fast with all the people around."

Bailey followed down the hill on Sydney's heels. The truck bumped slowly down the road, honking occasionally at people who didn't move off the path. It wasn't as hard to keep up with it as Bailey thought it would be. Soon, it turned down the path toward the Tunnel of Love. The truck stopped at the facility entrance to the tunnel. Mr. Bubble hopped out of the truck and opened the tailgate. Grabbing the bag, he slung it over his back, looking over his shoulder before entering the back door.

"Did you see that?" Sydney asked.

"He wanted to make sure no one saw him, just like he did before going into the Underwater Theater with the detergent."

"Well, yeah, but that's not what I meant."

Bailey cocked her head. "Then what?"

"I could have sworn I saw his bag move."

"Move? You don't think he had someone in there, do you?" Bailey wiped her sweaty hands on her shorts.

"Not someone. The bag wasn't big enough to hold a person, unless it was a tiny child." Sydney licked her lips. "But I think it was alive, whatever it was."

"Are you sure your imagination isn't going bonkers?"

Sydney's hands flew to her hips. "Yes, I'm sure! That bag moved. I saw it!"

"Okay, okay. I was just checking. Maybe it was something new for the boat ride. You know, like maybe new fish to swim in the water."

She shot Bailey a look. "Wouldn't that require them to be kept in water instead of in a burlap bag?"

Bailey laughed. "Oh yeah. I guess so."

Sydney playfully shoved her friend. "Oh well. Looks like the show's over here. We may as well move on."

A half-smile played at Bailey's lips. "Listen, I know you'd rather go with Stephen, but will you go to the Tunnel of Love with me tonight?" Bailey tried to hide her smile.

Sydney's face reddened, then she saw that Bailey was about to explode with laughter.

"I guess since we have the coupon, we may as well," Sydney answered. "Of course it won't be nearly as fun with you, but maybe we'll get some more clues as to what was in Mr. Bubble's bag."

Bailey burst out laughing. "Oh Syd. You're a good sport. I couldn't resist."

"Just stay on your own side of the boat," Sydney teased right back.

● — ● — ●

That evening as Bailey and Sydney stepped into the boat, they noticed that artificial vines with pink roses adorned the edge of the boat and romantic music played. The girls rolled their eyes as they saw other passengers snuggling closely in their boats.

"This is going to be good," Bailey said. "Thankfully it will be dark enough that we don't have to watch everyone getting all mushy."

"Besides, the boats will move farther apart once we get going."

Bailey peered over the side. "Hey, look! A fish just swam by!"

Sydney gave Bailey a sideways glance. "Probably glad to get out of that bag Mr. Bubble had him in."

Bailey laughed. "All right, I know you'll never let me live that one down."

"Bailey! Sydney! Is that you?" The boy's voice from the platform where they'd climbed onto the boat startled the girls.

"Stephen!" Bailey waved wildly. "It's us!"

She nudged Sydney, who sat with her mouth hanging open.

"What are you doing here?" he asked.

"We got some coupons today and decided to use them," Bailey explained. "Wanna join us?"

Sydney elbowed Bailey and gave her a warning glare.

"Sure! Hang on a second while I pay."

Bailey saw him hand money to the cashier and in seconds he stood beside the boat.

"Scoot over, Syd, so he doesn't have to crawl over you."

Sydney shot daggers with her eyes at Bailey, her cheeks flaming.

"What did you guys do this afternoon?" Stephen squeezed in beside Sydney.

"We just hung out here at the park," Bailey said. "The most exciting thing, I guess, was running into a couple of snakes."

"Here?" Stephen said. "I've never known there to be snakes at the Mermaid Park."

The mention of snakes seemed to bring Sydney back from the dead. "That's what Bailey said. Seems weird to have seen two in one day, don't you think?"

Stephen flashed his movie-star smile. "Definitely weird."

The boat lurched, and they began gliding slowly through the Tunnel of Love. Small white lights zigzagged above them providing dim, romantic lighting. Sydney scooted closer to Bailey, clearly uncomfortable with having Stephen sitting so near.

"We saw a fish in the water before we saw you," Sydney told Stephen. "Not that you were in the water like the fish, but you know, we saw it, then we saw you."

She looked away and squeezed her eyes tight.

"What Sydney is trying to say is that we saw a fish."

Stephen laughed. "That's what I thought she said."

The romantic music swelled as they rounded a corner and saw a beautiful waterfall with dancing colored lights.

"Wow," Sydney said. "That's gorgeous!"

Bailey felt her friend's body relax as the boat continued floating. Soon, they saw a tunnel ahead with roses, hearts, and cutouts of Cupid on the top. Mermaid statues flanked either side.

"Uh-oh," Bailey said. "Here it comes. Get ready, guys, this could be gross!"

"We might want to cover our ears so we don't have to hear all the kissing." Sydney's voice sounded apologetic.

Stephen laughed. "Not me. I'd rather listen!"

As their boat entered the pitch-black tunnel, someone in a boat behind them started hooting, his voice echoing off the walls. Someone else howled like a coyote.

Suddenly, something dropped into Bailey's lap and she screamed.

"What?" Sydney asked. "What's wrong?"

"Something fell on me! It's moving!"

Bailey felt Stephen's hands by her knees. "Where is it?"

"It fell onto the floor of the boat."

Sydney and Bailey scrambled to tuck their legs up on the seat. They heard terrified screams from other boaters punctuate the air.

"What did it feel like?" Stephen asked.

"It was like a heavy rope, b—but it moved." Bailey choked back a sob. "I think it was a snake."

"That's impossible!" Stephen said. "How could snakes get in here?"

"Sabotage," Sydney whispered. "Mr. and Mrs. Fuller were right. It has to be sabotage."

Sydney felt something brush the front of her leg and screamed. "It's on the floor in front of me!"

"I'll catch it and throw it overboard." Bailey heard Stephen's hands groping along the floor.

"Ugh! Every time I touch it, it moves away. I wish I had more room to move!"

The boat rocked as the search continued.

"Yeah, now he's over here by me again." Bailey started to cry. She clung to Sydney's arm.

Another snake dropped, landing on Sydney's shoulder. "*Aaaaeeeeek! Get it off me!*"

Stephen grabbed the reptile and flung it into the water. The first one still wiggled at their feet.

"We're almost to the end of the tunnel, then we'll be able to see better." He stretched a protective arm around the terrified girls.

Gradually, the light returned as they exited the tunnel. Bailey saw people in the boat ahead of them toss a snake into the water.

"I see him by your feet, Stephen," she told him.

Stephen felt around the bottom of the boat and came up with a snake in his hand. Both girls screamed before he threw it overboard.

Sydney shivered. "Someone had to have put those snakes in there."

Bailey squeezed Sydney's hand. "Or worse. Someone must have hid in the dark and thrown them as we passed."

"We need to let Mr. and Mrs. Fuller know about this right away," Stephen said. As boats stopped at the dock people quickly scurried out of them. Young men hugged their terrified, sobbing girlfriends.

"Let's go!" Stephen pulled Sydney and then Bailey from the boat. "We should get our money back!"

"We can do that later," Bailey said. "Mr. and Mrs. Fuller will take care of it for us."

"Come on!" Stephen motioned with his arm.

The girls ran after Stephen, who was already several strides down the path.

Bailey glanced back at the Tunnel of Love. Panicked people still leaped from their boats, bombarding the poor cashier with angry demands.

"Poor lady," Bailey muttered. Then a flicker of movement caught Bailey's eye by the back door where they'd seen Mr. Bubble earlier. "Look!"

Shondra and Mr. Bubble were walking arm in arm down the pathway, giggling and whispering.

Snakes Alive!

Stephen, Bailey, and Sydney raced to Mr. and Mrs. Fuller's office. Bailey knocked, then entered.

Mr. Fuller struggled to get out of his recliner when he saw them. "You kids look like you just saw a ghost!"

"Worse," Bailey said. "We just rode the Tunnel of Love and snakes fell all over everyone! Ugh!"

She shivered at the memory.

"What?" Bailey's grandma flew from the kitchen to the living room. "Are you okay?"

"What in heaven's name?" Mrs. Fuller joined them, wiping her hands on her dish towel.

"We're all right, but it freaked us out. People were screaming and crying," Sydney said. "It was like a scene from some horror flick."

Stephen stepped forward. "I'm glad I rode with them. They would have been all alone in that dark tunnel having to fend for themselves with those snakes."

"I'm grateful you were there to help," Grandma told him.

"But how in the world could snakes get into the Tunnel of Love?" Mr. Fuller asked. "We've never had a snake problem before."

"We don't think they *got* in," Bailey said. "We think they were *brought* in."

Mr. Fuller frowned so hard his eyebrows met in the middle of his forehead. "Brought in? How?"

"We don't know for sure," Sydney said. "We think people were in the tunnel throwing them at boats as they passed, but it was too dark to be sure."

"It had to have been more than one person, because snakes fell on us at two different places in the tunnel." Stephen slowly combed his fingers through his thick black hair.

Sydney nodded. "Besides, snakes don't attack people unless they feel threatened. Their natural instinct is to stay away. That's why I think they were being thrown at us."

Mrs. Fuller covered her mouth. "Ewww! The very thought of it horrifies me! Never in a million years did I think something like this would happen at our park."

"Did you see any suspicious characters around there before the ride?" Mr. Fuller asked. "Anyone who made you wonder what he was up to?"

Bailey nodded. "Just Mr. Bubble."

"Who?" Mr. Fuller asked.

"We think it was the same man who may have put the bubbles in the Underwater Theater," Bailey said. "We call him Mr. Bubble."

"Was he driving the golf cart again?" Mrs. Fuller asked.

"No. This time he had a Mermaid Park pickup truck," Sydney replied.

"And we saw him haul a burlap bag of something into the back entrance to the Tunnel of Love."

Sydney nodded. "Something that moved."

"You saw the bag move?" Mrs. Fuller grimaced.

"Well, I didn't but Syd did," Bailey said.

"And the guy looked over his shoulder again, like he wanted to make sure no one saw him."

"Did you see him too, Stephen?" Mr. Fuller asked.

"No. I didn't get there until the girls were already in the boat."

Ed stroked his chin. "Are you sure it was the same man?"

Bailey nodded. "Definitely. He had that same bushy mustache."

"Oh, and Shondra was handing out fliers with half-price coupons for the Tunnel of Love just before we saw Mr. Bubble."

"What? I never authorized that!" Mr. Fuller paced the small room.

"We got a few extras from her if you want to see." Bailey dug in her pocket and handed a crumpled flier to Mr. Fuller.

"Well, I'll be." He shook his head. "Mind if I keep this?"

"You need a half-price coupon?" Bailey teased. The room's tension lightened with their laughter.

"No," Mr. Fuller replied, still smiling. "But I'd like to spring it on Shondra when I have a little talk with her tomorrow. Plus, I need to find out who her friend is. She must be supplying him with keys to our vehicles. That alone is grounds for dismissal, much less if any of the rest of this proves true."

"Oh, and one more thing," Bailey said. "After we got off the boat we saw Shondra and Mr. Bubble together. He had his arm around her and they were laughing as they left the Tunnel of Love."

"So her friend may be more than just a friend," Mr. Fuller said.

Bailey shrugged. "Sure looked like it to me."

"I don't know why Shondra Ellis would want to sabotage our park," Mr. Fuller said. "She's always been a good employee."

"I'm sorry you have to deal with this nonsense." Grandma Cora stood. "But I'd better get these girls home. After a night like they've had they ought to sleep well."

"Of course." Mrs. Fuller whooshed over to them. "I'm so sorry about what happened. I wish we could make it up to you somehow."

"No problem," Bailey said. "We weren't hurt."

"I'd better go too." Stephen nodded his head toward Bailey and Sydney. "Maybe I'll see you tomorrow."

Mr. and Mrs. Fuller walked them all to the door.

"Good night!" Bailey waved as she climbed into Grandma's PT Cruiser.

●—●—●

At Grandma Cora's house, Bailey and Sydney flopped onto the bed in the spare bedroom.

"Do you have your phone handy?" Bailey asked.

"Right here." Sydney pulled it from her pocket.

"We need to fill in the other Camp Club Girls about the day." Bailey dialed Elizabeth's number, then conferenced in the rest of the girls.

After some initial chitchat, Sydney sat up and crossed her legs. "We called because we have some updates on our mystery."

"Let's hear it!" Kate said.

Bailey and Sydney told them about seeing the snakes on the pathway and then running into Shondra handing out fliers.

"Oooo!" Alexis hooted. "The Tunnel of Love!"

"Don't you mean, 'Ewww, snakes'?" McKenzie corrected.

"McKenzie's right," Sydney said. "Just wait until you hear what else happened and you won't be so thrilled by the Tunnel of Love, Alex."

Bailey picked up the story. She told them about seeing Mr. Bubble with the burlap sack in the Mermaid Park pickup truck and how he acted suspiciously when he went into the back entrance.

"And now comes the best—or worst—part." Sydney cleared her

throat and sat up straight. "We were sitting in the boat waiting for the ride to begin and Stephen joined us."

"Oh man," Alex said. "Did you freak, Syd?"

"No, I didn't freak."

"But she jabbed me good and hard in the ribs when I invited him to ride with us." Bailey winked at Sydney.

"So he climbs in and there's barely room for all three of us so we're squished together." Sydney picked up the story. "The ride started and almost as soon as we got into the pitch-black tunnel, Bailey screamed."

"What happened?" Elizabeth asked.

"You won't believe this," Bailey said. "A snake fell into my lap."

"A snake?" Kate squealed. "A real one?"

"A real snake." Bailey paused. "Stephen tried to get it off, but it had already slid onto the floor of the boat."

"So there Bailey and I were with our feet on the tiny bench seat while Stephen tried to find the snake in the dark."

"He wasn't having much luck, and we started hearing people in other boats scream too." Sydney shivered. "And the next thing you know, I heard *myself* screaming because another snake landed on my shoulder."

"I'm about to scream now, just thinking about it!" Alexis said.

"Stephen grabbed it off her and threw it into the water," Bailey said. "By this time we were coming out of the tunnel and there was better lighting. Stephen found the other snake on the boat floor and tossed it overboard too."

"I'm sure I would have died on the spot," Elizabeth said. "I'm terrified of snakes."

"Listen to this, though," Bailey continued. "We got off the boat and headed to Mr. and Mrs. Fuller's to tell them what happened. Then we saw Mr. Bubble and Shondra walking arm in arm away from the Tunnel of Love."

"And they were laughing like they'd just pulled off the funniest joke of all time," Sydney added.

"No way!" Kate said.

"Those two are up to no good for sure," Elizabeth said.

"But why?" McKenzie asked. "What would their motive be?"

"That's the big question," Bailey said. "Mr. Fuller said Shondra has always been a good employee."

"So we need to figure out what's changed recently that would bring about a change in her," McKenzie said.

Kate piped in. "I'll see what I can find out about her. Do you know her full name?"

"Mr. Fuller called her Shondra Ellis," Sydney said.

"Good memory, Syd!" Bailey gave her a thumbs-up.

"Great," Kate answered. "I'll Google her and let you know what I come up with."

"Sounds good," Sydney said.

"Hey, guys," Alex said. "I have some big news."

"About the mystery?" Elizabeth asked.

"Not exactly," Alex replied. "But sort of."

"Well, spill it!" McKenzie said.

"I'm doing a documentary for my cable column, 'It's a Kid's Eye View,' about. . .drum roll please. . .the Mermaid Park!"

"*Our* Mermaid Park?" Bailey shrieked. "Here in Florida?"

"The one and only!"

"That's awesome!" Sydney said. "Do you get to come here to visit?"

"Yep," Alex said. "I leave on Thursday. But my mom won't make my plane reservation until she knows if I can stay with your grandma. Would you mind asking her, Bailey?"

"I'm sure it will be fine. But I'll find out for sure and let you know."

"I'm totally jealous," Kate said.

Elizabeth laughed. "We all are! But really, Alex, that is so cool."

"We're going to have a blast!" Bailey exclaimed.

Sydney stretched. "I hate to spoil the party, but I've gotta say good-night. I think the drama of the day is catching up with me."

Bailey yawned. "Yeah, me too. And we've got mermaid rehearsal in the morning. I'll call you tomorrow about your trip, Alex. Good night, everyone!"

Wednesday morning Grandma Cora drove the girls to their practice.

"Grandma, our friend Alexis is doing a documentary on her cable column about the Mermaid Park. Isn't that amazing?"

"It sure is," Grandma replied. "When does it air?"

"I'm not sure, but she's supposed to fly in on Thursday to film it and her mom wondered if she could stay with us."

"Well, my place isn't very big, but I don't imagine she is either!" Grandma laughed at her own joke. "Of course she can stay with us. It'll be fun to meet another one of your friends."

"Thanks, Gram! You're the best."

Grandma parked in front of Mr. and Mrs. Fuller's office. "Here we are. Have fun at your practice."

"Okay. See you later." Bailey planted a kiss on her grandma's cheek before starting down the path to the Underwater Theater.

"I wonder if Shondra will be there today," Sydney said.

"Yeah, and if she is, I wonder if she'll act any different." Bailey kicked a rock.

Their question was answered as soon as the Underwater Theater came in view.

"There she is!" Bailey whisper-yelled.

"Where?"

Bailey pointed. "Over there, by the back entrance to the ballet show."

"Doesn't she ever go in the front entrance like everyone else?" Sydney asked.

Bailey chuckled. "Well, in all fairness, lots of the employees use the back door."

"I guess." Sydney sighed. "It's just that I don't trust her anymore, so I always think she's sneaking around."

"Hmmm." Bailey grew quiet. "Guess that's what my mom tried to tell me once."

"What do you mean?"

"I'd been on the computer when I wasn't supposed to be and I told her I was just turning it off. But she knew better. She said trust is the most important thing a person can bring to others. Without it, she said, people are always suspicious of what you're doing, even if you're doing the right thing."

"I see what you mean," Sydney said. "Shondra may have simply been coming to work, but I thought she was up to something because of what she'd done before."

"It's not so bad when it's someone you don't really know, like Shondra." Bailey dabbed on some pink lemonade lip balm. "But when it's your parents or someone else you care about, it makes you feel bad. I had to prove to my mom that I was trustworthy for weeks afterwards, just because of one bad choice."

Jessica and the other girls were already gathering for rehearsal. Sydney joined GraceAnn and Zeke backstage. Bailey and her fellow junior mermaids changed into their swimsuits and slid into the warm water.

"No bubble bath today," Bailey joked with a girl who looked about her age.

"The secret of being a realistic mermaid is to swim silently through the water with grace and ease." Jessica demonstrated by swimming across the tank. "Did you hear my feet kicking the water?"

"No."

"They kick under the water, so they don't make a sound," Jessica told them. "No splashing allowed when you're a mermaid. Now you try it."

The girls swam underwater, keeping their feet away from the surface where they'd make noisy splashes.

"Good!" Jessica beamed at her students. "That will be even easier in your mermaid suits because your feet will be in the tail fin. It will glide you effortlessly through the water."

Bailey could hardly contain herself. *I'm a junior mermaid in a show at the Mermaid Park! This is my dream come true!*

"The other thing you need to remember to be a natural mermaid is breath control. Johnson over there has a stopwatch and will time us to see how long we can hold our breath. Everyone take a big breath and hold it as long as you can." Jessica took a breath and held it too.

So did Bailey. Not moving, she watched the other girls' faces turn red after several seconds, and wondered if hers was too. Soon, girls began blowing their air out, unable to hold it any longer. Jessica still held hers, as did Bailey and a few other girls. Finally, it came down to only Jessica and Bailey. She felt sure her face was beet red by now. She was running out of air. Finally, when she was about to explode, she blew hers out with a giant whoosh!

Jessica, whose face was just starting to get pink, still held hers. She looked around at her students, her eyes asking the silent question, "What's the matter?" The girls clapped and urged her on.

"How long so far?" one girl asked Johnson.

"Fifty-four seconds."

"Wow! Almost a minute!" Bailey could hardly believe it. She thought sure she'd held her breath for over a minute. Or at least that's how it felt.

Finally, Jessica let her air out. The girls cheered and Johnson pressed the stopwatch button. "One minute, eighteen seconds."

"This is an exercise you can practice out of the water too," Jessica told them. "You can have breath-holding contests with your friends."

"How did you hold yours so long?" a red-haired girl asked.

"It takes a lot of practice. The more you hold your breath, the stronger your lungs will get and the greater your lung capacity will be. It's harder to hold your breath under water because of the water pressure around you, so you need to work up to longer and longer periods of time."

A small girl raised her hand.

"Yes, Charissa?"

"When you're swimming under water, do you run out of breath like when you run around the block?"

Jessica smiled. "Good question. You sort of do, but it's different. Charissa raises a good point. When you're actively swimming, you use more energy and your lungs naturally want more oxygen. That's why you need to work at increasing your ability to hold your breath for longer periods of time. Any other questions?"

Bailey looked around the group, but no one responded.

"All right." Jessica swam over to Bailey. "Bailey was our champion breath holder today so she gets to be the first to choose her mermaid costume after class."

Bailey bounced up and down in the water making little waves. She had chosen the costume she wanted when Jessica showed them to the class the first day. She couldn't wait.

"We have to choose costumes today so there's time to have them altered to fit each of you before next week's show," Jessica told them as they climbed out of the water tank.

Just then a siren pierced the air, followed by the sound of a blaring fire truck horn. Sydney came out from backstage as Bailey stepped, dripping wet, from the tank. Their eyes met, both girls wondering what had happened, as the wailing siren sped past the Underwater Theater.

CHAPTER 6

Mayhem in the Morning

"Sounds like something's happened!" Bailey said. "Let's go!"

"Not so fast!" Jessica caught Bailey by the arm. "You need to choose your costume first."

"I already know which one I want," Bailey said. "The blue-green one with the long flowing fins."

"Ahh." Jessica nodded. "Nice choice."

Bailey turned her attention to the open door of the Underwater Theater. She craned her neck hoping to see what was going on.

"Since I can see you're in a hurry to get out of here," Jessica said, "I'll let you postpone your fitting until tomorrow."

Bailey hugged Jessica spontaneously, then she and Sydney rushed for the door. Suddenly, Sydney stopped in her tracks and swung around toward Jessica. "Are we excused?"

Jessica laughed. "Yes. Class dismissed! And Bailey, don't forget to change your clothes."

Bailey looked down at herself. Water dripped from her hot pink-and-green swimsuit. She burst out laughing. "Thanks!" She ran to the dressing room and came out wearing dry clothes.

Outside, Bailey and Sydney ran in the direction the fire truck had gone. People crowded the path to the water ballet show, and Bailey spotted the big red engine parked in front.

"What happened?" Sydney asked a woman in the crowd.

"I'm not sure." She stood on tiptoe trying to get a good look. "I heard something was in the water at the ballet show."

"Something like what?" Bailey asked. "Mean fish? Bacteria? Poisonous plants?"

The woman shook her head. "I think it was some kind of animal."

Just then an ambulance parted the crowd like the Red Sea, horn blaring.

"Man, it must be bad," Sydney said.

"Did you notice Shondra wasn't at practice today?" Bailey raised her eyebrows at Sydney.

"Maybe she was too busy getting someone killed in the water ballet show." Sydney didn't crack a smile. Bailey saw intense concentration mixed with anger on her friend's features. She imagined that was how she looked before her Junior Olympic competitions—fierce and determined.

Sydney pushed her way to the front of the crowd. Bailey hooked her finger through Sydney's belt loop and followed her. When they reached the front, Bailey pulled out her cell phone and called Mr. Fuller.

"Lenore and I are already on our way there," Mr. Fuller told her. "The fire department called as soon as they got the 911 call. We were still at home, so we're fighting traffic even as we speak."

"Did they say what happened?" Bailey asked.

"Said someone turned a small alligator loose in the water ballet tank during the morning's first show and the performers had to scramble to safety. Not sure how they pulled that stunt off, but they did. Boy, if I get my hands on who's responsible for this. . ."

"I don't blame you for being mad," Bailey said.

"Mad? I'm furious! Not to mention worried sick over what this news will do for business." Bailey thought she heard Mr. Fuller pound the steering wheel.

"If it makes you feel any better, Sydney and I are in the front of the crowd and the people's injuries don't look too bad." Bailey surveyed the scene. "They just took two people out on stretchers, but they were talking and seemed all right."

"Hopefully they're just taking them to the hospital to check them over." Mr. Fuller's voice sounded weary, his anger deflating like air from a tire. "Lenore and I are almost there. I'll talk to you later."

Bailey returned her phone to her pocket. "Mr. and Mrs. Fuller are on their way."

"I bet Mr. Fuller's about to lose it," Sydney said.

"Yep," Bailey said, "and I can hardly blame him. He and Mrs. Fuller have worked so many years to make this a wonderful, family-friendly place, and now all this bizarre stuff keeps happening."

"It's bound to hurt their reputation." Sydney watched as the paramedics lifted the stretchers into the ambulances.

"We've got to figure out why someone would do this to them," Bailey said. "Maybe they've made some enemies along the way that they don't even know about."

"I can't imagine why anyone wouldn't like the Fullers, but obviously, someone's got it in for them."

"I'll be glad when Alexis gets here on Thursday. We could use a fresh take on this case."

After the performers were put into the ambulances, the crowd began to drift away. Minutes later, Bailey heard Mr. Fuller's big voice behind her.

"Coming through, coming through!" Ed Fuller stomped his way through the thinning crowd until he reached the emergency vehicles. He put his hand on Bailey's shoulder as he passed and gave her a quick smile.

"I'm Ed Fuller, the owner of Mermaid Park. What's the latest?" Bailey heard him ask the paramedic.

"The injuries aren't serious," the man said. "The victims were more shaken up than hurt. But we want to take them in to make sure everything checks out."

Ed nodded and turned to a police officer holding a clipboard. "Any more information about what happened here and who's responsible?"

"No, sir." The officer stuck his hand out. "I'm Officer Gallagher."

"Ed Fuller, owner of the Mermaid Park." The men shook hands.

"We're still working on the information we have, which isn't much." Officer Gallagher flipped pages on his clipboard. "All we know for sure is probably the same things you already know. A small alligator was put into the tank at the ballet show this morning."

"How small is small?" Mr. Fuller questioned.

"About three feet long."

Mr. Fuller shook his head. "That's big enough to cause injury if it got hold of someone."

"Absolutely," the policeman replied. "That's why we'll press charges of assault on whoever did this."

"Good. Stick whatever charges you can on them."

"Do you have any idea who would do something like this?" the policeman asked. "Any enemies who might want to do your business harm?"

Mr. Fuller rubbed his chin. "None that I know of, but we have had a couple of people we've wondered about lately with all that's been happening."

"I heard about the tank full of bubbles and the snakes in the Tunnel of Love," Officer Gallagher said. "Were there other incidents too?"

"No, just those lately."

"Tell me about the people you've been wondering about." The officer had his pen ready to jot down notes.

Bailey's ears perked up as she listened to the conversation.

"Mainly just one of my employees, Shondra Ellis."

The officer wrote the name on a pad of paper. "Does she have something against you?"

"I don't think so," Mr. Fuller told him. "It's just that she's been seen at the scene of almost every incident we've had around here in the last week or so. But she's always been a good employee in the past."

"I see. Anyone else?"

"I can't think of anyone," Mr. Fuller said.

"Mr. Fuller!" Bailey tapped his arm. "What about Mr. Bubble?"

"Mr. Bubble?" The officer looked like he was trying not to smile.

"Officer Gallagher, this is Bailey Chang and her friend, Sydney Lincoln. They're visiting their grandma who's a close friend of ours. Tell him what you saw, Bailey."

"We've seen Shondra with a man who has a big, dark mustache. He's usually driving one of the Mermaid Park's vehicles, but Mr. Fuller says he doesn't work here."

Officer Gallagher looked over his shoulder and said quietly, "Is Shondra here now?"

Bailey's heart dropped. "No. We haven't seen her at all today."

"And she wasn't in our mermaid rehearsal today like she usually is either," Sydney added.

"Do you know Mr. Bubble's real name?" the officer asked.

Bailey shook her head. "Sorry. We haven't been able to get close enough to read his name tag. But he might be wearing someone else's uniform anyway."

Officer Gallagher grinned. "Pretty good detective work there."

"Thanks. Sydney and I like to solve mysteries."

"If you get any more clues, you give me a call, okay?" The officer handed Bailey his card.

She studied it, a huge smile on her face. "You bet!"

Back at Grandma's house that afternoon, Bailey called Alexis and put her on speakerphone so Sydney could hear.

"My grandma said you can stay with us when you come!" Bailey told Alex.

"Awesome!"

"When do you get in?" Sydney pulled out her planner.

"Thursday afternoon at 3:25."

Sydney jotted down the information.

"Great," Bailey said. "We'll be done with our mermaid rehearsal by then."

"You won't believe what happened here today." Sydney told Alex about the alligator in the water ballet performance.

"That's unbelievable!" Alex said.

"We're hoping you can help us figure out this mystery while you're here." Bailey tucked her hair behind her ear.

"We can't imagine why anyone would want to do this kind of stuff to Mr. and Mrs. Fuller," Sydney said. "They're so nice!"

"I can't wait to meet them," Alex said. "Have you seen any more of Stephen?"

"Not since the snake episode," Bailey replied. "I don't think he even knows about what happened today."

"I hope I get to meet him while I'm there."

"I'm sure you will," Bailey said.

"Maybe you can go on his sponge diving boat with us." Sydney's eyes sparkled at the idea. "That reminds me, Bales, we're supposed to go over there this afternoon while his dad is out fishing. Remember?"

"That's right! With all the excitement, I almost forgot."

"We can't wait to see you, Alex," Sydney said. "We'll pick you up at the airport Thursday afternoon."

"I can't wait to see you either," Alex replied. "It will be fun to work together face-to-face on a mystery again."

"See you Thursday!" Bailey hung up just as Grandma Cora bounced into the room, her bright blue eyes shining beneath her baseball cap.

"I'm heading over to Mermaid Park to have a cup of coffee with Lenore. Wanna come?"

Bailey looked at Sydney and shrugged. "Sure. I guess."

"I'll be leaving in about two minutes." Grandma left the girls' room.

"Maybe we'll be able to get a few more clues to the mystery before Alex gets here so we have more to work from," Sydney said.

"I hope so," Bailey said. "All we have right now is Shondra and Mr. Bubble, but no motive or concrete evidence."

● — ● — ●

The aroma of hot coffee greeted the girls and Grandma Cora when they entered Mrs. Fuller's office-house.

"This smells like the right place." Grandma got a mug from the cabinet and helped herself to a cup of the dark brew.

"You girls want a soda?" Mrs. Fuller offered.

"Can we, Grandma?" Bailey seldom got soda at home, except for special treats.

"Sure. You're on vacation so you may as well live it up!"

Through the front window, Bailey noticed Mr. Fuller's pickup truck crunch its way up the gravel driveway and park in front of the house. He entered, the screen door slamming behind him.

"Anything new, dear?" Mrs. Fuller asked.

"Nope." He poured himself a cup of coffee. "Guess we just have to wait now until the police come up with—"

He was interrupted by the office telephone ringing. "Hello. . .yes. Who's this. . .oh really? Where'd you hear that?" Mr. Fuller's face suddenly turned red like a tomato about to burst.

"Listen here, sir. I don't know who you've been talking to, but they don't know anything about me or my business. I'm not interested in selling no matter how many problems we run into. Goodbye, Mr. Goodrich!" Mr. Fuller slammed the phone back onto its stand.

"Who was that?" Mrs. Fuller asked cautiously.

"Another developer wanting to buy the Mermaid Park." Mr. Fuller paced in circles around the small room like he was on a mini racetrack. "John Goodrich from Barron's Commercial Development, to be specific. He said he heard we've been having some trouble at Mermaid Park and that we may be considering selling it."

"*Another* developer? You mean you've been getting other calls like that?" Grandma asked.

"Off and on over the past few months, especially since they started building that fancy new amusement park on the edge of the next town. They think they can buy us out and rebuild the Mermaid Park on some grand scale with thrill rides and all."

"Are they offering a good price?" Grandma Cora asked.

"The price doesn't matter. I'm not selling. This place is my lifeblood, like one of my own children. We've raised it and nurtured it into the happy place it is today."

"I don't blame you, Mr. Fuller," Bailey said. "I love this place and I know a lot of families would be sad if you sold it."

"Not only that," Mrs. Fuller added, "but a lot of the townspeople aren't too thrilled with the idea of having a big, fancy amusement park here.

They don't want to deal with the traffic and noise that would come with it."

"It's good to know you've got the support of the locals if you should need it." Grandma Cora sipped her coffee.

Ed nodded and the room grew quiet.

Bailey cleared her throat. "Grandma, we told Stephen we'd come back to the Sponge Diving Park today so he could show us around. Can we go now?"

"Sure. Go ahead." She waved them off. "Tell Stephen hello for me."

"Thanks." Bailey kissed her grandma's cheek before the girls rushed out the door.

●—●—●

As they approached the Sponge Diving Park, Bailey and Sydney saw Stephen on the sponge diving boat with Andrew.

"Stephen!" Bailey called, but the boat engines in the bay swept her voice away.

Stephen turned to leave and saw the girls nearing the boat. He waved, a huge grin spreading over his face. "You came!"

"Of course we came," Sydney said. "We told you we would, didn't we?"

"Yeah, but I wasn't sure if you were just being nice."

"Is it okay that we're here?" Bailey asked warily.

"My dad's out fishing, if that's what you mean," Stephen said. "He won't be back until sundown."

Bailey felt her muscles relax. "Good. Can you show us around?"

"You bet. Let's start over here."

The girls followed Stephen to an area where oxygen tanks, wet suits, and flippers hung. There were also several two-pronged hooks with long handles and some kind of drawstring bags hanging alongside them.

"What are those?" Bailey asked.

"Those are the divers' hooks and string bags. They use the hooks to pry the sponges off the rocks or reefs, and they put them in these string bags to bring them up out of the water."

"Then what do they do with them?" Sydney asked.

Stephen walked a little further to the main deck of the boat. "They dump them out on the deck here and cover them with wet burlap sacks. That lets them dry out slowly. After they're partly dry, the harvesters wash them and string them together on a long, thin rope and hang them in the sun to dry out completely. When they're totally dry, the harvesters wash them several more times to make them ready to sell."

"Wow. You sure know a lot about this business."

Bailey smiled at the admiration in Sydney's eyes.

"I'd like to know more, like stuff you can only learn from diving for the sponges." Stephen looked away.

"You can't give up on your dream, Stephen." Bailey patted him on the back.

"I have no choice," he replied. "My dad will never let me dive."

Andrew came up beside Stephen. "Never say never."

"What do you mean?" Stephen's eyes blazed. "You know how he feels about it."

"I know." Andrew put an arm around Stephen's shoulder. "But I have a plan."

CHAPTER 7

Revelations

"A plan?" Bailey turned her face from a blast of salty wind that blew a faint smell of fish in with it.

Andrew nodded thoughtfully, looking intently at Stephen.

Bailey thought Stephen's dark eyes would bore holes through Andrew. Finally he said, "Well, what is it?"

"It'll take some patience and a bit of craftiness too." Andrew raised his face to the wind.

Stephen bit his lower lip, shifting his weight from one foot to the other. Then he cleared his throat. "Okay, we can be patient and crafty. So let's hear it."

After looking around, Andrew bent toward the group of youngsters and said, "Here's what we'll do."

He spoke softly. "When Stephen's dad, Cyrus, gets back from his fishing trip, I'll do my usual chitchat with him about how it went and so on. Then I'll start reminiscing about his dad and how happy he always was after a good dive."

All three kids nodded, eyes wide.

"Then what?" Sydney urged.

"I'll remind him of his own childhood and how proud he was of his dad." Andrew rubbed his weathered hand over the gray stubble on his chin. "I'm not going to bring Stephen into this until later. I just want Cyrus to remember and relive those warm feelings awhile."

"Good idea," Bailey said. "It might start to soften his heart a bit."

"That's my hope." Andrew's eyes sparkled.

"How can we help?" Sydney asked.

"Tomorrow, I'd like you girls to come back over here and meet Stephen's dad."

Sydney frowned. "Are you sure that's a good idea?"

"Cyrus is a good man," Andrew said. "Right, Stephen?"

"Yes, sir," Stephen agreed. "He just worries about me a lot and is overly protective. I'm all he's got. That's why he gets mad—he's afraid something will happen to me."

"He's as gentle as a mouse with everyone else," Andrew assured them.

"What should we do?"

"I'll introduce you as some gals who came to learn about sponge diving," Andrew said.

"Which is true," Sydney added.

"Very true." Bailey nodded. "We just happen to be friends with Stephen too."

Stephen puffed his chest out, his dark eyes twinkling. "You can tell him you met me at the Mermaid Park and were interested in learning more about the sponge diving business and came over to check it out."

Bailey scrunched up her nose at Andrew. "You really want us to become friends with Stephen's dad?"

"Yes," Andrew said. "I know he'll get a kick out of you, just like I do."

"If you think it will help Stephen get to sponge dive someday, then it's worth it," Sydney said. "Even if it does make me a little nervous."

"I'll be with you the whole time," Andrew assured her. "And Stephen, I want you to make yourself scarce while they're here. We don't want your dad thinking you're up to something."

"No problem." Stephen pushed his windblown hair from his face. "Thanks for doing this for me."

"We're glad to help," Sydney said. "I just hope it gets the results you want."

"We'd better get back," Bailey said. "There's a wild bird performance at four o'clock at Mermaid Park, and we don't want to miss it."

"Do you want to come with us?" Sydney asked Stephen.

He looked at Andrew, who nodded. "Sure!"

"Let's go!" Bailey said. "Bye, Andrew!"

●━━●━━●

Stephen, Bailey, and Sydney climbed into second-row seats at the Wild Birds in Action show in the partially covered outdoor arena.

"I've never seen this show before," Bailey said. "It's new since last time I visited."

"I have, but it's been awhile," Stephen said. "You'll love it."

"I love all wildlife, but I don't know much about birds." Sydney giggled. "I hope I'll learn something."

The trainer appeared on the stage and welcomed the crowd. He wore thick leather gloves that reached almost to his elbow.

"I'm Jim," he began, "and I'd like to introduce you to my assistant, Hopscotch."

Jim extended his arm and an eagle glided from backstage and landed on it. As the audience oohed its approval, the trainer rewarded the bird with a bite of raw meat.

"This is awesome!" Bailey grinned.

"That bird looks nervous," Sydney said. "I may not know much about birds, but I know when one's uneasy. See how he's pacing up and down the trainer's arm?"

"I'd be nervous too in front of all these people," Stephen joked.

"But he does these shows all the time," Sydney countered. "He should be used to it."

Another bird trainer came onstage, bringing with him a bright macaw.

"Look at him," Bailey said. "He's gorgeous! His tail is so long!"

The royal blue-and-red bird began squawking so loudly the trainer gave it an extra piece of meat to try to quiet him down. His yellow head bobbed up and down.

"Something's upsetting those birds." Sydney looked around trying to spot the problem. She turned her attention to the stage again when she heard the audience gasp.

"Look out! Here they come!" someone yelled.

The large birds left their trainers' arms and swooped over the crowd, which collectively ducked and covered their heads with their hands.

"I don't remember this being part of the act!" Stephen said.

The trainers blew special bird whistles to try to get the birds to return to their arms, but the feathered flyers continued circling over the audience. A moment later, several more birds flew out from backstage and joined the flight.

"Someone let the birds out of their cages!" a stagehand yelled.

Bailey looked overhead just in time to see the huge eagle fly out of the arena. Several smaller birds followed.

"They're escaping!" Bailey cried.

"Come on! We have to tell Mr. Fuller." Sydney sprinted across the arena.

Bailey snatched her cell phone out of her pocket and dialed. "Mr. Fuller, the wild birds were let out of their cages and are getting away. We're just leaving the show and will be at your office in a minute." She didn't wait to hear what Mr. Fuller would say, but flipped her phone closed and stuffed it back into her pocket as she ran.

When they reached Mr. Fuller's, he was just opening the door to leave. "Tell me what happened."

Bailey recapped the whole chaotic scene at the outdoor arena. "Birds were flying everywhere and the trainers couldn't capture them. People were screaming and running."

"Between the birds squawking and the people yelling, you could hardly hear your own voice," Sydney added.

"I hate to ask this," Mr. Fuller said, "but did you see Shondra or her friend there?"

"No," Bailey replied. "Not this time."

"But a stagehand said someone opened the birds' cages and let them out during the show," Stephen said. "How else could they all have gotten out? But, of course, we couldn't see who was backstage."

"Those birds are worth a small fortune." Mr. Fuller rubbed his hand over his head. "I'd better get over there. I'll be back later."

●—●—●

That evening, Grandma Cora invited Mr. and Mrs. Fuller over for supper. "After the day you've had—or should I say the *week* you've had—you don't need to be worrying about fixing meals when you get home."

"We can't thank you enough, Cora," Mrs. Fuller said. "I hadn't given a single thought to what I was going to make for dinner tonight."

Grandma Cora placed a steaming chicken casserole on a hot pad in the center of the table. A bowl of bright green broccoli with cheese sauce sat close by and the smell of hot rolls filled the room.

The group joined hands around the table and Grandma prayed. "Father, we thank You for these friends and this food. We ask You for wisdom for Ed and Lenore as they deal with these people who intend to harm their business. May they be caught and dealt with according to Your perfect justice. Amen."

"Your prayer makes me think of the Bible story of Joseph when his brothers sold him into slavery," Sydney said. "Remember what he said to his brothers when they were reunited?"

"Refresh our memories," Mrs. Fuller said, chewing a bite of casserole.

"He said, 'You intended to harm me, but God intended it for good to accomplish what is now being done, the saving of many lives.' "

Bailey buttered a roll. "I don't get it."

"The people are trying to hurt the Mermaid Park's business," Sydney explained, "but God might use this situation for some greater good that we can't see yet."

"Ohhh." Bailey nodded slowly. "Like maybe it will turn out to be good publicity for the Fullers and they'll end up getting more business than ever?"

"You never know!" Sydney scooped some casserole onto her plate.

"Mr. Fuller, did you call the police about the birds being let out?" Bailey asked.

"Yes, I spoke with Officer Gallagher again since he worked on this morning's incident." Mr. Fuller took a bite. "By the way, Cora, this food is delicious."

Mrs. Fuller nodded. "These things are happening more often." Worry edged her voice.

"If it doesn't stop, we'll have to close the park." Mr. Fuller shrugged his shoulders and shook his head. "I don't know what else to do. We can't continue to risk innocent people's safety."

"No!" Bailey's hands balled into fists. "You can't close Mermaid Park. We just have to figure this out, that's all. Then you can keep your business."

"It sounds easy enough," Mr. Fuller said, "but we both know it's harder than that."

"Hard doesn't mean impossible," Sydney said gently. "It just means we have to lean on God more to get it done. Remember, 'With God all things are possible.' "

Mrs. Fuller smiled. "You're absolutely right. We can't give up."

Mr. Fuller nodded. "We have to think of a way to bring our customers back. Attendance has dropped steadily over the last few months. If we stay open, we need some fresh ideas to attract more business."

Bailey stuffed some cheesy broccoli into her mouth. *How can we get more people to come to the Mermaid Park?* she thought, then clapped her hands and swallowed her food. "I've got it!"

"You do?" Mr. Fuller's eyebrows rose.

"We just need to give people a reason to come back."

"Huh?" Mr. Fuller's eyebrows dropped. "I'm not following."

"Think about it," Bailey explained. "The birds got away today. All your customers feel bad about it, not just us."

"Okay. . ." Mr. Fuller said.

"So we make a contest or incentive of some kind." Bailey scooted to the edge of her chair. "We could advertise that if someone spots one of the birds and calls to tell us where they saw it, they get a free all-day pass to Mermaid Park. We'll have the whole city looking for your birds!

The people who give us tips on where they saw the birds will come back because they got a free pass—that's their reason. And so many people like to help and feel needed—that would give them a purpose."

Mr. Fuller looked at his wife, a smile starting at the corners of his mouth. "It just might work."

"We could even take it a step further," Sydney added, grabbing another roll.

"How?" Grandma Cora asked.

"What if we offered free day passes to anyone with valid information about the incidents that have been happening around Mermaid Park?" Sydney explained. "And if one of the tips leads to the arrest of the people who are responsible, they get a one-year pass?"

"Great idea!" Bailey said. "That way, all the customers will be on the lookout for suspicious activity while they're here instead of just Sydney and me."

"Sort of like a community Block Watch," Grandma Cora said. "I think it's worth a try. What do you think, Ed?"

Mr. Fuller pushed back from the table and began pacing—as the girls noticed he usually seemed to do when he was thinking. "I think young minds are a wonder, that's what. Why didn't I think of that?"

"And if a tip about the location of a bird leads to its capture, the caller could get a one-year pass too," Bailey said.

Ed leaned over and hugged the girls. "You two are a bright spot in this tough time for me. Thank you."

"Glad to help," Bailey said. "I just hope it leads to some answers to this mystery."

"And I hope you get your birds back," Sydney added.

"Me too," Bailey said. "What if we called the newspaper and told them about the new incentive programs you're offering?"

"Now there's a thought," Mr. Fuller said.

"They might want to interview us and we could become famous!" Bailey said.

"Now hold your horses, Bales," Grandma Cora said. "I know you've always wanted to be a star, but this is about publicizing the Mermaid Park, not Bailey Chang."

Bailey sighed. "I guess you're right." She struck a dramatic pose. "Someday my star will rise. . ."

Sydney giggled and playfully shoved Bailey. "You'll be a star if you can solve this mystery."

Just then Bailey's phone rang. "Hello? Oh, hi, Kate. . .you did? What did it say? Uh-huh. . .interesting. Okay. Thanks for the info. Bye."

"Who was that?" Grandma Cora asked.

"It was our friend Kate." Bailey cleared her throat, unsure how much information to give about the Camp Club Girls.

"What'd she say?" Sydney asked.

Bailey looked at Mr. Fuller, Mrs. Fuller, and Grandma Cora. "We've kept our friends from camp informed about what was going on around here. There are six of us who met at camp. We call ourselves the Camp Club Girls and have solved more than twenty mysteries together. Kate, one of our friends, volunteered to do some checking on the internet about Shondra."

"What?" Mr. Fuller said. "I'm not sure that's a good idea."

"Did Kate find anything out?" Sydney asked.

"As a matter of fact, she did." Bailey looked at the group. "I think you'll want to hear this, Mr. Fuller."

"Seems like we're snooping into other's people's business." Mr. Fuller's pacing increased.

"It's public record or Kate wouldn't have access to it." Sydney said as she picked up her plate and carried it into the kitchen.

"Syd's right." Bailey followed Sydney's lead and stacked her plate with Grandma Cora's. "It isn't bad stuff. Just facts."

"Oh, all right." Mr. Fuller blew out his breath. "What did she find out?"

Mrs. Fuller took the plates from Bailey and added her own and Mr. Fuller's to the pile. She carried them to the kitchen and returned.

"Shondra used to live in Racine, Wisconsin," Bailey told him. "She moved to Florida two years ago and started working for Barron's Commercial Development."

Mr. Fuller swung around to face Bailey. "What? That's the company that called me yesterday asking me if I wanted to sell Mermaid Park!"

"How long has Shondra worked for us, Ed?" Mrs. Fuller asked. "A year or so?"

"Yeah, probably at least a year." Mr. Fuller resumed pacing. "I'd have to check the hiring records to be sure."

Sydney moved into the living room and the others followed. "So she was working for them, then she started working for you."

"Wonder why she quit over there?" Mr. Fuller asked. "I'd think she would have made better money working for John Goodrich."

"She didn't quit," Bailey replied. "She still works for them."

Lights! Camera! Action!

"Shondra Ellis works for John Goodrich at Barron's Commercial Development?" Mr. Fuller's mouth dropped open in astonishment.

"Afraid so," Bailey said.

"What's her position there?" Mrs. Fuller asked.

Bailey tucked her hair behind her ears. "Kate called there and couldn't find out her exact job title, but she works in the sales department."

"I'm betting her friend, Travis, works there too," Mr. Fuller said.

"Travis?" Sydney cocked her head, causing the beads on her cornrows to clack.

"Oh, that's right, I forgot to tell you," Mr. Fuller said. "I spoke with Shondra this morning."

"You did?" Bailey's eyes about popped from their sockets.

Mr. Fuller grinned and nodded. "I asked her about the new friend she's been seen with on the grounds."

"What'd she say?" Sydney asked.

"Said he was her new boyfriend, Travis Wingate."

"She gave you his name and told you he was her boyfriend just like that?" Bailey was beyond surprised.

"Well, with a little coaxing," Mr. Fuller admitted.

"Is he Mr. Bubble? The guy with the mustache?" Bailey asked.

Mr. Fuller sat in an easy chair and laced his fingers behind his head. "I specifically asked her about her new mustachioed friend and that's what she told me."

Bailey nodded thoughtfully. "So it must be him."

"Maybe we can dig into Travis's background next." Sydney pulled a pen and a pad of paper from her pocket and jotted down a note.

"Good job, Mr. Fuller," Bailey said. "You got some good information today. We'll figure this mystery out yet!"

"I hope so," Mrs. Fuller said. "I just hope the business doesn't go under first."

Bailey yawned. "It's been a busy day. I'm going to get ready for bed."

"Me too," Sydney said. "Good night, everyone!"

●—●—●

Thursday morning, Grandma Cora's phone woke Bailey.

"Yes," she heard her grandma say. "Of course. . .we'll be there within the hour. . .I just have to get the girls up and fed, okay? Bye."

Grandma knocked on the bedroom door. "Bailey? Sydney?"

"Hmm?"

Grandma cracked the door open. "That was Lenore on the phone. The newspaper just called them and wants to do an article on what's been happening at Mermaid Park. Ed told them about you girls thinking up an incentive for getting the birds back and boosting business. They'd like to interview you!"

"Us?" Bailey sat upright in her bed and rubbed her eyes. "That's awesome!"

"*Mblfrm,*" Sydney mumbled and buried her head under her pillow.

"Sydney, wake up!" Bailey shook her friend. "The newspaper wants to interview us! We'll be stars!" Bailey jumped up from the bed. "I have to figure out what to wear. Good thing we showered before bed last night."

Sydney yawned. "How can we become stars by getting our words put in the newspaper? They won't even see us."

Bailey dug through her clothes looking for just the right outfit. "Don't you see? That's where it all begins—name recognition!"

"Well, don't take too long," Grandma Cora said. "I told them we'd be there in an hour and you still need to eat breakfast."

A few minutes later, the smell of cinnamon toast drew Bailey and Sydney to the kitchen.

"Smells yummy in here." Bailey closed her eyes and lifted her nose to savor the sweet aroma.

"I thought the cinnamon sugar scent would get you out here in a hurry," Grandma Cora said. "Never fails." She placed a plate of the stacked toast slices between the girls on the table. "Eat up. We need to leave in fifteen minutes."

●—●—●

Bailey almost fainted when Grandma Cora drove up to the Mermaid

Park. Besides the waiting newspaper reporter, two local news vans sat outside Mr. and Mrs. Fuller's office. The antennas on each van reached high toward the crisp, blue sky.

"Do you think we'll get to be on TV?" Bailey smoothed her silky, black hair. A small strand on each side was held back with a pink, sparkly butterfly clip. She wore her favorite jeans embroidered down the leg with lavender flowers, even though she feared getting too hot in them. She didn't care. What mattered was that she looked her best for her big interview. Her purple-and-white T-shirt completed her look. She quickly smeared on some ruby grapefruit lip gloss.

"Maybe. Who knows?" Sydney stepped out of the car, dressed in tan shorts and a green, sleeveless, button-down blouse.

Bailey thought bright colors looked beautiful against her friend's dark skin and had suggested the shirt when Sydney asked what she should wear. "That green shirt will look great if the newspaper takes our picture!"

"Unless it's in black and white," Sydney mumbled.

"They wouldn't!" Bailey stuck out her lower lip.

Grandma knocked on Mr. and Mrs. Fuller's door, then opened it a bit and called, "Lenore?"

"We're in here, Cora." Mrs. Fuller called from the crowded kitchen. "Come on in!"

Bailey followed Grandma Cora and saw lights and cameras positioned in the living room, filling the tiny space. People milled about in the gaps around the equipment, some of them holding clipboards or microphones.

"Ron, this is Cora Chang, her granddaughter, Bailey, and Bailey's friend Sydney," Mrs. Fuller said. "And this is Ron Williams from the local news."

Bailey clapped her hands to her cheeks. "We saw you on TV last night!"

"It's a pleasure to meet you." Ron shook their hands. "We're about to begin our interview with Mr. Fuller. Then we'd like to interview you girls, if that's okay, and if it's okay with Grandma here."

Bailey saw Mr. Fuller getting his nose powdered at the kitchen table. "That would be awesome!"

"As soon as Mr. Fuller is finished there, you'll need to get your makeup done." Ron motioned toward the table. "You may think we put too much on you, but trust me, it'll make you look great on camera."

Bailey nodded. The makeup technician removed the oversized bib from around Mr. Fuller's neck and he stood.

"Right this way, Ed," Ron told him.

As Mr. Fuller passed by Bailey and Sydney, he wagged his finger at them and said with a smile, "No wisecracks about the makeup."

"You look beautiful!" Bailey teased.

"Yes!" Sydney added. "Positively stunning!"

Mr. Fuller scowled at the girls and sat on the couch where Ron indicated.

Bailey took her turn in the makeup chair. The woman smoothed a light tan foundation on Bailey's face and commented on her great bone structure. Then she brushed pink blush on her cheeks and applied a soft rose lipstick.

"There!" the makeup lady said. "You're done."

Sydney sat in the chair next and had the same thing done to her. By the time the two of them were made up, Mr. Fuller's interview was ending.

"Coming up," Ron said to the camera, "we'll talk to two girls who intend to boost the Mermaid Park's business and make it worth your while to come out. Stay tuned."

The bright lights turned off and Mr. Fuller rose from the couch. "Can I go wash off this makeup now?" he growled.

The TV station crew laughed. "Yeah, you're all through."

Ron ushered Bailey and Sydney into the living room and positioned them on the couch.

"You're on in three, two, one. . ." At the signal, the lights came back up and Ron stood in front of the girls and began speaking.

"If you're just joining us, we're at Mermaid Park where several incidents have occurred in the past month that have hurt their business. I have here with me two young ladies who witnessed some of the events firsthand." Ron turned and sat on the couch beside Bailey.

"This is Bailey Chang and Sydney Lincoln who are visiting from out of state. They're friends with the owners of Mermaid Park, Ed and Lenore Fuller. Can you tell us about what you've seen happen since you've been here?"

Bailey smiled and blinked. Sydney nudged her, but Bailey just kept smiling.

"Uh, well," Sydney said, "we were there when the snakes were dropped in the Tunnel of Love and we were at the Wild Birds in Action show when the birds escaped."

"Did any snakes fall on you?" Ron poked his microphone back toward Sydney, who looked at Bailey, whose smile had frozen.

"Yes, we had two snakes fall on us, right, Bailey?" Sydney elbowed her friend.

Bailey came out of her trance and said, "Yeah, right."

Ron gave a relieved smile. "Bailey, Ed Fuller told us that you have come up with an idea to get the escaped wild birds back and help increase attendance at the Mermaid Park all at the same time. Can you tell us your plan?"

"Sure." Bailey blinked and swallowed. She felt Sydney squeeze her hand. "Well. . .if anyone sees one of the wild birds, they can call The Mermaid Park and report it. If the bird is seen where the caller said it was, they get a free day pass to the park. But if the bird is actually captured as a result of a caller's information, that caller will receive a one-year pass."

Sydney jumped in. "The same thing goes for anyone who calls with information about the incidents that have been happening around here. If someone calls with a valid tip, he will receive a day pass. And if a tip leads to the arrest of the ones responsible for causing the trouble around here, the caller will get a one-year pass."

"Outstanding!" Ron said. "That should keep people on the lookout for those birds and for any suspicious activity around Mermaid Park."

"We hope so!" Bailey beamed, her stage fright gone. "Oh, and one more thing. Tomorrow, our friend Alexis Howell from Sacramento, California, will be here filming an episode for her cable column, 'A Kid's Eye View.' So come on out if you'd like to watch. Maybe you'll even get to be on the show!"

"I'm sure your friend will appreciate that plug." Ron looked directly into the camera. "There's a lot going on out here at Mermaid Park. Remember, photos of the missing birds are posted on the Mermaid Park's website. If you spot a bird you believe escaped from the Wild Birds in Action show, or if you have any information about the unfortunate events that have been occurring here, call Ed Fuller. The number is on your screen. You could win free passes to Mermaid Park as a result! This is Ron Williams, live at the Mermaid Park."

The bright lights went off and Ron stood. "You girls did great. Thank you."

"Thank *you*!" Bailey replied. "I've never been on TV before, though I've always wanted to be. I guess I was a little shy at first, but then I felt fabulous!"

Sydney laughed. "Good thinking about mentioning Alex's cable column!"

"I don't know where that came from," Bailey said. "It just popped out of my mouth."

"Well, it was genius," Sydney said. "It could help draw more people in tomorrow. That alone could help Mr. and Mrs. Fuller's business."

The girls stepped outside where it wasn't so crowded with people and equipment.

"Are you the girls who saw some of the horrendous events that have been happening at Mermaid Park?" a well-dressed woman asked.

"Yes, we were here for some of them," Bailey replied.

The woman stuck out her well-manicured hand. "Angela Downs, from the *Florida Chronicle*. I'm here to interview you."

"Oh yeah! I almost forgot with all the TV stations here!"

"Why don't we sit over there on that bench away from all the commotion?" Angela motioned toward a nearby park bench and the three sat down. Flipping open a leather folder with a pad of paper inside, she then asked Bailey and Sydney many of the same questions the TV interviewer had and jotted down their answers. But she concluded the interview with a different one. "Who do you believe could be responsible for these incidents?"

Bailey and Sydney stared at one another a moment.

"Well," Bailey began, "we don't know who's doing them for sure."

"But you have an idea of who it could be?" Angela pressed.

"We have some ideas, but that's all they are at this point," Sydney said. "We can't give you any names."

Angela's face fell.

Bailey nodded. "But the police are working on the case and I'm sure they'll figure out who it is."

"Well, thanks for the interview," Angela said.

"Do you need any pictures?" Bailey asked.

"No, thanks." Angela closed her notebook and stood. "It was a pleasure meeting you." She shook their hands.

"When will the article be in the paper?" Sydney asked.

"Tomorrow, in the Florida Life section."

"Okay, we'll watch for it," Bailey said. "Thank you!"

Angela waved before getting in her car.

Bailey waved back. "Hey, what time is it?"

Sydney looked at her phone. "Almost ten thirty. Why?"

"We're supposed to go to the Sponge Diving Park to meet Stephen's dad sometime today. We have to put Andrew's plan into action."

Sydney made a face. "Oh yeah. I'm not looking forward to that."

"I know, me neither, but if it will help Stephen, we should do it."

"May as well go now and get it over with," Sydney said.

"Let's go inside and wash off this makeup. Then I'll tell Grandma Cora we're leaving."

Minutes later, with fresh faces, the girls started walking to the Sponge Diving Park.

"You know what I said earlier about not looking forward to this?" Sydney asked.

Bailey nodded.

"Don't get me wrong, Bales. I want to help Stephen. I'm just nervous about meeting his dad, that's all."

"I know. I feel the same way." They waved at the man at the entrance, who had been told the girls were coming. "But I have a feeling we'll be surprised. From what Andrew and Stephen said, he sounds like we might have seen him at his worst the other day."

"I hope you're right."

The smell of fish wafted through the air as the girls reached the fishing boat. Stephen spotted them and jogged over.

"Hey! How's it goin'?" He flashed his million-dollar smile and offered his hand to help them aboard.

"Good!" Sydney wiped her sweaty palms on her shorts and took his hand. Then she turned and steadied Bailey as she climbed up while the boat bobbed in the water.

Stephen grinned. "Are you ready?"

"As ready as we'll ever be," Bailey confessed.

"I'll go get Andrew and then I'll stay out of sight." Stephen looked around. "I don't see my dad right now, but he's here somewhere."

"Okay," Sydney said. "We'll wait here."

Stephen gave both girls high fives, then left to find Andrew.

Bailey inhaled the ocean air and listened to the seagulls calling overhead. Lifting her face to the sun, she said, "I could get used to this."

"I know what you mean," Sydney agreed. "This place is nothing like Washington, DC."

"Or Peoria, Illinois," Bailey added. "But I suppose there are things about home that this place doesn't have either."

Andrew approached them, his rubber-soled shoes silent against the wooden deck. "Hi, girls!"

"Andrew!" Bailey called. "We were just soaking up this wonderful weather."

"Yep, the wind has died down. It's a beautiful day." He squinted into the sun. "Are you ready to meet Cyrus?"

"I think so," Bailey replied.

"We're feeling a bit nervous," Sydney admitted.

"Naturally," Andrew said. "But I assure you he's a pussycat." He winked at the girls. "He had a successful fishing expedition yesterday so he's in a good mood. I told him we may have a couple of young guests today. Come on. Follow me."

Bailey's eyes met Sydney's as they trailed behind the old fisherman. They followed him down a short flight of stairs into the belly of the boat.

"Cool!" Bailey said. "It's like we're underwater!"

"You are," Andrew said. "Look out the portholes and you'll see a whole different world."

The girls pressed their noses to the round windows and watched fish swim by. "Will we see any sponges?" Bailey asked.

"No, they live deeper," Andrew explained.

A deep voice interrupted their ocean viewing. "Andrew?"

Andrew swung around. "Cyrus! We were just looking for you."

"Out the window?" Cyrus asked.

Bailey didn't know whether to laugh or not.

"Well, that's where you were yesterday!" Andrew joked.

Mr. Christou's face softened. He smiled.

"These are the guests I told you might stop by today," Andrew said. "This is Bailey and this is Sydney."

Mr. Christou stuck out his calloused hand and the girls shook it. "It's a pleasure to meet you both."

"Thank you," Sydney said.

Bailey nodded. "It's nice to meet you too."

She saw that Stephen looked a lot like his dad. Mr. Christou's thick, dark hair and bright smile were also duplicated in his son, except for thin streaks of silver starting at each temple. But Stephen was already as tall as his father. Mr. Christou's build was shorter, stockier compared to his son's leaner frame. And salt-and-pepper whiskers shadowed the man's face.

"So you're interested in sponge diving?" Mr. Christou rubbed his stubble.

"Well, we're interested in learning about it," Bailey said. "But I don't know if we'd want to try it."

"I'd love to try it," Sydney said. "Does it take a lot of training?"

"It does." Mr. Christou's eyes darkened. "And there are many risks involved."

"Like what?" Bailey asked.

Andrew coughed and barely shook his head at Bailey. But it was too late.

"Like dying, that's what." Mr. Christou spat on the deck and walked away.

The Threat

Bailey swallowed hard and blinked back tears as Mr. Christou walked away, his hands swinging in fists by his sides. "I blew it!" she wailed when he was out of sight.

"It's okay." Sydney put her arm around Bailey's shoulder. "I'm sure we'll get another chance."

"I'll go talk to him," Andrew said. "I'll remind him that you're our guests and just wanted to ask some questions. Nothing more."

Bailey nodded and wiped her eyes. "I want to help Stephen if we can."

"I'll be back in a few minutes, hopefully with Mr. Christou." Andrew touched Bailey's arm. "In the meantime, dry your tears and put that sparkle back in your eyes. He'll never be able to resist that."

Bailey smiled weakly. She really wanted to make this work. Stephen shouldn't have to give up his dreams of sponge diving because of an accident that happened years before he was even born.

"You okay?" Sydney asked when Andrew left.

Bailey sniffed. "Yeah, just mad at myself. I should have thought before I spoke."

"We have to trust God with the results of all this. We can only do so much ourselves. The rest is up to Him."

"I know," Bailey replied. "Maybe that's the problem. I forgot to pray. I just plunged ahead without asking for God's help." Her cell phone vibrated in her pocket. She pulled it out and looked at the display. "It's Elizabeth!" She pushed the TALK button. "Hi, Beth! Hang on, I'll put you on speaker so Sydney can hear too." She punched another button. "There."

"Hi, Sydney, can you hear me?" Elizabeth asked.

"Loud and clear," Sydney replied.

"What are you doing?" Bailey asked.

"I hadn't heard from you lately so thought I'd check in to see how the mystery solving is going."

"Slow, that's how," Sydney said.

"But we *are* making progress," Bailey added. "Kate did some checking on Shondra Ellis and found out she works for a developer who's been trying to get Mr. and Mrs. Fuller to sell out."

"And we found out Mr. Bubble's real name," Sydney said. "It's Travis Wingate and Shondra admitted they were dating."

"And guess what?" Bailey scrunched up her shoulders. "We got to be interviewed by the newspaper *and* we're going to be on TV!"

"No way! How'd that happen?" Elizabeth asked.

The girls filled Elizabeth in on all the news. "It was awesome!" Bailey squealed. "But right now we're on Stephen's dad's fishing boat."

"We're hoping to convince him that he should let Stephen sponge dive," Sydney said. "It would be his dream come true if we can pull it off."

"But I just put my foot in my mouth and reminded Mr. Christou— that's Stephen's dad—about the risks involved and he stormed away." Bailey's voice trailed off.

"He'll be back," Sydney assured her. "Andrew went to talk to him."

"Wow," Elizabeth said. "Sounds like you're keeping busy!"

Bailey's enthusiasm returned. "We are! After this we have mermaid practice, and Alexis gets in this afternoon. I can't wait to see her."

"Well, I just had you on my mind and sometimes when that happens, God's reminding me to pray for you," Elizabeth said. "So I thought I'd see if there's anything in particular you need prayer for."

"You could pray that we can convince Stephen's dad to let him try sponge diving," Sydney suggested.

"And that we look good on TV," Bailey added with a giggle.

Elizabeth laughed. "That's our Bailey. Always looking to be a star!"

"Oh! Here comes Andrew with Mr. Christou," Bailey said. "We've gotta go." She stuffed her phone back into her jeans pocket.

Andrew fell behind Mr. Christou as they neared and was intercepted by a younger fisherman who apparently had a question for him. Mr. Christou continued walking toward them and stopped only a step away from the girls. His eyes narrowed and his fists rested on his hips.

Bailey felt a drop of sweat run down her back. A seagull's shrill cry pierced the silence as Mr. Christou stared them down. Bailey shifted her weight to the other foot, barely daring to move. Finally, she couldn't take it any more. "I'm sorry if I upset you, Mr. Christou."

Bailey remembered Andrew's advice, and smiled brightly at the fisherman. "I hope you'll forgive me."

Mr. Christou dropped his arms, closed his eyes and shook his head toward the sky. "There's nothing to forgive. I'm the one who should be asking forgiveness."

"You?" Bailey's mouth fell open.

"You are guests on my boat and I treated you rudely," he said. "I was reminded of a difficult time in my life and it caused me to overreact. I'm sorry."

"We just wanted to know a bit about sponge diving," Sydney said. "We didn't mean to say anything that would—"

Mr. Christou waved his hand at her, his face softening. "Never mind. I'll tell you whatever you want to know. Ask away."

"Okay then." Sydney drew in a deep breath. "You said it took a lot of training to learn to sponge dive. How long would it take someone like me?"

"First you have to learn to scuba dive," Mr. Christou said. "There are lots of different diving courses, and it depends on the level of certification a person wants as to how long it takes. Could be as little as twenty hours of classes for a basic open water certification. Or if you want to become a master diver, you'd have to do all the basic requirements and several advanced classes and diving hours."

"Do you have to be an adult to do it?" Bailey asked.

"Not to get started, but most require you to be fifteen or older to do the more advanced certifications."

"Have you ever sponge dived?" Sydney asked.

"I did when I was younger." Mr. Christou looked away.

"Did you like it?" Caution edged Bailey's voice, afraid she'd set him off again.

Mr. Christou stared across the ocean, his face raised to the wind. He slowly nodded, then looked at the girls. "Yeah," he said softly. "I loved it."

"What's it like underwater?" Sydney asked.

"Heaven." Mr. Christou's voice grew husky. "It's the most beautiful place on earth. The colors are vivid and bright, the motion fluid, the sounds soft and muffled. It's calm, peaceful, like nowhere else in the world."

"But you switched to being a fisherman," Sydney said. "Why would you leave something you loved?"

"I thought I loved sponge diving more than life itself," Mr. Christou said. "But then a terrible underwater accident killed my father on one of his dives. I knew there were dangers, but I didn't realize how real they were until that day."

"I'm sorry," Bailey said. "That must have been awful."

"I decided I wouldn't dive again and I wouldn't let anyone I loved dive either. Too much risk."

The threesome stood quietly at the boat's rail and watched the water churn below.

"Do you miss it?" Sydney asked.

"More than I can say," Mr. Christou admitted.

The sounds of the waves slapping the side of the boat filled the moment.

"Mr. Christou, you lost your dad because of a sponge diving accident." Bailey put her small, smooth hand over Mr. Christou's big leathery one. "But you don't have to lose yourself because of it too. Seems to me your heart is out there in the water."

Sydney nodded. "You could honor your father's memory by diving again, by doing something you enjoyed so much together."

Mr. Christou shook his head. "Divers have to have a partner. It isn't safe to dive alone."

"So get a partner," Bailey said. "I'm sure you have friends who would go with you."

"My friends are busy with their own lives. None of them are interested in diving."

"What about your son?" Sydney asked softly. "He's old enough to take diving lessons. I bet he'd love to have the same adventures with his dad that you had with yours."

"We met Stephen a few days ago," Bailey added. "He loves working with you and helping out with your fishing business. I bet he'd love to be your diving buddy."

Bailey noticed tears pool in Mr. Christou's eyes. He cleared his throat.

"I can't risk it," he said sternly. "If anything happened to him. . ." Mr. Christou rubbed his whiskery chin and abruptly pushed back from the railing. "It was a pleasure meeting you, but I have to get back to work."

He shook the girls' hands.

"I'm glad we had a chance to talk," Sydney said.

"Thank you for answering our questions." Bailey wished she could hug the grumpy man. Surely that would cheer him up, but she couldn't muster the courage before he turned and left.

"Well, at least we tried," Sydney said.

Bailey sighed. "Doesn't sound like Stephen will ever get to sponge dive."

"You never know." Sydney shrugged. "Maybe it just isn't God's plan for Stephen right now."

"Yeah, maybe." Bailey shrugged. "We'd better get back to Mermaid Park," Bailey said. "It's almost time for rehearsal."

●—●—●

Bailey lowered herself into the Underwater Theater tank and felt the lukewarm water lap around her. Treading water, she closed her eyes and tipped her head back, smoothing her hair slick against her scalp. When she opened her eyes, Shondra floated up to her.

"Well, I hope you're happy." Shondra's red lips curled in a deadly smile.

"Happy? About what?" Bailey replied.

"You and your little friend almost got me fired."

"What? We didn't do anything!"

"Whatever." Shondra looked around before swimming closer and hissing in Bailey's ear. "Just remember I know what you're up to."

She swam off like a great white shark that had just decided not to eat the angelfish after all.

Bailey froze. She didn't know what to do. She lowered herself to her neck in the water and bobbed there, deep in thought about what had just happened.

"Okay, class." Jessica clapped her hands to get their attention. "For those of you who still haven't been fitted for your costume, today is the last day. That leaves only a day for alterations. Let's start by reviewing what we've learned, then we'll run through our mermaid routine with the music."

Jessica's voice faded into the background of Bailey's mind as it replayed Shondra's words. *"You and your little friend almost got me fired. Just remember I know what you're up to."* She shuddered, and heard Jessica call her name.

"Bailey, are you going to join us?"

"Oh, yes," Bailey stammered.

She made her way through the review and the rehearsal as if she were wading through syrup. Her mind felt fuzzy. As she changed back into her clothes after rehearsal, Sydney joined her.

"You feeling okay?" Sydney asked.

"I guess," Bailey lied. Then she whispered, "I have to talk to you after we get out of here."

Sydney's eyes widened and she nodded.

Bailey toweled her hair and stuffed her wet swimsuit into her bag. "Let's go."

Once outside, Sydney asked, "What's wrong?"

"Shondra accused us of trying to get her fired."

"What? We didn't do that! We just told Mr. Fuller what we saw."

"I know, and that's what I told her, but of course she didn't believe me." Bailey bit her lower lip. "She said for us to just remember she knows what we're up to."

"Bailey, that sounds like a threat!"

"I don't think she'll do anything." Bailey tucked her wet hair behind her ear. "I think she just wants to scare us."

"We should tell Mr. and Mrs. Fuller." Sydney grabbed Bailey's arm and pointed her in the direction of the Fullers' office.

"There's nothing to tell," Bailey said. "She hasn't done anything. They can't fire her because she said she knows what we're doing."

Sydney slowed her pace and sighed. "Maybe not."

Bailey pulled out her phone and checked the time. Her face brightened. "Besides, it's almost time for us to meet Grandma Cora to go pick Alex up from the airport!"

"Good! We could use another investigator on site!"

●—●—●

Bailey and Sydney waited by the security checkpoint at the airport, eagerly looking for Alexis Howell.

"There she is!" Sydney squealed.

Bailey waved wildly at the slender girl with dark curls and electric-blue eyes pulling a red-flowered carry-on bag.

Alexis waved back and broke into a run, weaving around other passengers who moved way too slowly for her. When she reached the girls, the three wrapped their arms around each other, words and laughter flowing simultaneously.

"How was your flight?"

"I can't believe you're here!"

"You can't imagine the cute guy I sat next to on the plane!"

The chatter ended when grandma Cora put her arms around their shoulders and smiled. "I assume this must be Alexis?"

"Yes!" Bailey said. "Alex, this is my grandma Cora."

Grandma tipped her backwards baseball cap at Alex.

"Nice to meet you." Alexis shook Grandma's hand. "What should I call you?"

"Everyone else calls me Grandma, so you may as well too." Grandma Cora grinned. "And what shall I call *you*?"

"Alex is fine," Alex replied. "Mostly only my mom calls me Alexis."

"Alex it is then," Grandma Cora replied. "Do you have other bags?"

"No, I just brought this carry-on." Alex pushed down the handle and lifted the small suitcase. "It holds more than it looks."

"All right then," Grandma said. "I guess we're ready to head home."

Bailey grabbed Alex's hand and swung it. "Yeah, we've got lots to talk about!"

●—●—●

The next morning, the smell of bacon and cinnamon toast brought the girls down the hallway to the kitchen table.

"Good morning, girls," Grandma Cora chirped. "Get any sleep last night or were you too busy talking about that cute guy Alex sat next to on the plane?"

All three girls blushed and bit back smiles. Bailey forgot that her grandma had heard every word they said at the airport.

"We're too excited about Alex's cable column today to think about boys, Grandma." Bailey grabbed a slice of bacon and started to munch.

"Sit down and we'll have a prayer like civilized people before you eat everything in sight." Grandma winked at Bailey and they all sat and bowed their heads.

Grandma folded her hands beneath her chin. "Thank You, Lord, for this beautiful day and these beautiful girls to share it with. Thank You for the sharp smell of bacon and the sweetness of cinnamon toast. Be with Ed and Lenore, Lord. Encourage them and give them wisdom. Help us to shine Your love everywhere we go today. Amen."

"Eat up," Alex said. "We have to be at the Mermaid Park in less than an hour for filming."

The girls inhaled their breakfast and dressed for the red carpet. "I'm so excited!" Bailey said. "I've never been on TV two days in a row before. Besides," she added, "you never know when a talent scout might be there waiting to discover us!"

They chattered nervously in the car all the way to Mermaid Park. Grandma Cora whipped her PT Cruiser into a parking space and disappeared into Mr. and Mrs. Fuller's office. When Bailey got out of the car she inhaled sharply. "Look!"

Shondra was chitchatting with a news crew. They'd come to catch the human-interest story of Alex and her cable column visiting Florida. Sweetness and charm oozed from Shondra's every pore.

"This can't be good," Sydney said.

"Who is that?" Alex asked.

"It's Shondra, the one we think has been causing a lot of the problems here at Mermaid Park," Bailey said. "Remember? We told you about her."

"I remember," Alex said.

The girls walked up to Shondra and the film crew of two men and two women.

"Hi, Shondra," Bailey said.

"Good morning!" Shondra gave Bailey a stiff hug. "I was just getting acquainted with these media people. I heard on the news they were going to be here to do a story on your friend's cable column."

"Yes," Sydney motioned to Alex. "Shondra, this is Alexis, and Alex, this is Shondra."

The two shook hands. "Nice to meet you, Shondra." Alex looked at the film crew. "I guess we should get to work."

"Yes, I won't keep you." Shondra turned to leave. "Good luck on your show. Toodles!"

The girls watched her leave.

"Toodles?" Alex asked.

"I know." Sydney gagged.

Bailey's eyes narrowed. "If I know her, she's up to something and it won't be something good."

CHAPTER 10

Crocodile's Lunch?

After the media people had interviewed Alex and left, the girls started getting ready for Alex to actually tape her show.

"It makes me sick how Shondra's so sweet when other people are around and so mean when no one's looking." Bailey made a face.

"I know," Sydney said. "But we can't focus on that. We just have to make sure we don't become two-faced like her."

"We'd better get to work." Alexis said to Bailey and Sydney. "Where do you want to do your makeup?"

"We had ours done in Mr. and Mrs. Fuller's kitchen yesterday," Bailey said. "I'm sure they'd let us use it again."

"That would be great," Alexis said. "I want to film the column outdoors so we get some great shots of the park. I took a virtual tour of the place online before I came so I'd have a good feel for it."

Bailey went to ask the Fullers if they could use their kitchen for a makeup studio.

"Of course." Mrs. Fuller bustled around the tiny kitchen. "Just let me clear this table and wipe it down. Then it's all yours."

Moments later, Bailey sat with her eyes closed while Alexis rubbed a makeup sponge across Bailey's flawless cheeks. Her hair was pulled back in a ponytail. Then she put makeup on Sydney. After that, Sydney put makeup on Alexis.

"Where do you think we should start filming?" Alexis asked. "We want someplace with great scenery."

"The Tunnel of Love is really pretty," Sydney said. "It has lots of lush plants and colorful flowers. There's even a waterfall on the far side of the lagoon."

"That sounds perfect," Alexis said. "Lead the way to the Tunnel of

Love and I'll figure out where the best lighting is when we get there."

Bailey and Sydney took Alex to the most scenic view of the park. The high trill of birds in the trees made it sound like they'd arrived in the Amazon rain forest. Alexis began setting up lights and the camera. Since Bailey had helped Alex with her cable segments before, and Sydney didn't like to be in the spotlight, Bailey was chosen to be interviewed. Alex quickly showed Sydney how to operate the camera, which was on a rolling stand to keep it stable, but also able to move.

Microphone in hand, Alex stepped in front of the camera, while Bailey waited a few steps away.

"You're on in three, two, one. . ." Sydney signaled.

"Hi! Welcome to 'It's a Kid's Eye View'! I'm Alexis Howell and I'm coming to you live from Mermaid Park in Golden, Florida." We're here to discover what kids think are the best attractions at this fifty-year-old theme park." Alexis walked over to Bailey. "Excuse me," Alexis said. "Have you been to Mermaid Park before?"

Bailey answered, "Yes, I have. This is my third time."

"I see," Alexis replied. "What brings you back?"

"I love the mermaid shows in the Underwater Theater and the other shows are spectacular too." Bailey looked right at the camera, her smile splitting her face, in case a talent scout spotted her. "The bird show is one of the most interesting displays you'll see in all of Florida"

"I heard there was a problem with that. Will you tell us about it?" Alex said.

Bailey quickly filled Alex and her viewers in on what had happened. Then she added, "If someone calls saying they've spotted a bird and it's found where the caller said it was, they get a free day pass to the park. And the owners are offering a free one-year pass to anyone who calls with information that leads to the capture of one of the birds."

"So they may be getting calls this morning about possible wild bird sightings?" Alexis asked.

"We hope so," Bailey said.

Alex looked directly at the camera. "We're going to take a break, but when we come back we'll walk through this beautiful, historic park and point out some of its highlights. Don't go away."

"Alex!" Sydney squealed when Alex shut off the camera. "You were awesome! You're just like a real TV person!"

Alexis laughed and pulled her hair behind her ears. "Well, I *am* a real TV person when I'm doing my cable column."

"I wish more people knew about your show," Sydney said. "It would be great publicity for the Mermaid Park."

"I know what you mean," Alexis said. "I've got to get back on air. Sydney, will you keep running the camera for me?"

●━━●

When the girls were finished taping Alex's show, they flopped down on a park bench.

"That was fun!" Bailey said.

"Yeah, but I'm glad we're done so we can just goof around now," Alexis said.

Sydney picked up a newspaper someone had left on the bench. "Hey! Check it out. Here's the article about us!"

"Let's see!" Bailey reached for the paper, then scanned the page. "Wait a minute! This isn't what we said!"

"What's it say?" Alexis asked.

"It says we know who's doing the bad stuff at the park, but wouldn't give any names." Bailey moaned.

"Talk about twisting the news." Sydney took the paper to read it for herself.

"If Shondra sees this, she'll think we really did try to get her fired." Bailey's stomach started churning.

"We aren't trying to get her fired," Sydney said. "We just told Mr. Fuller that we saw her and Mr. Bubble together. He put the rest of the pieces together."

"With Kate's help," Alexis said. "She's the one who figured out they both worked for that development company."

"What a mess," Bailey wailed. "Shondra will kill us if she gets wind of this."

"Come on." Alex stood. "Let's forget about the mess and go do something fun. We only have a couple of days to be together, you know."

"Good idea," Bailey said. "What shall we do?"

"Let's go on the Jungle Cruise," Alexis suggested.

"Okay," Sydney said. "I haven't ridden it yet."

The girls stood, locked arms, and walked off, keeping step with each other. The Jungle Cruise had several small boats in which three kid-sized visitors could ride together, or two adults. It followed an underwater track, and a man's voice told all about the plants and animals that lived in this "jungle." Mechanized animals swung from trees and peeked out from behind bushes as visitors floated past. Jungle "animals" squawked and hooted throughout the lush green waterway.

The girls decided on a red boat, the last one in the line, and squeezed in together.

"Good thing we're not any bigger or we wouldn't fit!" Bailey muttered, squeezing in between Sydney and Alexis.

Mysterious jungle music began to play as the boat jerked forward.

"Here we go!" Alexis said.

Fake monkeys and birds hovered in the trees, looking so real the girls were tricked for a few minutes. As they rounded a corner, a crocodile in a box with wooden bars snapped at its enclosure making the people in the front boats shriek.

"That one always looks so real," one of the passengers in a yellow boat said. "The way it snaps at people as they go by is so believable!"

The girls' red boat came closer to where the croc grunted and bit at its rickety cage.

"If I didn't know better, I'd say he wants to eat us for lunch!" Alexis joked.

"I know," Sydney agreed. "Listen to those awful sounds he makes."

When Bailey, Sydney, and Alexis's boat reached the animal, it opened its powerful jaws wide and bit a gaping hole, tearing the bars from the crate. It hesitated for a split second, then ran out of the box that held it.

The girls screamed.

"It *is* real!" Bailey thought her heart would pound right out of her chest, but there was no way to hurry the boat along its track.

The crocodile stood on its stubby legs, looking stunned that it was free. It began to inch forward until it reached the edge of the water. The girls' boat floated past the prehistoric-looking beast. They collectively held their breath, not daring to move. Bailey prayed the animal wouldn't follow them into the water. She reached for her friends' hands and squeezed.

"What's the matter over there?" a voice blared on a two-way speaker.

Bailey turned to look at her terrified friends. "They must have heard us scream."

"We need help!" Alexis called.

"The crocodile got loose!" Sydney yelled.

The man chuckled. "The animals are mechanical. They won't hurt you."

"Not this one!" Alexis shouted back. "Help!"

Bailey looked back at the crocodile's broken cage and saw the animal was no longer on the shore. She started to cry. "The crocodile is in the water! Come get us!"

As they rounded another bend, Bailey saw a young man put on a lifejacket and get into a small motorboat. Soon, he was zooming toward them. His boat stopped beside theirs, making waves that wobbled their little red boat. "I'll toss you each a life vest. I want you to put it on, tighten it around you, and climb into my boat."

Bailey caught her bright orange vest and put her head through the hole, then strapped the belt around her waist. The other two girls did the same.

"Did you say a crocodile got loose?" The man smirked.

"Yes!" Alex's blue eyes were filled with fear as she stepped into the rescue boat. Sydney and Bailey followed her, clinging to one another.

"But there aren't any live animals on this cruise," the man explained. "They look very lifelike, but—"

Just then the croc raised his body to the surface of the water. Only his eyes and back showed.

"Th–that's a real crocodile!" The man threw the boat into gear and roared off to the loading platform. "Call the authorities! Close the ride! There's a live crocodile in the water over there!" he shouted to his fellow employees.

The girls stepped out of the boat, quickly removing their life vests.

"I'm calling Mr. Fuller." Bailey speed dialed his number and explained the situation.

"I'm on my way," Mr. Fuller said.

●—●—●

That evening, Bailey, Sydney, and Alexis sat in Grandma Cora's living room with her as Mr. and Mrs. Fuller chatted about the day, brows furrowed.

"I don't know what to make of all this." Mr. Fuller rubbed his chin. "Someone could have been seriously hurt or even killed if that crocodile had gotten hold of them."

"The weird part is that no one saw anyone bring him in," Mrs. Fuller said. "How does a person sneak a six-foot crocodile into a theme park?"

"I'm just glad animal control could capture him and haul him off." Mr. Fuller smoothed his thinning hair.

"We didn't see Shondra or Mr. Bubble hanging around this time either," Bailey said.

"Doesn't mean they weren't involved, though," Sydney said. "They may have been in the shadows."

"I'm just glad no one was hurt." Grandma Cora stood. "Anyone want some coffee?"

"I'll pass," Bailey teased. "Can we be excused to go to our room?"

"Sure," Grandma said. "Why don't you get ready for bed and you can have a pajama party. I'll bring some popcorn in later if you'd like."

"All right!" The girls jumped up and ran down the hall.

They giggled and chattered as they changed into their PJs.

"Let's call the other girls to fill them in," Alexis suggested. "They'll be so jealous that I'm here with you!"

All three pulled out their phones and settled in for a nice, long chat. Bailey laid on one twin bed and Sydney on the other. Alex's sleeping bag was spread out between the two and she sat on the floor leaning against Bailey's bed.

"I'll call and conference everyone in this time," Sydney said.

In minutes, they were all connected. Biscuit barked when he heard their voices.

"We almost became a crocodile's lunch today." Bailey launched into the whole terrifying story.

"We didn't think he was real at first," Alex explained after Bailey had told the basics, "until he came out of his cage at us."

"Sounds like God was looking out for you," Elizabeth said.

"Definitely!" Bailey said.

"You sure have had a lot of excitement since you've been there," McKenzie said.

"You don't know the half of it!" Sydney replied. "We got interviewed for the newspaper and the local news station yesterday!"

"You were on TV?" Kate asked.

"Yep," Bailey said. "But they misquoted us in the newspaper. They said we told them we knew who was doing all this bad stuff at Mermaid Park." The smell of buttered popcorn drifted down the hall.

"We're afraid Shondra's going to blow a fuse," Sydney said.

"Her fuse is already blown if you ask me." Bailey shifted her phone to the other ear. "She was so mean to me at practice yesterday."

"What happened?" Elizabeth asked.

Sydney jumped in. "She threatened Bailey, saying she knew what we were up to and accused us of trying to get her fired."

"How is that a threat?" McKenzie asked.

"I guess it wasn't exactly a threat," Bailey admitted.

"Her words weren't terribly threatening," Alexis said. "But evidently her tone and evil smile were like Cruella De Vil's." She snuggled into her sleeping bag.

"Whose?" Elizabeth asked.

"You know, the villain who stole the 101 Dalmatian puppies," Alexis clarified.

"Eww," Kate said. "She always gives me the creeps." Biscuit whined in the background.

"Alex, have you met Stephen yet?" McKenzie asked.

"Not yet," Alexis replied. "But I hope to before I leave."

"How's it going with him and his dad?" Elizabeth asked.

"We met his dad yesterday. We tried to convince him to let Stephen learn to sponge dive," Bailey said.

"And?" Kate asked.

"And I don't think he's going to." Bailey sighed.

"You never know," McKenzie said. "He may still be thinking about it—unless his fears are so deep that he can't let them go."

"That's what we're afraid of." Sydney stretched out on her bed.

"So is there any way we can help you figure out who's causing all the trouble at Mermaid Park?" Elizabeth asked.

"Kate did a great job getting info about Shondra and that she works at Barron's Commercial Development Company," Bailey said. "We could use some help digging up information about Mr. Bubble next."

Sydney piped in. "We know his real name is Travis Wingate and that he's dating Shondra. But we don't know if he works for the development company too or if he's just helping Shondra."

"I'll look into that," McKenzie said. "Shouldn't be too hard."

"I'm worried about you," Elizabeth said. "Between Shondra's mean spirit and the events happening at the Mermaid Park, I think we need to say a special prayer for you right now before we hang up."

"We'll take all the prayers we can get," Bailey said.

"That's for sure," Alexis added. "I don't know when I've ever been as scared as I was when that crocodile came at us this afternoon."

"I think we need to pray for Shondra too," Sydney said quietly, "and that we won't be nasty to her just because she's mean to us."

"Good thinking," Elizabeth said. "Jesus said in Matthew 5:44 to love your enemies and pray for those who persecute you. I'd say this qualifies."

The line grew quiet except for Biscuit's panting.

"Dear Lord," Elizabeth prayed. "Thank You for protecting our friends through all the weird things that have happened this week. We know You're taking good care of them. Please don't stop. Guide them and keep them safe. We ask You to change Shondra's heart so she isn't so mean. And help Bailey, Sydney, and Alexis to follow in Your footsteps and become more and more like You. It's easy to be nice to people who are nice to us, but it's hard when they're not. Help them to shine for You even when it's hard. In Jesus' name. Amen."

Grandma Cora knocked on their door just as Elizabeth finished praying.

"Come in!" Bailey called.

Grandma opened the door. "You'll never guess who just called Ed."

Mermaids in Action!

Bailey sat up straight on her bed. "Who?"

"NBC." Grandma Cora smiled.

"The TV network?" Sydney asked.

"The one and only!" Grandma crowed.

Now Alex sat up on her sleeping bag on the floor. "What'd *they* want?"

"They saw your cable column on the Mermaid Park and have decided to do a special about it!"

"No way!" Bailey could hardly believe her ears.

"All because of my little cable column?" Alexis's voice rose to a toddler's pitch.

"Well, partly because of it, anyway," Grandma said. "They've heard the reports of all the trouble the park's been having and how Ed and Lenore are struggling to keep it afloat. Then when they saw your tour and how beautiful the place is, they decided to come see for themselves."

"That's awesome!" Sydney said.

"When are they coming?" Bailey ran a trembling hand through her hair. *Maybe I should get a new outfit—or a new hairstyle,* she thought. She imagined being interviewed by a famous news anchor. After all, she'd already been warmed up by the local news station.

"Not until sometime next month," Grandma Cora said. "They still have to schedule it, but I'm afraid it will be after you've already gone home."

Bailey felt like someone had just let the air out of her. She slumped as she watched her visions of stardom disintegrate before her eyes.

"Can't they get here this week?" she wailed. "It could be my big break!"

Grandma sat on Bailey's bed and hugged her granddaughter. "I know you're disappointed. It's largely because of you girls that this is even happening, and Ed and Lenore are so grateful. You've really put the Mermaid Park on the map this week."

Bailey sighed. "I guess I'll have to settle for being a star in the mermaid show tomorrow."

"That's my girl!" Grandma said. "I can't wait to see you perform. Get to bed so you'll be well rested for your show."

"Yeah," Bailey said. "We only have one more rehearsal and then the live performance. I'm so excited!"

●—●—●

The next day, Alexis became an audience of one at Bailey and Sydney's mermaid rehearsal. Bailey made sure she pointed Shondra out to Alex before practice began. "She isn't in the show, but keep an eye on her," she warned.

Alexis clapped as the lights dimmed, knowing Sydney was backstage flipping switches. She applauded and whistled when the junior mermaids swam out, and gracefully dipped and twirled to the beat of the music. At the end of the rehearsal, she gave her friends a standing ovation.

After she changed into her dry clothes, Bailey met Sydney and Alexis in the auditorium.

"Bailey, you were awesome!" Alex exclaimed. "I didn't know you could swim like that!"

"Thanks." Bailey loved being in the spotlight. "It was fun. I'm glad you could watch us practice."

Clapping her hands to get her class's attention one last time, Jessica announced, "Just a reminder, I want you all back here at three o'clock this afternoon to get into your costumes for our four o'clock performance."

"Okay!" Bailey twirled in excitement.

"Boy, if you were this good during practice, you'll be even better at the show this afternoon," Alex said. "And, Sydney, those lights! They were so dramatic!"

Sydney laughed. "Zeke, my teacher backstage, says the show without lights is just a bunch of girls swimming in one-legged costumes."

Bailey threw her head back and snorted. "He's right about that. You really make us look spectacular with all the colored lights."

"Did Shondra say anything to you in practice today?" Sydney asked.

"No, she didn't have much chance to since she's not actually in this show," Bailey replied. "She was only there before to teach us the mermaid moves. But I could still feel her looking at me a time or two."

"She gives me the creeps," Alex said, "and I haven't even met her."

"I'm glad she didn't cause you any trouble today." Sydney put her arm around Bailey's shoulders. "Or she would have had to deal with me!"

Bailey laughed. "Yeah, you could drop the curtain so no one could see her throw a temper tantrum." The girls giggled and walked outside.

"So now what?" Alexis asked.

"We could see if Stephen's at the Sponge Diving Park." Sydney winked at Alex.

"Great idea!" she replied.

"Yeah, we wanted you to meet him," Bailey said.

"Let's go!" The three took off toward the Mermaid Park exit.

"Stephen!" Bailey called as they approached his father's boat, but the wind carried her voice off to sea. The smell of fish and salt swept over them.

They came closer to the boat and waved.

"Hey!" Stephen waved when he spotted them. "Come on aboard."

The girls climbed onto the big weathered boat.

"We wanted you to meet our friend Alexis from California," Bailey said. "Alex, this is Stephen."

Stephen shook Alex's hand. "It's nice to meet you. Bailey and Sydney have been so excited about you coming."

"It's nice to meet you too." Alex smoothed her shirt over her shorts. "I've heard a lot about you and your Sponge Diving Park and fishing boat."

"Stephen will be a great sponge diver himself someday," Sydney said.

"I hope that works out for you," Alex said.

Sydney shaded her eyes with her hand. "It *has* to work out."

"Thanks." Stephen lowered his dark eyes and stuck his hands into the pockets of his khaki shorts. "I hope my dad will think about the things you said to him the other day. I never got the chance to thank you."

"No problem," Bailey replied. "I don't think we accomplished much."

"Yeah," Sydney said. "He didn't seem too receptive to our suggestion that you be his sponge diving buddy."

"Well, I appreciate your trying." Stephen flicked his dark brown hair out of his eyes. "Nothing ventured, nothing gained, right?"

"I guess you're right," Sydney said.

"I hear you have a cable column that filmed at Mermaid Park yesterday." Stephen smiled at Alexis. "How'd that go?"

"Great!" Alex replied. "It's a beautiful setting and I hope we generated some business for them. There are so many great shows there too."

"Like the Junior Mermaid Show! We just got out of our last rehearsal." Bailey held up a strand of wet hair. "In case you couldn't tell."

"I should have guessed." Stephen laughed. "Isn't your performance soon?"

"Yeah, at four o'clock this afternoon." Sydney cocked her head. "Wanna come?"

"I'll have to check with my dad," Stephen replied.

"You could keep Alex company along with my grandma Cora and Mr. and Mrs. Fuller." Bailey bounced excitedly on her toes.

"I'll try to be there." Stephen glanced at Alex. "That would be fun."

"Stephen!" Mr. Christou emerged from the belly of the boat.

"Over here, Dad." Stephen waved his arm.

Mr. Christou came up to their group and stood with his beefy hands on his hips. "Hello, girls, good to see you again," he said crisply.

"Good to see you too, Mr. Christou." Bailey gestured toward Alex. "This is our friend Alexis."

"She's visiting from California," Sydney added.

"Nice to meet you," Alex reached to shake his hand.

Mr. Christou tipped his cap. "My pleasure."

He turned his attention to his son, and a smile played on his dry lips. "Do you suppose you could break away from entertaining these girls to help me get the fishing gear ready for the next trip?"

Stephen's face reddened. "Sure."

Mr. Christou walked off.

"I've gotta go," Stephen said reluctantly. "But maybe I'll see you later. I'm glad I got to meet you, Alex."

"Me too." Alex waved goodbye and watched him walk away.

"I see what you mean about Stephen's dad," she said. "He's kind of gruff."

"But I have a feeling that inside that tough fisherman is a cuddly teddy bear just waiting to come out," Bailey giggled.

"I hope you're right, for Stephen's sake."

●━━●━━●

Three o'clock rolled around and Bailey put on her blue-green sequined costume with long flowing fins. Only they didn't flow very well out of the water. She looked at herself in the full-length mirror. "I need some makeup."

"Yes, you do," a woman said behind her. "I'm Sue, the makeup artist. Come with me and we'll make you up with our special waterproof products."

Bailey grinned from gill to gill, now that she was a junior mermaid. "Come on, Syd and Alex. You can watch." With her feet already in her mermaid tail, she hopped behind Sue. Sydney and Alex each took an arm to help her along.

"It was nice of Jessica to let Alex come back here with us until the show starts," Bailey said. "She said it's usually off-limits to nonperformers."

Sue sat Bailey in a chair and slipped a paper bib around her neck. "This chair is like the one I sit in when I get my hair cut. It probably goes up and down, right?"

"Yes, it does." The lady pumped a pedal under the chair with her foot to raise it higher. "There. Now I can reach you better."

Soon Bailey had red lips, blue eyeliner and mascara, and sparkly turquoise eye shadow to match her outfit. Her cheeks were rosy pink.

"Wow!" Alex exclaimed. "You look fantastic!"

"You're as pretty as Jessica!" Sydney added.

"Okay, ladies!" Jessica called. "In your places!"

"That's my cue to leave," Alex said. "Good luck! I'll be saying prayers for you both from the audience!"

The girls hugged each other, careful not to smudge Bailey's makeup. Alex went out to sit with Grandma Cora and Mr. and Mrs. Fuller while Sydney took her place with GraceAnn and Zeke at the lighting booth.

Bailey floated in the water tank with Jessica, two other adult mermaids and six junior mermaids, awaiting the musical cue for their show to begin. Goose bumps pricked her skin as the music crescendoed and the curtain rose. Applause reverberated throughout the auditorium. She searched the crowd for Grandma Cora and spotted her and the Fullers three rows back, front and center. She was glad to see Stephen sitting beside Alex.

Beaming her best mermaid smile, Bailey focused on the show. She swam and twirled, feeling every bit as graceful as a real mermaid. Her tailfin moved effortlessly, propelling her smoothly through the water. As she swam in precise rhythm with the music, everything was going perfectly.

Suddenly, the purple adult mermaid broke out of the routine. Bailey wasn't sure what to do. Should she keep swimming like nothing was happening, or stop and make sure everything was all right? The purple mermaid swam the opposite direction of where she was supposed to, then broke through the top of the water gasping.

Bailey heard muffled words, but couldn't make them out from underwater. She saw Jessica, wide-eyed, signal for all the girls to get out of the tank.

Fear churned in Bailey's stomach. Mr. Fuller jumped up from his seat in the audience and charged toward the backstage door. The curtain dropped in front of the water tank and the show was over. Bailey felt hot with anger and disappointment.

Climbing out of the tank, she asked "What happened?"

At the side of the water tank, dripping mermaids clung to one another, shivering with cold and fear.

"Someone cut Angela's air line," Jessica told her. "She couldn't breathe."

Gasps escaped all around. "Is she all right?" a small yellow mermaid asked.

"I think so." Jessica stroked the wet hair of the little girl. "She's being checked over now."

Sydney came out from behind the lighting panel. "I'm sorry your show got ruined, Bales."

"I'm so mad I could spit!" Bailey said. "Who would do such a thing?"

"I don't know, but I saw Mr. Fuller running by here. He looked like he was determined to find out."

Bailey shivered. "I'm gonna go change clothes before I freeze."

"I'll wait with Alex in the auditorium," Sydney said. "We'll meet you there."

As Sydney started to leave the room, something shiny by the door to the mermaid tank caught her eye. "Hey, what's that?" she said.

Bailey moved closer. "Looks like scissors." She started to pick them up.

"No, wait!" Sydney cried out. She looked around and saw a hand towel on a chair. Gently, she used the towel to pick up the scissors by the blade.

"If someone cut the cord, chances are they might have used scissors," she explained.

"And we need to give them to Mr. Fuller for the police, in case they left fingerprints on the handle," Bailey filled in.

"Yes," Sydney agreed. "We'll loosely wrap them in the towel so any fingerprints aren't disturbed."

As if on cue, sirens sounded in the distance as Sydney left the room. While she hunted down Mr. Fuller to give him the scissors, Bailey changed out of her costume into her dry clothes. She combed her wet hair, washed off her makeup, and then went to the auditorium.

"You were spectacular!" Grandma Cora wrapped her in a soft grandma hug.

"I've seen plenty of junior mermaids in my time," Mrs. Fuller began, "but none as natural as you. And you looked absolutely beautiful!"

"Yeah, Bales," Alex said. "You were awesome!"

Stephen joined in. "The way you swim underwater, I bet you'd be a great sponge diver!"

"It was so exciting to be able to perform like that, even if it got cut short." Bailey turned at the sound of sirens pulling up outside the Underwater Theater. "Sounds like an ambulance. I hope Angela is okay. Come on."

The group hustled outside and found not ambulances, but two police cars blocking the back exit.

"Wonder what that's about?" Sydney asked.

"Ed must have called them," Mrs. Fuller said.

They passed the time chatting and keeping an eye on the back door of the Underwater Theater. About a half hour later, the police emerged from the building with Shondra and Mr. Bubble. Both were in handcuffs and were arguing loudly enough with each other for anyone to hear.

"I told you not to touch anything with your bare hands!" Mr. Bubble shouted.

Shondra wagged her platinum blond head as she shouted back, "It's a little tough to look natural in a swimsuit and gloves!"

"You shouldn't have left them laying around!" Mr. Bubble shouted. The girls wondered what he was referring to.

"Maybe the scissors," Bailey whispered.

The police escorted them to the waiting police cars and helped Shondra into one and Mr. Bubble into the other. They glared at each other through the windows.

"It's Shondra!" Sydney shouted.

"And Mr. Bubble," Bailey added. "We must have been right about them all along."

"Surely they couldn't arrest them without some proof that they were involved in criminal activities," Grandma Cora said.

Mr. Fuller joined them in time to hear her comment. "Oh, they're working on getting proof," he said. "The police have been running fingerprints from the previous incidents. When they heard about this one, they showed up with their dusting powder and their laptop and are busy dusting backstage right now in hopes of finding a match. In fact, young sleuths, initial tests show what they believe are Shondra's fingerprints on a pair of scissors that may have cut Angela's air line. And they're checking to see if Travis Wingate's were on the equipment too."

"Looks like they finally got caught," Bailey said. "The police should also trace the trail of where the snakes came from."

"Hmm. You know our friend Kate told us about the development firm the two used to work for," Sydney said. "Maybe she should check to see if the development firm has been building in any areas that might have lots of snakes. If they've been working in swampy areas, they might even have come across some crocodiles."

Mr. Fuller threw back his head and laughed. "You girls are full of ideas! I'll mention that one to the policemen too."

Mr. Fuller stuck his hand out for a high five and Bailey slapped it. "Thanks to your help, if the police find what they think they will, the two will be charged with a whole list of things from assault to vandalism to possibly even attempted murder for letting that crocodile out at the jungle cruise yesterday."

Sydney shook her head. "It's hard to believe people could do such things."

"Especially people you've known and trusted," Mrs. Fuller added.

"Yeah, that must be pretty hard to take." Stephen shook his head.

"Did they say why they did it?" Alex asked.

"They haven't actually admitted to any of it yet," Mr. Fuller replied. "They're being taken in as primary suspects now. I'm sure they'll be thoroughly interrogated." His cell phone rang. "Ed Fuller here."

The girls and Stephen chatted as Mr. Fuller talked on the phone. Soon he hung up and returned the phone to its holster on his belt. "Good news," he said. "Come on. I'll tell you about it back at the office."

Good News!

"So let's hear it!" Bailey said as she sat on the living room floor at the Fuller's office. "What's the good news?"

"Someone spotted two of our wild birds on forty-eighth Street and Watson," Mr. Fuller replied. "I'm going to round up my bird handlers and meet the caller there so she can show us where they are."

"All right!" Bailey and Sydney exchanged high fives.

"That's great news, Mr. Fuller!" Stephen said. "Hopefully more people will start calling."

"Thank you, Stephen." Mr. Fuller thumped the young man on the back and then looked at his watch. "Oops! I'd better get going. Need to meet those people about the birds and then I have to go to the police station to answer some questions about Shondra and Travis."

"If the police want to talk to Sydney and me, we're available." Bailey grinned. "We're getting pretty used to being interviewed."

"I'll keep that in mind," Mr. Fuller said. "They just may have a few questions about what you saw."

"And keep us posted on the birds," Bailey said. "That bird show was my favorite. I'll be glad to know when any are returned."

"Will do." Mr. Fuller waved, kissed his wife, and was off.

Grandma Cora and Mrs. Fuller excused themselves to the kitchen to enjoy fresh cups of coffee.

Bailey and her friends strolled outside. "So what do you want to do?"

"We could go to my dad's boat," Stephen suggested. "I never did get to show Alex around."

"That would be fun!" Alex turned a flip.

"Whoa!" Stephen said. "Where'd that come from?"

"I don't know." Alex shrugged and giggled. "I'm a cheerleader and I sometimes do stuff like that when I'm happy."

"I'd kill myself if I tried to do something like that." He turned a wobbly cartwheel, making everyone laugh. "See what I mean?"

"I think you'd better stick to fishing," Sydney said.

"Or sponge diving," Bailey added with a wink. "Grandma, is it okay if we go to Stephen's boat?" she called into the kitchen.

"Sure," she replied. "Just take your cell phone."

The four kids took off toward the Sponge Diving Park, the slapping sound of girls' flip-flops accompanying their every step.

"Is your dad fishing today?" Bailey asked.

"No, he's still getting ready for a trip later this week." Stephen kicked a rock, then caught up to where it landed and kicked it again.

When they reached the fishing boat, Stephen climbed aboard first, and then helped the girls. He gave Alex the same tour he'd given Bailey and Sydney a few days earlier.

"Over here is the diving equipment—oxygen masks, flippers, and wet suits."

"Wait a minute," Alex said. "I thought your dad didn't dive anymore."

"He doesn't," Stephen replied, "but he still has divers who harvest sponges for him."

"What are these big hooks?" Alex touched one of the long handles.

"That's what the divers use to pry the sponges off the rocks." Stephen pointed to some drawstring bags hanging next to the hooks. "They put them in these bags to bring them up out of the water."

"See a wet suit that would fit you?" a husky deep voice behind them asked.

Stephen spun around to see his dad. "Huh?"

"The wet suits," Mr. Christou repeated. "Do you see one that would fit you?"

"I—I don't understand," Stephen stammered.

"I heard you're interested in diving," his dad said. "You need the proper equipment to do it."

"You're going to let me dive?" Stephen's face was a mixture of joy and confusion.

Mr. Christou wrapped his arm around his son's shoulders. "It's time I faced my fears—and the truth."

Bailey beamed at Sydney and Alex.

"I've denied you the joy of diving because I was afraid something would happen to you like it did to my dad." Mr. Christou stared into the distance. "I've lived in fear most of my life. But you're a capable, strong young man with a dream." He glanced at the girls. "I realize now I don't have the right to take that from you."

Bailey whispered a silent prayer of thanks.

Stephen and his dad embraced. "Thank you, Dad. I won't disappoint you. I'll be so careful."

"I know you will because I'll teach you myself." Mr. Christou clapped his son on the back. "We'll be diving buddies. I won't worry as much if I can be with you myself."

"*You're* going to dive too?" Stephen whooped and turned to the girls. "My dad's going to teach me to sponge dive!" He grabbed all three in a group hug.

"That's so cool, Stephen!" Bailey said. "I'm so happy for you both."

"Me too," Sydney said.

"I owe you girls a huge debt," Mr. Christou said. "If you hadn't reminded me about my love for sponge diving and what I was missing with Stephen, I never would have considered this."

"I'm glad you're going to give it a try," Bailey said.

Sydney laid a hand on Mr. Christou's arm. "I'm sure you won't regret it."

"I already feel like a huge weight has been lifted from me," Mr. Christou admitted. "I didn't realize how heavy it was until I took it off."

"I didn't know fear was heavy," Alex said.

"It is if you carry it around long enough," Mr. Christou replied. "And the weight of anger is just as bad."

"When can we start my lessons?" Stephen asked his father.

"How about tomorrow?" Mr. Christou pulled a booklet from his back pocket. "I want you to read this booklet about diving safety before we start the actual classes. It will help you better understand the importance of our underwater procedures."

Stephen took the booklet and flipped through it, a smile plastered on his face. "I can't believe this is really happening. It's too good to be true." His gleaming brown eyes met his dad's. "Thank you, Dad. You don't know how much this means to me."

"Oh, I think I do," he said. "Funny, but I suddenly realize it means the world to me too."

"We'd better get going," Bailey said. "You've got reading to do and I'm anxious to see if Mr. Fuller's back from the police station."

"Thanks for the tour, Stephen," Alex said.

"Good luck on the diving!" Sydney called as they turned to leave.

The girls walked in silence on the way back to Mermaid Park, each lost in her own thoughts. Finally, Bailey spoke up. "I still can hardly believe how well that all turned out."

"I know," Sydney replied. "I *never* thought Mr. Christou would give in and let Stephen dive."

"I'm sure he's going to make a great diver," Alex said. "Did you see his muscles?"

Bailey and Sydney laughed. "Oh Alex," Bailey playfully shoved her friend. "You *would* notice that!"

"Well, I *am* twelve," Alex teased back. "I'm practically a teenager."

Bailey's cell phone vibrated in her pocket. She pulled it out and looked at the display. "It's McKenzie!" She pushed TALK and sat in the shade of a huge oak tree. Sydney and Alex sat on the ground beside her.

"Hi, Mac! Hang on. I'll put you on speaker so Sydney and Alex can hear." She pushed the SPEAKER button. "There."

She held the phone out so it would pick up all their voices. "Can you hear us?"

"Hi, guys!" McKenzie said. "I can hear you. Can you hear me?"

"Loud and clear," Sydney replied.

"I wanted to let you know what I found out about Travis Wingate, also known as Mr. Bubble," McKenzie said.

"Wow! You were quick in researching that!" Bailey said. "Should we get the other girls on the phone so they can hear too?"

"Good idea," McKenzie said. "I'll conference them in."

Moments later, Bailey had filled them in on her mermaid show that was cut short because of Angela's air line being sliced. She told them about the police hauling Shondra and Mr. Bubble away. All six girls chattered excitedly until McKenzie cleared her throat and said, "Okay, girls, here's the scoop, and it may help explain Shondra and Travis' motive in doing all that stuff. Travis Wingate has worked at Barron's Commercial Development for the last two years. He's the right-hand man to the company's president, John Goodrich."

"John Goodrich is the guy who called Mr. Fuller the other day to try to get him to sell Mermaid Park!" Bailey said.

"That makes perfect sense," McKenzie replied. "Sounds like he's been using Travis and Shondra to do his dirty work for him to try to run Mr. and Mrs. Fuller out of business."

"Of all the rotten things to do!" Sydney's eyes flashed with anger.

"I can't imagine why Shondra would go along with a plan like that,"

Bailey said. "From what Mr. and Mrs. Fuller have said, she's been a model employee until recently."

"Let's think about that. What do we know about Shondra?" Elizabeth asked. "And why would she change so much?"

"We know she's working at Mermaid Park at the same time she's working for John Goodrich." Sydney scratched her head.

Alexis jumped in. "She admitted to dating Travis Wingate."

"She might be tight on money since she was working an extra shift at the Tunnel of Love." Bailey's forehead creased. "And she likes to be in the spotlight," she added. "She hated it when Jessica was in charge and she had to play second fiddle to her. She'd rather be the star than the assistant."

"I think we're getting warmer," McKenzie said thoughtfully.

"You lost me," Kate admitted. Biscuit panted into the phone.

"Think about it," McKenzie began. "Mr. Goodrich must have offered her something to make it worth her while to turn against Mermaid Park and the Fullers."

"Oh, I think I see where you're headed," Elizabeth said. "Maybe Mr. Goodrich is paying her a lot more than the Fullers if she'll do this stuff to run Mermaid Park out of business."

"They say everyone has their price," Alex said.

"And if she needed the money, that could be her motive for changing," McKenzie said.

"You know Mr. Fuller said that if he sold out, another company would build a bigger, more elaborate mermaid park," Sydney pointed out. "Maybe John Goodrich offered to let her be the star of his show!"

"I bet that's it!" McKenzie exclaimed. "With Shondra's personality that would probably be even more important than money!"

"We were just on our way back to Mr. and Mrs. Fuller's to see if there is any more word on the case," Bailey said.

"Let us know what you find out." Kate giggled. "Biscuit! You're tickling me!"

"Give Biscuit a belly rub for me," McKenzie said.

"Oh wait!" Bailey said. "We almost forgot to tell you some big news!"

"Bigger than Shondra and Travis getting caught?" Elizabeth asked.

"Well, sort of." Bailey grinned at Sydney and Alex and paused for dramatic effect. "But this is happier news. Stephen's dad is going to teach him to sponge dive!"

All the girls cheered and talked at once.

"How'd that happen?"

"Were you there when he got the news?"

"How did you convince Mr. Christou to do it?"

"That's unbelievable!"

Bailey told them the whole story, with Sydney and Alex adding the details she forgot.

"Wow!" McKenzie said. "It's like a miracle!"

"I'd say it was a direct answer to prayer," Elizabeth said.

"I'll say!" Kate added. "And it happened so fast!"

"It seems fast to us," Sydney said, "but I know Stephen has been waiting years for that answer."

"Guess that shows how God can change things in an instant when all the pieces are in place." Elizabeth sighed. "He sure is a good God."

"We'd better get going," Bailey said. "Thanks for getting the info on Travis for us, McKenzie. We'll keep you posted on how things turn out."

Bailey tucked her phone into her pocket. "Come on. Let's go see if Mr. Fuller's back yet."

When the girls entered the Fullers' office, Mrs. Fuller was just hanging up the phone.

"That was Ed," she reported. "He's on his way home from the police station. Said he'd be here in five minutes."

"Anything new?" Bailey asked.

"I think he has something, but he said he'd tell me when he got here," Mrs. Fuller said.

Bailey nodded. "In the meantime, we have some exciting news to tell you about Stephen."

Grandma Cora clapped her hands after hearing Bailey's story. "You're kidding!"

"I always knew Cyrus was an old softie," Mrs. Fuller said. "I'm glad he's starting to show it."

The gravel outside crunched beneath the tires of a car. The girls heard a door slam. Seconds later, the screen door opened, and Mr. Fuller entered.

"So what happened?" Mrs. Fuller asked.

"Pretty much what we expected." Mr. Fuller plopped into his easy chair and put his feet up. "They booked Shondra and Travis into the county jail. The fingerprints they found backstage matched theirs as well as the prints they got at the scenes of the other incidents. Sounds like John Goodrich hired them to sabotage our business when we kept rejecting his offer to buy us out. They're investigating him now too."

"Goodrich is the perfect name for him," Bailey said. "He was trying to get 'good and rich' even if he had to do it underhandedly."

Ed chuckled. "Guess you're right there."

"But why would Shondra fall for such an awful plan?" Mrs. Fuller asked. "She always seemed like such a nice girl before this all started."

"We think we know," Sydney exclaimed. "Mr. Fuller said the people who wanted you out of business wanted to build a bigger park. The Camp Club Girls think they've promised Shondra the chance to be the star of the show."

Mr. Fuller looked at her in amazement. "How did you come up with that?"

"McKenzie pointed out that it had to be a strong motivation. And that's the strongest motivation we could think of!"

"Well, you Camp Club Girls are absolutely right. The police said she gave them a statement saying Barron's Commercial Development promised to make the Mermaid Park into a major theme park within the next year. And when they did, they'd make her the star in the biggest, flashiest mermaid show of all time and pay her more money than she'd ever seen."

"Ah." Mrs. Fuller nodded her head. "The oldest trick in the book. The promise of fame and fortune."

Bailey looked at Sydney and Alex. "It's just like McKenzie figured."

The group sat quietly for a moment. Then Bailey spoke up. "Hey, Mr. Fuller. What about the birds you went to see? Were they from the Wild Birds in Action show?"

"As a matter of fact they were," Mr. Fuller ran a hand over his head. "And it wasn't just the ones she called about."

"What do you mean?" Sydney asked.

"Seems like the birds that escaped were more attached to each other than anyone knew," Mr. Fuller explained. "By the time I got there, a lot of the other escaped birds had gathered in the trees too and were staying together. Those trees were dotted with the brilliant blues, reds, and yellows of the birds' feathers. It was a spectacular sight."

Sydney's black-brown eyes popped. "No way!"

"So I called my bird trainer, Jim, and had him bring the trucks we use to transport the birds." Mr. Fuller smiled and shook his head. "Jim met me there and put on his leather glove. Those birds came to him like they were on stage. It was a beautiful sight."

"I wish I could've seen that," Bailey said.

Mr. Fuller laughed. "You may have missed it, but a lot of other people didn't. A crowd started to gather as they saw the huge birds putting on an impromptu show right there in the public park. It was quite a spectacle. As a bird landed on Jim's arm, he rewarded it with a chunk of meat and caged it in the truck. Then he'd wait for another bird to fly to his arm. I've never seen anything like it."

"That's awesome!" Alex said. "I can't believe we missed it!"

"Next thing you know," Mr. Fuller continued, "the local news station showed up and started filming. Funny thing about it is that even with all that equipment and people around, the birds only seemed to see Jim. They just kept flying one by one to him." Mr. Fuller shook his head and said softly, "It struck me as a holy moment—like Noah's animals coming into the ark or something. And that's when I knew everything was going to be all right."

"It's another miracle!" Bailey clapped her hands.

"Another?" Mr. Fuller's forehead creased.

Bailey gave him a quick recap of Mr. Christou letting Stephen dive.

"Well, that is a miracle if I ever heard one." Mr. Fuller shook his head and then looked at the girls. "I owe you a lot myself."

"Yes." Mrs. Fuller went to stand by her husband. "We couldn't have gotten all those birds back without your idea of having people call in to report them and receive free passes."

"And we would have never found out what Shondra was doing if you hadn't figured that out," he said. "I think you can count this as another mystery the Camp Club Girls have solved!"

"Whatever we did, we were glad to do it," Bailey said.

"Hopefully, once people hear how the other company was trying to drive you out of business, they'll realize it's safe to come back and have fun here again." Alex tucked a strand of hair behind her ear.

"It's almost news time," Grandma Cora said. "Do you suppose they'll have anything on this early about Mermaid Park?"

"Maybe, since they taped it while I was there a little bit ago." Mr. Fuller turned the TV on to the news station. Immediately, a shot of Mr. Fuller, with Jim gathering birds in the background, came on the screen. In the foreground, a reporter was interviewing a bystander.

"Do you think Mermaid Park is a place you'll visit?" the reporter asked.

"Definitely," the man replied. "They've been a part of this community for so long we've got to get out and support them to get their business back on their feet."

"How can we do that?"

"By taking our families to the Mermaid Park and encouraging everyone we know to do the same. It isn't right that good people like Ed and Lenore Fuller should be treated like they were. And you can see right here by this bird display the quality of the shows they offer their guests." The man looked at the crowd that had gathered. "Come on, everyone! Let's go give the Mermaid Park some business!"

Hearing noise outside Mr. and Mrs. Fuller's office, Bailey got up to look out the window. "Mr. and Mrs. Fuller! You've got to come and see this!" she yelled.

Everyone joined Bailey at the front window where throngs of people poured through the park entrance.

"Thank You, Lord," Mr. Fuller choked out. "Thank You!"

He put his arms around the girls and said, "Let's go enjoy the park with all these supporters."

Bailey hugged him with all her might. She'd never been so glad to have solved a mystery, and in the process, help save a park. It truly was a miraculous day!

Check Out More Camp Club Girls!

Camp Club Girls: Elizabeth

Whether the Camp Club Girls are uncovering a decades-old mystery at Camp Discovery Lake, investigating a bag of mysterious marbles in Amarillo, untangling a strange string of events in San Antonio, or solving the case of a missing guitar in Music City, you will encounter six delightful, relatable characters who combine their mystery-solving skills to crack the case.

Paperback / 978-1-68322-767-0 / $9.99 / Now available!

Camp Club Girls: Kate

Whether the Camp Club Girls are saving the day for a Philadelphia Phillies baseball player, investigating the sabotage of a Vermont cheese factory, going on a quest to uncover phony fossils in Wyoming, or solving the case of twisted treats in Hershey, Pennsylvania, you'll encounter six charming, relatable characters who combine their mystery-solving skills to save the day.

Paperback / 978-1-68322-854-7 / $9.99 / March 2019

Camp Club Girls: McKenzie

Whether the Camp Club Girls are in the middle of a Wild West whodunit, investigating a mysterious case of missing sea lion pups, uncovering the whereabouts of a teen girl's missing family member, or unearthing clues in an Iowa history mystery, you'll encounter six charming, relatable characters who combine their mystery-solving skills to save the day.

Paperback / 978-1-68322-879-0 / $9.99 / April 2019